SEPTEMBER'S MOONLIGHT SERENADE

A NOVEL

L. B. JOYCE

September's Moonlight Serenade – 1st edition
Print ISBN: 978-0-9600311-1-5
Cover by Soxsational Cover Art

ALSO BY L. B. JOYCE

This book is the seventh book in the series -

Twelve Months, Twelve Love Stories

A Million Decembers

For the Love of July

February's Angel

Promise Me November

An Unexpected June

A January to Remember

September's Moonlight Serenade

Goodbye Heartbreak, Hello May

Holidays in White Oaks Valley

A Grand Slam Kind of Christmas

God gave us two ears to hear,
two eyes to see and two hands to hold.
But why did he give us only one heart?
I think this is because he wants us to find
the other one.
~ Anonymous

* * *

Definition of serenade (ser-e-nade) ~
A complimentary vocal or instrumental performance,
given outdoors at night for a woman being courted.

As for me?
Nothing to say this time... except enjoy!

CHAPTER 1

Wherever you go
no matter how long you're gone,
there's no place like home.
~ Anonymously Yours

"Come on... open, *damn you.* I don't feel like dealing with this right now ..." Muttering this under his breath, Jason Bennett was not in a good mood.

Yeah, he was grouchy. He was exhausted. And completely done in after six weeks on the road. With a schedule that left no time to even think, let alone relax.

He definitely wasn't up for this, standing on his front porch in the middle of the night, trying to bust open his door. No, he should be inside already, in his own bed. Where he could finally get a decent night's sleep.

Was this too much to ask?

He didn't think so ...

He took a deep breath, ready to try again. "Come on... work with me here." This coming through gritted teeth, he gave the key once more hard twist, finally bringing on that telltale click.

He pushed at the door.

But, as he expected, it didn't budge, not even a fraction of an inch. After leaning against it for a few seconds, he gave it his all, shoving as hard as he could.

The door flew open, sending him barreling into the darkness. After more muttering and a lot of groping for the light switch, the room was flooded with light, almost blinding him.

You need to get the damn door taken care of before you break your neck. You are way past the limit of excuses. It's been over two years since you bought the house.

He glanced over to where Paul was waiting in his jeep, the motor running. He raised his hand, sending him a thumbs-up.

With a short beep of his horn, Paul was off. Flying down the driveway, his tires squealed in protest as he made a sharp turn onto the street.

Jason shook his head.

The guy was going to kill himself one of these days.

But he understood. Paul had a wife waiting for him at home, with the promise of a home cooked meal.

And even better ... someone to kiss goodnight.

Trying not to think about this, he grabbed his bag and, after lugging it down the hall and up the stairs to his bedroom, he tossed it on the floor. He gazed around the room, giving a huge sigh of relief. His bed had never looked more welcoming.

It had been a rough trip and everyone in the band, including him, had about reached their limit. It didn't help this had been one of those days that felt like it would never end. They should have been home hours ago, but he'd be willing to bet they had spent more time sitting in traffic than actually driving.

One can only spend so much time in a van, packed to the hilt with five guys and all of their paraphernalia, and not be a little snarky. This coming after traveling from one booking to the next, one hotel after another and consuming more fast food than one should even think about.

Add to that, more than their share of over-zealous and needy fans.

Not that he was complaining, but it got a bit much after a while. How many times had they come back to their hotel to find women camped out in front of their rooms? Most of them, at an age they should know better.

So that everyone was more than eager to get home would be an understatement. Cleveland had never looked so good.

Yeah, well ... maybe to everyone except you. Because what do you have waiting for you?

Nothing ... just an empty house.

Heck, he didn't even have a dog. Not that he could, with the little time he spent here. Though it would be nice.

Yep, it's just you and your guitar. Talk about pathetic.

Massaging the back of his neck, he groaned. This wasn't him, this feeling sorry for himself. Nope, this wasn't something he'd normally do. He had a good life. He was young. Healthy. He had friends. He was successful at what he did.

Yeah, you've made a name for yourself, more than what most people could only imagine.

So, why the sudden low spirits? Was this a sign he was getting too old for this traveling bit?

You're only thirty-one

Well, right now he felt like he had passed thirty-one years ago. Way too many years ago.

He dragged his hand through his hair. He was beat. And he was hungry. Once he had something to eat, he'd feel better. Then, after a good night's sleep, he would be fine.

This is when it occurred to him, the chance of finding anything edible in his kitchen after his long absence was pretty close to zero.

Great ... this means you might possibly starve to death.

And again, here came the dramatics ....

Unhappy with this mood he was in, he decided to take a shower. Maybe after scrubbing away the travel grime that seemed to stick like glue throughout the entire trip, he would be in a better frame of mind. Then he'd search the kitchen and see what he could find.

Who knows?

Maybe he'd get lucky.

Refreshed from his shower, Jason made his way downstairs to the kitchen. His eyes squeezed shut and a prayer on his lips, he yanked open the refrigerator door.

He slowly opened his eyes. *"Yesssss ..."*

A loaf of bread, a carton of eggs, orange juice and a package of bacon were lined up on the shelf in front of him. This, along with a bunch of bananas and what appeared to be a plate of homemade cookies, was enough to make him a happy man.

After he grabbed a cookie, almost inhaling it in one bite, he pulled off the note stuck to the orange juice carton.

> *Hey,*
> *I picked up a few groceries for you,*
> *knowing how you always get home at*
> *some insane hour. It's not much, but*
> *at least you won't go hungry.*
> *I don't even want think about what*
> *kind of garbage you've been eating*
> *over the past six weeks.*
> *I gave your refrigerator a good clean-*
> *ing. I threw out some things because*
> *they were way past their expiration*
> *date, a few almost two years ago.*
> *Seriously? Jason, you should know*
> *better.*
> *Anyway, enjoy the groceries. Think of*
> *them as my welcome home gift to you.*
> *p.s. I'm leaving tomorrow morning for*
> *that river cruise I told you about. I'll*
> *be home in about a week. You should*
> *be fine, since I gave the place a good*
> *cleaning. It definitely needed it.*

Signed with a smiley face sticker and dated yesterday, the note was from Caro, his next door neighbor. Besides one other person, she was the only one who called him Jason instead of Jazz.

He frowned, thinking of that other person. He didn't want to go there, not now. There were too many memories.

Instead, he glanced down at the note again. It was one of the infamous sticky notes Caro was always leaving somewhere around his house.

He grinned, shaking his head. She had to be the only person on earth who got excited about sticky notes. But this was because she loved to write notes.

Notes about everything and anything. Notes she had the habit of leaving all over his house.

Jason had known Caro, short for Caroline, since he moved into his house.

She lived in the house next door. In her early sixties, she fussed over him like she would a son. Since she never had children and his own mother had died when he was around eight years old, they had quickly developed a close relationship.

He would be the first to confess he enjoyed the attention she showered on him.

Just as she would admit she loved giving it to him.

Well, occasionally you like the attention. But she has the tendency to get a little bossy. And you never want to be the reason for her anger. No, sireee ...

A nurse for many years, five months ago, she decided she needed a break. The hospital gave her a six-month leave of absence. Once this time was up, she had to either return or retire.

She told Jason she left her job because she was becoming too emotionally attached to her patients. He wondered if there was something more going on, but he wasn't going to ask.

If she wanted to confide in him, fine. If not?

Again, fine.

They had met when she stopped by to drop off his mail, delivered to her by mistake. Appalled at the unkempt bachelor-like state of his house, she returned, ringing the bell way too early the following morning. She had a proposition for him. She wanted him to hire her to clean his house, and she wasn't going to take no for an answer. Half asleep, but knowing this was a deal he couldn't afford to pass up, he had jumped at her offer.

She now claimed she had never been happier. Believe it or not, she was in her element when she was cleaning, no matter what it was. She liked there was no stress involved, no problems to take home at the end of the day.

Nope, there was only the satisfaction of a job well done.

She also liked the extra money. With all her new free time, there were so many things she wanted to do. Art classes. Joining the gym. Traveling. Whatever struck her fancy.

A good example would be this river cruise she was on.

Jason would never tell her this, but he was hoping she decided not to go back to nursing.

His house had never been so clean.

Caro was also a good friend of his sister, Steffi, also a nurse. They had met when working the same shift at the Children's Hospital.

Speaking of Steffi, this was a reminder he needed to let her know he was home. She always worried about him when he was on one of his road trips, claiming she didn't sleep well until she knew he was back in town. As she had told him many, many times, as the only two left of their family, they needed to watch out for each other.

He grabbed his phone from the counter and sent her a text. Then he grabbed another cookie, and after taking a big bite out of it, he leaned back against the counter.

He shook his head, just thinking about her.

Wow.... what can you say about Steffi?

Steffi... this was short for Stephanie. Three years younger, she would always be his baby sister. She meant the world to him.

Everything about Steffi was what he would have to describe as, well, the only word he could think of?

This would have to be delicate.

Her hair, silky and an almost luminous blond, she wore long and free. He'd swear it floated around her like strands of light when she moved. Her complexion was like fine porcelain, her cheeks always tinted with a slight blush. She had these enormous hazel eyes that seemed to look right into your soul. And her smile, if you were lucky enough to get one from her, could light up a room.

She had an aura around her that reached out to everyone who she came in contact with, making it almost impossible to be in a bad mood.

She was also the kind of woman every man felt this sudden need to protect. Jack, the drummer, and all around talented musician in his band, had harbored a crush on her since he first joined the band a little over two years ago.

Steffi was also painfully shy, to the point she almost worked herself into a panic when faced with any kind of social interaction. She had been like this for as far back as he could remember.

He tried to help her, boost her confidence. Starting by getting her more involved in his life. With the popularity of his band rising over the past few years, there was always some kind of special or charitable event he could use her help. Unfortunately, every time he mentioned something like this, she refused, using her job as an excuse.

But he was wondering if this was beginning to change. During this last road trip, she had sent him a text to let him know she had signed up to be on the committee for the Moonlight Madness Masquerade Ball.

Held at The Regency Party Center on the last Saturday of September, this was an annual fundraiser for the Children's Hospital. Now, in its eighth year, it had become one of the most popular events in the city, tickets selling out the first day.

Jason's band had provided as the entertainment for every single one of those eight years, something he was very proud of.

He didn't know what had finally persuaded Steffi to volunteer, but he was glad she did. He needed to ask Caro. If anyone would know the answer to this, it would be her.

Jack is going to be happy about this. Since you appointed him as the official band spokesman for any committee meetings, this might give him more time to spend with her.

This could be a chance to work his magic.

He laughed out loud at this. This would be a tall order for Jack.

Because with the act he put on while on stage, you would never guess he was almost as shy as Steffi.

Another blast of cold air came right at him.

Jason realized he had left the refrigerator door wide open for who knows how long. If Caro was here, she would be handing out another lecture. This was one of her pet peeves.

A guilty expression on his face, he grabbed the bacon, bread, and carton of eggs. After slamming the door, he set the food on the counter.

This was when he saw there was another one of Caro's sticky notes, along with a photograph, on the counter. Creased, and with one corner torn off, the photograph looked like it had been crumpled into a ball at one time.

A memory pushing its way into his mind, an uneasy feeling took hold of him.

Ignoring the photo, he picked up the note.

> *I found this when I was cleaning your bedroom, stuck to the back of the dresser. I thought it might mean something to you... you might wonder where it was. She's beautiful. Was she someone special?*

His heart pounding like a jack hammer in his chest, he was suddenly finding it difficult to breathe.

Come on, you're being ridiculous. Just look at the damn photo.

He swallowed, and gripping the edge of the counter, his gaze dropped to the photo.

Then he swiftly looked away, closing his eyes. He groaned, raking his hand through his hair.

Why is this coming back to haunt you? And why now?

After he exhaled a long, steadying breath, he opened his eyes, his gaze again going to the photo.

And in less than it would take to snap his fingers, he was right back in that time, reliving everything about that day.

It had been early afternoon on a wintery day in late January.

They had just left this little restaurant where they'd shared a very late and leisurely breakfast. Huddled close together in the cozy warmth of the little restaurant, they hadn't noticed it had started to snow.

And boy, was it cold. A bitter, penetrating and freezing your eyebrows cold.

Swirling around them, the snowflakes were like fine particles of glitter stinging their faces.

But he hadn't cared about the weather.

Or, to be honest, you hadn't even noticed.

Laughing and holding on to each other, they had made a run for his truck. In an impulsive move, he had waved down a passerby, asking if he could take their picture. He had been filled with this sudden need for proof of the moment, something he could carry with him.

He wanted more than only a memory.

And now you can't help but wonder if this was a warning of what was to come...

The camera had caught him smiling down at her as she leaned against him. Her arms wrapped around him and her face turned up to his, she was also smiling... maybe even laughing?

He studied the photo more closely.

Yes... now you remember. She had been laughing. You were teasing her because she kept complaining about the cold. You said something corny about the best way to warm her up would be with a kiss.

And right after the photo was taken, the kiss he gave her was one he would never forget.

He raised his head and, staring into space, he fell right back into that moment, that kiss.

He groaned, closing his eyes. He could remember every single second of that day.

Hell, you remember every single second the entire time she was with you.

Was she someone special?

Yeah, she was.

But not anymore.

If you searched even deeper into your memory, you would also remember how she made it very clear ... a future together? This was never going to happen.

He pushed away from the counter. For a moment, he hesitated. Then he picked up the photo, and in almost one step, he was at the trash container. He tossed the photo inside and slammed down the lid.

He stared down at it, breathing hard. Then he groaned.

Damn ....

He lifted the lid and fishing the photo out of trash, his voice was like a roll of thunder in the silent kitchen. "*No, dammit ....* You will not throw this away. You're going to put it somewhere as a reminder of what happened. So you don't make the same mistake again."

He glared down at the photo, shaking his head. "Not with her, not with anyone."

He gazed around the kitchen, two new magnets on the refrigerator catching his eye. A scarecrow and a pumpkin. He knew Caro was responsible for this. It was an early hint of the fall decorations she was planning to clutter up his home.

Hadn't she already made it known how disappointed she was with his pathetic display of holiday decorations? The magnets, along with the arrangement of pumpkins he noticed on his front porch, were just the beginning. Where she found these in all different colors was beyond him.

Who knew there was such a thing? Aren't pumpkins supposed to be orange?

There was no doubt in his mind, if she had her way, she would deck his place out like an advertisement for a party store. And this would become a year-round production.

Well, he was going to put one of these magnets to good use. The photo was going on his refrigerator, right at eye level and in full view. It would be a reminder to be more careful in the future.

This accomplished, he stepped back and viewed his handiwork.

He nodded.

Perfect. You'll see it every time you walk into the kitchen.

He was suddenly consumed by a bone-tired weariness. His hunger no longer a priority, he loaded everything back in the refrigerator and headed upstairs.

He needed to catch up on his sleep.

But even as exhausted as he was, this was a long time coming.

The photo?

It just wouldn't leave him.

CHAPTER 2

*D*arcey Hollister watched the screen saver pop up on her computer. It was a photo of the mountains, taken from the window of her office back in California. A place and time suddenly looking a lot more inviting than she remembered.

Whatever made you think you could do this? Evidently, you weren't thinking straight.

Wearily massaging her forehead, she took another deep breath before she leaned in closer to her phone. Propped up on the desk in front of her, she had set it on speaker mode.

She clearly and slowly enunciated her words. "Yes, it's understandable you're worried. But I assure you nothing like what you're suggesting is going to happen. We have a crew of very dedicated employees here at The Regency and their top concern is every event —"

This was as far as she got before the caller's voice became even louder, bordering on hysterical anger. Now more than loud enough to be heard outside of her office, Darcey switched off the speaker mode. Bringing the phone to her ear, she leaned back in her chair and closed her eyes.

As far as she was concerned, this problem, if it could even be considered a problem, had been resolved in the first five minutes of the call. Why she was even still on the phone with this woman was beyond her. Yes, her daughter was getting married in less than two weeks. And yes, she had been told the event planner was no longer with the party center.

But Darcey could handle this. A fact she'd already told this caller at least five times.

You need to hire an event planner and you need to do it soon. Very soon.

She frowned. This was her father's fault. She was still furious with him for firing both the current event planner and her assistant all in one swoop. Yes, they weren't doing their job and hadn't for quite some time. But he should have let her hire someone to take their place before stranding her with no one.

You are not an event planner. You're meant to be a silent partner. Your job is to check in occasionally to make sure everything is running smoothly. This was the agreement you and your father made.

Hadn't he assured her the operation of the party center would be solely in her hands?

Yes... absolutely, he had promised this. Maybe not in writing. But hey, it was her father. If she couldn't trust him, who could he trust?

But no ... what does he do? He comes barreling into Cleveland and sweeps through every department, firing people right and left. Then he hops back on a plane and flies off to California.

Leaving her to clean up the mess.

You know he was right with what he did. It was a move long overdue.

She sighed, glancing down at her watch. It wasn't even noon, and she was already wishing she could call it a day.

It didn't help she'd been here since before six this morning. But this had been her choice. She'd thought the early morning hours could work to her advantage, with fewer interruptions. But almost from the moment she entered the building, she had been hit her with one problem after another.

Seriously, it was as if the staff had sent out some kind of alarm as soon as you drove into the parking lot, eager to get in their complaints.

And what problems had they thrown at her?

A sink in the women's lounge was leaking. The carpet was soaked, the water beginning to spread into the hallway.

There was a burning smell in the kitchen, but what was of more concern, no one could figure out where it was coming from. The electrician wasn't answering his phone and his partner was out of town. And the usual back-up option? It was suddenly not an option.

Last night, the chef and his sous chef had become embroiled in a huge argument, nearly causing a scene in front of the fifty guests gathered in the Garden Room for a retirement party.

So, it hadn't been a surprise to find both men waiting outside her office door when she'd arrived. Still riled up over what happened, they had both come to hand in their immediate resignations. It had taken her over an hour of fast talking and pleading to get them to call a truce.

But she had a feeling this wasn't going to last very long.

She checked the time again.

"Hello? Hello? Are you still there?" This came in a loud yell from the phone.

Darcey sat up straight up in her chair.

Oh geeez ... you forgot you were still on the phone...

Her response came flying out almost as loud. "Yes, yes ... I'm here and once again, let me assure you everything will be beautiful for your daughter's wedding. Even though the ownership of The Regency has changed, the services we provide haven't. Our plan is to make everything even better. I promise you won't be disappointed."

When this was met with silence, she quickly ended the call. Pushing the phone as far away on the desk as she could, she reached for the pad of paper in front of her.

She had a lot of work to do. So, this required a list.

Number one, hire a new event planner and assistant. She underlined this. Staring down at this, she underlined it again.

Number two, she had already decided it might be a good time to hire a new chef, too. Along with a sous chef. Underneath this, she wrote in all caps, must be compatible.

She also heavily underlined this.

A loud yell suddenly came from the courtyard located right outside her office window. This was from one of the landscaping crew who were in the midst of completely overhauling the area. The plan was to have it party-ready for an upcoming annual charity event, always held the last Saturday in September.

The favorable weather had allowed them to work non-stop, and they were now ahead of schedule. Unfortunately, this also meant she had to work with these constant disruptions ever since she and her father arrived a little over a week ago.

She threw her pen down on her desk, giving a frustrated sigh. Yeah, believe it or not, it had only been a week. A week that felt more like months as she tried to make sense out of the many problems the past owners had left behind.

This reminded her … picking up her pen again, she wrote a note she needed to meet up with the committee involved with the charity event.

She left her desk and wandering over to the window, she watched a truck unload a huge pile of mulch before it backed out into the parking lot. She didn't notice the man who in turn, was watching her. It was only after the truck left, she glanced over, meeting his gaze.

She gave a sharp intake of breath.

It was Rob Johnson, the contractor her father hired to oversee the new improvements to the property.

You don't like him.

He scared her. She felt like he was always watching her, his deliberate gaze enough to make her shiver, but not in a good way. No, it was more of an uneasy, you-need-to-trust-your-intuition-and-stay-away-from-him kind of shiver.

The impression he gave was of a man who was used to being in control. Though domineering might be a better choice of word. This was obvious with how tightly he gripped her hand when they first met. To the point, it was almost painful. And in the way he narrowed his eyes, as if he was waiting for her to cower under his gaze.

When her father informed Rob that she was the person in charge, his soft, mocking laugh, low enough for only her to hear, made her angry. But it was his comment that sealed her dislike.

He had leaned in close, definitely more than was acceptable in a business situation, his breath had brushing over her cheek as he spoke. "I have a feeling you are a woman who never goes down without a fight. But I'm up for the challenge. Only because I know the result will be more than worth the wait."

What? What kind of remark was this? A challenge? Worth the wait? For him ... never. Absolutely not.

Quickly stepping back, she had sent a glance over at her father, But he had taken a call, oblivious to what was going on.

So, after she sent Rob a glaring look, sputtering out the excuse she needed to get back to work, she left. The knowledge he was probably watching her as she walked away had been very unsettling.

Later, she had asked her father what made him decide to hire Rob.

His answer? Rob had come highly recommended by one of his close business associates. His qualifications were exemplary. Out of all the candidates he had interviewed, Rob was the only one to give all the right answers. Since good contractors were hard to find, he hoped she would trust his judgement and work with him.

After studying her for a few moments, he then reminded her that she was the one who pushed for this project. To have it done right, she needed to concentrate solely on the job, avoiding any outside distractions. No matter how tempting they were.

And he was counting on her to do this professionally.

With that being said, he moved right on to the next item on his list. For him, the subject was closed.

She was a little puzzled. She didn't know what distractions he was talking about. But she wasn't worried. When it came to the company, she was always professional.

If this was some kind of test your father is giving you, you plan to pass it with flying colors. No one, not even Rob Johnson, will distract you.

But now, even with the glass separating her from Rob, she felt her skin crawl. Slowly backing away from the window, she scurried over to her desk. But not before she caught his arrogant smile.

16

Her phone rang. She almost pounced on it, thankful for the diversion.

What a coincidence, it was her father.

"Okay, but you have to remember you put me in charge. So, let me try my plan first. I'll call you when I have more information to give you."

This being said, Darcey ended the call, a wry smile on her face. She had been on the phone with her father for almost forty-five minutes. Evidently, once he was back in California, he realized he had left without giving her the talk.

And, no, this wasn't a lecture about men or sex.

Heaven forbid ...

Though he had made one attempt at this back when she became a teenager. He had called her into his office and, after a great deal of throat clearing and nervous fidgeting, told her absolutely nothing. Instead, his talk had turned into more of a lecture about her role as a woman in a man's world. With no reference to what she really wanted to know about the mysterious subject of sex.

He had rambled on about how boys were not as mature as girls at this age, their needs were much stronger. But no matter what they tried to tell her, she should never feel pressured to give into their demands.

At the time, he had her totally confused. What exactly were these strong needs? And what demands were boys going to make? Rather than ask him, prolonging his discomfort, she had nodded at everything he said.

From that point on, she avoided boys as much as possible.

It was finally June, her father's secretary, who explained everything. This, along with what she and her friends figured out, eventually gave her a good idea of the whole girl, boy, sex thing. And the next time her father brought up the subject, now even more uncomfortable because she was older, she was able to tell him she got it, she understood, she would be fine.

As you have probably figured out by now, Darcey's father wasn't what you would describe as a loving and doting parent. Her brother Niles told her this was because after their mother cheated on him, he put a tight rein on his emotions and became married to his work instead.

Darcey didn't know where Niles got his information. But at three years older, he had her convinced he knew what he was talking about.

So, she believed him.

But back to the lecture her father just gave her over the phone. It was one she already knew by heart, having heard it many times over the course of her life.

This would be his speech about honesty. After all, this was what Hollister Industries was known for. According to her father, achieving success came down to honesty on all levels. This was the key to earning respect not only in the business world, but your personal life as well. And she was never to forget this.

There was more he had to say on this subject… so much more, but she didn't want to hear it. Because, seriously? She found it hard to agree with him. She could come up with a long list of people who were successful, yet their integrity rated low on the list.

Take David, for example.

But she didn't want to waste her time thinking about him. Eight months had passed since she walked away from what she had believed was a mutual commitment in their relationship. Catching him kissing another woman, who happened to be her best friend, was what finally convinced her David would never be the man for her.

She sighed. Even now, David was still calling, leaving messages. About how much he missed her and how sorry he was for what happened. Yes, he realized he had made a huge mistake. But he also found it hard to believe she thought the kiss had meant something.

It was just a kiss. Think of it as a friendly kiss between friends, he had told her.

So, he wanted her to seriously think about giving him a second chance. Things had been so good between them. So, why give up so easily?

Yeah, they would make a fresh start, take it slow.

A fresh start?

She didn't think this was possible.

At first, she had listened to his messages, almost pulled in by his pleas. Maybe he was right, they should give it another try.

But now? She was over him, the hurt no longer there. And when he called? She deleted his messages without reading them.

That part of her life was over, her focus now on The Regency. She intended to show her father she could turn the venue into the best Cleveland had to offer.

Lost in thought, she fingered the ring hanging from the delicate sterling silver chain around her neck. Her father was right. It had been her choice to take on this new venture. This meant no outside distractions, and no time for dreaming.

Her phone started to ring. She picked it up to see it was the employment agency.

So, for the time being, it appeared she was right on track.

Yeah ... you're going to be just fine.

CHAPTER 3

Challenges are not sent to destroy you,
they're sent to strengthen you.
~ Anonymous

If his phone rang one more time, Jason was going to throw it right out the window.

And yeah, he was serious about this.

Dead serious.

What time was it, anyway?

Squinting over at the clock on the nightstand, he shot up to a sitting position. Dragging his hand down over his face, he reached for his phone.

He checked the time there. Just to make sure.

Yep, same result … 11:14 a.m.

Holy cow, how did you sleep so late? And why do you feel as if you haven't slept at all?

He got out of bed and gave a long stretch. Staring down at his phone, he waited. But it appeared the caller had given up.

Thank God …

After splashing cold water on his face and throwing on some

clothes, he made his way to the kitchen. Where he set about making coffee. But his mind still not quite awake, this was slow going.

He was also having a dickens-of-a-time trying to avoid the refrigerator. But the photo was like a magnet, pulling him in.

He grabbed the bread from the refrigerator. After he popped two slices in the toaster, he leaned back against the counter.

Dragging his hands back through his hair, he closed his eyes. There were plenty of other things to worry about instead of an old photograph.

Such as how he should be at the party center right now. In fact, he should have been there over an hour ago. The plan had been for the band to meet up this morning to do a quick equipment check. Followed by an overview of their upcoming schedule, starting with the wedding reception scheduled for tomorrow night.

So far, the bride and groom had been easy to work with. But from experience, he knew how quickly this could change. The closer it came to the actual event, this is when even the most well thought out plans suddenly came under question, emotions running awry.

He didn't like surprises.

And you don't want any surprises. None. Period.

So, to get a heads up on all of this, he had made it very clear to the guys they would meet early this morning.

He scratched his head, following with a loud sigh

They're probably not too happy right now, wondering where the hell you are.

Well, they could wait.

He was going to drink his coffee and enjoy his toast. And he was going to take his good old time doing this.

As he opened the cupboard door to grab a cup, his gaze drifted over to the photo again.

He groaned, raking his hand through his hair.

This was a bad idea. You need to take it down. Out of sight, out of mind ... isn't this what they say?

Right after he yanked the photo off the refrigerator door, he heard the front door open.

"Jazz …" This loud bellow was followed by the slam of the door.

"Here, in the kitchen." Tossing the photo on the counter, he waited.

Paul came bursting into the room. His hair sticking straight up and his anxious expression gave off the vibes he was worked up about something.

His gaze sweeping over Jason, his look became angry. "Jesus…. what are you trying to do to me? I've been calling and texting you all morning. I didn't know what was going on when I got to The Regency and you weren't there. Then after you didn't show or answer any of my calls, I really got worried. If you remember, you're the one who made such a big deal about meeting so early this morning."

Jason held his hands up in surrender, shaking his head. "Yeah, sorry, man. I'm really sorry. I never heard my alarm. After you dropped me off last night, I went straight to bed. But once there, I was wide awake. When I finally fell asleep, it was close to dawn and I guess I slept like the dead. A lot on my mind, I guess."

He massaged the back of his neck, sending a furtive glance over at the photo. Paul caught this and, being Paul, always sticking his nose into everything, he moved closer to get a better look.

But Jason beat him to it and grabbed the photo, stuffing it in his jeans pocket.

You should've thrown the damn thing out. The last thing you want right now is Paul asking you a lot of questions.

Nonchalantly taking a cup out of the cupboard, he filled it with coffee and slid it across the counter to Paul. "Here, I just made it."

Paul took a deep gulp, wincing at the hot beverage. "Man, that's hot."

When Jason had nothing to say to this, not even a sarcastic remark at his stupidity of not checking to see if it was hot in the first place, he studied him, a puzzled look on his face. "Is something wrong?"

Busily buttering a piece of toast, Jason shook his head. "Nope."

After Paul settled on one of the counter stools, he studied him. That Jason was refusing to meet his gaze had him worried.

He gave an exasperated sigh. "Well, you're sure acting like there is."

When Jason remained silent, he shook his head. "If you had shown up at The Regency this morning like the rest of us," here he cleared his throat, sending Jason a sarcastic look, "you would have seen there were some changes made while we were gone. From what I could find out, the company who took over doesn't mess around. They move in quickly and get right down to business. The venue will remain the same, a place for parties and events. And there are absolutely no plans to tear it down or make any drastic changes. A long-needed freshening up to the place is what they're aiming for."

He took the piece of toast Jason handed him. "Thanks. You got jelly?"

Without a word, Jason took a jar of jelly out of the refrigerator and slid it across the counter to him. He did this with enough force to send it almost sailing off the edge.

At Paul's raised eyebrow, he took a knife out of the drawer, and handed it to him, too. "Anything else?"

Spreading jelly on his toast, Paul shook his head, deciding to ignore the sarcastic tone of his voice. "Nope, this is fine."

After taking a generous bite, he began to talk. "So, the one area they've already started working on is the outdoor courtyard space. The plan is to spruce it up, add lots of lighting, seating areas, plants, and trees, I guess. They hired some architectural genius, slash, contractor for this and all the other improvements. Probably has some fancy college degree. Jack already met him and doesn't care much for him. He got the impression the guy is full of himself and not at all pleased about being here. My guess is Cleveland wasn't in his plans."

He chuckled, shaking his head. "He tore into Jack this morning for showing up late for work, not even bothering to apologize when he found out Jack wasn't part of the landscaping crew. Jack is still fuming about this."

He snorted. "Yeah, like Jack could handle a job like that. I don't think he knows a bush from a tree, let alone how to plant one. Anyway, I guess this guy is someone they brought with them from California, where the company's headquarters is located."

Jason's response came out almost in a yelp. "California?" His hand hit his cup, knocking it over.

They both watched as a stream of coffee spread across the counter before Jason grabbed a paper towel and began mopping up the spill. His jerky movements concerning Paul, he cautiously continued talking. "Yeah, a company by the name of Hollister Investments. From what I hear, they've been around for a long time. Reputable company, no one seems to have any complaints about them."

"Damn ... you've got to be kidding me." Throwing down the paper towel, Jason dragged his hand through his hair. The look on his face one of stunned disbelief, he leaned back against the counter and closed his eyes.

Now Paul was really worried. Jason could tell him he was fine until he was blue in the face, but he wasn't going to believe him. Something was going on and he wanted to find out what it was.

Starting with the photo he had tried to hide in his pocket.

He waited until Jason opened his eyes. And even though he was looking right at him, Paul knew he was somewhere else ... in another place, another time.

He cleared his throat. "Jazz, I've known you now, for what, almost two years? So, I know when you're not telling me something. Like right now. So, come on... what is it? Because, believe me, I don't plan to let up until you spit it out."

A closed look coming over his face, Jason shook his head. "There's nothing to tell." He glanced over at the clock on the microwave and, after taking one last gulp of coffee, he sent Paul a curt nod. "Are you ready? I'll follow you to The Regency. Late or not, I still need to check you got everything right."

At Paul's murderous look, he gave a short laugh. "You know I'm kidding. But I still have to do this. If only for my sanity."

Absentmindedly reaching into his pocket for his keys, he pulled them out. This sent the photo fluttering down to the floor and right at Paul's feet.

Paul was on it in a flash, with Jason only able to watch as he held it out of his reach to study it more closely.

After what felt like a long, tense, filled moment, he sent Jason a curious glance. "It's sort of blurry with all the snow blowing around, but I can definitely see it's you. But who is the woman? And what did you do that she isn't around anymore? You find a woman like her and you do whatever you can to keep her. Because from what I can see, she's a knockout."

Jason shrugged. "Yeah, I thought she was mine. Unfortunately, she didn't agree, didn't think I measured up. So, in answer to your question, no matter what I did, for her it never would've been enough."

He jerked his head towards the door. "Come on, let's go. We have a lot of work to do."

He walked out of the kitchen.

Paul set the photo on the counter.

His wife Sasha would be the first to tell you he wasn't the most romantic guy in the world. But in the two years since they got married, he had learned a few things.

He didn't want to brag, but he could tell when someone was in love. Even if they weren't aware of this themselves.

And by the look on Jason's face when he talked about the woman in the photo?

Whoever and wherever she was?

He was still in love with her.

Rubbing the back of his neck, he groaned. Why did falling in love involve so much drama?

After stuffing the last of his toast in his mouth and taking one last gulp of coffee, he took off after Jason.

He told Sasha this would only take a couple of hours, and when he came home, they could do whatever she wanted. He knew how he would like to occupy their time, but this would be her call.

After being on the road for six weeks, just being with her would be enough for him.

But now it looked like any plans were on hold.

Damn ...

CHAPTER 4

*If you asked me how many times
you've crossed my mind,
I'd have to say once.
But this is because you never left.*
~ Anonymous

Jason was leaning against his truck waiting for Paul.

He knew he was acting like a complete idiot, but he didn't want to walk into the party center alone. Again, he blamed this on he wasn't one for change. From what little Paul had told him, this is what would be waiting for him when he went inside.

Briefly closing his eyes, he dragged his hand down over his jaw.

Let's be honest here, it's not the state of the party center you're worried about. It's more about who you might find there.

A few minutes later, Paul's jeep came roaring into the parking lot, the audio system on full blast, country music floating through the air.

Jason shook his head.

His hands jammed in his pockets, Paul came sauntering over to where Jason was waiting. He searched his face. "Hey, what's up? Don't tell me you're afraid to go inside. After the way you tore out of your parking lot, breaking every speed limit to get here, I thought for sure you'd already be inside, checking things out."

When Jason only gave him a dirty look before he began walking towards the party center, Paul groaned aloud. "For god's sake, tell me what's bothering you. It has something to do with that photo, doesn't it?"

Avoiding his gaze, Jason shrugged. "You know I don't like surprises. And, let's just say I'm tired and leave it at that, okay?"

He began walking even faster, giving Paul no choice but to tag along.

Paul let out a long, resigned sigh. "Okay, I get it. You're not talking. So, we'll only talk about work. Before I left for your place, I told the guys to take a break, so they should be back by now. But, Jazz, I'm warning you, with this mood you're in, you can't take it out on them. You need to let them have some off time before we're back here for tomorrow night's wedding. You gotta know this is the last place any of us want to be right now."

Jason opened the door, gesturing for Paul to go in before him. "Yeah, I know. Don't worry, we'll keep it short."

He sent a furtive glance around the main lobby. It was empty. In fact, it felt deserted, as though they were the only two people in the building.

He let out a slow sigh of relief.

If Darcey was here, you'd know it, right? At least in the past, this would've been the case. You could always sense when she was anywhere near. In a heartbeat.

But there wasn't any sign of this happening now. Leaving him suddenly more disappointed than relieved.

So, which is it? Make up your mind. You either want her here or you don't...

He groaned, and raking his hand through his hair, he sent Paul a fleeting glance. "I can't believe I'm saying this, but it feels good to be back here. I gotta tell you, the way I felt last night, I started thinking maybe I'm getting a little too old for this touring stuff."

He shook his head. "I thought we might have made the wrong

decision cutting back on the bookings here. But with all the time we spend down at the studio, doing backgrounds, recording new releases and whatever else comes up, we have more than enough to keep us busy. And it doesn't look like it's going to let up."

Paul's laugh was more of a snort. "You think you're old? Since I'm six years older than you, what does that make me? Ancient? Believe me, I'm all for cutting back. As long as the money keeps coming in, I'll be happy."

He laughed. "I only know I don't want to be one of these aging musicians trying to keep up with the times." His hand went to the back of his head. "It's not looking good back here ... thinning out. Doesn't seem fair you have more than enough for both of us."

Jason shot him a look. He was grinning. "They say bald is the new sexy."

Paul laughed. "Then it looks like I'll be giving you a run for your money."

They were both laughing as they made their way past the staff offices, the route they needed to take to reach the room they kept all the equipment they needed for events.

A woman walked out into the hallway. Her attention was focused on the papers she was holding in her hand.

Jason came to an abrupt halt.

He gave a sharp intake of breath. To then release it in one slow, shaky swoosh.

His one word was barely a whisper.

"Darcey ..."

Darcey leaned back in her chair, tossing her pen down on the desk. She finally felt like she'd made a breakthrough on some of the more urgent items on her to do list.

She had the employment agency searching for a qualified event planner and assistant. Unfortunately, a chef and sous chef would be a little harder to find, but the agency was confident something would surface soon.

She had even found the time to go over the answers to the questionnaire for the catering staff. Besides a few petty gripes, she found nothing that couldn't be fixed.

She glanced down at her watch. Already past noon, this could explain why she was starving. The bagel and lukewarm coffee she had when she first arrived had worn off a long time ago.

The possibility she might convince the catering people to give her a light lunch, she decided she would stop by the kitchen. She would use the questionnaire as an excuse.

She grabbed the questionnaire and left her office.

At the sound of laughter, she turned to smile at the two men who were coming down the hall.

She froze in her tracks, her heart almost leaping out of her throat.

It was him …

Standing right in front of her, only a few feet away.

Jason …

The silence seemed to go on forever. Her heart now pounding so loud and furious, Darcey couldn't even think. It was the sound of someone clearing their throat, shocking her back to reality, she dropped the papers she was holding.

In a daze, she watched them flutter to the floor. Then she panicked, diving after them. As she began picking them up, she tried to collect her thoughts, searching her mind for something to say.

But with Jason standing right in front of her, everything about him so familiar and coming at her all at once, she knew there wasn't a chance this was going to happen.

You were worried you might have a hard time when you ran into him again. But never, ever had you expected to feel like this.

Once she had gathered up all the papers, she stood, clutching them to her chest. She took a deep breath and glanced over at him.

A bad move, a really dangerous move.

His expression was closed, angry. That this was because of her, she wanted to turn around and run.

As far away as possible.

Instead, she sent him an overly bright smile, her voice coming out too loud. "Hi, Jason. It's been a while, hasn't it?"

Then she could only wait.

Jason didn't respond.

How could he?

The second their eyes met, it was as if this had sucked everything out of him, leaving him completely drained. This was followed by a rush of memories flooding his mind, all having to do with her. With all of this going on, he doubted, even if he tried, he'd be able to say a single word.

Not even a simple hello? Come on ... say something.

He slowly shook his head.

No, you need to be careful... you don't want to say something stupid.

Instead, he studied her, drinking in every detail.

She was everything he had tucked away in his memory, more beautiful than he remembered. Her hair, a warm sun-kissed blonde, was styled the same, falling to her shoulders in a combination of soft waves and curls. He closed his eyes, the memory coming to him so vividly of how he loved tangling the silky strands in his hands when he kissed her. If only to bring her closer.

Her eyes ... what could he say about her eyes? Hazel, with flecks of gold, he could write a song about them alone. In fact, he had maybe even a dozen or more, storing them away in his mind. Shining like the stars in the sky, they pulled him in, taking him to a place he never wanted to leave.

Her mouth was made for kissing, her lips intoxicating and sweeter than any wine.

And yes, he was responsible for every one of these descriptions.

This is what she had done to him. She had allowed him to believe everything he had ever heard about being in love. The love he had written about, yet never truly understood.

She's everything you had ever dared to dream. And you thought she was yours.

Slowly shaking his head, he opened his mouth, his intention to respond.

But, no ... he still couldn't get out a damn thing.

For Darcey, the silence between them seemed to drag on forever. Wasn't he going to say something? Not even a hello?

Evidently not.

She wanted to curl up and die.

Never did you think this would happen. Maybe anger or sarcasm, but never did you expect this ...

She sent a frantic look over at the man who was with Jason, but he only gave her a tentative smile. Growing even more distraught and fumbling with the papers, she glanced over at Jason again.

Her smile was bright, forced. "I ... I'm ... sorry, I really need to go. I ... well, have a nice day."

She turned and almost ran down the hall.

After he watched Darcey disappear around the corner, Jason let out a long, measured breath. Struggling to push his memories to where they belonged, deep in the back of his mind, he slowly shook his head. "Well, that didn't work out all that great, did it?"

Paul was silent, unusual for him. This was because he was trying to figure out what just happened between Jason and this woman. And why she looked so familiar. Had he met her at one time? Maybe at one of their shows?

Then it hit him. An incredulous expression on his face, he just blurted it out. "Damn ... she's the woman in the photograph, isn't she? Come on, give ... who is she? What is she doing here? And where did she come from?"

His gaze slowly shifting over to Paul, Jason ran his hand slowly through his hair before he shrugged. "Her name is Darcey ... Darcey

Hollister. She is the daughter of Steven Hollister. The same Steven Hollister, who is the head of Hollister Investments. And who you said is now the new owner of The Regency."

Pinching the bridge of his nose, he groaned. "I don't think I can do this again. What am I saying? I know I can't."

He abruptly began backing away, shaking his head. "You know what? You keep telling me you want more of an equal partnership in the band? Well, you've got it. Starting right now. Here's your chance to prove yourself. You know the schedule and you know what needs to be done before tomorrow night. So, go for it. Yep, from this moment on, you're in charge."

He turned to walk away, his next words barely audible. "I've gotta get out of here. I need to think, or do something. I only know I can't stay."

Paul watched Jason leave.

Yeah, he could have gone after him, but what good would this do? Obviously, the guy was upset, the state he was in no use to him or the rest of the band.

Paul would later tell his wife it was the strangest thing. He'd swear he had never seen anything like it. Except, maybe in one of those TV romance movies she was always trying to get him to watch.

And here you thought they over-exaggerated everything in those movies.

The only way he could think to explain it, Jason and this woman had taken one look at each other and BAM! They had become frozen in place, as if they had been struck by lightning.

Again, he wasn't much of a romantic, so this was the best description he had.

He told his wife it was a good thing he was there, though. Because if he hadn't cleared his throat to get their attention, who knew what would have happened. They might still be standing there in the damn hallway.

Yep, what happened was proof of what he had thought earlier. Jason was still in love with this woman... this Darcey.

It was also obvious whatever went on between them had ended badly.

But she's a Hollister? Could this get any more complicated?

Massaging the back of his neck, he groaned.

You know this will make a mess of things. This is what had you leaving the last band you were in.

Nope, he didn't want to go through all of that again … the drama, the fighting. Why was it, every time a woman was involved, trouble came barreling in right behind?

Except for Sasha. She was different. Even though, when he told her about the photo, she thought it was the sweetest and most romantic thing she had ever heard. A dreamy smile on her face, she'd told him this was probably fate, Jason and Darcey's second chance at love. Maybe they would get it right this time.

She then had to ruin it, telling him this was proof she had been right all along. All these romance movies she watched? They weren't silly at all.

He shook his head. Okay, he would give her this one time, she could very well be right.

He smiled, just thinking about this.

This had him almost breaking into a trot to get to the equipment room. He needed to get this meeting started and over with if he wanted to spend more time with her.

But before he left the party center today, he was going to stop by this Darcey's office and introduce himself. Somehow, he was going to find out what was up with her and Jason. He didn't know how, but he sure as hell was going to try.

He quickened his pace.

This was going to be the shortest meeting on record.

He wanted to go home.

Standing on the front steps of the party center, Jason watched as a sudden breeze scattered leaves across the steps, sending them swirling at his feet.

It was a beautiful autumn day. The sky was a clear, crystal blue, the temperature a perfect seventy-two degrees. The lake behind him was calm, almost like glass.

Since it was a weekday, it was pretty quiet, the parking lot almost deserted. But he welcomed the solitude.

When he realized his hands were clenched at his sides, he jammed them in his pockets. Closing his eyes, he exhaled a long breath.

He felt like he had been hit by a truck, the life knocked out of him.

Yeah, he'd known there was the possibility he might see Darcey again someday, but he didn't expect this to happen now. Or even in the next decade, for that matter. Nor did he think the sight of her would hit him so hard. But then he also hadn't had the chance to process the news Hollister Investments now owned The Regency.

Because, come on ... what were the chances a billion-dollar company like Hollister would want to invest in a small and family owned party center?

He shook his head ... it made little sense. Their headquarters were in California, for god's sake. There had to be plenty of properties there for them to take on. The Regency was a drop in the bucket for them, nothing like what they were known to scoop up, revitalize and then sell for a handsome profit.

And, after what happened between them, why was Darcey the one to take on the job? He'd think Darcey's father would have encouraged her to stay as far away from Cleveland as possible.

If only to avoid any contact with him.

Yeah, you ... the typical musician, always on the make, as he so vehemently once told you. He couldn't have made his dislike of you any more obvious.

Jason would never forget the last time he talked to Steven Hollister.

It had been the one and only time they had a conversation, if you could even call this. He had made it very clear he hadn't devoted his entire life, working twenty-four-seven to provide security for his family, to then have his daughter throw it all away on some rock star.

Jason actually cracked a smile, thinking about this.

Rock star ... you can't even remember the last time you dreamt of being called a rock star. Maybe when you were in high school? But those plans flew right out the window. Along with the dream of making it big in LA or New York...

Nope, he found out this was not what he wanted at all.

He stared down at his boots, shaking his head as he watched another batch of leaves swirl around his feet.

He didn't understand ... why was Darcey even here? Why would she even agree to come back to Cleveland? Was she here to stay? And if she was, exactly what role would she have with The Regency?

Even more importantly, what did this mean for him? For them?

The possibility he would have to interact with her in a purely business manner had him shaking his head.

No.

As he had told Paul, this was something he couldn't do.

What you refuse to do, you mean.

Jason was reaching for his keys when a SUV pulled up in front of the party center.

He could hear a baby crying even before the driver's door flew open. He began to smile as he watched a woman jump out and, after opening the back door, disappear back inside the SUV to reassure the crying infant.

"Madeline Rose, what is going on that you're making such a fuss? You can't possibly be hungry. And I changed you right before we left, so I know that can't be the problem."

Jason was still smiling as he made his way down the steps.

Abby Kardell.

He'd recognize her anywhere, her copper-penny hued hair glowing like fire in the afternoon sun. Friends since grade school, they had stayed close over the years. This was in part because of their association with the party center.

At one time, Abby had been the event planner for The Regency, but she quit to open her own business selling custom decorated sugar cookies. One of her biggest fans, Jason was always quick to tell everyone she was the best baker in town. And she reciprocated in return, handing out praise for him and his band.

After she'd married Kevin Kardell, who played for Cleveland's professional baseball team, she moved her cookie business out of her home into a much larger facility to accommodate her growing customer following.

Only recently, she had also started taking on orders for custom wedding cakes.

And now, she and Kevin were the new parents of a baby girl, Madeline Rose. The same Madeline Rose who was now making so much noise.

Jason reached the SUV as Abby emerged from the car. "Hey, Abby... do you need help?"

She turned, holding the baby in her arms. A miniature version of Abby with her curly red hair and hazel eyes, her sobs came to an abrupt stop when she saw Jason. Ducking her face against Abby's shoulder, she smiled as she peeked at him from behind her fingers.

Abby laughed. "Oh geeez ... will you look at this. Even as young as she is, she's taken in by your good looks."

She grinned. "You're back. Did you just get home? How was your trip? Did you leave another trail of broken hearts behind like you usually do?" Not waiting for his answers, she thrust Madeline Rose into his arms. "Here... hold her for a minute, will you?"

Before he could protest, she ducked back inside the SUV, still talking. "I need to get her diaper bag. It fell over and I want to make sure her bottle didn't roll under the seat. Every little thing has set her off today. And if we lose that bottle, I don't even want to think about what will happen."

Her eyes wide, Madeline Rose was studying Jason.

Since he knew little about babies, his experience with them very limited, he gave her a nervous smile.

It was when he shifted to get a better hold on her so he could swipe away the one lone tear lingering on her cheek, she broke into a big smile.

He chuckled. "Well, thank you for that beautiful smile. I take it this means you approve?"

Her answer was to reach over to pat his cheek.

Hmm ... look at that. A piece of cake. Goes to show you can handle a baby. Think how good you'd be at it after a little practice.

A sudden memory flashed in his mind, bringing on his look of pain. A completely different pain.

One that went deep.

Then Madeline Rose completely surprised him by grabbing hold of his hair and giving it a good pull.

Who would've thought someone so little could be so strong?

He let out a yelp. "Hey, let go."

He was trying to ease her fingers from his hair when Abby finally emerged from inside the SUV.

He glanced over at her. "Boy, for such a little thing, she's pretty strong."

She was laughing as she untangled his hair from Madeline Rose's fingers before taking her from his arms. "Oh no, I'm so sorry. This is her latest thing, grabbing on to your hair and giving it a good yank. I think it's because she's teething and the pain makes her want to lash out at something. I don't dare wear earrings."

Settling the baby on her hip, she glanced over at the entrance, a long sigh coming from her. "My trunk is full of cookies. I need to go inside and see if I can get someone to take them to the Grand Ballroom. They're for Jake and Grace's wedding tomorrow night."

She smiled at Jason. "By the way, you should know they're thrilled you could make it back in time to play for their wedding."

She made a face. "That reminds me, I also have to go back to the kitchen. I need to make sure the cake is still in the refrigerator and in one piece. I'm not looking forward to this since I heard the chef isn't in a good mood. He's not happy about Jake's restaurant crew taking over the kitchen tomorrow night. But, from what I've heard, he might not be here all that much longer after the scene between him and his sous chef last night. Not a good way to impress new management, get in a big fight while you're in front of a roomful of guests."

She chattered on, not even giving him a chance to get a word in. "You've probably already heard they've let Pam and her assistant go. But, I'm not surprised. Ever since Jenny left, it seems like we've gone through one event planner after another. I think even Pam realized this was coming."

She shook her head. "It looks like these new owners certainly aren't wasting any time, are they? Have you ever heard of them? Hollister Investments? They base their headquarters in California, I've been told. They're supposed to be a decent company to work for."

Jason remained silent, merely nodding.

Noting the sudden look of uncertainty on his face, she patted his arm. "You know you have no reason to worry, right? They'd never let you go. There would be a riot if that happened."

Jason opened his mouth to say something, then abruptly shut it.

If she only knew there could be a riot if someone, namely Darcey's father, were to find out you're still around …

A sudden grin lit up her face before she laughed. "Don't you just love how everyone knows everything that goes on here? There are no secrets, that's for sure."

She made a face. "But I'm just as bad, talking your ear off when you probably want to get going. I imagine you're beat after your long trip."

Finally getting his chance to speak, he cleared his throat. "No, I'm okay. In fact, let me deliver the cookies. You have enough to handle with your little one. Give me your keys. After I drop off the cookies, I'll lock your car and bring you the keys. This way, you can head right on over to the kitchen and check on your cake. I'm sure this is the last place you want to be on a beautiful day like this."

He squinted, looking up at the sun. "I hope it stays nice for the wedding tomorrow."

He grinned. "It makes for a happier bride. And you know how we all feel about that."

Abby nodded, giving an enormous sigh of relief. "Oh, Jason … you're such a sweetheart. I'd love if you did this." For a moment she studied him, a serious expression on her face. "I just don't get it. How is it you haven't been snatched up yet? You're every woman's dream."

About to answer, he hesitated, gazing out at the parking lot. Then he shrugged. "Aw Abby … unfortunately, I don't think that's going to happen. At least not with the woman I want."

Realizing he may have said too much, he grabbed her keys and went to the back of the SUV to open the trunk. "Go on, check on your cake. I'll take care of this for you."

As Abby made her way to the kitchen, she was thinking about Jason. Something wasn't right. Not only because of his dejected mood, but also because of his comment.

What did he mean, the woman he wants?

Seriously? If there was some woman out there who wouldn't jump at the chance to be with him, there had to be something radically wrong with her. Or she was a complete fool.

Because not only was Jason devastatingly handsome, he was also one of the sweetest guys she knew. And so talented with that voice of his. Why, as soon as the words came out of his mouth, it was enough to send you into a trance. Not only when he sang... but when he spoke, too. His deep, husky drawl had a way of turning even a simple string of words into a romantic lullaby.

Not for her, of course. Oh, no … she had Kevin. From the moment they first met, and even though she had tried to deny the attraction between them, Kevin was the only one who captured her heart.

But Jason? She couldn't even count the number of women who, once they found out she and Jason were friends, begged for an introduction.

Yep, it was insane how women chased after him. To have him merely shrug it off, making him even more desirable.

She was going to ask Sophie about this woman he hinted at. Maybe on Monday night, when they met for their once a month girl's night out. If anyone would know what was going on in Jason's life, it would be Sophie. She wasn't shy about asking anyone about anything, personal or not.

Madeline Rose let out a string of baby talk. Evidently, she was beginning to feel neglected.

Shifting her more securely on her hip, Abby pressed a kiss in her hair before she gazed thoughtfully at her. "I wonder who you will fall in love with when you get older?"

She laughed. "What am I thinking? I have a feeling it will be a long, long time before daddy even lets you get within ten feet of a boy."

She was smiling as she turned down the hall leading to the kitchen.

CHAPTER 5

*D*arcey was a mess.

Standing outside the door leading to the kitchen, she gave a quick glance down the hall. Once she saw there was no one around, she leaned against the wall and closed her eyes.

She needed time. If only to calm down. She couldn't catch her breath, she was trembling and her heart was pounding out of control. If she could, she would slide right down the wall onto the floor, put her head down on her knees, and stay there.

At least until she got herself under control.

You have made a terrible mistake. That you actually thought you could come here and be fine when you saw him, well ... this has to be the most stupid assumption you have ever made.

She let out a long, shaky breath. If only she could get Jason's angry expression out of her mind. Even though she wasn't all that surprised at his reaction. She knew that look. It was almost the same one he gave her after they last argued. One she hadn't been able to forget, even after all this time.

She had so hoped, idiotically it now seemed, when they met again, they could at least be civil to each other.

Well, you tried. What more can you do?

She let out another long, shaky breath.

Maybe she should take this as a sign she should pack up and return to California? In fact, this is exactly what she was going to do. She would casually inform her father she'd changed her mind. He would have to find someone else to take over this project.

Yeah, you thought you were ready for this, you'd tell him, but now realize you were wrong.

Filled with a sudden anger, she vehemently shook her head. She was an adult. Jason was an adult. The two of them should be able to put their past behind and do their jobs.

If he had a problem with this, well … he could take his band and go somewhere else.

She groaned, and gazing up at the ceiling, she spoke her thoughts aloud. "*Oh, no* … you can't let this to happen. Just imagine the uproar… everyone would go crazy. Almost the entire city of Cleveland idolizes Jason, considers him as their own private rock star. The last thing you want is to become the villain here."

"Hello?"

Startled, she almost dropped the papers she was still holding. A woman, a worried expression on her face, was standing only a few feet away. A baby in her arms, it was obvious they were mother and daughter because of the same curly red hair.

Shifting the baby to her other hip, the woman smiled, inching closer. "Are you okay?"

The concern in her voice was almost enough to push Darcey over the edge, tears building in the back of her eyes. Since she had arrived, her father had kept her so busy, there had been no time to meet or even carry on a conversation with someone unless it was work related. And now, the fact someone was actually worried about her was almost too much to handle.

You're tired, under a lot of stress … get a hold of yourself.

Managing a faint smile, she shook her head. "Thank you, I'm fine. It's been one of those mornings where everything keeps going wrong. I think I just need a break, maybe grab a quick lunch. Breakfast is feeling like it was a long time ago."

The realization she was rambling, not the best way to make a first good impression, she took a deep breath. "I'm sorry. I'm sure you don't want to hear all about my problems."

The woman held out her hand. "No, it's okay. I'm Abby Kardell, the owner of Sweet Abby's. And the unofficial dessert caterer for The Regency. I supply the cookie favors, desserts and wedding cakes for the events. I'm guessing you are the new event planner?"

Darcey shook her head. "No, no … I'm not. I'm Darcey." She was hesitant to tell Abby who she was. Because everything about this woman had her wishing they could be friends, with the party center out of the picture. So, hen she saw the uncertainty on Abby's face because of her vague reply, she sent her a bright smile.

"Your daughter is beautiful. How old is she?"

As Abby was about to answer, Madeline Rose held out her arms, reaching for Darcey.

Abby laughed. "She always does this. She's pretty spoiled. My husband, Kevin and I believe she thinks everyone has been put on this earth to hold her. So, don't feel obligated. I'll understand."

Before Darcey had the chance to respond, a deep voice came from behind her. A voice until now, she had heard only in her dreams. A voice with the power to make her forget who and where she was.

"I'm pretty sure she doesn't, Abby. If I recall correctly, Darcey isn't all that comfortable around children. Am I right, Darcey?"

Surprised at his behavior, Abby sent him a puzzled glance. This wasn't the Jason she knew.

Darcey had gone completely still, watching as Jason sauntered over to them. His arms crossed, his expression was unreadable.

She opened her mouth to reply, to then promptly close it. In a panic, she turned to Abby. "I should go. I told the chef I would stop by and I'm already late as it is. It was nice meeting you."

She yanked open the door and disappeared into the kitchen.

Abby looked over at Jason.

His eyes closed and his arms falling to his sides, he looked totally deflated.

She sprang into action, her words coming out almost in a hiss.

"Jason Bennett, what was that all about? What did that poor girl ever do to make you come out with what you just said? I've never, ever seen you act like this before."

He dragged his hand through his hair, a pained expression on his face. "It's a long story. One I had hoped to keep in my past. But this doesn't seem like it's going to happen now."

He closed his eyes.

"*Damn ...*"

Before he even had a clue of what she was planning, Abby came at him, shoving Madeline Rose in his arms. "Here, you're in charge of her for the next few minutes. I need to check on my cake. After that, I'm going to find Darcey and invite her to dinner on Monday night. It's our girl's night out. *Oh my god, Jason ...* I don't want her to think everyone in this town acts like you."

At his sheepish expression, she shook her head. "And when I get back, you and I are going over to the coffee shop across the street and you're going to tell me what happened between the two of you. What turned you into this person I've never seen before."

With that being said, she also vanished into the kitchen.

Jason glanced down at Madeline Rose. She was gazing up at him, the telltale trembling of her bottom lip alerting him she was about to cry. Bouncing her up and down in his arms, he strolled over to where there was a bulletin board on the wall, hoping the photos and bright notices would grab her attention.

He was explaining one photo to Madeline Rose when he heard someone open the door to the kitchen.

Thinking it was Abby, he turned to see it was Darcey.

For a brief moment, their eyes met.

She started toward him. Then she abruptly turned and walked away.

Jason groaned, closing his eyes.

What the hell is the matter with you? For the past three years, you've done nothing but dream of seeing her again and now this is the way you act?

He briefly considered going after her, but remembered he had Madeline Rose. Abby wouldn't be too happy if she found them gone.

Looking down at the baby in question, she surprised him with a big smile.

He couldn't help it … he laughed. "You are a little sweetheart, aren't you? I pity the boys when you get older. They won't have a chance."

He turned back to the bulletin board, pointing at another photo. "Look, here's another baby who looks like she's almost the same age as you, I'd think."

Madeline Rose leaned in to gaze at the photo before she turned to give him a solemn look. He nodded back just as seriously as he brushed the hair back from her forehead. As if he was about to share something very confidential, his next comment came as a whisper in her ear. "Yep, I know … you're a lot cuter."

After this brought on another one of her big smiles, he moved to the next photo. *"Hmm* … now let's look at this one…"

And this is how Abby found them when she returned.

But this didn't surprise her. This was all Madeline Rose.

She won over everyone who came into contact with her.

CHAPTER 6

You've got to take a chance,
you've got to risk losing it all.
You've got to close your eyes and leap,
because it might just be worth the fall.
~ Anonymous

"And there you have it. The whole story."

With these words, Jason stood and grabbing their cups, he made his way over to the counter to get coffee refills.

As he made his way back to the table, he saw Abby was watching him, a serious expression on her face. This had him wondering if he told her more than he should have. But after holding everything inside for so long, it felt good to share with someone.

He was also hoping to get a woman's take on the whole sorry mess.

Glancing over at Abby, he shrugged. "So, now I need you to tell me what you think. And I want you to be honest."

Settling Madeline Rose more comfortably in her arms as she drank her bottle, Abby watched Jason play with his coffee stirrer, twirling it between his fingers.

Slumped in his chair, he had a look of complete hopelessness about him. Yet he still looked so darn sexy, if not even more so with his forlorn expression. She would bet every woman in the coffee shop had noticed him. And they would be more than happy to help him forget whatever brought him to this miserable state.

She sighed.

Then she cleared her throat. "Do you still love her?"

His head jerking up, for a moment, he stared at her. Then, dragging his hand over his jaw, he groaned. "Abby, I've loved her from the very first moment I saw her. At least, I'm pretty sure it's love. I only know I never felt like this before. When we were together, everything was so right, what I'd always imagined being in love would be."

He frowned. "But I thought love would be a joyful experience, not this unsettled feeling I've been carrying around since she left. And now she has dropped back into my life and I have no clue why or what she's thinking."

He grimaced. "She's back, yet she's not. So, I'm confused, angry."

Giving a short laugh, he shook his head. "I know I've said the same thing, a dozen times or more in a song. Sorry ..."

"That's okay, I'm used to you going off like that, composing in your mind." She smiled. "How did the two of you meet?"

He gazed around the room, a wistful smile on his face. "We actually met right here in this coffee shop. She was standing in front of me in line for coffee. She turned around, our eyes met, and something clicked. Or I'd describe it more like this sudden explosion of feelings. But in a good way."

He shook his head. "I think we were both so surprised, we didn't know what to do. But it was her turn to place her order, so she turned back to the counter. This had me in a panic, trying like the dickens to think of some way to strike up a conversation with her."

He sent her a shy smile. "You know I'm not good around women, Abby. But with her, it was different. It was so important I didn't let her get away. So, when she started searching through her purse for money, I insisted on paying for her coffee. But I told her this was under one condition, and this was she would share a table with me."

He shook his head, a baffled expression on his face. "I swear, this isn't something I'd normally do. The words just came out. As if I had no control over them, my mind fixated on one thing. And this was I wanted to know more about her. I wanted to know everything."

Abby smiled at the bewildered look on his face.

He returned her smile before he nodded over at the window. "We sat right over at that table for over two hours. Our coffee growing cold, we talked about everything. I could tell she didn't want to leave, and I didn't either. So I asked her out to dinner. When she said yes, I remember thinking it was like I won the lottery."

He chuckled. "Bewitched, bothered and bewildered... that was me. A truck could have run me over and I would have jumped right back up to go running after her."

He began fiddling with the coffee stirrer again, refusing to meet her gaze. "I don't know, maybe I'm holding on to a dream. Or it's one of those—since I can't have her, I want her even more—kind of thing. I ... *oh heck, Abby* ... I'm a guy. You know how we are. We're slow to catch on. And completely clueless with something like this."

He tossed the stirrer on the table, a wry smile on his face. "How ironic... I can write about it, sing it and convince other people they can find love, but I can't do it in my own life."

Abby removed the bottle from a now sleeping Madeline Rose's mouth and after tucking her more comfortably against her, she smiled at him. "Jason, you're going to think I'm nuts, but I gotta say, I'm thrilled to see you like this."

He burst out laughing. "What? You like to see me miserable?"

She held her finger to her lips, shaking her head at him. "Shh... this little one is not a happy camper when her nap gets disturbed. What I'm trying to say... I'm happy to see how much in love you are with Darcey. Because from what I've witnessed, I'm pretty sure she feels the same about you. Otherwise, you both wouldn't be so cautious with each other. I see it as you both care so much, but are afraid of getting hurt again."

She grinned. "I thought I despised Kevin the first time I met him. But I think I was trying to protect my heart. Like you, I didn't want to get hurt again."

She frowned. "Peter breaking off the engagement less than a month before the wedding did it for me."

"Yeah, I remember. Not a good time." He shook his head, his eyes on the coffee stirrer he was twirling between his fingers again.

She cleared her throat. "She's very pretty."

His head jerked up, a wistful smile on his face. "She is, isn't she? Like sunshine on a cloudy day."

When Abby laughed, his face reddened with embarrassment. Then, despite himself, he grinned, too. It was one of those grins he was so well known for, bringing women ready to pledge their life and everything else to win him for their own. "Aw... Abby, stop it. You know I can't help it."

Abby nodded. "I know. And this is why we all love you."

She reached for what was left of the cookie they had decided to share. Though, for the record, she ate most of it. This was even after they both agreed the cookie in no way measured up to one of hers.

After she popped the piece in her mouth, she studied him.

This had him wary, sitting up straighter in his chair. "What are you drumming up in that crazy mind of yours?"

Smoothing back the wispy curls from Madeline Rose's face, she nodded, her expression thoughtful. "Do you know why Darcey's here? Or how long she's planning to stay?"

Her eyes went wide. "Maybe she was the driving force behind buying The Regency. This gave her the excuse to come back to Cleveland and see you again."

Shaking his head, he threw the coffee stirrer in his cup. "After the last conversation we shared, I can't imagine she would ever want to come back to Cleveland, at least not to see me." He shrugged. "And I know there is no way her father would encourage this."

He sighed. "And there you have it... when it comes to women and what they want, I'm clueless. If anything, they scare me."

He grinned. "Except for you and Sophie. I guess this is because we've known each other for so long."

Abby sighed. "Oh, Jason ... you amaze me. You could have any woman you want. My gosh, when you put on a show, you have them all dreaming about you when they go to bed that night."

When he ducked his head, embarrassed, she shook her head. "But forget about that. Let's get back to Darcey. If you want to get her back, you need to keep showing up wherever she is."

She frowned. "But not to the point you're stalking her. That would be creepy. No woman likes that. The best scenario would be if you could re-enact the time you first met. Women love that kind of stuff."

She grinned. "I know I do."

She watched him smile at this before she continued. "Before I left the kitchen, I told Darcey about our girl's night out on Monday and she said she'd try to come. If I see her tomorrow, I'll remind her again. Maybe we'll be able to get some information out of her."

Her eyes lit up. "We'll scheme up an accidental meeting between the two of you."

He groaned. "Abby ... I don't think —"

She grinned, cutting him off. "Don't worry, we'll come up with such a good plan, she won't even know we're involved."

She stood, gently settling Madison Rose in his arms. "Hold her while I go to the restroom. She's out, so she'll be fine. I have to hand it to her, she's a good sleeper. Be right back."

Jason gazed down at the sleeping Madeline Rose. He had held a baby in his arms more times today than he had in the past few years combined.

And it was starting to grow on him.

Yeah, it's turned out to be a lot easier than you thought.

Maybe it could be the same with Darcey? He shook his head.

Deep in thought, he gazed down at Madeline Rose's innocent little face, watching as she slept.

And this is how Abby found them when she returned.

Paul's meeting with the band at The Regency had lasted longer than he intended, so now he was in a hurry.

In fact, he almost passed right by Darcey's office before he came to a quick halt. He glanced in to see she was at her desk. Working on her computer, she didn't notice he was there.

He loudly cleared his throat. "Hey ..."

Lifting her head, her smile was tentative. "Hey..."

Taking this as an invitation to enter, he sauntered over to her desk and held out his hand. "I can see you're busy, so I won't take up much of your time. But I wanted to introduce myself. I'm Paul Adams, a member of the band, Banded Together."

He paused for effect. "You know, Jason's band. Earlier, when we saw you, I got the impression you and Jason know each other, right?"

She shook his hand. "Hello, Paul. I'm ..." As before with Abby, she paused, unsure about sharing her identity. But since she didn't know what Jason might have told Paul about her, it might be better to be upfront.

She sent him a bright smile. "I'm Darcey ... Darcey Hollister. It's so nice to meet you. I'm sorry I haven't made the rounds yet, but I've been so busy trying to sort things out. It's been a little overwhelming."

She shrugged. "But I'll get there."

His goal to work as much charm as possible into the conversation, Paul gave her his best smile. He also hoped this would make her forget about the cool reception she received from Jason. Don't think he hadn't noticed how she ignored his comment about her connection to Jason.

He nodded. "I'm sure you will. So, Darcey, tell me... are you here only to help with the transition, or are you planning to stay on?"

Darcey slowly sat back in her chair. She hesitated before she shrugged. "I guess you could say I'm the person in charge, at least for the time being. So, I'm not sure what my title is, or if I'll even have one. I only know my job is to bring The Regency back to the successful venue it once was."

She smiled. "But don't worry, I won't meddle with the band. I know a good thing when I see it. So it's safe to say you'll find nothing will change, and you'll be able to carry on as you have all along."

"Thanks, that's good to know." Paul's expression was as non-committal as he could manage.

But in his mind?

There he was like... *damn,* wait until Jason hears this.

Making his move towards the door, he smiled. "This is good to hear. Know that you can count on our help. Any time."

He paused, turning back to her. "Here's a suggestion, why don't you stop by the equipment room before the reception tomorrow night? You can meet the rest of the band members and see what a great bunch of guys we all are. Jason included."

He smiled. "But I guess you already know that... about Jason, that is. And you don't have to give me an answer right now. Just think about it, okay?"

He was halfway out the door when she called out to him. "Paul? Can I ask you something?"

Ah ha ... Thinking he was going to get the scoop on Jason, he was smiling as he turned to her. "Sure, ask away."

"I heard one of your band members had a run in with Rob Johnson. Will you let me know if something like this happens again?"

He nodded. The look passing between them confirmed they both had the same opinion about the contractor. They didn't trust him.

This made Darcey feel much better. "And Paul?"

He turned back to her again. "Yes?"

There was the hint of a smile on her face. "I agree with what you said about Jason ... he is a great guy." Her gaze dropped back to her computer.

He was smiling as he left.

Once he was in his jeep, Paul sent Jason a text.

He was chuckling as he turned on the engine. He had a pretty good idea what Jason's reaction was going to be.

Yep, things are going to get very interesting.

The windows down and his favorite country mix turned up loud, he drove out of the parking lot, heading for home.

But there were two quick stops he had to make. The florist, then the wine store.

He had less than twenty-four hours to spend with Sasha before he had to be back at the party center.

His plan was to make the most of this time.

As Jason watched Abby start up her SUV, his phone buzzed. He pulled it out of his pocket to see he had a text from Paul.

> Seems we have a new boss. At least for now. Darcey Hollister. I got this out of her before I left The Regency. Not sure how you feel about this.

He groaned, dragging his hand through his hair.

Abby glanced over at him. "*Uh, oh ... what's wrong?*"

He handed her the phone, watching a big smile spread across her face as she read the text. "Well, this is going to make everything a lot easier, isn't it?"

She handed back the phone, giving him a nod. "I promise you, I'm on this. But right now, I need to get going. We lucked out and got a babysitter, so it's a rare date night for me and Kevin. See you ..."

After Abby drove off, Jason sent a glance over at the party center. Should he swallow his pride and go talk to Darcey? At least apologize for his unacceptable behavior?

No, not yet. You've got to think this through. You need to be sure.

Because if there was one thing he knew, this time he couldn't make any mistakes.

CHAPTER 7

From her office window, Darcey watched the electrician connect the last string of lights before he shouted out an order to hit the power.

The courtyard was instantly transformed into a magical fairyland, thousands of miniature lights meticulously strung through the bushes and trees, randomly beginning to twinkle.

This was followed by the pop of lights lining the newly installed stone walkways.

With a panoramic view of Lake Erie in the background, the high-topped tables and benches were arranged for casual conversation. Large stone pots, holding mums in deep vibrant hues of yellow, burnt orange and purple, added just the right touch of warmth and color.

It was a perfect outdoor reception area.

Darcey gave a sigh relief. The completion of this project was her first chance to prove she was capable of heading the renovation. And with the limited time they had to work with, it was amazing everything had been finished ahead of schedule. That it would be available gathering space for the wedding reception scheduled to start in less than an hour, was a bonus.

The electrician, aware that Darcey had been checking their

progress throughout the day, sent her a thumbs up. As she was about to respond, Rob Johnson slowly sauntered over to speak to him.

Quickly ducking from view, she returned to her desk.

Closing her eyes, her sigh was frustrated.

You're acting like a child. You can't ignore him forever. After all, he is the head contractor.

As if he had read her mind, something almost too frightening to think about, she opened her eyes to see he was standing in the doorway to her office, his hand raised about to knock.

As had happened the first time they met, his gaze traveled slowly over her before he spoke. "Hey ... Ms. Hollister, can I have a minute of your time?"

A minute?

Fine. She'd give him a minute. But this was all he was going to get, not a second more. If anything, a minute with him was ten times more than she wanted to give him. Maybe a hundred times more...

Pasting a bright smile on her face and adopting her most business-like tone, she gave him a quick nod. "Sure, what's up?"

He appeared amused as he moved to stand in front of her. Placing his hands on the desk, he leaned in closer.

Too close.

Between this and the overpowering scent of his cologne, it took everything she had not to back away as he began to speak. "As your father requested, I wrote up a list of my recommendations. When I called him about this, he was quick to remind me you're the person in charge. I should be going over this list with you, not him. So, it looks like we need to set up a time to get together. Since I'm still waiting for quotes on a couple of things, this coming Tuesday would probably work best. Preferably late afternoon."

Here he stopped to shake his head, a mocking smile on his face. "This, of course, all depends on your schedule. I imagine you're finding all of this a little over your head."

At first, she didn't respond. Her anger wouldn't let her.

So he doesn't think you know what you're doing, does he?

Her first instinct was to tell him there was no need for them to meet, just get the work done and leave her alone.

But this would send the message he was right, she didn't know what she was doing. Or worse yet, he had free rein.

Absolutely not. This is the last thing you want.

Her nod was curt. "Sure, Tuesday will be fine. Around four?"

Having already determined he was the type who liked to call the shots, she wasn't the least bit surprised when he shook his head. "Let's make it around five, plan on doing it over dinner."

Before she could respond, he gave her a mock salute and slipped out of her office. As silently as he had arrived.

Like a snake.

She put her head down in her hands and groaned.

You only have yourself to blame. You're the one who convinced your father you could handle this.

She pushed away from her desk. She was going to take Jack up on his offer and stop in to meet the band.

After briefly wondering if she should touch up her make-up, she shook her head. There was no need for this. She wasn't trying to impress anyone. And if Jason was there?

Well, he'd just have to suck it up.

Flipping off the light and closing her office door, she went marching down the hall.

CHAPTER 8

Life is a song.
Love is the music.
~ Anonymous

*H*er shoulders thrown back and a determined look on her face, Darcey went marching around the corner to the room designated for the band as their office and to store their equipment.

She slipped past the partially opened door. From what she could see, there was no one was in the room. It appeared the band members had already left for the Grand Ballroom to set up for the wedding reception.

Well, you tried.

She turned to leave when she heard music… guitar music.

Now, the logical thing to do would be to call out, announce her presence. But for some insane reason, she felt a sudden need to hide. So, she cautiously squeezed in between a rack loaded with the band's costume changes and a large up-right keyboard. From there, she could see someone was in the back of the room.

It was Jason.

Seated on an old leather couch, this and a desk the only furniture in the room, he was working on a song.

She watched as he sang a few words. Then, after writing something on a notepad, he played a few notes on his guitar.

The familiar sound of his voice floating over to her, she closed her eyes, a wistful smile on her face. The memory of three years ago, the one and only other time she had been in this room, was still so clear in her mind.

The band had finished up for the night and everyone had left, leaving only her and Jason. Waiting for him to finish a phone call, she had sat down at the piano, idly fingering the keys.

He had sat next to her, smiling down at her. It was a smile that held her spellbound, her fingers dropping from the keys.

Her head on his shoulder, she had watched as his hands skimmed across the keys. His voice like velvet, he made up the lyrics as he sang. It was a song dedicated to her.

When she asked him how he could do this so effortlessly, he had studied her, a bemused smile on his face. Then, after he framed her face in his hands, his mouth brushing over hers, he told her as long as she was around, he would never run out of songs.

She inspired him.

She sent the words flowing right out of him.

The kiss that followed was one she would never forget. She was pretty sure this was when she fell in love with him. Deeply and forever in love.

Not that this did you any good, as you were soon to find out.

Because, in love or not, in less than a week she was back in California. Trying to convince herself she had made the right decision to leave.

But when she finally realized she'd made the biggest mistake of her life, she called him to leave the message she needed to talk to him.

But he never returned the call.

It was as though the distance between Ohio and California had become unreachable, millions of miles apart instead of a few thousand.

So, he was lost to her.

And what had she wanted to talk to him about? She wanted to know what he would think about her moving to Ohio.

She wanted to be his inspiration ... for his songs, his life, for everything. But now, watching him at work on a new song, she wondered if she was too late.

Maybe he had already found someone else to inspire him.

More than she ever could.

Jason was restless.

He had been feeling this way all day.

Right now he should be in the ballroom with the rest of the guys, helping set up. But Paul had been insistent they didn't need his help.

Hadn't Jason told him it was time he took on more responsibility? Well, in that case, this is what he was doing. Starting out by offering Jason this opportunity to relax.

A bonus of sorts. This way, he would be refreshed and ready for the night ahead.

After all, he was the star.

You're the star? What the ...?

He set his guitar on the couch. Coming to his feet, he massaged the back of his neck, a wry smile on his face.

There was no doubt about it... Paul was up to something.

Jason's sudden move had Darcey swiftly ducking behind the clothes rack.

Her plan, to leave the same way she came in, never had a chance. She bumped into the keyboard. On wheels, this set it in motion, rolling across the floor. She tried to make a grab for it, but lost her balance and wound up shoving it instead.

And this, she would have to say, was when everything began to go so terribly wrong.

The keyboard picked up speed as it began rolling across the room.

Horrified, she could only watch as it crashed into the wall and toppled over, hitting the floor with a loud bang.

Now in a panic, she backed right into the clothes rack. Only to find it was also on wheels.

The next thing she knew, she was on the floor, watching the clothes rack weaving erratically across the room. The hangers wildly swinging from side to side, sending clothes flying everywhere.

"Oh, no, no, no ..."

Now she was even more determined to get out of the room. In her attempt to scramble to her feet, she found she was at eye level with a pair of jeans-clad legs. Along with what appeared to be a very expensive and custom-made pair of leather boots.

Jason's jeans ... Jason's boots ...

It briefly flashed through her mind, this was one of the many little things she remembered about him. He was always so well-dressed.

But right now? This was the last thing she should even be thinking about.

She groaned, closing her eyes.

Oh my god... can you please just die? Or at least, disappear?

Slowly sitting back on her heels, she waited.

To say it scared the hell out of Jason when the keyboard went flying into the wall would be completely understandable. Frozen in place, he watched as it tipped over, hitting the hardwood floor with a sound comparable to that of a mini explosion.

Still in shock, he then watched as the clothes rack began rolling in the opposite direction, sending clothes and hangers flying everywhere and onto the floor.

Everywhere...

What the ...? What just happened here?

A faint cry was his answer. This was followed by silence.

He groaned

You've got to be kidding me.

As he slowly made his way towards where the cry had originated, he didn't know if he should be concerned or angry. He hoped it wasn't some young girl who had sneaked in, hoping to get a photo or autograph. He didn't even want to think about how many times this had happened in the past.

But until now, this had only happened when the band was on the road.

Never here at The Regency.

Cautiously moving even closer, he saw someone sitting on the floor.

It was a woman.

Seriously?

Dragging his hand through his hair, he exhaled a long, irritated breath. His voice was an angry bark in the silent room. "For crying out loud, who are you and why are you even in here? This area is off limits, only staff members allowed. Didn't you see the sign outside in the hallway? It's there as a warning for people like you. Because, look what happened. Not only have you made a mess of things, you could have hurt yourself."

When this was only met with silence, he grew concerned. As mad as he was, you have to remember Jason is basically a good guy. The last thing he wanted, was for someone to get hurt.

And now, knowing it was a woman as he had suspected, he didn't want any tears or hysterics.

God, no...

He moved closer, the tone of his voice much softer. "Hey, you're okay, right? You didn't get hurt, did you?"

This is when Darcey finally lifted her head.

For a few seconds, he stared at her, incredulous.

When he spoke, it came out almost in a croak. "Darcey?"

She shook her head.

And she kept shaking it. And the whole time she tried to explain, she couldn't seem to quit shaking it. If only because she was so embarrassed.

So, so, so embarrassed.

"Jason, I'm sorry. I ... well, I ... what I mean is, Paul asked if I'd like to stop by before the reception, introduce myself to the guys in the band. And well ... at first, when I walked in, I didn't think anyone was here. But then I heard music, and I saw it was you ... and ..." She clamped her mouth shut.

She certainly couldn't tell him, once she realized it was him, she couldn't tear herself away. Instead, she glanced frantically over to where the keyboard was upside down on the floor.

Her distress escalated. "*Oh my God*, I hope I didn't break your keyboard. If I did, I'll pay for the repairs. And the clothes that got knocked on the floor, I'll pay to have them cleaned."

She reached up to run her hand through her hair, horrified to see it was shaking. Averting her gaze, her next words were just barely audible. "Again, I'm so, so sorry. I don't know what I was thinking..."

A long silence was his only answer.

It felt like an eternity.

She didn't understand, why wasn't he saying anything? Was he still angry at her from before, to the point, he now wasn't going to talk to her at all?

Again?

You want to just die...

As you can imagine, there was a lot going on in Jason's mind.

Most of this had to do with Paul. How he was going to knock his block off when he saw him.

Paul was giving you this opportunity to relax, was he?

Nope, this was Paul's plan to get him and Darcey together.

He invited her to meet the band?

What could he have been thinking?

Because look at the outcome, not even Paul could have dreamt up this one.

But why was he surprised? Ever since Paul had married Sasha, he'd been on this let's-get-everyone-married campaign. How many times had he gone off on a lecture about this? Along with his annoying reminder, at his age, Jason should start thinking about settling down.

As far as you're concerned, this is not a big priority in your life right now.

Again, he was only thirty-one.

But now, here in the equipment room, he found he was having a hard time trying to deal with the fact Darcey was only inches away ... on the floor and at his feet.

Not only was his mind scrambling, this had his body on complete alert.

The hint of her perfume alone was enough to take him right back in time. A scent that, for the longest time, had flooded his senses every time he walked into his bedroom.

He'd swear the fragrance had lingered, haunting him for months after she left. And now it was back, a sensuous reminder of so many memories of her.

But remember, you need to be careful ... you can't let yourself get sucked back in again.

His arms crossed and gazing down at her, Jason tried to hide his smile. He wondered what would happen if he tried to joke around a little, get her to laugh.

Maybe something corny about her falling for him?

Nah...

He shook his head. This could be a mistake. The Darcey he used to know would have laughed. But he wasn't sure how this Darcey would respond. And to be honest, he rather liked she didn't know what he was thinking.

He held out his hand. "Here, take my hand so we can get you up off the floor. You didn't hurt yourself, did you?"

She shook her head, refusing to look at him.

When he saw she was still so obviously embarrassed, he decided he might have been wrong. Maybe a little humor would be the better choice after all. He cleared his throat, a smile twitching the corner of his mouth. "You could've just made yourself known, you know. Instead of sneaking around. Let me give you a hint, this isn't a good way to gain your employee's trust."

He suddenly pulled his hand back and crossing his arms back over his chest, he glared down at her, one eyebrow raised. "Wait a minute

… are you spying on me?"

Her head jerking up, she scowled at him. "No, of course not. I have no reason to spy on you. Why would you even think this? If you had been listening earlier, you'd remember what I told you. I'm here because Paul suggested I meet the rest of the band. How was I supposed to know you'd be the only one here? If I had, I guarantee you, this is the last place I'd want to be."

Unfazed by this outburst, darn if he wasn't grinning.

Uh, oh …

She eyed him warily, watching as he slowly shook his head. "My, my, my … someone seems to be a little angry here. And if anyone were to be mad, shouldn't it be me? Look around you." He waved his hand towards the keyboard and the clothes rack, "I'm certainly not the one who caused all of this destruction."

When her face crumpled, as though she was about to cry, he swiftly changed course. "Hey, I'm only kidding." He held out his hand again. "Come on, at least let me help you up off the floor before someone comes in here, thinking who knows what. Believe me, information travels fast around here. Rumors about the two of us making out behind the clothes rack probably isn't something you would want to happen, being the new kid on the block and all."

When she still held back, refusing to take his hand, he sent a quick glance around them, shaking his head. "*Umm* … you have to admit, it looks like we had here a wild time. Clothes all over the floor, you at my feet and …"

This galvanized her into action, grabbing his hand. Careful to avoid any further contact with him once she was back on her feet, she made a big deal out of brushing any possible dirt from her dress.

He watched this, taking in the perfect fit of her dress, short enough to show off her fabulous legs. Legs he could remember tangled with his when they shared his bed, loving each other with a passion he had never shared with anyone.

A slow heat traveling through him, he drew in a ragged breath.

My god … you want this again. You want this with every single inch of you. Right here and now, if you could.

After dragging his hand through his hair, he sent a quick glance at the mess surrounding them before he looked over at Darcey.

Their eyes locked, the intensity in his sending a flood of memories through her.

Oh god, it's like you never left him. Get out of here before you do something stupid. Such as telling him you wouldn't mind giving everyone something to talk about.

She glanced down at her watch before she slowly began to back away. "I should be going. I want to greet the bride and groom when they arrive. I know a lot of people have expressed concern with all of the changes being made. So, I like to reassure them the best I can. As far as I know, there's no issues with the wedding tonight, which is good. But I still want to be there."

And now she was babbling. "But I can't leave without helping you clean up this mess. I don't think anything is ruined. Except maybe for that?" She nodded over at the keyboard. At the same time, she began gathering up the clothing scattered across the floor.

And yes, she kept right on chattering, non-stop. "I'll just straighten up what I can before I go. I'm not sure if you had these in any special order, but—"

Jason was scrambling, his mind in overdrive. Because, truthfully? He couldn't care less about the keyboard. Or the clothes. That he and Darcey were even talking to each other was all that mattered. And something he considered a miracle.

In one swift move, he was next to her, his two fingers pressed to her mouth. This simple touch bringing on a tremor that vibrated through both of them, he trailed his fingers in a slow path down over her jaw before he reluctantly dropped his hand to his side.

A smile slowly curved his lips. "Darcey, stop. Don't worry about it. I'll take care of the clothes. And the keyboard? We haven't used it in so long, I'm not even sure it works anymore. We should have given it away a long time ago."

He glanced over at the keyboard. "I think the only reason it's even still here is because it was the first major purchase we made as a band. When we thought we were so cool, big things to come."

A smile flashed across her face. "Just so you know, you still are cool... very cool." With this, she took another step back, her feet almost getting tangled up in a hanger thrown from the clothes rack.

Oh, geeez ... you'd think you would have learned your lesson and left the way a normal person would. But, no ...

"Hey, be careful there." He reached out to steady her, his hand lingering on her arm.

Again, his touch sent a shudder racing through them.

Now she was beyond flustered. "*Ooops* ... if this isn't the proof I need to get out of here before I do more damage, I don't know what is."

She turned to leave. "Please tell Paul I stopped by, okay?"

"Darcey ..." He called out just as she reached the door.

She turned. "Yes?"

She did this so quickly, he wondered if she had been waiting for this.

And even though he knew he was grasping at something that probably wasn't there, he was filled with a sudden rush of hope.

He smiled. "I'll tell Paul you stopped by. And ..." he hesitated slightly, "I want you to know, it's good to see you, too."

For a long moment, she searched his face, the warmth of his smile reaching her all the way across the room.

Then she nodded, realizing this was his way of apologizing for the silent treatment he had given her yesterday outside of her office.

After she gave him one more smile, she turned and walked out of the room. While he watched her go, a song already forming in his mind.

He couldn't fight it ...

She really was his inspiration.

Darcey was walking on air.

She didn't even notice she passed right by Paul on the way to her office.

Once there, she closed the door and leaned back against it. Her arms wrapped around herself, she didn't move, waiting for her heart-beat to settle back to normal.

But, for the first time since she returned to Cleveland, she felt like maybe, just maybe, she had made the right decision.

Or maybe this was fate? She had finally stumbled onto where she was meant to be?

Whatever it was, she was going to enjoy the moment

A few minutes later, she left her office. She wanted to do a last check of the Grand Ballroom. Everything needed to be perfect for the bride and groom.

Now even more than ever.

True love deserved the best.

Paul walked into the equipment room to find Jason hard at work, struggling to get the keyboard back on its stand.

At least, this was his intention. But who would have thought the damn thing was so heavy? And so awkward to maneuver?

Definitely not what you would call a one-man job.

After gazing around the room and noting the unusual location of the clothing rack, with almost all of what had been hanging on it scattered across the floor, Paul scratched his head. "Jesus, what happened here? Did you get into a fight with someone?"

Jason glanced over at him. "Nope, no fight. Let's just say there was a minor accident. And how did this happen, you ask? I'm going to put the blame on this little plan you cooked up to get me and Darcey together. As you can see, it almost turned into a complete fiasco."

Picking up a hanger and a jacket from the floor, he tossed them to Paul.

After Paul put the jacket on the hanger and hung it on the rack, he shrugged. "Me? What did I do?"

His attempt to appear clueless fell flat, a telltale smile twitching at the corner of his mouth.

Jason chuckled. "You know damn well what I'm talking about.

Now, just don't stand there... help me get this thing back on the stand. I swear it weighs a ton."

Once they accomplished this, Jason pulled out his phone to check the time. "Whoa, I didn't know it was so late. We'll have to clean up the rest later. Right now, we need to get over to the ballroom."

As he headed for the door, Paul groaned. "So... you're not going to let me know what happened?"

Jason stuffed his phone back into his pocket. "Nope. I'm not. You should know by now I prefer to keep my personal life private. Especially when there is a member of the opposite sex involved."

Paul grinned. "A member of the opposite sex, eh? So, it looks like my plan may have worked?"

Already out the door, Jason's response was brief. "Again, you'll never know."

But, by the confidence in his stride and his sudden good mood, Paul had the answer he needed.

He was also feeling pretty proud of himself.

Because it sure looked like his plan had worked.

Big time...

CHAPTER 9

It's time to drink champagne
And dance on the table.
It's our time to celebrate.
~ Anonymous

Slowly bringing the kiss to an end, Jake Martin lifted his head to fall right into his wife's eyes.

A deep crystal blue, today they appeared even more stunning, shining from the tears she couldn't seem to stop for the life of her.

And, yes, you heard right.

His wife ...

"Hmm ... we've been married for," he pushed back the sleeve of his tuxedo to look at his watch, his next words coming out in an unsteady whisper, "not even an hour and already I love you even more, Gracie Martin. That we are finally husband and wife is the best feeling in the world."

"I know." She sighed against him before she began to laugh. "Even though I do believe Bella stole the show when she ran up to you, clamoring for you to pick her up."

She shook her head. "And, when she yelled out 'I do' with me, I thought everyone in the church was going to give her a standing ovation."

She grinned up at him. "I bet you never thought you'd be holding a child while exchanging wedding vows."

She reached up to give him a kiss, her voice shaky. "I can't believe how lucky we both are to have you. I love you so much."

Linking his fingers with hers, he brought her hand to his mouth for a kiss. "*Ah …* I believe I'm the lucky one."

The limo had now come to a stop. After sending a glance out the window, he pressed a quick kiss to her cheek. "It appears we're the last to arrive. Sam and Livy are waiting for us on the steps."

He grinned over at her. "Sam is carrying Bella. I swear, the two of them have become the best of friends. He was grinning from ear to ear when she informed him from now on she was going to call him Uncle Sammy."

After the driver came around to open the door and Jake helped Gracie out of the limo, the photographer gestured for Livy, Sam and Bella to join them. "I need to get photos of all of you with the lake in the background. With the blue sky and the sun hitting the water, it's the perfect backdrop."

Later, when they were able to view all of the wedding photos, they both agreed the photo of Jake bending Gracie back over his arm to give her a passionate kiss, was one of their favorites.

But their most favorite?

This would be of Jake holding Bella in his arms, with Gracie next to him and her head on his shoulder. Their smiles were as bright as the sun shining down on them.

It was this kind of day, perfect in every way.

The sound of a child's excited chatter a sign the wedding party had arrived, Darcy left her office.

She had been told the bride and groom were Jake and Gracie Martin. Four years old, the flower girl's name was Bella and Gracie and Jake were in the process of adopting her.

But Darcey was most interested in the only other two people in the wedding party, the maid-of-honor and the best man, Livy and Sam Bridges.

This was the same Livy who sent the ring Darcey wore hanging from a sterling silver chain around her neck.

Sam and Livy had just become engaged when Livy sent the ring. They had also purchased the house that once belonged to Darcey's grandparents. Now married, they were renovating it, one room at a time.

In the letter that accompanied the ring, Livy explained how she and Sam had found the ring on the floor when they saw the house for the first time. It was the initials engraved on the inside of the band, and where it was found, that made her think it might be Darcey's.

This is why she was so interested in Livy and Sam.

She wanted to thank them.

For sending her the ring and keeping one of her fondest memories alive.

Darcey was suddenly wrapped in a big hug from the knees down.

This came from Bella. Gazing up at Darcey, she had a huge grin on her face. "Daddy said there is going to be a cake, a *really* big cake. Can I see it?"

"Sorry about that. Let's just say she's very excited." This came from Jake who was laughing as he scooped up Bella.

He extended his hand. "I'm Jake Martin. You must be Darcey?"

Darcey smiled at the incredible happiness on his face. "Yes, I am... Darcey Hollister. Congratulations from all of us here at The Regency. You all look so happy. Gracie, you look absolutely beautiful and Jake, so handsome."

She smiled down at Bella. "And you ... how pretty you look. In answer to your question... yes, there is a cake, a big one. With lots of frosting. After you have a piece, you'll have to tell me if you liked it, ok?"

After she received a very vigorous nod from Bella, she turned to

Jake. "You'll be glad to know your staff is hard at work in the kitchen. And everything else is ready ... appetizers, bar, the works. So, enjoy."

"Good... and thank you."

Jake reached for Gracie's hand. "Come on, beautiful ... I promised everyone we would stop by the kitchen so I can show you off."

Darcey turned to Livy and Sam, impulsively reaching out to give Livy a hug. "Livy, I don't know how I can ever thank you enough for your letter and the ring. I honestly thought I'd never see the ring again. It's very special to me."

The relief on Livy's face was instantaneous. *"Thank goodness ...* at first I wasn't sure if I should send it, but since we did find it in your grandparent's house, my intuition told me it had to be yours." She searched Darcey's face. "I hope the memories it brought are happy ones?"

Darcey nodded. "Yes, and it made me think about what I want in life." A wistful smile on her face, she shrugged. "What I really need."

She turned to Sam. "And you... how can I ever thank you for what you're doing with the house. The last time I saw it was about three years ago, when it was in such disrepair. When my father put it on the market, I was so afraid the buyer's only interest would be in the land, eventually demolishing the house."

Sam pulled Livy close, smiling down at her before he responded. "Well, you have this woman to thank. She was the one who convinced me the house was calling out to be saved. All because of a birthday party she attended there when you were children. You'll have to come by and see the progress we've made."

Livy was nodding. "I know you'll love what Sam has done so far. I only wish I could be as talented as he is. And, yes... feel free to visit anytime."

"I will." Darcey gave them both a smile. "But right now, I need to check on a few things. And you need to get a drink and something to eat. It was so nice meeting you."

Once she left, Sam pressed a kiss to the top of Livy's head. "Well, she seems nice. And she was happy to get the ring. So, everything is good."

He took hold of her arm. "I don't know about you, baby... but I can use a drink." He grinned. "And I'm starving. I haven't been able to stop thinking about the appetizers Jack was describing earlier. They sound amazing."

On their way to the Grand Ballroom, they passed by Jason. Surrounded by a large group of wedding guests. Livy wasn't surprised to see they were all women.

A few seconds later, she came to an abrupt stop.

"Oh my gosh ..." she gazed up at Sam, a shocked expression on her face.

Puzzled, Sam glanced around them, wondering what he'd missed. Seeing nothing out of the ordinary, he searched her face. "What is it, sweetheart?"

Her hand going to her mouth, her eyes were wide. "Sam... did you see who we just passed?"

He nodded, a slightly confused expression on his face. "Are you talking about the guy you and all of your friends carry on about ... the hot-band-leader-guy, Jason-what's-his-name?"

He frowned. "Though I don't see what you all see in him. He's okay and everything, but I just don't see what the fuss is all about."

She sent him a startled look. "Sam, are you jealous?"

At his guilty expression, she laughed. "You are, aren't you? Well, don't worry, as far as I'm concerned, he doesn't even come close to you when it comes to being hot."

Her vote of confidence, making him happy, merited a kiss. This also had him completely forgetting what they had been talking about.

Again, he was hungry. So, all his focus was on the appetizers waiting for them right around the corner.

But she hadn't forgotten. "Sam, do you understand what I'm getting at?"

No, he didn't. If anything, he was now even more confused. See what?

He cleared his throat. "I'm not quite sure ... you tell me."

Raising her face to the ceiling, she groaned. "Sam, *come on* ... think about it. Jason Bennet, what are his initials?"

Comprehension crossing his face, he began nodding. *"Hmm ... J. B. Ah ...* now I get it. The same initials on the ring."

Livy was nodding like crazy. "Yes, yes ... Oh my gosh, I wonder..."

Her jaw dropping, she stared up at Sam. "Could this be why Darcey came back to Cleveland? Maybe at one time, there was something between them. So, she persuaded her father to buy The Regency, hoping this would be her chance to rekindle their relationship. You do know her father owns Hollister Industries, don't you?"

Sam was shaking his head. "Baby, I don't know about that. I'm pretty sure this isn't how her father runs his business, buying party centers across the country just so his daughter can link up with former boyfriends."

Livy didn't agree. "Nope, it all makes sense now. Whatever happened between them didn't end well. And now she wants another chance."

Sam groaned. This poor Jason didn't have a chance. Once Livy and the rest of the girls got involved, they would go all out to help Darcey get what she wanted. He could only pray this Jason wanted the same.

Taking her hand, he planted a quick kiss to her mouth. "How about we talk about this after we get that drink and something to eat?"

Listening and nodding as Livy continued to chatter on about this new theory of hers, he quickened his pace.

Now he was definitely ready for that that drink.

It was late in the evening and the reception was close to the end.

Slipping unnoticed into the Grand Ballroom, Darcey sat at one of the empty tables towards the back of the room. Even though she was exhausted and there was really no need for her to stay, she was drawn by this need to watch Jason perform.

If only for a little while.

She gazed around the room. Judging by the large number of people who still remained, the majority on the dance floor, the night had been a complete success.

There was no doubt in her mind a big part of this was because of

Jason and his band. It was a reminder of not only how popular he was, but of how good he and the band really were. The show they put on was always right up there with the best of the best.

As the leader of the band, Jason didn't only get up on stage and sing, he became the song. Through a lot of hard work and using a system he had devised on his own, he managed to turn any song into something better, his version making it sound brand new.

For him, there were no rules. No boundaries.

Known for leaving the stage to mingle with the dancers, he would work the floor, taking the time to teach new moves and dance steps. It was nothing for him to hand over his microphone to give a guest the chance to sing. He joked, told stories that made them laugh. And he shared the memories, both good and bad, that were the inspiration for the songs he wrote.

During every performance, he gave the impression there was nothing else he would rather be doing.

This had the crowd crying out for more, everyone clamoring to dance with him.

And he loved this.

Yes, Jason Bennett wasn't only a member of a band... he *was* the band. An entertainer in every sense of the word, he loved what he did, and this showed.

And he was *so* much more talented than he gave himself credit for.

But that he remained so humble was what made him even more loved and adored.

After the band ended their song, Darcey watched Jason run back up on stage. Scanning the room, when his eyes met hers, he stilled. She could feel the intensity of his gaze all the way across the room.

For what felt like forever, he held her gaze. Then after giving a slight nod, he spoke to the crowd. "Okay, everyone... I hope you're all danced out because this next dance will be the last of the evening. It will be a slow song, a chance to wind things down with the one you love."

He paused, again sending another glance in her direction, this one longer. Then he cleared his throat. "Make sure you hold them tight, let them know how much they mean to you. Because we all know how things can change in a heartbeat. You could wake up and find them gone. Not everyone is lucky enough to get that second chance."

Abruptly, he turned, giving the band the sign to start.

Darcey was afraid to move. She was pretty sure it wasn't her imagination his words had been directed to her.

And if they were?

Was this his way of telling her he, too, wanted that second chance?

As his voice began to fill the room, she listened, almost in a trance. Her chin in her hand and her eyes closed, she let the music carry her away.

With you in my arms,
I could dance all night.
Your head on my shoulder,
Has everything feeling so right.

I want this moment to last forever,
Your heart beating next to mine.
Together, this love we share,
Only growing stronger with time.

With you in my arms, baby
This is all that I'll ever need.
For this is as real as it gets,
So much better than any dream

I want this moment to last forever,
Your heart beating next to mine.
Together, this love we share,
Only growing stronger with time.

I want this moment to last forever,

Let this moment with you last forever,
Forever ...

Once the last chords of the song faded into silence, the lights flickered once, twice, and then a third time to announce the night was over. Too exhausted to even ask for more, the guests began drifting off the dance floor.

Jason sent a quick glance over to where Darcey had been sitting. She was still there.

But he knew this. Only because from the moment he had realized she was in the room, he hadn't been able to think of anything else, unable to keep from glancing over at her while he sang.

You almost forgot the words to the damn song.

In fact, he was pretty sure he had left a couple out. Or even added a few.

Untangling himself from his guitar, he sent a quick glance over at Paul. "Give me a few minutes, okay?"

Not even waiting for an answer, he jumped off the stage and cut his way through the maze of tables to where Darcey was seated. Her eyes closed and her chin resting in her hand, he wondered if she had fallen asleep.

He cleared his throat. "What's this? My singing has put you to sleep? This isn't exactly the reaction I hope to get when we introduce a new song. Especially, not from you."

Her lashes flying open, she watched as he grabbed the chair next to hers and straddled it. Wrapping his arms around the back, he rested his chin in his hands.

And darn if he didn't aim one of his smiles right at her.

It was a smile that sent everything she remembered about him rushing right back at her. A smile she had forgotten how powerful it was.

It was also the same smile he gave out so easily, a smile that had women of all ages swooning over him.

Yes, you need to remember this important fact.

But it was when he reached over to tuck her hair behind her ear, she knew she was in trouble. Because, believe it or not, even though he had worked up a sweat from performing, he smelled absolutely wonderful.

All because of the cologne he wore.

She wanted to close her eyes and breathe it all in.

The first time she had commented on this, he had laughed, shaking his head. He told her that his sister had suddenly decided he needed a signature scent if he wanted people to remember him. So, when she found this little shop specializing in custom fragrances, she insisted he go with her to have one made especially for him.

He found this amusing.

A signature scent? What did this have to do with anything? If he wanted people to remember him, he hoped this would be for his music.

Not because of the cologne he wore.

But she had insisted.

So now he was the owner of his own custom-blended cologne. It was a masculine scent in every sense of the word. a combination of cedar and sandalwood, with just a hint of musk.

Jason still didn't understand the draw. And having grown used to the scent, he honestly couldn't even smell it anymore. Most of the time, he wasn't sure if he had even remembered to put it on.

Darcey could confirm he had put it on tonight. And the scent still remained just as potent.

She sighed. "You still wear the same cologne. And it still smells just as heavenly. What I mean is …" With not a clue where she was going with this, she began playing with a place card left on the table, tapping it on the table.

When she got up enough nerve to glance over at him, she found him watching her, a faint smile on his lips.

She sent him a bright smile. "Well, I guess what I'm trying to say, your sister was right about having a signature scent. Because it's so you. Not that I've been thinking about your cologne… or you …"

Her lips pressed together, she frowned down at the place card before pushing it away.

As if it was responsible for her behavior.

What are you doing? You need to change the subject. Before you say something really stupid.

She began talking a mile a minute. "I liked the last song you played. Is it one of your own? If it is, I can see why your band is so popular. Do you still go on tour?"

His gaze still intense, his only answer was a nod.

Then, as if he suddenly realized she expected an answer, he shrugged. "Yes, to both questions. But we've been slowly cutting back on the tour circuit and bookings at the Regency. Our priorities have changed. With two of the guys in the band recently getting married, one with a baby on the way, we've become even more selective with what we take on."

When she only nodded, he became concerned. He certainly didn't want her to think he was getting lazy, slacking off.

No, if anything, he was doing far better than he thought he would in his life. Between the recordings and his songwriting, the band had more than enough work to keep them busy.

His intent to make this clear, he smiled. "Touring is not the thrill it used to be. I've slowly been going back to doing what I like most, writing the lyrics. Paul, who you've met, has a real knack for matching the right music to the words. The song we just played is one we've been collaborating on for quite a while. We also have another one in the works."

He shrugged. "Paul thinks it's our best one yet. I guess we'll see."

"Hey Jazz, can you come over here for a sec? I need your help." This summons came from Paul. He was signaling for Jason to join him on the stage.

After he reluctantly unfolded himself from the chair and gave a long stretch, the smile Jason gave her was resigned. "I don't know what he wants, but I better go and check it out before he breaks something."

His hands stuffed in his pockets, he began backing away, an almost shy smile on his face. "Thanks for sticking around to listen to us. I guess I'll see you around."

He took a few steps before he glanced back to see she was watching him.

He came to a stop, sending her a smile.

"Sweet dreams, gorgeous."

After that, he didn't dare look back, almost sprinting the rest of the way to the stage. The gorgeous comment had come from him so easily, it scared him.

Calling her gorgeous had settled in his mind almost from the very first moment he set eyes on her, standing in line at the coffee shop. This had been the one and only word he could think of that was worthy to describe her.

And now? He had fallen right back under her spell, the endearment flowing from his mouth the most natural thing in the world.

Did he still have that right?

He shrugged.

Why try to change something you can't control?

So, he was smiling as he walked over to Paul. "What's up?"

Looking up from the tangle of wires he was holding in his hands, Paul frowned. "The sound was cutting in and out again when we got to the end of the last song. I don't have a clue what's wrong. But if I remember correctly, you fixed this the last time this happened."

Then he grinned, shaking his head. "But I have a feeling you didn't notice anything, too caught up in a certain someone who stayed to watch us play." He cleared his throat. "I also knew if I didn't get your attention while I still could, you could end up sitting there with her all night."

He chuckled. "She's got your number, Jazz. You don't stand a chance."

Jason had no comment. Instead, he grabbed the wires from Paul and headed for the sound system.

Paul just shook his head. Again, it looked like he wasn't going to get even a trickle of information out of the guy.

A few minutes later, Jason glanced over to where Darcey had been seated.

The table was deserted.

He looked down at the wires in his hand.

Never had he felt so completely alone.

Darcey had made a hasty retreat right after Jason called her gorgeous.

She had to... reality had begun to feel more like a dream. What was happening, and what she wanted, coming too easily.

While brushing her teeth, her confused expression staring back at her from the bathroom mirror, her gaze fell on the promise ring. Hanging from sterling silver chain around her neck, it had been a part of her ever since Livy sent it to her.

She reached up to finger the ring, wondering if Jason had noticed it.

But he couldn't have. Otherwise, he surely would have said something.

Right?

About to unfasten it, she abruptly changed her mind.

She liked that the ring was so close to her heart.

Call her silly, but this made her happy.

It also gave her hope.

CHAPTER 10

*J*ason opened his eyes to the sunlight filtering through the blinds and falling across the bed. This told him it had to be somewhere around mid-morning on this second Monday in September.

Slowly rolling out of bed, he gave a long stretch. Yawning, he ambled down the hall to the kitchen.

While leaning against the counter, waiting for his coffee to heat, he realized this was the first in a long time he could honestly claim he had slept through the night. That he actually woke feeling refreshed was a bonus.

Back to sleeping in your own bed probably has a lot to do with this.

Along with the little spark of hope, hovering in his mind ever since Saturday night.

Just thinking about Darcey sprawled out on the floor of the equipment room, he chuckled.

The look on her face?

If you had been thinking clearly, it would have been the perfect opportunity to pull her up off that floor and kiss her. Yep, play the element of surprise. If only to remind her of what she had left behind.

Shaking his head, he poured out a cup of coffee. He needed to stop thinking of her, concentrate on his work. As with every other time he came across any bumps in his life, he invariably turned to his music. This had always helped him in the past.

Not this time ...

Memories had taken over... so many memories.

But they were good ones this time.

It had taken him longer than usual to get into his latest song. This was the same song he had been working on when Darcey interrupted him with her surprise visit to the equipment room.

Yesterday, he had finally looked over what he had written, only to find it was all wrong. So, he started over. And the new lyrics came at him so fast, he almost couldn't keep up. Even now, they were still sounding off and re-arranging in his mind.

Eager for Paul's input, he had almost called him yesterday, suggesting they meet up at The Regency to pool their talents. But just as swiftly, he vetoed the idea.

Paul deserved to have some time off, spend some time with Sasha. It was Sunday, for god's sake.

The song could wait.

And what was he going to do now? After he figured out what he wanted to eat, he was going to take a break from song writing. He needed to catch up on all the other work waiting for him. The bills certainly weren't going to pay themselves.

After a big gulp of coffee, he grabbed the bacon and eggs out of the refrigerator.

First things first.

He was starving.

It was later that evening Jason made a trip to the party center. Unable to shake the feeling he was forgetting something important with this newest song, he wanted to check the notes he had left behind in the equipment room.

When he pulled into the parking lot, the sun was about to sink into the lake, the first stars of the evening coming to life in the darkening night sky.

He unlocked the door to the party center and headed down the hall. The eerie silence, a complete contrast to the usual bustling daily activity, had him a little uneasy, quickening his steps.

Yep, the place almost feels haunted. Add the right music and you would have the perfect setting for a horror movie.

After he opened the door to the equipment room, and was about to turn on the light, he heard footsteps.

He turned, coming face to face with Rob Johnson, the contractor.

He almost groaned aloud.

This was the last person he wanted to see right now.

Even though their prior meeting had been brief, he had to agree with Jack's opinion of him. And it wasn't a good one.

Let's face it, Rob Johnson sent out bad vibes. His entire demeanor hinted at trouble.

Proof of this... why was he at the party center, sneaking around in the dark? On a Monday night?

Never mind, you're essentially doing the same thing.

He exhaled a long, drawn out breath. "*Damn* ... you just about scared the bejesus out of me. With the place all locked up for the night, the last thing I expected was to find someone wandering around. Just what the hell are you doing here?"

Rob's response was brief. "I could ask you the same thing."

When Jason remained silent, he shrugged. "I needed to check on something. I've got a big meeting tomorrow with the boss and I realized there was something I might have overlooked." He shrugged. "I don't want to start off on the wrong foot. Especially when the boss is a woman and also the daughter of the man who hired me. Have you met her?"

Jason's only answer was a curt nod.

Rob grinned. "She's hot, that's for sure. Makes me want to get to know her a lot better, if you know what I mean. Yeah, she's a little uptight, but from my experience, I've found this is typical of most career-minded women. You learn quickly how to deal with that."

Giving Jason a once-over, he shook his head. "But I'm sure I don't need to tell you this. In your line of business, I'm sure you've had a lot of experience dealing with women."

The muscle twitching in his jaw was only a hint of the anger Jason was holding inside, surprising even him with how fierce it was. That he was actually considering the possibility of shoving Rob up against the wall, to make it perfectly clear Darcey was off limits, was something that surprised even him.

This wasn't his style.

But this didn't mean he wasn't tempted.

Jamming his hands in his pockets, if only to prevent this from happening, his anger was more than clear in his voice. "Since you're an outsider, you're probably not aware of how much this venue needs someone like Darcey to get things back on par. No one wants her to leave. In order for this not to happen, she needs to know everyone is one hundred percent behind whatever plans she puts in place."

His voice hardened. "Not only is Darcey undoubtedly smarter and more qualified at her job than the two of us put together, the last thing she needs is unwanted attention from someone like you. So, I'm going to warn you, once and only once… leave her alone."

A silence stretched out between them.

It was Rob who finally spoke first. "I don't know why, but I'm getting the impression you don't like me. I also think Darcey's involvement with the party center isn't the only reason for this warning you're giving me."

He slowly shook his head. "Nope, I'm thinking you and I might be in competition for the same woman. If that's the case, may the best man win." He was laughing as he turned to walk away.

Jason watched him leave.

After grabbing the notes that were the reason for this visit and locking the door behind him, he made his way back to the front entrance. He walked outside just in time to see Rob's car leaving the parking lot.

He felt uneasy about the whole encounter. There was something fishy about the guy, as if he had something to hide. There was no reason for him to be wandering around the party center after it was closed for the night.

What was so important it couldn't wait until morning?

He frowned.

Who are you trying to kid? This isn't what you're concerned about.

No, it was what Rob said about Darcey he found so upsetting. Absolutely furious would be the best way to describe how he felt.

Evidently, he now had even more of a reason to do what Abby had suggested. He needed to keep showing up wherever Darcey was... if only to keep an eye on things.

But remember, you have to do this without coming across as a stalker.

Well, after this encounter with Rob, he didn't care if Darcey thought he was a stalker.

Sometimes a man's gotta do what a man's gotta do, right?

His drive home was a quiet one.

He had a lot to think about.

As Rob drove out of the parking lot, he could see Jason in his rearview mirror. Standing on the front steps of the party center, he was watching him.

He frowned, dragging his hand through his hair. What were the chances they would run into each other like this?

It was obvious the guy didn't like him.

Since most people felt this way about him, he wasn't too concerned.

Now he was starting to regret his agreement with Steven Hollister. Yeah, he had been asked to do a lot of strange things in his life. But this time?

This took the cake.

But he could really use the bonus promised to him, the sooner, the better. He had some debts he needed to pay off.

It looked like he needed to be more careful in the future.

CHAPTER 11

So, when you feel like trying again,
reach out, take my hand.
Baby, take a chance with me.
~ Anonymously Yours

The pillows propped up against the headboard behind him, Sam Bridges was lounging on the bed.

He was working on his laptop.

He lifted his head. Did he just hear a car door slam?

Head tilted, he listened. Nope, he must have imagined it.

This meant no Livy yet.

Tapping his fingers on the keyboard, he looked down at the screen to check the time.

11:36 p.m.

Damn ...

He should be asleep right now. He needed to be well rested for the full day he had scheduled for tomorrow. Then he was off to Quebec for four days. This was for the long-delayed dedication ceremony for the historical renovation project he and Carrie had worked on two summers ago.

The project had dragged on much longer than expected and he was looking forward to finally wrapping it up.

He smiled. Originally planned as a one-night stay, with only him and Carrie making the trip, Chris had secretly arranged for all four of them to go, extending the trip for another three days.

Just yesterday, Livy had bemoaned the fact they should've done something like this. But he had pretended to shoot down the idea, using his busy schedule as an excuse.

And now he was looking forward to her excitement when she found out she would be going with him after all.

He loved surprising Livy. But then again, he loved doing anything for her.

You love her. Period.

He checked the time again.

11:39 p.m.

After an enormous yawn, he stared down at the design he was working on. It was a plan for their kitchen. This had suddenly become a number one priority when only yesterday, the sink had sprung a major leak.

Leak probably wasn't the best word to describe what happened… flood would be a better fit. Even though they got the leak repaired, he knew this was only a temporary fix. Once you passed the fifty-year mark with any kind of plumbing fixture, a guarantee on repairs was pretty much non-existent.

Old houses were famous for this. He would know.

So, while Livy was out with her friends, his goal was to come up with a rough draft of the kitchen layout for her to approve when she got home.

A good time as any. Since you know you won't be able to fall asleep until she returns. Not only because you're concerned about her safety, but because you want her with you.

He leaned back against the pillows and closed his eyes. His intention was to take a brief rest, lasting maybe five minutes at the most. Just enough to rest his eyes. At least this is what he told himself.

Twenty minutes later, he was jerked awake by the sound of the front door closing.

Ah, finally ... she was home.

After saving the work on his laptop, he shut it off.

He waited, a smile on his face.

When the taxi pulled into the driveway, Livy noticed the light was on in their bedroom.

Good.

This meant Sam was still awake.

After dinner and two glasses of wine with her friends, she was in a good mood. Singing as she ran up the steps, she burst into the bedroom.

Met by Sam's warm smile, she kicked off her shoes and, crawling across the bed, she planted a big kiss on his mouth.

"Hi ... did you miss me?"

He chuckled, his arm going around her before he pressed a kiss in her hair. "I did. Very much. I take it, with this good mood you're in, your girl's night out was a success? You had a good time?"

She nodded, leaning against him. "I did. Have a good time, that is. But I couldn't wait to come home to you." She sighed. "Especially since I know you'll soon be off to Quebec. Before I forget, Carrie told me June sent you an email with all the travel info."

He was smiling as he pulled her closer. "*Ah ...* it's only one night. Think of all the quiet time you'll have to work on your writing."

Her only answer was another sigh. A longer one this time.

He pressed another kiss in her hair. "So, what did you girls talk about tonight? Or should I say, who did you talk about tonight?"

She leaned back to look at him, a smile on her face. "Oh, we're not that bad. We only have nice things to say." She laughed. "At least about each other."

She reached up to plant a kiss on his chin. "We only discuss those who deserve our attention."

He nodded, smiling. "*Hmm ...* if you say so."

She snuggled closer. "Darcey came. I think she had a good time. At least she said she did. And everyone seemed to like her. But I had to kick Sophie under the table twice when she started asking so many questions."

She was shaking her head. "Honestly, Sophie is something else. She doesn't have any qualms about getting information out of someone, no matter how personal. But, she doesn't mean any harm, she's only just really interested."

She gazed up at him. "I'm so glad we didn't tell anyone about the ring. Or about the initials J. B. Sophie would have picked up on this right away, figuring out they were Jason's. Who knows what she might have said to Darcey."

Sam tucked an errant strand of hair behind her ear. "Baby, we don't know for sure that's true."

Livy was skeptical. "Sam, come on … I'm willing to make a bet with you it is."

He chuckled. "You are, are you? *Hmm* … this is a very tempting offer. You do know you have lost just about every single bet you've made with me, don't you?"

She laughed. "How could I not? You never let me forget. But this time I know I'll win, hands down."

Sam shook his head. "Whatever you say. So, what else did you talk about?"

She filled him in about the rest of her evening.

How Abby brought Madeline Rose and how absolutely adorable she was with her enormous eyes and curly red hair.

How Madeline Rose sat on her lap, refusing to go to anyone else until Kevin came and whisked her off so Abby could enjoy her dinner.

She also told him how nice it was to see Lisa, who stopped by for a brief visit, bringing Chloe and three-week-old Jonathon Lee with her.

Jonathon was such a cute baby and so good, he slept the whole time. And Chloe was such a proud big sister. It was so obvious she was besotted with him.

At first, Sam was very interested in what Livy had to say. As was always the case, lulled by the smoky sound of her voice, she had him sinking into this place only she could take him.

But it was when she rested her hand on his stomach, her fingers slowly tracing the waistband of his pajama pants, his attention quickly switched gears.

Because honestly?

It was driving him crazy.

Every nerve in his body had jumped to attention, his body craving what he was pretty sure she was hinting at.

Then again, maybe this touch of hers was merely coincidental?

But remember, she had two glasses of wine. And she did say she missed you ...

Her fingers had now slipped under the waistband, drifting lazily over his skin in a caress. This was enough to convince him her touch was definitely not a random move. Nope, this was a hint she wanted more.

More than willing to go along with this, he was about to make his move when she suddenly pulled her hand away. Her kiss brushing his jaw, she began scooting off the bed. "I really need to take a shower. I'm sure I smell like French fries."

He reached out and had her tucked back next to him in an instant. After he took her hand and tucked it back under his waistband, his lips traveled in a leisurely trail up to her ear. The shiver racing through her at the huskiness of his voice had him pulling her even closer. "*Oh no, baby...* you're not going anywhere. Not until you finish what you started. Only then may you even think of taking that shower."

The heat in his gaze had her closing her eyes, the kiss he pressed to her jaw, bringing on her soft sigh. She reached up to link her fingers behind his neck. "*Umm ...* you always know what I'm thinking."

His breath brushed across her cheek. "And I always will. I would also like to make that bet with you."

A smile tugged at her lips. "Okay ... and what are your terms?"

After another kiss, one that had her pressing closer, he was also smiling. "I'll bet you're absolutely right about the initials."

She laughed. "But that's not fair, because you're repeating exactly what I said."

He was smiling. "I know. So, this means, once again, I win."

She was shaking her head. "I don't know how you figure this. Again, you're not playing fair."

"*Hmm* ... I always play fair. Especially with you." He was now unbuttoning her shirt, doing this so slowly, almost to the point she wanted to help him.

She sighed. He was right. This is exactly what she wanted. But now, after spending the evening holding Madeline Rose on her lap, she knew she wanted even more.

She didn't even hesitate, blurting it out.

"I want a baby."

He slowly leaned back to study her, his expression one she couldn't quite decipher. Hardly daring to breathe, her gaze didn't falter from his.

That it was taking him so long to react was because he would be the first to tell you, he was a little shocked. She had completely thrown him with this announcement, especially since this was the same thing he had been thinking ever since she told him how she loved her time with Madeline Rose.

This is what he had been waiting for, trying so hard to be patient. He had wanted a child with her ever since she had lost the baby she conceived with Zack.

But he was also confused. Lately, this was a subject he was so sure she was trying to avoid. When he brought up having a child of their own, he was pretty sure it wasn't his imagination how quickly she changed the subject.

Not because he kept bringing it up. Oh, no... at the most, he only gave a casual hint here and there. More of brief reference to what he hoped for their future.

Never did he pressure her, not once. Because even though he was more than ready to take on this next step in their lives, he got the impression she wasn't.

So, he had backed off.

But, now he got it.

Yep, he had a pretty good idea what was going on.

Yeah, it took you a little time... okay, more than a little, but now you're pretty sure you know what the problem is.

Livy was scared. After losing the baby, she convinced herself this was going to happen again.

He carefully tucked her hair behind her ears, his gaze fixed on her face. "Livy, baby ... you have to know I want the same. Having children with you is something I've had tucked away in my mind ever since I first fell in love with you. But you have been sending mixed messages lately. You want a baby, but at the same time, you need more time."

He framed the side of her face in his hand. "Or, maybe it's that you're afraid?"

She closed her eyes, her nod so faint, he almost didn't catch it.

He studied her, searching for the right words. "*Aw, Livy* ... open your eyes ... look at me, sweetheart."

Once he was looking into her eyes, what he wanted to say came easy. Reaching for her hand, he pressed it over his heart. "I have a feeling, deep here in my heart, this time everything will turn out the way it should. And, perchance, it doesn't? I'll still be right here, like I was before and like I always will be. So, you have no reason to be scared."

Caressing her cheek with his thumb, he smiled. "And just so you know, if things don't work out, I'm willing to keep trying. Again, and again, if need be."

He kissed her again, his lips lingering over her mouth as he spoke. "We're in this together, baby. I want what you want. I can't wait to fill this house with all of those family celebrations you've been dreaming about."

That he could sense what she was thinking and knew what to say to make her feel so safe and loved was a feeling unlike Livy had ever known before. And one, she vowed, she was never, *ever* going to take for granted.

He waited, watching as the worry slowly faded from her eyes before he smiled. "Okay?"

She nodded, and lifting her face to his, she gave him a kiss. "I love you ... so, so much."

"Oh, baby ... I love you, too."

He kissed her back, slowly, almost reverently.

Then, resting his forehead against hers, a huskiness took over his voice. "So, does this mean we're going to make a baby?"

In the brief silence that followed, he found he was holding his breath.

Tears brimming, she nodded again.

And, right before his mouth swooped down to cover hers in another kiss, she was able to say what she had so desperately wanted not that long ago

"I hope it's a little boy... just like you."

CHAPTER 12

arcey unlocked the entrance door to the party center on this dreary Tuesday morning. The sky was overcast, with rain in the forecast for later in the day.

She had decided to come in early. So, for the first hour she had the luxury of being the only person in the building. Then the sound of voices signaled the arrival of the catering employees. The crew hired to re-finish the floors of the Grand Ballroom were the next to trickle in.

She closed her office door, hoping to muffle the noise. She also wanted to discourage any visit from Rob Johnson when he finally made an appearance.

She had no desire to see him.

Dropping her head down in her hands, she groaned. She couldn't believe she was acting like a child, hiding away in her office.

Come on, you need to figure out your best way to deal with him and go with it.

Her plan was to make their meeting as brief as possible, covering only what was absolutely necessary. Then it would be his responsibility to get the work done. If he was as good as her father claimed, there should be no reason for them to meet again.

And this idea he had about holding their meeting over dinner?

This is not going to happen. The meeting will take place right here. In your office, with the door open.

Confident she now had a plan in place, she got down to work.

By noon, she had overseen two interviews for the position of event planner. The first candidate was qualified, but her long and detailed list of questions and demands showed she would be extremely difficult to work with. The second candidate was not as experienced, but personable. As a new mother, she made it a point to tell Darcey the baby would always come first, her job second. She also preferred not to work on weekends.

Darcey understood about the baby, but no weekends? This had her mentally crossing the woman off the list halfway through the interview.

Because, come on ... wasn't this when most of the events took place?

She could only pray the two interviews lined up for the afternoon would have better results.

She closed her computer and, leaning back in her chair, she watched the wind blow the leaves around the courtyard. Since it wasn't raining yet, she was going to walk over to the little coffee shop across the street and order takeout for lunch. This wasn't something she wanted to do.

Not with the many memories there to haunt her.

But she was hungry. It was close. And it was only lunch.

What could possibly happen?

Jason was meeting the rest of the band at The Regency. His plan was to do a trial run through the new song while it was still fresh in his mind.

He had just pulled into the parking lot when Darcey came running down the steps. He watched as she headed towards the coffee shop across the street.

Massaging the back of his neck, a thoughtful look came over his face. He pulled out his phone and sent a text to Paul.

> Running a little late. Start without me. You've
> got the lyrics, go with them.

After Darcey entered the little shop, he slipped his phone back in his pocket and got out of his truck.

Casually strolling across the parking lot, he also headed for the coffee shop.

When Jason entered the small shop, the line for takeout reached almost to the door. He smiled when he saw Darcey was the last in line.

Déjà vu ... again.

But after he walked over to stand behind her, panic set in.

Geeez ... if she turns to find you standing almost on top of her, smiling like an idiot, she's going to think you're exactly what Abby warned you not to be. A stalker. Think ... do something.

He dug his phone out of his pocket and slowly began scrolling down through his messages. It didn't come as a surprise to see the latest text, sent only minutes ago, was from Paul.

> Running late, huh? I pulled in right after you
> and saw you follow Darcey over to the coffee
> shop. You sly dog, you.

He shook his head. He couldn't pull anything past Paul, and he probably never would.

Chuckling, he began scrolling down through the rest of his messages.

Darcey was reading the menu above the counter when the sound of a familiar laugh came from behind her.

This sent a shiver zipping right through her.

Come on ... it couldn't possibly be who you think it is. You're imagining things, right?

Determined not to turn around, she concentrated even more on the menu, even though the words now came across as a foreign language, making absolutely no sense.

The person behind her moved closer. This was when she knew it was Jason, the scent of his cologne nudging her senses, bringing a smile to her face.

Unable to resist, she turned around.

When he didn't even look up, engrossed in his phone, she took the time to study him.

He was so close, she could see the small nick on his cheek from where he must have cut himself shaving. This told her he still refused to go with the current casual, bearded trend in honor of his father. A military man, he had believed a clean shave showed a man who was not only serious about his appearance, but had nothing to hide. A man you could trust.

But his hair was a whole different story. A shade somewhere between a deep mahogany and midnight black, he still wore it slightly long, spilling over his collar in the back. In the front, it fell in a sweep to one side.

This gave him a sexy, almost mysterious look. Or more like a dare-devil-come-and-get-me kind of image. It was his own personal interpretation of how he believed a lead singer of a band should look.

And it worked ...

Big time.

Her sigh was long and dreamy...

Let's face it ... He was just too perfect.

Jason wasn't really checking his messages.

He was more than aware Darcey was studying him.

Trying not to smile, it was only when she gave such a dramatic sigh, he finally looked up and right into her eyes.

For the longest moment, it was as if they had fallen right back to when they first met.

Three years ago, in this very coffee shop. Almost in the exact same spot.

That this time and this place was now being offered to them as a chance to start over again?

This was almost too impossible for either of them to comprehend.

His gaze holding hers, Jason smiled.

"Hey, Darcey..."

He watched as a blush slowly filled her cheeks,

"Jason ... hi."

She continued to smile up at him, not moving. While unbeknownst to hers, the line had now moved forward.

He cleared his throat, nodding towards the counter. "Hey, you need to pay attention, gorgeous... this is a hungry lunchtime crowd and you don't want to get them riled up."

Gorgeous? Did he really just call you gorgeous again?

Flustered, she stepped back, bumping right into the man in front of her. After a much longer apology than was necessary and her cheeks now even more flushed, she turned back to Jason.

He was watching her, his expression giving nothing away.

She glanced away, trying to compose herself. Or give herself a mini pep talk of sorts.

Come on, don't let him get you all rattled. Keep the conversation casual. You don't want him to know he has you all tied up in knots.

Clearing her throat, her voice came out much louder than she intended. Enough to have the nearby customers glancing over at her. "So, you're here to pick up something for lunch?"

Oh, for heaven's sake. Of course he's here for lunch. It's lunchtime.

Before he could even respond, she rambled on. And this would be about ... yeah, you guessed it, basically a lot of nonsense.

"Silly me. Of course, you are. Me, too. I'm going to get takeout so I can eat in my office. From what I remember, they have the best salads here."

When he only nodded, she kept right on talking. "It's great we can walk from The Regency. So convenient not having to drive." She gave a nod in the direction of the party center. "Truthfully, I'm just happy to be away from all the noise. They've been sanding the floors all morning, so it's been crazy loud."

She shrugged, sending him a smile. "But I'm sure the end results will be fantastic. The Grand Ballroom needed a facelift. They've already replaced the old wallpaper and after they finish painting, everything will look new." She shook her head. "Well, maybe not brand new, but it will certainly be an improvement."

As Jason watched her struggle on, he wouldn't be able to tell you a word she said. This was because the possibility of pressing his mouth to hers in a kiss was really all he could think about.

He wanted to experience that same emotional connection they had shared the first time they kissed.

He wanted to feel her lips on his again.

Yeah, if only to see if they're as soft as he remembered.

Admit it ... it's more like what you haven't been able to forget.

Hadn't Abby suggested he should try to re-create the time he and Darcey first met? Well, here it was ... this was the place. If they were to make a movie out of this moment, they could almost follow the same script.

It's true they had been sitting at a table, not standing in line. But chattering away like she was now, this was when he had impulsively leaned in to kiss her.

It had been the start of everything wonderful.

He frowned.

At least you thought it was...

To Darcey, the distracted expression on Jason's face was a sign he was more interested in getting his lunch order so he could get back to whatever he had going on.

And the frown? Maybe he wanted to get away from her?

She watched him slip his phone into his pocket before he moved closer, his gaze slowly traveling over her face.

Stuffing her hands in her pockets, she sent a glance out the window before she turned back to him. She began talking even faster, her words running into each other. "They're predicting rain for later. I see it's pretty cloudy. It's getting windy, too."

She shrugged. "Believe it or not, this is the kind of day I missed the most in California. One can only take so much sunshine. The sound of rain–"

He leaned in, pressing his lips firmly to hers. Before she could react, he pulled away, a smile hitching the corner of his mouth at her shocked expression.

Her lips parted, Darcey stared up at him.

He cleared his throat. "Sorry, I didn't know how else to stop you from talking." He gave a slow nod. "I see it worked."

He nodded again, this time towards the counter. "I believe you're up."

After she somehow gave her order, she realized Jason had come to stand next to her. He smiled at the woman behind the counter. "Hi Janice."

She smiled. "Hey, Jason ... what can I do for you?"

"Janice, I'd like you to meet Darcey Hollister. If you could put her order and mine on the same bill, I'd appreciate this. I'll be paying for both."

Darcey turned to him, about to protest, but he shook his head.

"Nope, I've got this. Consider it a welcome back lunch from me. And the guys in the band."

He turned to give Janice his order while Darcey stood by, listening to their good-natured banter. Another employee, arriving with their drinks, smiled at Darcey. "So, do you work at The Regency, too? Is this how you know Jason?"

Jason answered for her. "Darcey is now my boss. In fact, she is everyone's boss over at the party center. But this is okay, Darcey and I go way back, so we understand each other."

He grinned over at her. "Right?"

Thinking about the kiss he just gave her, Darcey wanted to say no, maybe they didn't understand each other at all. Because she had no clue where that came from. Or why he even did such a thing.

Don't think she didn't like it, because she did. If anything, she wished it hadn't been so brief.

She glanced over at him.

He raised an eyebrow, a familiar twinkle in his eye.

She took a deep breath. "*Ah, Jason* ... you will always be your own boss. You're too much of a free spirit to let anyone tell you what to do."

He stuffed his wallet in his back pocket before he slowly shook his head. "I disagree. Every free spirit needs someone ready to step in and ground them."

Their orders paid for, Jason took Darcey's arm, leading her over to a less crowded area to wait for their number to be called.

She glanced up at him. "Thank you for the lunch. You really didn't have to do that."

She took a sip of coffee, slowly shaking her head. "I must say, coming here to get my lunch has turned out to be a much different experience than I thought it would."

Jason leaned up against the wall and half turning to her, there was the hint of a smile on his lips. His gaze locked with hers. "Oh? How so?"

She took another sip of coffee, hoping to hide the shiver that ran through her at the message in his eyes. It was one she remembered so well.

It was a sign he was completely aware of the effect he had on her.

Wrapping her hands more securely around her cup, hoping the heat might calm her, or possibly even knock some sense into her, she gazed up at him. "Oh, I don't know. Maybe it's the little thing you did. I don't know if you meant it as a kiss or what. But I know it was the last thing I expected."

He smiled as he reached over to tuck her hair behind her ear, his fingertips going on to graze her jaw. "Sometimes the least expected things are those that are the most memorable. If I recall, you were the one who felt planning is over-rated. Spontaneity made for a happy life, you told me."

He tilted his head, studying her. "*Hmm* ... you no longer feel this way?"

He remembered this?

She nodded. While telling herself not to read too much into this sudden attention from him. "Yes, of course I do. Though I've become a bit more cautious now." She frowned. "I've also come to accept most plans don't always turn out as you hoped they would."

He moved closer. "Darcey…"

She glanced up at him, eager for what he was going to say.

Instead, he handed his cup to her. "Here, that's our number. You stay here and I'll get our orders."

When he returned, he abruptly handed her one of the bags. "I'm sorry, but someone I know just walked in and I need to talk to him. He does the videos for our songs. So, I have to cut this short."

He leaned in to press a kiss to her cheek. "Let's plan on finishing this conversation at a later date. It was getting interesting. I'll see you around, gorgeous. Enjoy your lunch."

Before she could thank him or even say goodbye, he left.

The little coffee shop now almost filled to capacity, Darcey skirted her way through the crowd to get to the door. As predicted, it was raining. And by the time she reached the party center, it was pouring.

Once she was back in her office, she hung up her dripping coat.

She sat at her desk, and for the longest time, she stared at the bag with her lunch. Her mind going around in circles, she searched for an explanation of what exactly happened in the coffee shop.

Don't even go there. Don't start looking too much into this. You're different now. He's different.

With an exasperated sigh, she grabbed the bag and reached inside for her salad. Instead, she pulled out Jason's turkey sandwich.

Oh, geeez … maybe you should take it to him?

She put it back in the bag, then changed her mind.

After all, he was the one who cut things short, leaving everything up in the air between them.

She unwrapped the sandwich and took a big bite.

She hoped he liked salad.

CHAPTER 13

Sometimes the people you think
don't want to talk to you,
are the people who are waiting
for you to talk to them.
~ Anonymous

Steffi Bennett was in the third-floor hospital staff lounge, entering her patient reports on the computer

She was taking her time at this, one eye on her work and one eye on the door to the hallway. This was so she could keep track of everyone who walked by.

Most notably, Dr. Davis. Dr. Noah Davis.

Or, as she referred to him in her mind … Noah … just Noah.

She had been smitten ever since her first glimpse of him when he joined the hospital staff about a month ago. And they had yet to share a single word.

Not even a hello.

So, it was highly possible he didn't even know who she was.

When she had pulled into the parking lot earlier, she saw his car was in his reserved parking space.

This had her remaining in her car for the next fifteen minutes or so. Giving herself a serious pep talk.

And what was her plan of action if this Noah stopped in for a much-needed break?

Today was going to finally be the day she would introduce herself, carry on an actual conversation with him.

And why did this have to happen today?

She wanted to find out if he was planning to attend the meeting for the upcoming masquerade ball at The Regency. It was when she heard he'd volunteered to be on the hospital staff committee, she had also offered to help.

She hadn't volunteered only because of him. Of course not. At least this is what she was telling herself. No, she knew how much this event benefited the Children's Hospital. And she also wanted to show Jason she was finally ready to step out of her shell, get more involved. How many times had she promised him this?

Too many. Way, way, too many ...

She looked up from the computer when she heard voices out in the hall. But none belonged to him.

After a sigh, she gazed around the room. She had chosen the staff lounge to finish her reports because this was where Noah usually came to get some quiet time or review his patient charts.

A glance over at the coffee station confirmed the plate of cookies she brought were still there. They were chocolate chip cookies. Noah's favorite.

And how did she know this?

Earlier in the week, she had overheard a conversation he had with one of the other nurses. He was talking about his mom and how he missed her homemade chocolate chip cookies. So, yesterday on her day off, after reading what she would swear were hundreds of recipe reviews for chocolate chip cookies, Steffi found one she liked.

Two hours later, her kitchen smelled heavenly, the counter covered with rows of just baked cookies. She had even added extra chocolate chips, the one thing Noah had mentioned he liked best about his mom's cookies.

In fact, she had almost doubled the amount. So, how could she go wrong?

But now she was wondering if making the cookies might have been a mistake. Why had she ever thought she could measure up to his mom's cookies?

She glanced over at the door, thinking she heard someone coming.

But again, it wasn't Noah.

Hopefully, he would come by soon.

She couldn't stay in the lounge forever.

Steffi had almost finished with her reports when she heard Noah's voice out in the hallway. She watched out of the corner of her eye as he came into the room.

He let out an enormous sigh, and sinking down into a chair, he closed his eyes.

Her fingers hitting the computer keys the only sound in the room, she chanced a glance over at him.

He looked exhausted.

But this didn't surprise her. From what she had learned from other members of the staff, he was at the hospital twenty-four-seven.

You need to let him get some rest.

Reluctantly signing out of the computer, she turned to leave. Only to find Noah was looking right at her.

His expression unreadable, she gave him a tentative smile. "Are you okay, Dr. Davis?"

Dragging his hand through his hair, he shook his head. "Hmm … am I okay? Well, let me see … can you promise you won't tell anyone I said this?"

Her look was cautious. "I guess?"

He was trying not to smile at her worried expression. "My answer would be I don't know that I'm okay right now. But this might not be the best time to ask. It's been a long day. More like a long week."

After a sharp laugh, he closed his eyes again.

Steffi wasn't sure what to say. Or what to do. Should she leave? Offer to get him some something? Maybe coffee? Or, she wondered ... when was the last time he ate?

Could this be a good time to offer him a cookie?

Or maybe you should leave and let him rest.

Since it appeared a break was what he needed the most, she slipped out of the room.

Noah wasn't resting.

He couldn't, even if he tried. Not with all the charts, procedures, and consultations whirling around in his head.

He dragged his hand through his hair again. His workload had become so heavy, he was worrying he would forget something important and make a mistake. But he didn't know what to do about this. Every time he turned around, someone was seeking his help and he couldn't turn them down.

After all, this was the life he had chosen. He was fulfilling his dream of being a doctor, something he wanted ever since he was a child. How many times had his parents told the story of how, when he was only eight, he had tried to operate on a dead mouse he found in the backyard?

Unfortunately, as far as his mother was concerned, now this wasn't enough. She wanted him to settle down, get married, and have children.

So, this past Valentine's Day, he had asked Michelle, his high school sweetheart, to marry him.

But here it is September, and you're still refusing to set a date for the wedding.

How could he have known, before he even finished his internship in Boston, they would offer him this position in Cleveland? Then, before he even had time to process this, he was making patient rounds here at the Children's Hospital.

He tried to convince Michelle this was only a minor setback to their plans, but their last conversation about this had escalated into an argument. Leaving the both of them still angry when they ended the call.

The situation wasn't good. He knew this. And he sensed she did, too. But he didn't know how to resolve this.

And sometimes … like right now?

He didn't care.

The buzzer on his phone went off.

Popping up into a sitting position, he reached for his phone.

He groaned. It was Elenore Cromley.

Or, as he had nicknamed her, The Queen.

A woman of unlimited resources, she believed the world revolved around her. She also insisted she had every single ailment possible.

Yes, she was a die-hard hypochondriac.

So why did he put up with her eccentric ways?

Mrs. Cromley had a soft spot for children. Especially those with any kind of disability or life-threatening illness. A devoted and very generous benefactor of the Children's Hospital, she was always quick to grant their most difficult requests. Even more so when it came from one of the younger patients.

According to her message, her status wasn't an emergency. She only had a few questions for him before he left for the day.

He ran his hand through his hair.

This is not how you pictured your life as a doctor would be.

Stuffing his phone back in his pocket, after a huge yawn, he gazed around the room.

This is when he realized the pretty little nurse had left.

But the word pretty couldn't even begin to describe her. Beautiful would be a much better fit. Even though this still didn't seem good enough.

He had first noticed her about a week ago. But as far as her name or anything else, he was batting zero. He had tried, but every time they crossed paths, she went out of her way to avoid him, her shyness so obvious.

She also had this uncanny way of disappearing before he even realized she'd left.

Like now.

He smiled. He wanted her to stop fluttering, settle down. And he preferred this to be right next to him.

If only for a little while.

And what did he want to happen after that?

He didn't know.

You don't like to think that far ahead.

As if she knew what he was thinking, she came back into the room. She was holding a mug in one hand and a plate in the other. She moved very slowly, her concentration all on the cup.

When she realized he was watching her, she came to an abrupt stop, sending the hot cocoa sloshing over the rim and onto her hand.

She closed her eyes, a flash of pain crossing her face. "Ouch, that's hot."

He was out of his chair in an instant. He set the cup on the desk and reached for her hand. After a thorough examination, he glanced up at her. "We should put some ice on this. Does it hurt?"

The usual blush in her cheeks was now an even deeper shade of rose. Avoiding his gaze, she vigorously shook her head. "*No, please ...* don't worry about it. I'll be fine."

After easing her hand from his, she nodded over at the cup. "I made hot chocolate for you. I thought it might be a welcome change from all the coffee you drink."

A big smile lit up her face. "I'm sorry there are no marshmallows. I was told a few of the children pirated the entire bag from the kitchen and had a marshmallow fight. Then they gobbled up all the evidence."

At a loss for words, he didn't respond.

His silence making her think she must have done something wrong, her smile faded. "I'm sorry, maybe you don't like hot chocolate. You don't have to drink it. I can take it back to the kitchen."

Noah was trying to pull himself together. Her smile had hit him hard, but in a good way. As though he had been given a shot of pure sunshine.

But his silence now had Steffi beyond a state of panic. She set the plate of cookies in front of him, her words flying out of her mouth. "I brought these cookies in today. I try to make a different kind each week. The children look forward to this. They have even made up a chart with their likes and dislikes."

She shrugged. "It makes them happy, if only for a little while."

She nodded towards the cookies. "These are chocolate chip. They seem to be a big hit from the reviews I saw on the chart. You're more than welcome to have one."

She sent him another smile. "Eat all of them if you'd like."

Honestly? You wouldn't care if he ate the whole plateful.

Embarrassed by the way she was rambling, she made a move for the door. "I'll leave you alone now."

She turned and was halfway out the door when his hand fell on her shoulder.

She froze.

"Hey, don't leave." Fearful he may have scared her, he removed his hand. "Please, stay. I would really enjoy your company. Even if only for a little while."

An almost shy expression on his face, he shrugged. "One tires of eating alone all the time. And I could use some everyday conversation. With no talk about illness, shots, medicine or the like."

She nodded. "I guess I can, for a little while."

And darn if she didn't smile at him again.

He closed his eyes. She needed to stop doing this.

He reached for her hand, a thrill running through him when her hand relaxed in his. Once they were both seated, he smiled. "So, tell me about yourself. Since you already know my name is Noah, why don't you tell me yours?"

Tucking her hair behind her ear, she gave him a nervous smile. "It's Stephanie. But most people call me Steffi."

His direct gaze making her blush, she watched as he nodded. "Well, I don't consider myself like most people. So, if you're okay with this, I'm going to call you Stephanie. It's a beautiful name, and it fits you."

She nodded, giving him another smile.

This causing havoc with his mind, he was momentarily at a loss for words. He took a big gulp of the hot chocolate to hide this..

It was hot ... almost boiling hot.

His face scrunching up, he ran his hand down over his jaw.

Dear Lord, you need to figure out what's going on here before you kill yourself.

He didn't know what it was ... but she did something to him no woman ever had.

And just like that, a voice in the back of his mind was quick to bring him back down to earth.

What about Michelle?

He groaned.

Yeah, this was going to be a problem. A big problem.

CHAPTER 14

*D*arcey glanced up from her computer, watching another gust of wind send the leaves sailing past the window. The sky had turned so dark, she checked her phone for the time, thinking it might be later than she thought.

Nope, it wasn't even five yet.

She shut off her computer, and leaving her desk, she walked over to the window. Resting her forehead against the glass, she closed her eyes. She had such an awful headache. No doubt this was because of the strong fumes from what they were using to seal the ballroom hardwood floor.

She sighed. It had been a disappointing afternoon. Through no fault of her own, she had accomplished very little. The first candidate scheduled to interview for the event planner position had never showed. The second applicant was fifteen minutes late for her appointment. But this didn't matter, since she didn't have any of the qualifications for the job.

No sooner had Darcey finished with the second interview, the current Regency chef knocked on her office door. He had come to hand in his resignation. He had a job offer he couldn't pass up, and would have to leave in two weeks.

Then after ending her call with the woman at the employment agency, who promised both jobs would be filled by the end of the week, she received an email about the Grand Ballroom seat covers and draperies she had on order. The fabrics she had chosen were now on back-order for another six to eight weeks. With the possibility, they might not come in at all.

This had resulted in the rest of her afternoon spent on the phone with the interior decorator, searching for another option.

So, no … it had not been a productive afternoon. And now there was the meeting with Rob to deal with.

Could things get any worse? Right now, you would give anything to go home, put on your pajamas and do nothing.

Resisting the urge to repeatedly bang her head against the glass, she let out a long groan.

At the sound of someone clearing their throat, she whirled around.

Paul was standing by the door, a concerned look on his face. "Hey, are you okay?"

After massaging her forehead with her fingers, she gave him a faint smile. "I have a headache, but I'll be fine. I think I just need some fresh air."

She gave a frustrated sigh. "Unfortunately, in about ten minutes, I have a meeting with Rob. Hopefully, I can keep it short so we won't have to be here for long."

Paul shook his head. "Not a good idea. With these strong fumes, you should take the meeting elsewhere. As it is, I think we're about the only people left in the building."

And the bad news just keeps coming...

This is not what Darcey wanted to hear. It was bad enough she didn't want to have this meeting with Rob, but now she would be alone in the building with him?

You are not in the mood for this... not at all.

A crazy thought popping into her head, she glanced over at Paul. She wondered what he would say if she asked him to stick around, if only for a little while.

But Rob ruined any chance of this happening.

Sauntering into the room, he gave Paul a brief nod before he turned to Darcey. "I heard what Paul said, and he's right. I know a place we can get dinner not too far from here. It's not fancy, but it will work."

Her only goal to get the entire night over with, she pulled out her car keys. "Okay. I can follow you in my car."

Rob laughed. "Come on … be reasonable. There's no reason for both of us to drive. We both have to come back in this direction to go home, so why take two cars? I'll be more than happy to drive."

He sent her a challenging look. "Don't worry, I've been driving for a long time. Definitely longer than you have, I'm sure."

Darcey wanted to tell him his driving was the least of her worries, but she was suddenly too tired to care. She nodded, reaching for her coat. "Okay, then let's go."

Paul was frowning. He didn't like how this was going. He slipped his hands in his jacket pockets, casually nodding over at Rob. "So, where are you headed? Jake's Place?"

Rob shook his head. "Nah, but where we're going is right down the street from Jake's. Just not as fancy. Or loud."

When he turned to see Darcey was waiting, he pulled his keys out of his pocket. He was grinning as he gestured towards the door. "After you."

Paul watched until they turned the corner. Then he glanced back in the direction of the equipment room, a thoughtful look on his face. He knew it was none of his business, but he wasn't feeling very good about this plan of Rob's.

He rubbed the back of his neck, and after a long sigh, he turned and headed back down the hall. He hoped Jason hadn't left yet.

He nearly collided with him when he rounded the corner.

Jason's gaze went from Paul to Darcey's closed door. He looked back at Paul, an amused look on his face. "What are you doing now? Guarding her office?"

Paul shook his head. "No, she's gone. She just left with Rob."

Jason became dangerously still, the muscle in his jaw clenched. "What do you mean, she left with Rob? And why would you let this happen?" He was scowling as he jammed his hands in his pockets. "You know it's not a good idea for her to be alone with him. Do you know where they're headed?"

Any other time, Jason's reaction would have amused at Paul. That it was brought on because of a woman was something he never thought he'd live to see.

But now? He frowned. Why was Jason mad at him? "Hey, hold on here... I couldn't stop them. It's not like they're a couple of teenagers. But I did ask Rob if they were heading for Jake's place, and he said no. They were going to a place right down the street from there. Not as fancy or loud, he said."

For a moment Jason was silent, then he stared at Paul, incredulous. "The Corner Bar? Is he nuts?"

Paul shrugged. "I don't know any other bar around there except that hole-in-the-wall, do you?"

Jason shook his head, his expression furious. "Damn ... The Corner Bar is not the kind of place you conduct a business meeting. Or, for god's sake, take a woman. What the hell is he thinking? Most of the guys who hang there are questionable. You know this as well as I do."

With all the swear words Jason was throwing around, Paul knew he needed to calm him down before he went charging off after Rob like a madman.

He held up his hands. "I know, I know ... you don't have to tell me. Believe me, I know."

Jason abruptly turned to him. "What do you have going on right now?"

Dragging his hand down over his jaw, Paul groaned. "I have a feeling I'll be going to The Corner Bar. Maybe have a beer or two. You know, just to relax."

He watched the tension fade from Jason's face, a hint of a smile in his response. "I think I may join you."

Already on his way down the hall, Jason came to a halt. He turned to Paul. "Thanks. I know you probably think I flipped my lid, but I ..." He shook his head.

Paul grinned. "Hey, who am I to stand in the way of true love?"

The fact Jason had nothing to say, not even one of his usual dry remarks, was enough for Paul to know he had been right all along.

Jason Bennett had finally met his match.

In the form a beautiful blonde with eyes shining like stars.

To Darcey, it felt like Rob had been driving for hours. When in reality, it was probably closer to twenty minutes.

She tried to answer as briefly as possible the questions he kept throwing at her, ignoring those she thought were too personal.

This would account for at least seventy-five percent, if not more.

When Rob finally turned off the road and pulled into a parking lot, it was a relief to know they would soon be in the restaurant and she would no longer be alone with him.

Her relief was short-lived.

The Corner Bar?

After a quick glance at the building, one that would be better named The Corner Shack, she scanned the parking lot. Most of the vehicles were beat up and old vans or pickups.

This told her this was a hard-core guy's kind of hangout.

Now, Darcey wasn't a snob. Nor did she have anything against bars, old vans, or pickups. But there was one thing she was sure of... this was not the best place for them to have their meeting.

Certainly not by what she could see from the exterior of the place.

As she and Rob made their way to the entrance, he moved closer, his hand going to her back. He did this in a very casual move, as if he didn't think she would notice.

But she did.

And she didn't like it.

It was when his hand drifted lower, resting on her waist, she came to an abrupt stop, her voice curt. "Rob, *please* ... I'd rather you kept your hands to yourself. After all, this is a business meeting."

As soon as these words left her mouth, she knew she had made a mistake. He withdrew his hand, but not before he let it drift down over her hip. An amused look on his face, he laughed. "Darcey, come on. You need to lighten up a little."

At her angry expression, he held up his hands. "Okay, I get it... you don't like to be touched. It won't be easy, but I'll try to remember. After all, you're the boss."

She was furious. Wanting to slap him silly, furious.

Enough is enough. You need to make this the shortest meeting this guy ever had.

They had reached the entrance. Her lips still pressed together in anger, she yanked open the door. Stepping aside, she waved him ahead of her. "After you."

With a resigned shrug, he walked inside.

After quickly scanning the crowded room, Darcey sighed. The inside was as rundown as the outside, the raised voices and loud music making it hard to even think.

On a scale of one to ten, with ten being the loudest, she would have to rate it as an eight or nine.

If she could, she would turn around and walk right back out the door. But thinking about what Rob had said only minutes before, her confidence kicked in.

Big time.

She was the boss.

And once he accepted this, the better it would be for both of them.

Jason pulled into The Corner Bar parking lot.

Once he was out of his truck, he leaned against it, his gaze going to the street.

Where the hell was Paul? He should have been right behind you.

He felt a raindrop, then another. They were big drops... almost angry drops, he would have to say. A sign they were in for a heavy downpour.

He pulled up his collar, his focus on the street.

Paul's jeep finally came bouncing across the sorry excuse of a parking lot. If you could even call it that. By the number of potholes and crumbling asphalt, it was obvious the owner wasn't too concerned about appearances.

And from what he remembered of the one time he had been here, the inside wasn't much better.

He shook his head. He couldn't even imagine what Darcey must have thought when she saw this was where Rob planned to hold their meeting.

She doesn't belong in a place like this ... how many times have you seen it written up for some altercation or other in the police blotter?

Paul came up to him, shaking his head. "*Geeez* ... you were driving like a bat out of hell. That you didn't get stopped is a miracle."

He nodded over to the line of parked cars. "I see Johnson's car is here. I'm surprised you haven't already gone charging inside, ready to wage war."

On his way to the entrance, Jason's answer came out in a growl. "Darcey doesn't belong in a place like this. You know this as well as I do. He's an idiot to even consider bringing her here."

Paul grabbed his arm as he was reaching for the door handle. "Wait ..."

Jason stilled, an eyebrow raised. "What?"

"Promise me you won't get into a fight or something."

Jason actually laughed. "A fight? When have you ever seen me try to start up a fight?"

Paul shrugged, releasing his arm. "I haven't. But ever since Darcey came on the scene, I've witnessed a side of you I didn't know existed. And now I don't know what to think. The one thing I do know, whatever is going on between the two of you is awfully strong. I've seen you go from a calm, easygoing kind of guy to this ninja warrior type, ready to protect his woman at any cost. And to tell you the truth, it's beginning to scare me."

Then he grinned, hoping to lighten the moment. "So, being the good friend that I am, I don't want you to make a fool out of yourself. Rob has this way of starting trouble without making it look like he's the instigator. It's also obvious he would like Darcey to be his latest conquest."

Jason nodded. "You may be right. But, trust me, that isn't going to happen."

He pulled open the door, his words coming in a growl over his shoulder.

"She's mine."

CHAPTER 15

Being a knight in shining armor
isn't about being the strongest,
It's about taking a stand
between the enemy and who you love.
~ Anonymously Yours

*D*arcey was unaware that Jason and Paul had followed her and Joe to The Corner Bar.

Nor did she know they were at the bar with a perfect view of the table she and Rob occupied.

But this was understandable. Right now, she had more important things to worry about.

Beginning with the amount of alcohol Rob had already consumed, along with his complete lack of interest in getting their meeting started.

He was now on his second drink and they had been in the bar for only about twenty minutes. And even though she refused his suggestion of a drink, he still ordered her a glass of wine.

He told her this would do her some good. Get her to lighten up a little.

So, when the server set the glass of wine in front of her, she pushed it over to the far side of the table.

She did not want a drink. Least of all, with him.

And his comment that a drink might do her some good? This also hadn't set well with her.

Yes, again, she knew this was childish, but this was the reaction Rob brought out in her.

She. Just. Did. Not. Like. Him.

She pulled her laptop out of her bag and set it on the table. After she signed into her mail, she looked over at him, her brow furrowed in concern. "*Hmm ...* I don't see the itemized list I requested. Did you send it?"

Lounging back in his chair, he laughed, shaking his head. "Darcey, Darcey, Darcey ..." He pointed to his forehead. "I don't need a list. I've got it all filed away right up here."

She closed her eyes, a sudden fury building inside of her.

He has it all filed away? In his head? Is he kidding?

She watched as he reached over to close her computer. "We both know there's no reason to go over the list. I already have everything under control and the work will get done as promised. This is the way I handle all of my jobs."

He chuckled, shaking his head. "I might make some enemies along the way, but I don't care. I'm not in this business to make friends."

Settling back in his chair, he sent her a lazy smile. "Ah ... but I'd be more than willing to make an exception. With you, I'd like to make a deal... let me take over and you won't have to worry your pretty little head about a thing. Life will be a lot easier and who knows, maybe you'll see we have more in common than you think. So, what do you say?"

She was at a loss for words ... speechless.

She thought of grabbing the glass of wine and tossing the contents right in his face. Then, to make sure he understood, she would do the same with her glass of water.

Instead, she stared down at her laptop, trying to calm down.

Not at all bothered by her silence, Rob reached for the menus the server had left, placing one in front of her. He opened the other menu, scanning the choices. "*Hmm* ... I see there's not much of a selection. But it will do for now. Next time we'll go someplace nicer. There has to be at least one halfway decent place in this godforsaken city."

And now Darcey had reached her limit.

Slipping her laptop back into her bag, she removed a ten-dollar bill from her wallet. She was about to set it on the table when Rob looked up from the menu.

Reaching for his drink, he raised an eyebrow. "So, I take it by your silence, you agree with what I said?"

She stood and shrugged into her coat. She glared at him as she slapped the bill on the table. "That should cover the wine you ordered. Feel free to drink that, too."

Her voice became louder ... much louder than she intended. "No, I don't agree with anything you've said so far. In fact, I'm appalled by your behavior. That you have the audacity to call yourself a professional, let alone a gentleman, is beyond me."

She was unaware a silence had settled over the room. Not that it would have mattered if she had. No, she was all fired up, determined to make her point. "I expect to see a list of the work we agreed on, along with estimates, on my desk by five o'clock tomorrow. Once I approve what you have given me, only then may you start the work."

She began walking away, only to stop and glare at him once more. "And if you don't have this information to me by then? No problem. I'm sure I'll be able to find someone to take your place. And, what you said about a next time? This will never happen."

Her head held high, and a smile pasted on her face, she marched over to the door. She yanked it open and made what she thought was a very impressive exit.

It was only after Darcey slammed the door behind her and the noise level in the bar had returned to normal, Jason came to life.

He pushed away from the bar, almost sending the bar stool flying backwards onto the floor.

The anger radiating from him had Paul grabbing his arm. "*Whoa ...* you're not thinking of going after him, are you? Trust me, not a good idea. You can deal with him later. Right now, Darcey is your biggest concern. You need to make sure she's all right."

Jason turned to him. Some of the anger leaving his face, he gave a slow nod. "Yeah ... you're right."

Paul let go of his arm. "*Thank God* ... the last thing we need is you getting into a fight over a woman. Here, of all places."

He sent a quick glance over at Rob, who was talking to the waitress, his dispute with Darcey already forgotten.

He looked back at Jason. "So, what do you want me to do in the meantime? Ask him what the hell his problem is? Give him a warning? Let me know and I'm on it."

About to pull his wallet out of his pocket, Jason paused, glancing over at Paul. "You don't want me to go after him, but it's okay for you to take him on?"

Paul grinned. "Hey, fighting is in my blood. You don't spend time in the army without learning some moves. He wouldn't even know what hit him. Especially since I can see by the way he's inhaling his drinks, he'd be an easy target."

Shaking his head, Jason threw a bill on the bar. "Here, this should cover our beers. And, no ... neither you nor I will be reading him the riot act until after I talk to Darcey and find out what happened."

He walked away, only to turn back to Paul once more. "Hey ... and thanks. I owe you. I mean it."

"Just go ..." Waving him off, Paul watched him leave. As usual, he had been right on the mark ... A woman comes on the scene and here comes trouble ... following right behind her.

He shook his head. Now he was even more thankful that the new-dating-uncertainty-phase, always a hurdle in any relationship, hadn't been a big deal with him and Sasha. He wouldn't want to go through any of that again.

Nope, you're happy with the way things are... you wouldn't change a thing.

He took a big swallow of beer. After grabbing a handful of peanuts, he began watching the football game on the big screen TV.

He was going to give Jason and Darcey fifteen minutes.

Then he'd leave.

Huddled beneath the small roof covering the main entrance to the bar, Darcey was miserable. She shivered, watching as the big drops of rain multiplied in number.

Don't complain. Didn't you tell Jason you were looking forward to rain? Well, it looks like you're getting your wish.

Wrapping her coat more securely around her, she moved closer to the building when it began raining much harder, the wind blowing it in sheets across the parking lot.

Consumed by rage, and her only goal to leave the bar as quickly as possible, it had completely slipped her mind Rob had driven. This meant she was on her own, with no way to get home.

No, your car is in The Regency parking lot, about a twenty-minute drive from here.

But there was no reason to panic yet, right?

She would call a taxi.

Digging through her bag, she pulled out her phone.

It took only seconds for her to realize she had no reception. She groaned, knowing her only option would be to go back inside the bar and ask to use someone's phone.

Well, this wasn't going to happen. She had made her exit, and a darn good one at that. There was no way she was going to ruin it by slinking back inside, begging for help.

She frowned. Wouldn't Rob like to see this happen? No doubt he would tell her not to worry her pretty little head.

Now feeling even more overwhelmed, she huddled even deeper into her coat.

What are you going to do?

She closed her eyes.

Think ... think really, really hard.

The door to the bar opened and then closed. Even with her eyes closed, she could tell someone had come outside and was now standing only a few feet away. Hoping it wasn't Rob, she waited for the person to leave.

But it appeared they had no plans of going anywhere.

When Jason stepped outside and found Darcey huddled next to the door, he couldn't believe how relieved he was.

Yes, he knew she could take care of herself. Hadn't she made this perfectly clear only minutes ago? Not only to Rob, but to everyone else in the bar? But this hadn't erased this vision in his mind of her wandering off, lost and all alone.

He shook his head.

Was he a piece of work, or what?

You only want to protect her ... keep her safe. Anyone else would do the same.

He watched as she turned, huddling deeper into her coat to shield herself against the blowing rain. It was obvious she had no intention of acknowledging him.

Or whoever she thought he was.

That's okay, he could wait.

When he could see she was shivering, he slipped out of his jacket. Cautiously moving closer, he draped it over her shoulders.

For a few heavenly moments, Darcey sank into the warmth the jacket provided. It was the scent of Jason's cologne that had her turning to face him, her mouth dropping open in surprise.

"Jason ..."

Then, for some odd reason, that he was there, she was filled with such anger.

She stepped back, her greeting coming in a mad rush of words. "Oh my God, did you follow us here? What are you doing? Are you spying on me?"

This was not the reaction Jason expected.

No, a more positive response would have been much nicer.

Maybe even a smile, accompanied by a simple, but sincere, I'm-so-glad-you're-here kind of greeting.

Yeah, that would have worked. You'd be more than happy with that.

But to accuse him of spying on her?

Why would she think this? Granted, you followed her. But only out of concern.

So, now a little angry, this was how he responded. "Why would I be spying on you? If anything, you should be glad I was concerned enough to come to your rescue."

Her fists clenched to her sides, she came at him, her face almost up to his. "You think I need to be rescued? Well, I don't, not from you or anyone else. I can take care of myself. This includes not only the decisions I make about the party center, but in my personal life, too. I don't need anyone. Most of all, I don't need you."

For a few moments, they remained locked in each other's gaze. It was the hurt she saw in his eyes that had her finally turning away. The wind now blowing the rain in her face, she pulled his jacket more tightly around herself, trying not to cry. If she did, this would erase everything she had thrown at him so passionately.

Even though in her heart she knew she didn't mean any of it. Especially her last words.

Jason was at a loss, not sure what to do.

She didn't really mean what she said, did she? At least not the part where she said she didn't need him.

He moved closer, her name coming from him in a long groan.

"Darcey ..."

She closed her eyes, her response barely audible. "Please ... just leave me alone."

He didn't even hesitate, pulling her into his arms, his response a whisper in her hair. "I'm sorry about what happened. But no matter how you feel about me right now, I'm glad I'm here. And I'm not going to leave."

At first, she didn't move, remaining rigid in his embrace. Then she broke down and, resting her head against his shoulder, she gave into all the frustration she had been holding in for so long.

"I can't do it, Jason. There is no way I can't work with him. I can't. At first, I tried. But only because my father seems to think so highly of him. But he's impossible. I realized tonight was going to be a complete waste of time when he started out by telling me he could never think of me as his boss. Then, even though I insisted I didn't want a drink, he ordered a glass of wine, suggesting it would help me relax."

She shook her head against him. "This made me so angry. But what finally put me over the edge was when he told me once I let him take over, I wouldn't have to worry my pretty little head."

She leaned back to look up at him, a look of disgust on her face. "My pretty little head? Is this something you'd say in a business meeting? I don't think so."

He opened his mouth to respond, but he didn't have a chance.

Her voice was shaking with anger. "This was when I knew I had to leave. But not before I informed him the information we were to go over tonight needed to be on my desk by five o'clock tomorrow. And if this didn't happen? I'd find someone else to take his place."

She sighed. "But I'm pretty sure you heard all this …"

A smile tweaked the corner of his mouth. "Darcey, I can assure you, every person in the bar heard you loud and clear. But I'm willing to bet everyone was on your side. I know I was. Paul, too."

"Oh, Jason … what am I even doing here? I'm seriously wondering if I was a fool to think I could handle a project like this."

His hands drifting up and down her arms, hoping to calm her, he was still smiling. She was clinging to him as though she planned to never let go. This wasn't how he had envisioned it would be when he held her in his arms again. But he'd take it … gladly. Even when standing on the rickety steps of this less than desirable establishment, the rain and wind blowing at them from all directions.

He pressed a soft kiss to the top of her head, taking a moment to inhale the familiar flowery scent of her shampoo he remembered so well.

His voice was a husky whisper. "You, Darcey Hollister, can do anything you decide on. Rob can't hold a candle to you. And don't you ever forget this."

Her head resting on his shoulder, she smiled. And for a brief millisecond, she let herself feel comforted by his support. Then she realized what she was doing, and becoming flustered, she pulled away.

Wrapping his jacket more securely around herself, she gazed out at the rain swept parking lot. "I tried to call for a taxi, but I couldn't get any reception on my phone." She gazed up at him. "Maybe I can borrow yours?"

Again, he was smiling. He couldn't seem to stop. Nor did he want to try. He cocked his head, his gaze traveling over her face. "You seriously think I would let you call for a taxi? There's no reason for that. I'll be more than happy to take you to wherever you need to go."

He raised an eyebrow. "Unless you think this is my way of telling you what to do."

"Jason ..."

He peered out at the pouring rain, taking a moment to assess the distance to his car before he pulled out his keys. "You stay right here, gorgeous. I'll come pick you up. There's no reason for you to get even more wet than you already are."

She grabbed his arm as he turned to leave and removed his jacket, handing it to him. "Put this on. Please don't argue, just do it. I don't want to be responsible for you getting sick."

A look passed between them, one that had them both reluctant to look away. Then he wrapped the jacket back around her and went sprinting to his truck.

Darcey was shaking her head. But she was smiling, too.

Gorgeous ...

Paul had finished his beer. Eager to get home, he threw on his jacket and headed for the door and pushed it open.

Damn ...

It was raining ... more like a monsoon, he'd have to say.

Zipping up his jacket, he was about to make a run for his jeep when he caught sight of someone huddled against the building.

What the ...?

He looked closer.

Damn ... it was Darcey.

He thought for sure she and Jason would be long gone by now. Together. Their differences forgotten and ready to live happily ever after.

But no, here she was. With no Jason in sight.

They didn't get into a fight and then he just left her here, did he?

Hoping he was wrong about this, Paul cleared his throat. "Hey, Darcey ... did you ... I mean, where ..."

She glanced over at him, a smile flitting across her face. "Hi, Paul. Yes, I've seen Jason. He went to get his truck. He's going to take me to pick up my car."

Paul let out a long sigh of relief. But then he didn't know what to say. Or more like what he shouldn't say.

He nodded a few times before he reached for his keys. After making a big production of clearing his throat again, he sent her a smile. "Well, that's good to hear. Funny we should run into you like this, huh?"

She nodded, trying not to smile. "Oh, Paul ... yes, funny. Thank you for that."

He studied her for a long moment before he spoke. "I guess you could say I came along for moral support. Maybe even more as a referee. With the way Jazz has been acting lately, I wasn't sure if he could be trusted to remain level-headed."

He hesitated, his gaze going to the parking lot before he turned to look at her. "I don't know what went on between the two of you in the past, but now I understand who he's been writing all his songs about."

He pulled up his collar before giving her a nod. "It would be nice to see him write one with a happy ending. Because if anyone deserves this, it's him. He's a good guy, Darcey. One of the best. Take care."

He took off, running to his car. Leaving her staring after him.

Did he mean what he said? The songs Jason wrote were about her? Or about them?

Oh, my ... maybe there's hope for you after all?

This explained why, when Jason pulled up in his truck and after she slid into the passenger seat, she gave him a big smile.

The smile he sent in return?

This had both of them forgetting all about the rain.

Darcey watched as Jason fiddled with the temperature controls, her whole body relaxing in one long sigh of relief when the heat came at them full force.

A teasing glint appeared in his eyes. "There, this should have you warmed up in no time. If I remember, you don't take very well to cold weather. Even though, by Cleveland's standards, tonight isn't what we locals would consider cold. The rain only makes it seem like it is. Now, when it snows, that's a whole different story."

The mention of snow had him transported back in time, the moment captured in the photograph Caro had found.

The same photograph he now had in his possession.

Yeah, the photo is in your wallet. You know it's crazy, carrying it around with you. But you don't want to take the chance of losing it again.

He glanced over at Darcey. He wondered, did she remember that day? Because, talk about cold. He was pretty certain it went down in history as one of the coldest and snowiest on record.

As if she had read his mind, a smile touched her lips. "Do you remember how I insisted you come with me to my grandparent's house? I'll never forget how cold it was that day. And snow ... it was like a blizzard. You were so mad when your truck got stuck in the driveway. Thank goodness for the snowplow driver, who stopped to help push it out. But I was so determined to show you the house, because I didn't know if I'd ever see it again."

She sighed, a wistful look on her face. "I loved that house. And I'll always remember that day. It was so perfect ..." Her voice trailing off, she stared down at her hands. If she had glanced over at Jason, she would have been surprised.

His hands resting on the steering wheel, he was staring at her, blown away by what she said. Not only had she read his mind, but like him, her memory of that day was just as fond as his.

He stared down at his hands. He wanted to reach out to her, keep this moment in place forever. Instead, he closed his eyes and took a deep breath.

They needed to take it slow. And maybe, just maybe, this time they could make it work.

Please ... you hope so.

"Jason?"

He glanced over to see she was studying him, a curious expression on her face. "Are you okay?"

He hesitated before he finally smiled. "Yeah, I'm fine. How about you? Drying out a little?"

Her eyes meeting his, she nodded. And again, something passed between them, but this time it was stronger.

And to be honest?

This was scaring both of them. Any anger between them seemed to have disappeared, now replaced with an overwhelming uncertainty.

And they weren't quite sure how to deal with it.

He put the truck in drive and headed out of the parking lot. His eyes on the road, the tone of his voice was casual. "I could use something to eat. How about we stop somewhere for dinner? It will help take the chill away."

She smiled. "I'd like that. Now that I've ruined my chances of dinner with Rob."

She sent him a quick glance. She didn't want him to think she had been okay with Rob's choice of meeting place. "Not that this was what I wanted. This dinner was all his idea. If I hadn't had such a headache, I don't think any of this would have happened. Obviously, I wasn't thinking clearly."

"Don't worry, I know it wasn't your idea. Paul let me know this." He smiled over at her. "I was thinking about Jake's Place. It's just down the road from here. I know you've met Jake and Gracie, but you haven't been to their restaurant yet, have you?"

"No, I haven't. But after hearing all the great reviews, I'd love to go there." Pulling down the visor, she studied herself in the mirror. Running her hands through her wet hair, she made a face. "But look at me, I look like I've been dragged through a puddle. I don't think I'm presentable for such a nice place."

She studied him before giving a dramatic sigh. "Where you ... well, you look fine. You look perfect, in fact." She shrugged. "But then, you always do."

A smile tweaked the corner of his mouth before he turned into the parking lot for Jake's Place. "Darcey, you couldn't look bad even if you tried. As far as I'm concerned, you'll still be the most beautiful woman in the restaurant."

He grinned over at her. "And shouldn't my opinion be the only one that matters right now?"

He opened his door. But before he got out of the truck, he hesitated, turning back to her. "Just so you know, when I think back to that day, I don't remember feeling angry when my truck got stuck in the snow. I only remember it as one of the best days of my life."

Before she could respond to this, he was out of the truck and on his way to open her door.

CHAPTER 16

The hostess kept glancing back over her shoulder at Jason as she led him through the crowded restaurant, a nervous giggle coming from her each time.

Once he was seated, she handed him a menu before nodding towards the large windows. "With the rain, you won't have much of a view tonight, but I promise our food will more than make up for this."

She gave another giggle. "Pam will be your server tonight. And don't worry, I'll show your date to the table as soon as she comes out of the women's lounge. In the meantime, would you like to order a beverage?"

"No, thanks. I'll wait." This delivered with a smile, he opened his menu to study his choices. The handful of peanuts he had at the bar having worn off a while ago, he was suddenly famished.

When he realized the hostess was still standing by the table, he glanced up from the menu, an eyebrow raised.

She blurted it out. "I was a guest at Jake and Gracie's wedding this past Saturday and I just had to tell you... your band is so, so amazing. You're amazing. My boyfriend and I had so much fun at the reception."

She waved her left hand at him, the flash of a diamond catching his eye, before she giggled again. "We just got engaged. And even though we aren't planning on getting married until we get our degrees, which won't be for another two years, we would love to have you as the band for our reception."

A frown crossed her face. "Oh, but wait … I guess this all depends on if you're still around." Then she gave him a big smile. "Anyway, I meant what I said. You're the best."

After one more giggle, she left.

Well … this certainly left him with mixed feelings.

But I guess this depends on if you're still around?

Did she actually just say that?

He sighed, running his hand through his hair.

Again, let it go on record, he was only thirty-one. Until lately, an age he still considered young.

And, come on … How old do you think she is? Nineteen? Twenty? So, of course, you must seem ancient to her.

Settling back in his chair, trying not to dwell on this sudden reminder he wasn't as young as he used to be, this was when he became aware of the whispered giggles and glances coming from the four women seated at the next table.

Aw, geeez …

He didn't dare look over in their direction. After what just happened? Nope, he didn't need any additional attention coming his way.

Not that he was complaining. Of course, he was flattered when people recognized him. Sometimes carrying on like he was a celebrity or something.

But it also embarrassed the heck out of him.

As far as he was concerned, he was no different from the next guy, trying to make a living. And this was by doing the one thing he knew how to do best.

Make music.

But, even though she had been very complimentary, this was the first time his mortality had popped into the conversation.

Don't forget, she did say you and the band are amazing …

So, this was a good thing, right?

He returned his attention back to the menu. Again, he was hungry. And more than ready to enjoy a leisurely and uninterrupted dinner with Darcey.

Only Darcey.

When she finally showed up, that is.

His gaze swept the restaurant. Nope, no Darcey in sight yet.

He glanced over at the rain-spattered window. The hostess was right, there wasn't much of a view.

Absentmindedly fingering his fork, a smile worked its way across his face. The view didn't matter. This wasn't why he was here. No, he was interested in only one thing, and this would be the woman who would soon be sitting next to him at this table.

He was very curious what direction this evening was heading. But he was also a little worried.

Pushing the fork away, he frowned.

Remember, just a short time ago when he was all talk, going on about taking it slow?

Well, this might have been his intention, but it wasn't happening. Already, it felt as though the past three years he and Darcey had been apart, had ceased to exist in his mind.

Poof ... just like that.

Yet, there were still just too many unanswered questions.

"Excuse me ... you're Jason of the group Banded Together, aren't you?

A woman from the foursome at the next table had come to stand next to him. The other three were watching, expectant smiles on their faces.

Sending them his best smile, he came to his feet. "Of course not. It would be an honor to be in a photo with such a group of beautiful women."

After she grabbed a passing server to take the photo, the women all crowded around him.

While Jason took the time to remind himself, this was all part of the job.

Darcey followed the hostess through the restaurant, her intention to attract as little attention as possible.

The rain had done a number on her. Everything... her coat, her dress and her shoes were soaked. But at least her shoes no longer made a squishing sound when she walked.

Her hair was now her biggest concern. The humidity had turned it into an explosion of curls, her attempt at bringing some order to this, failing completely. The only thing that might help would be a hat. Most preferably, a cowboy hat. Then she could pass as a country western singer from the sixties, big hair and all.

She certainly wasn't looking her best.

At least, this is how she saw it.

As Jason watched her approach the table, he was not of the same opinion. To him, she looked beautiful... more like stunning. He would even go as far to say she was still, and always would be, the most gorgeous woman he knew.

This was why the word gorgeous came out of his mouth so easily as an endearment when she was with him.

His gaze leisurely traveling over her, it was a few moments before his eyes met hers. He watched as a blush rose in her cheeks.

Coming to his feet, he pulled out the chair next to him with a flourish, gesturing for her to sit. "Here, gorgeous ... have a seat."

Between the warmth in his voice and genuineness of his smile, an unexpected shyness hit her. Avoiding eye contact, she slid into her seat where she made a big production out of moving her menu to the side, even going as far to align it just so with the silverware. This done to her satisfaction, she picked up her napkin. After giving it a good shake, she spread it over her lap, smoothing out any invisible creases in the fabric.

It was only after she clasped her hands together on the table, she glanced over at him.

He had watched all of this, a slight smile on his face. There was a playfulness in his voice. "I'm glad to see you made it. I was wondering if you had left, sneaking out the back door or something."

She smiled, shaking her head. "No, I would never run out …" Her words fading, her gaze shifted over to the window.

Oh, no … not a good thing to say.

And now she would give anything to snatch those words back. Because running out on Jason was exactly what she did the last time she was with him.

He had still been sleeping when she let herself out of his apartment so early that morning. She could still remember how cold it was when she ran out to the taxi, the pre-dawn darkness making it seem even colder.

Cold enough, she'd swear, to freeze the tears on her cheeks.

She would also swear, and just so you know, swearing wasn't something she'd normally do, without Jason to hold her, it had taken days after she arrived back home to feel warm again.

Even with the heat of the never-ending California sun.

This was when she made a vow she would never again love someone so passionately, to then miss them so desperately.

And now? She realized how wrong she had been, beginning with the never again…

"Darcey?"

She blinked. Jason was smiling as he sent a nod towards their server, waiting to take her drink order.

Once the server left, Darcey gave him a rueful smile. "I'm sorry. And I'm also sorry it took me so long. But the rain has wreaked havoc on my hair and it seems to have taken on a life of its own." She frowned as she ran her hand through her still damp hair. "Not my best look."

Again, he'd have to disagree. "You look fine. I'd even go as far to say you look perfect. But then, you always do." He winked as he said this. Then he shook his head. "I see some things haven't changed. You're still so hard on yourself." To soften his words, he reached across the table, his fingers grazing hers.

This simple contact had her completely unnerved. Fighting the urge to link her fingers with his, she shrugged. "I guess I've had too much happen to make me feel this way."

He studied her for a few moments. Then he gave a heavy sigh. "Darcey, I think we need–"

She pulled her hands from his so abruptly, she knocked her menu to the floor, almost sending her water glass along with it. She righted the glass and began mopping up the spill, all the while shaking her head. "Jason, please, can we talk about only simple things tonight? It's been a long day and I feel like I've accomplished nothing. I still have a headache. And what happened with Rob was almost enough to put me over the edge. So right now, I don't think I could handle anything serious."

This time, she was the one to reach across the table to link her fingers with his. "Please … can't we think of this as dinner shared with a friend? At least for now?"

He gazed down at their hands. He wasn't too happy about this. But he'd take it. Only because her words led him to believe there would be a next time.

So he nodded.

Their server set their drinks on the table, a white wine for her and a whiskey and tonic for him.

As she began rattling off the specials, little did she know, neither Darcey nor Jason heard a word she said. Their thoughts were only on each other.

It appeared some of the magic had already taken hold.

CHAPTER 17

$\mathcal{B}$ecause of the lateness of the hour, the main dining room of the restaurant had almost completely cleared out.

Only three tables were still occupied. Jason and Darcey were one of these.

After their served dropped off the bill, assuring them there was no hurry, Jason glanced over at Darcey. Her hands cradling her coffee cup, there was a serious expression on her face.

She looked exhausted.

He reached over to take the cup from her and, after setting it aside; he covered her hands with his.

Just as he suspected, they were ice cold.

As he massaged her fingers to warm them, his words were teasing. "Cold hands, warm heart, I've been told."

A small smile flitted across her face. "You remember?" This was what she'd quoted to him when he had teased her about this in the past.

He nodded.

Do you remember? Of course, you do. Along with so many other things.

He cleared his throat. Even then, his voice was still husky. "You'd probably be surprised at what I remember."

After a slight hesitation, he let go of her hands. "There's something I want to show you." He dug his wallet out of his pocket and pulled out the photograph. The photograph Caro had found. After he smoothed it out, he handed it to her. "Remember this?"

For a few moments, she was silent as she studied the photo. Then she gazed up at him, slowly shaking her head. "I can't believe you still have this and you keep it in your wallet."

Now, Jason could have easily let her believe this. But if there was one thing he wasn't good at, this would be telling a lie. His guilty expression always gave him away.

In most cases, this would be a good problem to have.

But now?

He'd give anything to tell her that yes, he carried it around with him everywhere. And had done so, every single day, for the past three years.

Instead, he smiled, shaking his head. "To be honest, I thought I'd lost it a long time ago. But I have this friend, Caro, who lives next door and she cleans my house twice a month. She found the photo stuck behind the dresser in my bedroom the last time she cleaned."

His face brightened. "But, just so you know, it's been in my wallet ever since. Even before I knew you were back in Cleveland."

He fingered the stirrer from his drink, studying her. Close enough to get caught up in the scent of her perfume, it was suddenly all so clear why he had put the photo in his wallet.

This was what he had been hoping for. This moment … this place. Giving them a chance to figure it all out, find out what went wrong.

It had to be fate.

Or … what was it called?

Destiny? Yeah … what is meant to be, what's written in the stars, your inescapable fate.

That he even knew the definition of destiny was only because he had recently looked it up for a song idea.

But for them, it was a perfect fit.

Darcey is your destiny. Without a doubt, you know this.

This was when he decided, why not dive right in and share this with her? What did he have to lose?

He cleared his throat. She glanced up from the photo.

He shrugged. "I guess, well … I thought with the photo showing up like it did, out of the blue, maybe it was some kind of sign."

When she didn't respond, her gaze going back to the photo, he mistook this as she didn't agree. And now he felt foolish. Quickly scribbling his signature on credit card receipt the server had left on the table, his words were barely a mumble. "Forget it. I don't know why I even brought it up."

There was a reason Darcey didn't respond to him. For the second time during the evening, she was trying so hard not to cry. If she did, she knew she'd never be able to stop.

"We should leave. I think we've worn out our welcome. We're the only people still here."

At the sharp tone of Jason's voice, she finally glanced up to see he had already stood. Avoiding her gaze, he began pulling on his jacket.

She held out the photograph. "Here, you probably want this back."

For a moment, they remained as if suspended in time, staring at the photograph in her hand. Then he opened his mouth, only to close it. A wry smile on his face, he finally shook his head. "No, you can have it."

"Jason …"

He shook his head again. "No, I insist. Remember? This was to be a dinner shared with friends. If I recall, this is what you wanted. So, think of the photo as a token of our friendship."

After he helped her into her coat, he gestured for her to go ahead of him. "It's time we left. It's late and I'm sure you're exhausted."

Neither of them even noticed the photo was still on the table.

But this pretty much summed up how the evening had gone.

The drive from the restaurant to pick up Darcey's car at The Regency was a silent one. A lot of this had to do with Jason and how angry he was.

But his anger wasn't directed at Darcey. No, he was mad at himself because of his behavior.

What are you doing? Ever since you first saw her, you've been like a spoiled brat, pouting when things don't go your way. Could this be the reason she left in the first place?

But he was having a hard time. He wanted to take her into his arms and kiss her until they both couldn't even think anymore, put an end to this uncertainty between them.

Instead, the way he saw it, they were wasting time.

While Darcey had worked herself into such an emotional state, she was afraid to even open her mouth. She was pretty sure if she did, what came out would be everything she had been wanting to say.

But not in a good way. No, she would make a mess of it.

It was when she sneezed, four times in a row, he glanced over at her, a smile tugging at the corner of his mouth. "Bless you."

"Thank you …" This ended in a sneeze, followed by another.

He chuckled. "Again, bless you. I hope this isn't a sign you've developed an allergic reaction to me. Though I'd think this would have shown up before now."

She sighed. "I seriously doubt you're the cause of my sneezing. I'm sure the weather is to blame. Even now, my feet are freezing because my shoes are still wet."

He reached for her hand, linking her fingers with his. "I'm sorry I acted like such a jerk back there in the restaurant."

She glanced over at him. "It's okay. I think the photograph…" She clamped her hand over her mouth. "*Oh no, Jason* … the photograph. I left it on the table in the restaurant. I didn't mean to do that, I …"

She began to cry, a build-up of all the tears she had worked so hard to hold inside, coming out all at once.

Jason turned his truck into the first driveway he could find and put it in park. Reaching for her hand, his voice was soothing. "Darcey, take it easy, gorgeous. It's okay. It's just a photograph."

Now don't start thinking he was shrugging this off as though he didn't care about the photograph. Because he did … a lot. He hadn't put it in his wallet, just to carry it around on a whim.

In fact, he already had a plan all worked out in his head. As soon as he saw Darcey off safely in her car, he was going to return to the restaurant. Where they would still have the photograph. He'd tuck it back in his wallet and everything would be fine.

But now, his concern was for Darcey. A look of such misery on her face, her words came out in little gasps between sobs. "No, no... it's not okay. Everything you give me, I lose. That photo was everything that was so perfect about us. Do you remember what happened right after it was taken?"

Of course, he remembered what happened.

The kiss ...

It had definitely been some kiss. A fiery, passionate and joining of their souls kind of kiss. And in that moment, for him, everything had changed. She was all he'd ever want, all he would ever need.

This was also when she told him she loved him.

Engraved in his memory, these three little words had settled deep inside of him, right next to the kiss. Where they had remained ever since.

How could she even think you would forget something like that?

But before he could even open his mouth to tell her this, she continued. "You kissed me. And I remember thinking how wonderful it was. That we had fallen into this perfect moment. It was how I had always imagined it would be when I finally fell in love."

She took in a deep breath, a quiet anger taking over her voice. "But then I did something I know now I shouldn't have. I told you I loved you. To only wait, for what felt like forever, for you to say you loved me, too. Or to at least say something. I was desperate for anything at that point. Even a thank you would have been enough."

She took in a deep breath. "But you said nothing. This was when I wondered if I had made a terrible mistake. What we shared wasn't real. At least not on your part."

Jason was speechless. While in his mind, he was frantically reliving that moment, scrambling to find some proof she was wrong.

But he found nothing.

And this was when he realized what she was telling him was true.

Even though the words had been what he passionately believed in both his heart and in his mind, he had neglected to say them aloud.

Leaning his head back against the headrest, he closed his eyes.

My god ... what had you been thinking?

He finally found his voice. "Darcey, I—"

She cut him off. "*Oh Jason*, the last thing I want right now is for you to feel like you have to say something just to make me feel better. Or worse yet, something you don't mean."

She gazed over at him. "But maybe now you'll understand why I had to leave. I couldn't stay. For me, nothing was the same."

He was silent. He was confused. And he was angry. But most of all, he felt like a total jerk.

Without a word, he pulled his truck back onto the main road.

Besides his inquiry of whether Darcey was warm enough and her occasional sneeze, the rest of their drive was again a silent one.

This was because they were both afraid to say anything.

Even with his eyes glued to the road, with so much racing through his mind, Jason was having a hard time concentrating.

Clearly, this latest development had thrown him for a loop.

He didn't understand. Had he really been that shallow back then?

Or were you just plain stupid?

Whatever the reason, he now had to fix this. He had to prove to Darcey he was a different man from the one she'd known three years ago. But this could only happen if she agreed to give him another chance.

Thank goodness, he was smart enough to know this might not be the right time to bring this up. Not with the emotional state they were both in.

He glanced over at her. Her head resting back against the seat, her face was turned to the window. Not what one would call a positive response to the evening they shared. This had him even more determined.

He needed to come up with a plan. A foolproof plan.

. Yep, you're going to do whatever it takes. Even if it means starting all over again, wooing her, flowers, phone calls, dinners, the whole she-bang.

Darcey had never felt as vulnerable as she did at this moment. She had bared her soul to Jason by admitting, not only had she loved him then, her feelings now hadn't changed.

And how had he responded? Again, he said nothing.

So she was right back to where she had been three years ago.

Well, tonight you only have yourself to blame. You didn't give him much of a chance to defend himself.

But with her headache now back with a vengeance, she only wanted to go home, crawl into bed, and go to sleep.

Hit with another three sneezes in a row, she was thankful when Jason finally turned into The Regency parking lot.

Jason pulled up next to Darcey's car. He came around to open her door, a hesitant smile on his face. "I'm sorry, Darcey. Sorry about everything ... what happened after the kiss most of all. I don't know what I was thinking. Or what I wasn't thinking ... I ..."

He let out a long sigh. "And most of all, I'm sorry if this evening has made things worse."

Even though the rain had stopped, the wind had become stronger, making it feel much colder. Her teeth chattering, Darcey huddled deeper in her coat. "It's okay ... don't worry about it. If anything, I haven't even thanked you for dinner yet. So, thank you."

She sneezed.

And then she sneezed again.

Concerned, he peered more closely at her. "Are you sure you're okay? It sounds like you might be coming down with something." He cast a worried glance over at her car. "Why don't you let me drive you home? I'll get your car to you by morning."

"No, no ... I'll be fine." Unlocking her car, she slipped into the driver's seat, sending him a shaky smile. "I only need a hot shower and a good night's sleep. Again, thanks Jason."

He held out his hand. "Give me your phone."

Too tired to question this, she did as he asked.

After he handed the phone back to her, he smiled. "Now you have my number. When you get home, I want you to text me. So, I know you got home safe. Okay?"

She sighed. "Okay... but like I said, don't worry, I'll be fine."

He watched her drive away before he started up his truck.

She didn't look fine.

He briefly contemplated following her. You know, just to be on the safe side. But as this could land him in even more trouble, he decided against this.

Turning out of the parking lot, he headed back to Jake's Place.

Once he pulled into the parking lot, Jason checked his phone. There was a text from Darcey.

> I'm home. So, you can relax.

Even though he was shaking his head, he was smiling as he typed out his response.

> Sweet dreams, gorgeous.

Twenty minutes later, he walked out of the restaurant, the photo once again stashed safely in his wallet. He was also carrying a takeout box. Inside was a huge slice of the featured dessert of the day, Amber's Carrot Cake.

This was Darcey's favorite dessert. Another thing he had stored away in his memory.

Yeah, how crazy was it you remembered this, yet you failed to say I love you to the most important person in your life. At the most important time.

Yeah, what the hell was his problem?

CHAPTER 18

All I want to do is sit down for a few minutes
and not worry about a single. damn. thing.
Is this too much to ask?
~ Anonymously Yours

*D*arcey unlocked the door to her office and dropped her purse on the chair. After shrugging out of her coat, she momentarily eyed the coat rack over in the corner. Deciding the trip there wasn't worth the effort, she tossed her coat on top of her purse.

She checked her phone.

11:43 a.m. It was almost time for lunch.

But she wasn't hungry. No, right now the only thing that sounded good to her was the luxury of taking a long nap.

A really, really long nap.

For a few moments, she gazed into space, just thinking about the possibility of being able to do this. Then, after a long sigh, she slowly made her way over to her desk and sank down in the chair. For the next five, ten or maybe even fifteen minutes, she really couldn't say how long, she stared out the window watching the leaves blowing around the courtyard.

Startled by the sound of voices out in the hallway, she jerked her head up, sending a guilty look around the room. She needed to get some work done.

Already the morning was shot.

Sometime between when she went to bed last night and woke to the sun shining through her bedroom window, she had come down with a dreadful cold. Her head ached, she had a terrible sore throat and she couldn't breathe through her nose.

This was when she realized, with the position of the sun, it was a lot later than it should be. She grabbed her phone off the nightstand to see she had slept right through her alarm and it was after nine.

Fighting the urge to crawl back under the covers, she sat on the bed, again for an undetermined amount of time, before she finally stumbled her way into the bathroom to take a shower.

She was right in the middle of washing her hair when the hot water ran out. By the time she stepped out of the shower, the water was ice cold and she was shivering. Hoping to warm up while she dried her hair, she turned on the hairdryer.

Sparks flew from the nozzle and after one enormous blast of hot air, the dryer went deadly silent.

The discovery she was out of coffee had almost been enough to put her over the edge. But this was all quickly forgotten when she realized she had somehow misplaced her keys.

After a frantic search, she finally found them hidden under the mail she brought in when she returned home last night.

So, it wasn't a surprise it was already late morning when she finally left her apartment.

This didn't stop her from making a detour from her usual drive to the party center. After spending a very restless night, she was determined to return to Jake's Place to see if they still had the photograph she left on the table.

She couldn't stop thinking about what a romantic gesture it was for Jason to keep the photograph. So, she wanted to get it for him. Then he could put it back in his wallet.

But, with the way her morning had gone, she wasn't the least bit surprised the photograph wasn't to be found. This was even after the more than helpful staff had checked every possible place they thought it could be.

And now, finally in her office, she wished she was anywhere else.

She opened her planner.

She had two interviews scheduled in the afternoon and if she was lucky, Rob would come through with the information she had requested. Then she could call it a day, brief as it was, and go home.

She reached over to pick up her phone to call the employment agency to confirm the interviews. This was when she saw the folder on her desk.

The note attached was from Rob.

> *Ms. Hollister,*
> *This is the information you requested.*
> *Once you've okayed everything, please*
> *initial and get it back to me. Then I'll*
> *get started on the work.*
> *Rob*

If she wasn't feeling so miserable, she would be thrilled he had delivered the information to her so quickly.

Could this possibly mean he was finally ready to accept she was in charge?

She shook her head.

There was no way it could be this easy.

She opened the folder. The first page was an itemized list of the cost and installation of new hinges, handles, and locks for all the doors.

Abruptly looking up from the folder, she glanced over at the door to her office. She was confused.

If you had to use your key when you arrived, this means the door was locked. So, how did Rob get this on your desk?

Well, he certainly didn't knock the door down. Did this mean he had a key?

This sent a chill racing through her, one that had nothing to do with her cold. Rob had no reason to have a key to her office. She understood there were some rooms he might need to access, but her office shouldn't be one of them.

But how was she to address this without giving him the impression she didn't trust him?

Because you don't. But you also don't want to get on his bad side.

But she didn't want to think about this right now. Quickly scanning and initialing all the orders, she set the folder aside to deliver later.

She checked her phone for the time to see it was after one. In desperate need of a break, she rested her head down on her arms and closed her eyes.

She had no intentions of falling asleep.

No, of course not.

This would be just for a few minutes. Then she would get back to work.

But with the condition she was in?

It didn't quite work out that way.

Jason had told the guys in the band to take off the next two days. There was nothing going on until Friday, and it was a pretty low-key event, so there was really no reason for them to meet.

He sat back in his chair and gazed around at what was the second bedroom of his house. Unfortunately, his plan to turn it into a music room had not yet materialized. Instead, there was only a small desk, a sleeper sofa, and the chair he was sitting in.

Along with still a few unpacked boxes.

But this was a job for another day. Right now, he was hungry. He had been up since early morning and it was already past one.

Ambling his way into the kitchen, he opened the refrigerator. The first thing he saw, was the takeout container from Jake's Place.

The carrot cake for Darcey.

And his mind took a detour right back to last night.

But truth be known, it had never left.

He groaned, dragging his hand over his jaw. No matter what he did, there was always a memory of her that wouldn't leave him. Unfortunately, this time, it wasn't a good one.

He still didn't understand. How could he have unknowingly, or more like idiotically, made the mistake of jeopardizing what they had by not telling her he loved her?

Three little words ...

But how they would have changed everything.

After staring at the container, he groaned aloud.

This is ridiculous ... either stop thinking about her, or do something to fix it.

And his decision was made.

He was going to take the cake to her. Right now. And while he was there, he was going to ask her out on a date. A real date ... dinner, dancing, the works. Whatever it would take to show her how much she meant to him.

And if she said no?

He stared down at the box in his hand.

Well, you're not going to even think about this.

It just wasn't going to happen.

And how could he be so sure of this?

He just was.

On his drive to the party center, Jason spent the entire time going over what he was going to say to Darcey when he saw her.

When he pulled into the parking lot, he almost got out of his truck with the motor still running.

If this wasn't more than enough proof of his preoccupied state, he was halfway up the steps to the main entrance, when he realized he'd left the takeout container on the front seat of his truck.

Not good, since this is the reason for your visit.

So, he headed back and grabbed the cake, all the while giving himself quite a lecture.

Come on, you're acting like you have never asked a woman on a date before. Show some confidence. As though you're expecting nothing less than a yes.

Takeout box in hand, he entered the building and headed for Darcey's office. Relieved to see her door was partially open, a sign she must be in, he sent a cautious glance inside.

Yep, she was definitely there. But at the same time, she wasn't. Seated at her desk, with her head down on her arms, she was completely still.

Thinking she must have fallen asleep and not wanting to startle her, he called out softly as he entered her office.

"Hey, Darcey?"

She didn't answer.

He drew closer.

Her eyes closed and her mouth wide open, she appeared to be sound asleep. If he wasn't mistaken, it also sounded like she might actually be snoring.

He cleared his throat. Once. Then he cleared it again, louder this time. When she still didn't move, only mumbled some incoherent gibberish, he moved even closer.

He was finding it difficult not to smile. He had a feeling she was going to be embarrassed when she finally woke to find him in her office.

He moved closer. "Darcey, honey? Are you okay?"

Slowly lifting her head, she peered up at him. Only to drop her head back down on her arms with a long moan.

His smile faded, and making his way around the desk, he squatted next to her, his hand on her shoulder. "Hey, gorgeous ... are you okay?"

Barely opening her eyes, her gaze slowly traveled over his face. She seemed confused, her words slurred. "What are you doing here?" Her lashes then fluttered shut.

Concerned, he brushed the hair back from her face, his voice a soft murmur. "Hey, sweetheart, are you okay? Come on, look at me."

She opened her eyes again, attempting to focus on his face. She sighed, her answer barely audible. "Sweetheart? Am I really your sweetheart? Or are you only trying to be nice?" Then she frowned. "I went back. But it wasn't there. And now it's lost. I'm so sorry. It's all my fault."

Not sure what she was mumbling about, he saw her eyes were now filling with tears.

Oh, geeez ... you know how you can't handle her tears.

And lost?

What did she mean? What was lost?

Cautiously moving closer, he put his palm to her forehead. He wasn't sure if he should worry, but she did seem a little warm.

His voice was soft, soothing. "What's lost?"

Barely lifting her head, she gazed into his face. "The photograph. They couldn't find it."

She shook her head. "They looked everywhere, but they said it probably got thrown away. I'm sorry, I'm so sorry." A sob catching in her throat, she dropped her head back down on her arms.

Slowly coming to his feet, he put his hand reassuringly on her shoulder. "Let's not worry about that right now. I think it's more important we get you home."

She dragged herself up into a sitting position, her gaze following him as he picked up her coat from the chair and brought it over to her.

She shook her head. "I can't go home. I have two interviews this afternoon."

Three sneezes followed this. Then she blew her nose before giving him a pitiful look. "Don't worry, I'll be fine. I just need coffee or something."

He reached over to nudge her chin up with his finger. "Darcey, look at me."

Her eyes finally focused on his, she was lulled by the soft tone of his voice. "I don't think coffee is going to do it for you. You're sick. And I think you might even have a temperature. This means you need to go home, where you can get some rest. The interviews can wait, gorgeous."

A dazed look on her face, she stared at him.

How are you going to make him understand, for you, leaving isn't even an option?

She rested her forehead in her hands, her sigh coming out long and very dramatic. "Jason, I can't. I have too much to—" Abruptly lifting her head, she frantically scanned her desk before she snatched up the folder from Rob. "I need to get this to Rob. You can't let me forget."

Sending a furtive glance around the room, she scooted closer to him. Her forehead creased with worry, she spoke in an exaggerated whisper. "I think he has a key to my office. And this isn't right."

Again, Jason was confused.

Rob had a key to her office? Why would he have a key? And how does she know this?

"Jason? Darcey? Is everything okay?"

They both glanced over to find Abby standing by the door.

On her way out of the building after delivering a cookie order, she had hoped to ask Darcey a few questions regarding the menu for the upcoming Moonlight Madness Masquerade Ball. But now, having heard most of Darcey and Jason's conversation, she realized her questions would have to wait.

Jason motioned for her to come into the office. "Abby, I'm glad you're here. I need your help. Darcey isn't feeling well. So, I'm trying to convince her home is the best place for her right now."

Abby came over to put her hand to Darcey's forehead. She shook her head. "Darcey, Jason's right. You feel pretty warm. You should probably take some ibuprofen or something."

Darcey was shaking her head. "I already took something. I stopped at the drugstore on the way here and picked up some medicine. But it didn't seem to work, so I took another dose a short time ago."

When she saw Abby and Jason share a quick glance, she became irritated. "Oh, for heaven's sake, I asked the pharmacist, and this is what he recommended. It's not like I could overdose on cough medicine."

When this had Darcey and Jason sharing another glance, she

waved her hand towards her purse. "Go ahead, check it out. It's in my purse."

Abby dug the bottle out of Darcey's purse and after reading the label, her forehead scrunched up with worry. "This is to be taken at night. And, at the most, every twelve hours. It's made to knock you out so you can sleep."

They both looked over at Darcey.

Her head propped on her hand, her eyes were closed.

Jason released a long breath. "Well, that settles it. Come on, Darcey... I'm taking you home. If there are any problems here, Abby is more than qualified to handle them since she was the event planner here at one time."

He nodded over at Abby. "Are you okay with this?"

"*Ah* ... something tells me I don't have a choice in the matter." She softened this with a smile before she turned to Darcey. "But, it's okay. I can hang around for a little while. Fill me in on anything I need to know so the two of you can get out of here."

After Darcey gave her the contact information for the employment agency, she picked up the folder from Rob. "I need to deliver this to Rob. I want him to have it so he can start getting the work done."

Before she realized what he was planning, Jason had taken the folder from her and headed for the door. He spoke over his shoulder. "I'll be more than happy to deliver this to him. I'll be right back."

Darcey didn't even have the energy to protest.

Abby smiled at Darcey's worried expression. "Don't worry, it's better if Jason handles this. From what I've heard, Rob has already ruffled quite a few feathers around here. I haven't met him yet. Nor do I want to."

She strolled over to the window, gazing out at the view for a few moments before she glanced over at Darcey. "I can't believe how nice the courtyard looks. It's such a great space now."

"Yes, it is."

When Darcey had nothing more to add, only giving an enormous yawn, Abby decided this might be a good time to say what she'd been wanting to say ever since she and Jason had their little talk in the coffee shop.

Her hands stuffed in her jacket pockets, she smiled over at Darcey. "I don't know if he told you this, but Jason and I have been friends since grade school. He became like my personal bodyguard when the boys started teasing me about my red hair. He told me I had the prettiest hair of everyone in school and whoever didn't agree was just jealous. After that, I swore I would be his friend for life."

She laughed. "I followed him everywhere. I was such a pest."

She smiled at the memory. "He was so shy back then. And he's still shy. When he and his friends started the band and the girls all started going crazy over him, he honestly didn't understand why."

She shook her head. "Even to this day, I don't think he has a clue of how good looking he is or what a magnetic draw he has. And he doesn't care about being rich or famous. If he did, he would have left a long time ago, moving to either LA or New York. But he told me he was perfectly happy right here, writing his music and playing with his band. He needed nothing more in life."

After a slight hesitation, she continued. "But this all changed when he met you. Since then, he hasn't been able to get you out of his mind. So, I don't know how you feel about him, but whatever you do, please don't hurt him. He's such a good guy. And I can promise you, if he has decided you're the one, he will cherish you for the rest of your life."

She smiled. "You'll have a love like what he sings about in all the songs he writes."

Unfortunately, Darcey hadn't heard a word.

Her eyes closed and her head propped on her hand, her elbow was slowly inching precariously close to the edge of her desk, almost on the verge of sliding off.

Abby started towards her, reaching out to grab her arm. "Darcey... hey, you're gonna fall."

Her head jerking up and her lashes flying open, Darcey slowly sank back in her chair and, dragging her hands through her hair, she gave another huge yawn. "I'm sorry, I think I may have dozed off. What did you just say?"

Abby sighed.

All that brilliant advice ... wasted, just like that.

"It's okay. It's nothing that can't wait until later."

Darcey didn't even have the energy to nod. Suddenly, she couldn't stay awake for the life of her. She felt like she was drunk, too weak to even move. If she could, she'd curl up on her desk, close her eyes and go to sleep.

She was that tired.

Maybe Abby and Jason were right.

She needed to go home.

Umm ... and maybe you shouldn't have taken that second dose of medicine.

Jason found Rob in the Grand Ballroom, supervising the crew refinishing the floors. His intention to keep their conversation brief, he handed Rob the folder. "This is from Darcey. She signed off on everything, so you're good to go."

He turned and headed for the exit, but Rob's short laugh had him turning, a guarded look on his face.

Tossing the folder onto a chair, and crossing his arms over his chest, Rob appeared to be amused. "I see you and your sidekick felt it was necessary to play detective last night. So, you know our meeting didn't go that well."

He shook his head. "She's definitely a spitfire, that one. Daddy's little girl is tougher than she looks."

Jason would later claim he didn't remember approaching Rob. He had even surprised himself when he found he was only inches away.

The look of rage on his face had Rob taking a step back, while the threatening tone of his voice was loud enough to capture the attention of everyone in the room.

"I don't get you. What kind of man lets a woman walk away when he knows she will be alone in the parking lot of a questionable establishment? You didn't even have the decency to make sure she had a way home."

He dragged his hand through his hair. "And what made you chose The Corner Bar? The only business meetings taking place in that hole-in-a-wall aren't something you'd want to brag about."

Rob shrugged. "Hey, I didn't ask her to leave, she did that on her own. She had her phone, so she wasn't in any danger. And after the scene she made? I'd say she fit right in with the rest of the clientele who frequent the place."

His laugh was short. "I think it's about time she realizes I have a lot more experience and know-how than she does. And if she thinks I'm going to be checking in with her all the time, looking for her approval, she is in for a rude awakening."

Jason didn't say a word, his steely glance and the tight set of his jaw the only sign of the anger he was holding so tightly inside.

So, it wasn't really a surprise Rob was the first to look away. His glance sweeping the room, he zeroed in on the crew, who were still listening. "Nothing about our discussion is any of your business. So, it might be best if you got back to work."

His enraged expression sent them scrambling.

Already at the door, Jason had one more parting shot. "I'm going to tell you this just once... Stay away from Darcey. If you don't, you'll have me to contend with."

As furious as he was, he made the effort to calm down as he strode down the hall. As soon as he had a chance, he was going to dig up as much information about Rob as he could. And find out why he had the key to Darcey's office.

He'd be willing to bet his favorite and most expensive guitar, the results wouldn't be good.

Silence greeted Jason when he came striding back into the Darcey's office.

Abby was reading over the resumes of the interview candidates. Darcey, her head resting on her hand, was half asleep.

He grabbed Darcey's coat off the chair and walked over to her. "The folder is now in Rob's hands. So now you have no reason to worry."

This was the extent of what he was going to say. He saw no reason to share the conversation he had with Rob.

Not now ... maybe never.

He reached for Darcey's hand. "Come on, gorgeous. Let me help you with your coat. We need to get you home."

Don't worry, he made sure to grab the takeout container on the way out.

CHAPTER 19

*J*ason glanced over at Darcey. Her head resting against the seat, her eyes were closed.

But this was okay with him. More than happy to be taking care of her, he didn't feel the need to say anything.

While she couldn't find the energy to think of what to say.

When they had arrived at his truck in the parking lot, he hadn't even asked, scooping her up in his arms to settle her into the passenger seat. The thrill of having her in his arms, he had held on to her a little longer than necessary, reluctant to let go.

If you're not mistaken, she was holding on pretty tight. Maybe this was because she was afraid you might have dropped her.

He chuckled to himself. Like he'd ever let this happen.

He cleared his throat. When she slowly turned her head to gaze over at him, he smiled. "Hey, I need your address so I can put it in my GPS. Once I have that, you can close those beautiful eyes of yours and go right back to sleep."

A faint smile touching her lips, she gave him the address. Then, after a searching look, a long sigh escaped her. "I'm sorry I'm not the best of company."

"That's okay, you're fine." At his smile, her lashes fluttered shut.

As he drove, he was absentmindedly tapping his fingers on the steering wheel to a beat in his head, humming along.

Remember, Jason is a musician. Music made him who he was, which meant silence wasn't his thing. And if he did feel the need for peace and quiet? He still needed music, even if it was somewhere in the background.

And was there a certain style of music he preferred?

This would be classical music. In fact, some of his best songs had come about while listening to classical music.

He sent a glance over at Darcey and, thinking she had fallen asleep, he reached over to turn on the audio player.

This immediately sent Bolero, by Ravel, blaring from the speakers. Hastily turning down the volume, he shot a look over at Darcey.

She was staring at him, wide-eyed.

Oh, geeez ... not good. If she was asleep, you definitely put a quick end to that.

"Sorry ... I always play this song full blast."

He watched a smile flit across her face.

His head tilted, he smiled, too. "What?"

"I remember the same thing happened the night we made dinner at your place and... Pachelbel, Canon in..." She closed her eyes, her words trailing off.

He remembered this. So clearly, he did. How could he not? They had bought ingredients to make dinner at his apartment. Their plan to follow a DIY link Darcey found, titled how to prepare a romantic dinner for two. Or something like that. Opening a bottle of wine, they set out the ingredients and got to work.

It turned out this video was more than appropriately named. Their time in the kitchen, cut short by a romantic episode of their own, had delayed their dinner until much later in the evening.

Yeah, everything had been a little overdone, but you remember it as one of the best dinners you ever had.

After a brief silence, he cleared his throat. "I remember. Correct me if I'm wrong, but I believe it turned out to be a very memorable night. But now thinking about it, I'm surprised we didn't burn the place down."

A smile twitched at the corner of his mouth. "It was also the night we both discovered I'm a much better cook than you are."

She looked over at him, a faint smile touching her lips. "Yeah, I guess I'll give you that one little thing."

He smiled. "How generous of you."

The GPS giving the instructions to turn, Darcey pointed to the first building on the left. "My apartment is right there. The third one down."

Around to open her door before she even unbuckled her seatbelt, he reached for her arm. "Come on, let me help you. Pickup trucks aren't user friendly for the fashionably dressed."

Jason gazed curiously around Darcey's apartment.

He was a little surprised. It was a mess... even for him.

The dining room had boxes stacked high on the table. There were more boxes stacked against the wall in the hallway leading to the bedrooms.

He glanced over at her, clearing his throat. "*Wow*, it seems like a lot of stuff for just one person. And for such a small space. What could you possibly have in these boxes?"

She groaned. "I know. And the sad thing is, I can't even give you the answer to that. I think I went a little crazy, packing up everything I owned."

He raised an eyebrow. "A little?"

Now she was getting a little irritated. Who was he to judge her? She frowned. "In my defense, the photos the realtor sent made the apartment look a lot larger than it is."

She wearily ran her hand through her hair. "I've been trying to put away a little at a time. But I've been spending so much time at The Regency, when I finally get home, unpacking is the last thing I want to do."

He reached over to tuck her hair behind her ear, his fingertips grazing her jaw. This slight touch, brought on such a yearning for more, he quickly dropped his hand.

He cleared his throat. "Right now, unpacking is the least of your worries. I want you to get into your pajamas, hop into bed, and get some rest. While you're doing that, I'm going to make a run to the deli down the street. I've been told they make the best chicken soup. "

He shrugged, smiling over at her. "I know I've read somewhere this is the cure-all for everything."

The tenderness of his expression enough to send a gentle nudge to her heart, she wanted to tell him soup wasn't what she needed. Nor did she need sleep. What she wanted, what would make her feel better? This would be if he took her into his arms and held her close.

Yeah, this is exactly what you need.

Instead, she shook her head. "You don't have to do that." She glanced over at the kitchen. "I think there might be a can of soup or two somewhere in the cupboards."

He shook his head. "Nope, you deserve better." His gaze held hers. "Darcey, let me take care of you. I want to do this. Think of this as a friend helping a friend. Okay?"

His words came almost as a shock, her heart dropping to her stomach.

A friend? He still thinks of you as only a friend?

Suddenly, she was beyond exhausted.

Fine, soup and sleep it would have to be.

Twenty minutes later, Jason returned to find Darcey curled up on the sofa.

Wrapped up in a quilt, she appeared to be asleep.

Stashing the soup in the refrigerator, and the container of ice cream in the freezer, this last item highly recommended by the owner of the deli, he began searching for a pen and paper to write Darcey a note.

He glanced over to see she was awake, watching him.

Smiling, he walked over to her. "I thought you were asleep, so I put the soup in the refrigerator. Just so you know, the woman at the deli said they're famous for their chicken soup. She also talked me into bringing you a carton of their own brand of mint chocolate chip ice cream. Another customer favorite, she told me."

Shaking his head, he was grinning. "If I hadn't finally told her you were on the verge of starving to death, I would probably still be there, buying out the store."

He rubbed his hands together. "So, do you want me to warm up the soup for you?"

"Maybe I'll have some later?" More interested in what his plans were, she searched his face. "You're leaving?"

After he smoothed her hair back from her face and placed his palm on her forehead to check her temperature, he nodded. "Yes, but I'll stop back to check on you later. I'll bring a pizza or something."

Slipping into his jacket, he held up her keys. "I'm going to take these with me. This way, if you're sleeping when I come back, I won't wake you by knocking on the door."

He gave her a stern look. "And this is what you should be doing. Sleeping. I don't want you on your computer or making calls. Work can wait."

After a slight hesitation, he reached over and cupping her chin in his hand, he pressed a soft kiss to her forehead. "I'll see you later, gorgeous."

She watched as he left, closing the door behind him.

Gorgeous ...

He wouldn't keep calling her this if he thought of her as only a friend, right?

Too tired to even think about this, and dragging the quilt behind her, she headed for her bedroom.

During the time it took him to drive home, Jason thoroughly evaluated of his life.

And what had he decided?

It was time to make some changes, something he had put off for way too long.

Number one on the agenda? He was going to get serious about fixing up the rest of his house. When he moved in, the attic had already been converted into a master suite. But the rest of the house direly needed help.

He was going to call Paul's buddy Tom. According to Paul, he was the best around. Paul warned he was expensive, but there were no surprises. Something, according to Paul, was very important with a home remodeling job.

Well, bring it on then ... you're ready.

He pulled into his driveway. Resting his arms on the steering wheel, he gave the property a thorough once over. He tried to imagine how it would look in someone else's eyes.

Hmm ... and whose eyes would this be?

He shook his head, ignoring this subtle reminder.

From what he could see, it appeared there was a lot more work to be done than he had expected. Starting with a paint job and a new roof. And the yard, how had he not noticed how overgrown everything was?

Geesh ... you can hardly see the front door.

And then there was the front door itself. He was tired of fighting with it every time he wanted to get inside.

He pulled out his phone.

An hour later, the interior inspection finished, Jason was following Tom around the outside of the house. The long list of recommendations had Jason wondering what he had gotten himself into.

After scribbling something on his clipboard, Tom went over to his truck and pulled out a paint sample book. He handed it to Jason. "While I write up an estimate, you can start looking through these paint samples, get an idea of what you want. I suggest you get your girlfriend to help you out with this."

Jason was curious. "What makes you think a woman is involved?"

Tom slowly shook his head. "As soon as you told me you wanted to wait with the kitchen, it was obvious a woman was in the picture. Otherwise, you would've given me free rein to start the work."

He sent Jason a grin. "It's in your best interest to get her involved right from the beginning." He laughed. "Trust me on this, it will be a lot cheaper in the long run."

After Tom left, Jason flipped through the paint sample book.

Finding a color he liked, he read the name.

Billowy Clouds?

He checked out a few more samples.

Popped Corn? Clear View?

He laughed.

What the heck? How do any of these names make sense? Or give you an idea of what the color really is?

He made a quick detour back to his truck and threw the paint sample book on the back seat.

He was definitely going to need Darcey's help with this.

CHAPTER 20

Take time to enjoy the little things in life.
Because one day, you'll look back and realize,
Maybe they weren't so little after all.
~Anonymously Yours

Darcey hadn't planned to sleep on the sofa.

In fact, she had fallen asleep in her bed almost as soon as her head hit the pillow.

But then the dreams started up, one after another, each one sending her more into a panic than the last. Dreams, she couldn't seem to do anything right.

Or get to where she needed to go.

In her latest dream, when she began falling into this deep hole with no end in sight, she woke in a cold sweat. Sitting straight up in bed, she stared into the darkness, listening to the pounding of her heart in the late afternoon silence.

Once her heartbeat was almost back to normal, she wrapped the quilt around her and left the bedroom. She settled in more comfortably on the sofa and turned on the TV to an old Friends re-run.

It was when she began drifting off to sleep, she remembered

Jason's promise he'd be stopping by later to check on her. Knowing Jason, she could count on this.

She fell asleep, a smile hugging her lips.

After a long run, followed by a quick shower, Jason put a call into the pizza place down the street.

He hopped into his truck, his plan to pick up the order on his drive over to Darcey's.

It was a beautiful autumn evening, the sun just beginning its descent over the lake. Unseasonably warm for September, he had the windows down, sending the breeze rifling through his still damp hair as he drove. With the audio playing one of his favorite songs, he was feeling pretty good about life.

After a quick stop at Mama Jo's Italian Restaurant, he was back on the road. His truck now filled with the mouth-watering aroma of the hot-from-the-oven pizza, this was when he realized he hadn't eaten since breakfast.

And now?

He was starving.

Ten minutes later, he had parked in front of Darcey's apartment and was unlocking her front door.

Once he set the pizza on the counter, he glanced over to see she was sound asleep on the sofa.

The TV was on, the volume down low. He found the remote and turned it off.

When he picked up the quilt from where it had fallen on the floor to cover her, she mumbled something, but too softly for him to hear. He stilled, listening for more, but she only let out a deep sigh and burrowed deeper under the quilt. So, he headed back to the kitchen.

He was going to let her sleep.

But while he waited, there was no reason he couldn't have some pizza.

If you recall, he was pretty hungry.

When Jason opened the box, he saw they had neglected to cut the pizza into slices. But he wasn't too worried. Give him a knife and he'd take care of it.

He began searching through the kitchen drawers for the silverware. But there was a problem. He could only get the drawer to open about an inch. Thinking there was a piece of silverware caught up inside, he gave the drawer a good shake.

Nothing happened.

He gave the drawer a firm tug.

Again, nothing.

So, he tried shaking it again. But the drawer still refused to budge.

Frustrated, he rubbed the back of his neck.

Come on, you just want a piece of pizza. Is this too much to ask?

He tried again.

Nothing.

Now he was getting annoyed. Grabbing hold of the drawer handle with both hands, he gave it a hard yank.

Evidently, this was one of the few times he had underestimated his strength. Taking him by surprise, and before he even had time to react, the drawer came shooting right out at him.

He barely held on to it as it hit the floor, sending the entire collection of silverware sliding right out and flying in all directions. Bouncing off the cabinets and skittering across the tiled floor, this made enough noise to wake the dead.

To Jason's musically trained mind, it sounded like an unrehearsed rendition of percussion instruments, battling it out to see who could be the loudest.

He'd have to say it was a tie.

Damn ... damn ... damn ...

He was tossing the silverware back into the drawer when he remembered Darcey.

He whirled around to see she had come to her feet. She was holding the quilt up to her chin, a look of total shock on her face.

In his haste to get to her, he almost tripped over the silverware still scattered across the floor. Once he was close enough, he took her into his arms. "*Oh, sweetheart* ... I'm so sorry. The pizza place forgot to cut the pizza into slices. The drawer where you keep your knives wouldn't open. I pulled it, obviously harder than I should have and, well ... you heard the results."

Her response was muffled against his chest. "It's okay. That drawer sticks every time. It drives me crazy."

He chuckled.

She looked up at him. "What?"

He smiled down at her. "I was thinking you and I are about even right now, wouldn't you say? You left behind a trail of destruction in our equipment room and I answer by trying to top that here in your apartment. If this isn't proof we're two of a kind, I don't know what more we need."

He rested his palm against her forehead, relief filling his features. "*Ah* ... nice and cool. This is good."

At the warmth in his voice, she tentatively wrapped her arms around him. Breathing in the combination of shampoo, his cologne, of everything that was him ... it filled her lungs, sending her right back to how it had felt to be in his embrace. Resting her head against his shoulder, she closed her eyes.

Her mouth brushing against his shirt, her words came softly. "I feel so silly, causing all this trouble. I would have been better off drinking a couple glasses of wine."

He chuckled. "I assure you, you're no trouble. I enjoy taking care of you. And if I remember, one glass of wine is pretty much your limit, with two comes trouble. So, we'll save the wine for another time."

He adjusted the quilt, gently wrapping it around her. "Come sit at the kitchen island so we can talk while I clean up the mess I have going on. Then you can tell me what you want to eat. We've got quite an assortment, soup, pizza, ice cream, and I even got you a piece of that carrot cake you like."

He tilted his head. "I'm not sure. What is it they say? Feed a cold, starve a fever? Or is it the other way around?"

He looked so confused, she laughed. Gazing up at him, she shook her head. "You pick, anything is fine." Her smile was tentative. "The fact you're here is enough."

Again, they became caught up in each other's gaze. Finally clearing his throat, a flicker of amusement crossed his face. "Yeah, it turns out I'm not that bad of a guy after all, am I?"

He reached over to run his knuckles lightly along her jaw. "It's your call, whatever you want."

Jason had cleared away all signs of their dinner, refusing Darcey's offer of help.

He checked his watch. "Whoa, I can't believe it's so late. I've been here for over two hours. So, I think it's time for me to take off." He winked at her. "I believe my work here is done."

After he shrugged into his jacket, he pulled out his keys, fingering them. This habit of fiddling with his keys was one Darcey remembered as something he did when he was nervous or unsure.

She gazed up at him. "What's up?"

Shoving both the keys and his hands in his pockets, he cleared his throat. "This has been nice, spending time together. Hasn't it?"

She nodded. "Yes, it has. Again, thank you for everything, the pizza, the soup, your company. I'm feeling so much better now." She smiled. "And the cake. Thank you for the cake. I can't believe you remembered carrot cake is my favorite."

He nodded, a preoccupied nod. "You're welcome. But ..."

She tilted her head, waiting. "But?"

Shoving his hands in his pockets, he sat next to her on the sofa, his gaze searching. "I was wondering what you would think of the two of us going out on a date? You know ... a nice restaurant, a great dinner, or whatever you'd like. We'll go all out, make a night of it."

His next words came out in a rush. "I want to give us another try, Darcey. I want to start over. Maybe you'll think I'm crazy, but I feel like we're being offered a second chance. And I'd like to see where this could take us."

He shrugged. "It might turn out to be nothing. But again, it could be the start of something amazing." He sent her a rueful smile. "Unless I do something stupid and screw it up again."

She was shaking her head, "Oh Jason, I think we were both to blame for what happened. I often wonder …" Her words trailing off, she suddenly smiled. "I would love to go out to dinner with you."

Then she shuddered, wrapping the quilt more tightly around her. "As long as you promise we won't be going to The Corner Bar."

He was frowning as he came to his feet. "I don't know what the hell he was thinking. He … well, never mind. You don't want to know what my opinion is of the decisions he makes."

He pulled out his keys again. "Saturday night then? Since it's a rarity nothing is going on at The Regency." He raised an eyebrow. "Maybe another sign in our favor?"

He was watching her, waiting almost impatiently for her response. He suddenly found it very important he had her promise right here and now.

He would write it down and have her sign it if he could.

Yeah, he'd admit this was crazy.

But he wanted proof this was going to happen.

He cleared his throat. "Seven-thirty?"

She nodded.

"Seven-thirty. It's a date."

After Jason left, Darcey settled on the sofa with her laptop. Even though she felt a little guilty, since she had promised him she would take a break from work.

But it turned out she had nothing to worry about. After reading the same email at least four times, unable to remember a single word, it was obvious she wasn't going to accomplish anything. Shutting off the computer, she snuggled deeper into the sofa and pulled the quilt up around her.

She closed her eyes, allowing herself the luxury of reliving the time Jason had spent with her.

They were settling into this familiar camaraderie. Almost as if no time had passed, they had never been apart. But there was too much they weren't talking about, so much they were trying to avoid.

A few times during the evening, she had caught him studying her with a caution she hadn't seen before. Then he would hesitate, as if he was about to say something, only to change the subject.

But she was just as guilty, not asking him about the one thing that bothered her the most. And this would be why he had never returned her call after she went back to California.

Fingering the ring hanging from her necklace, she brought it up to her lips. There had been a moment during the evening she almost showed it to him. But then she changed her mind, not sure she if she was ready to let him know it was the real reason she had returned.

Resting her head back against the sofa cushions, she closed her eyes. The memory of Jason's face when he had slipped the ring on her finger was one she would never forget. The ring signified so much more than a promise, he'd told her. It was a solemn pledge he would always be there for her.

Always ...

And now?

She hoped he still felt this way.

CHAPTER 21

*A*cross town and a little over an hour into her shift, Stephanie Bennett was hiding out in the third-floor women's lounge.

She had been there now for at least twenty minutes. Her arms wrapped around herself, she was pacing back and forth, trying to calm down.

You are such a fool. By now, you should have figured it out. You'll never get this right.

Yes, this was what she kept telling herself. From this point on, she was through with love.

And what had brought this on? Or, more likely, who had brought her to this state?

Less than a half hour ago, she had found out Noah was engaged.

But wait, it gets worse. This information had come from, none other than, Noah's fiancée. In person and in the third-floor staff lounge.

This fiancé's name? Not that it mattered, but it's Michelle.

It seems this Michelle's intent was to surprise Noah by flying to Cleveland for a visit. She told Stephanie she knew she was taking a chance, springing something like this on him. But she didn't want to wait for his next trip home to Minnesota.

She missed him. After all, they had been dating ever since high school and this was the longest they had ever been apart.

So, when she arrived at the hospital, she asked the first person she saw if they knew where to find him.

What were the odds this person would be you? One in a Million?

Stephanie's mind had grabbed right onto the "I'm his fiancée" comment of Michelle's, and from then on, hadn't been able to let go. And now it was still bouncing around in her head, to the point she couldn't even think straight.

He was engaged? How could this be? His actions hadn't come across as an engaged man. And she definitely would have remembered if he had told her this very important fact.

She groaned, dropping her head in her hands.

A man who had already asked another woman to marry him should not be inviting another woman out to dinner.

Right?

Unfortunately, Noah seemed to think differently.

Because this was what happened only about an hour ago. Approaching her in the staff lounge Noah had asked if she would like to go out for dinner after the masquerade ball committee meeting tomorrow night.

Then, BAM! Only a short time later, his fiancée shows up.

You should have known he was too good to be true.

She glanced down at her watch. She needed to get back to work before anyone noticed she was missing.

After she splashed cold water on her face, she stared at her reflection in the mirror. Her eyes looked enormous, her face devoid of color.

How will you ever be able to face him? Or worse yet, both of them? What will you say?

Closing her eyes, she pulled out her phone. She needed to talk to Jason.

When Jason got home from Darcey's, he checked his phone.

He had had missed a call from Steffi about fifteen minutes ago. She had also sent a text.

> Can we meet for coffee tomorrow? I need to talk to you. Maybe around five at Café Latte? I'm at work now, so text me your answer. Thanks, XOXO

Since it was almost midnight, an unusual time for her to call, he wondered if he should call her back. But her text didn't seem urgent. And like she said, she was at work.

So, he sent a text.

> See you at five - Café Latte it is. You better not be late.

He was smiling as he tossed the phone on the counter. He knew this wasn't going to happen. There was a fifty percent chance Steffi would be late.

No, he'd take that back. More like a seventy-five, or even ninety percent chance.

Not that she was irresponsible. Her problem was she always put herself last. If someone asked for her help, she couldn't say no. Even if this meant she would be late for something else.

Unless it came to her work at the hospital. Her dedication to the children was second to none.

For a brief second, he wondered what it was she wanted to talk about. But the prospect of sleep won out, and he turned out the lights.

He was going to bed.

Darcey was with him in his dreams.

CHAPTER 22

God makes sure to give us dreams a size too big.
This way we can grow into them.
~ Anonymously Yours

At the sound of footsteps in the hallway outside of her office, Darcey glanced over at the door.

She waited, an expectant smile on her face. But, as had happened every time before, whoever it was?

They passed right by...

Again, it wasn't who she had hoped it would be.

Absentmindedly tapping her fingers on the keyboard, she stared at the computer screen.

You're pathetic. Seriously, what is wrong with you?

Even if Jason stopped by the party center, there was a chance he might not be too happy to see her.

Nope, he had made it quite clear he thought she should have taken the day off.

But this wasn't possible.

She had a lot of work to do. And, besides the occasional annoying cough or having to blow her nose every five minutes, she wasn't feeling all that bad. In fact, she had been in a pretty good mood ever since she woke up, sniffles and all.

There was also the committee meeting for the masquerade ball tonight, something she wanted to attend. Café Latte was the meeting place, six o'clock was the time.

Since this was the chief fundraiser for the Children's Hospital, it was very important the evening went without a hitch. And now, with the ball less than two weeks away, there were still a lot of details to be ironed out.

So, she wanted to help in any way she could.

With a thoughtful look on her face, she sat back in her chair. The ball did sound like it was going to be a fun evening.

Not that she was planning on attending.

This wouldn't be an option, since they had sold out the event months ago.

And if it wasn't sold out? Would you want to go?

But this meant she would have to go alone, since Jason and his band were the entertainment.

You're assuming a lot, aren't you? What makes you think he would want you as his date?

She pushed away from the desk, and wandering over to the window, she gazed out at the deserted courtyard. She needed to stop. She was getting ahead of herself, imagining something that probably wasn't going to happen.

"Darcey?"

Recognizing Abby's voice, Darcey was smiling when she turned to watch her walk into the room, Madeline Rose settled on her hip.

Abby grinned right back at her. "Well, you're looking much better than you did yesterday. At least, you seem to be more awake."

Darcey shook her head. "I am. Wide awake and feeling a lot better. Though, I'm a little embarrassed. I haven't been at my best the last two days."

She smiled. "I can't even tell you how much I appreciate you taking over. I see you even left some notes about the two people you interviewed, which is great."

Abby sat Madeline Rose on the desk, where she swiftly reached over to grab Darcey's phone, with Abby intercepting it just in the nick of time.

She sighed. "This little one ... she is going to be the death of me. She is so darn fast. She gets into everything. And now everyone keeps telling me it looks like she's going to be an early walker."

She groaned. "Lord, help us."

She handed Madeline Rose her keys to play with before she glanced over at Darcey. "So, about the interviews... I'd have to say Emma nailed all the requirements and had all the right answers. While Susan, the other candidate?" She shook her head. "She was nice, but she had such an anxious vibe going on, by the time the interview was over, she had me all worked up, too. And I didn't even know why. Not the message you want to send in this business. Especially with weddings."

Darcey reached down to pick up the keys Madeline Rose had pushed off the edge of the desk. She handed them back to her, rewarded with a big grin.

She turned back to Abby. "After reading your notes, I set up a second interview with Emma. The employment agency also informed me they had a lead on both a chef and sous chef. So hopefully, everything will come together. I'm keeping my fingers crossed this will all happen before the masquerade ball."

Giving a delighted shriek, almost as if she approved of what Darcey said, Madeline Rose flung the keys through the air, to have them land over by the door.

Clapping her hands, she sent Darcey another big grin.

Abby was shaking her head as Darcey retrieved the keys. "Thank you. It appears someone is getting a little carried away, so we should probably move on. I blame this new behavior on Kevin. Last night, he was trying to teach her how to throw this cloth baseball he got for her. And this is the result. She thinks she has to throw whatever she can get her hands on." She grinned. "I don't know who's worse, Kevin or this little monkey."

Heading for the door, she turned to Darcey. "Will you be at the committee meeting tonight at Café Latte?" At Darcey's nod, she smiled. "Good. I'll be there, too. I'm doing the cookie favors. The cookies are done, sealed and ready to go."

She frowned. "But I'm still working on the final design plan for the cake. I've come up with a few ideas, but still have some details to iron out."

She sent Darcey an inquiring glance. "Do you know if Jason will be at the meeting tonight?"

Feigning nonchalance, Darcey shrugged. "I don't know? Should he? I'm not really sure what his plans are." Then she began rambling, making little sense. "I'm referring to what part he has in the meeting, of course. Not about him and me. We really didn't talk about the meeting. Not that we talk all that much."

A smile twitched Abby's lips. "*Hmm ...* I was only curious. I got the impression you two were sort of close."

She shrugged. "But I guess he doesn't need to be there. For the band, it's like any other night. Though with this event, they do black tie."

She laughed. "Wait until you witness firsthand how the women go totally nuts over Jason in a tux. He has them stammering, falling over their feet just to get next to him. There has even been a few"

She shook her head. "But he takes it all in stride, as if nothing unusual is going on. And this isn't an act, it's just the way he is."

She took a few more steps towards the door, only to stop, tilting her head. "You are planning to attend, aren't you? As a guest, I mean. Not just to stand around and supervise. If not, you should. Around here, it's a big deal, a chance to get all dressed up. A lot of the women plan their outfits months ahead. And the masks... you should see how elaborate some of them are. It really is a magical evening."

After Abby's assessment of Jason, Darcey had heard little of what she said. She'd completely zoned out, her thoughts veering off in a whole other direction.

Jason in a tuxedo?

Because of her family's business and their involvement in the community, she had attended many formal events over the years. So, she'd seen her share of men attired in tuxedos.

But Jason?

In evening wear?

Oh my, you can't even imagine how spectacular a sight this must be.

"Darcey?"

Her mind still miles away, Darcey blinked. Then she looked over at Abby, giving a negative shake of her head. "I wasn't planning to attend. I didn't bring any formal dresses with me. And not that it matters, but I would feel out of place coming by myself."

The excuse about a dress was true. She had given away most of what she owned before she left California, this including a good number of glamorous dresses worthy of any formal occasion.

Her reasoning? She wanted to embrace this new start with a clean slate.

Abby was frowning. "Nonsense. Everyone mingles, the whole aim to have a good time and raise money for charity. Sophie, Hannah and I may be without our husbands for the first part of the evening, depending on how long their afternoon game goes."

Her frown deepened. "And when it comes to a dress? I'm sure you'll be able to find one at the boutique."

At Darcey's puzzled look, Abby nodded. "The Chic Boutique. Sophie and her Aunt Louise's dress shop." She smiled. "I'll tell you what ... I can talk to Sophie and—"

Darcey interrupted her. "Oh, no ... please, you don't need to do this."

Abby held up her hand. "Nope, we're going to find you a dress. A dress that will knock Jason's socks off." Now halfway out the door, she came to a halt. "I'll ask Sophie to call you. Finding the perfect dress is what she and her aunt do best."

She grinned. "Trust me, you'll love what they pick out for you."

With a wave, she was gone.

Darcey slowly sank down into her chair.

She was smiling.

Well, there you go. It looks like you'll be going to a masquerade ball.

But, come on … she couldn't miss this.

Again, Jason in a tuxedo?

She was going to fall right into that group of women Abby mentioned. Stuttering and falling over her own feet in order to get close to him.

You realize you've already done that. Remember? The fiasco in the equipment room?

Resting her chin on her hand and closing her eyes, she let her imagination take over.

In his arms, he whirls you around the dance floor, your steps in perfect harmony with his. The mask unable to hide the desire in his eyes, you dance like you've never danced before.

One dance. This is all she would need.

And yes, she actually believed this alone would be enough.

CHAPTER 23

*J*ason pulled into the Café Latte parking lot.

From what he could see, Stephanie hadn't arrived yet. At least he didn't see her car.

But why are you even surprised?

Once he was inside, his order of a coffee and a blueberry muffin in hand, he chose a table by the window. Settling in his chair, he took a big gulp of coffee, following with a long, satisfied sigh. They had the best coffee around.

He pulled out his phone. From experience, he knew he had about a fifteen-minute wait.

If you're lucky ...

He gazed around the half-filled café. The low hum of voices, along with the soft jazzy background music, gave the room a peaceful vibe. But he knew this would be short-lived with the soon-to-be arrival of the after-work crowd.

He was reading a message from his agent when he felt someone standing next to him.

He looked up to see a young kid, maybe about sixteen or seventeen years old, standing by the table. His hair flopping over his forehead, almost covering his eyes, he was holding a napkin and pen.

Jason set his phone down, sending him a smile. "Hey, what's up?"

Shifting from one foot to the other, the kid went to say something, to have it come out in a hoarse squeak. Turning a bright red, he shoved the hair out of his eyes before he cleared his throat. "Hey, I was wondering… can I get your autograph? And could you maybe make it out to Louie?"

"Sure." After taking the napkin and pen, Jason gave him a closer look. Maybe he was wrong, but this kid didn't look like a Louie. Tapping the pen on the table, he smiled. "Louie … is this you?"

Shaking his head, the hair flying back in his eyes, the kid grinned. "*Nah*, I'm Ben. Louie is my grandpa. He used to play guitar in a band with his friends, and he taught me to play, too."

Nodding towards the napkin, he grinned. "He collects autographs. And he follows you on social media. We both do. My goal is to play as good as you, have my own band someday."

His voice ended in another squeak. He turned an even brighter shade of red before clearing his throat again. "Sorry."

Jason studied him for a few minutes before he scribbled something on the napkin. He smiled as he handed it to him. "Something tells me you're going to pass me up, Ben."

He sent a quick glance around the room. "Is your grandpa here with you?"

Ben frowned, shaking his head. "No, he's at home. He started forgetting things. When it got worse, my mom convinced him to come live with us."

Then he grinned. "I come here a couple times a week and buy him something from the bakery. He loves sweet things."

Now he was on a roll, the words pouring out. "Me and my grandpa used to play together, but after he moved in with us, someone broke into his house and stole all the equipment he had. So, using the guitar he gave me a long time ago, we take turns."

He made a face. "It's okay, but not the greatest. So, I just started a landscaping business in our neighborhood so I can make some money to buy a new guitar … a good one."

Jason studied him for a few moments. There was something about this kid he liked. He picked up his phone. "Give me your name and address. I can't promise you anything, but maybe I can help you out."

After the information was in his phone, he rose from his seat and pulling out a chair, he nodded over at Ben. "Here, sit here for a few minutes, save my table. I'll be right back."

He went over to the counter and asked the woman to add another half-dozen bakery items of Ben's choice to his order. Handing her his credit card, he told her to charge this to his account. Returning to his table, he put his hand on Ben's shoulder. "You're all set. Give them my name when you place your order at the counter. My treat."

A huge smile lighting up his face, Ben thanked him at least a half dozen times before he sprinted his way across the room to place his order.

After Ben had come back to thank him one last time before he left the café, Jason sent a text off to Jack. If anyone would know the best way to get a guitar in the hands of Ben and his grandfather, it would be Jack. He didn't know how he did it, but he always found the right person for requests like these.

Taking another gulp of his coffee, he checked his phone to see it had now been fifteen minutes since he entered the café. But after his encounter with Ben, the wait no longer seemed an issue.

As he broke off a piece of the muffin and popped it in his mouth, he started thinking about Stephanie. He hoped she wasn't on one of her let's-go-live-in-London kicks again. A college roommate of hers had moved there about a year ago and she kept trying to persuade her to join her.

You hope this isn't what it's about.

He was frowning down at his phone when someone tapped on the window. He glanced over to see Stephanie's smiling face. After she gave him a quick wave, she headed for the entrance.

He watched her make her way through the restaurant before he stood, pulling out a chair for her. "Hey, good to see you. Here, sit. Tell me what you want and I'll go get it for you."

"Just a coffee." After she gave him a hug, she grinned. "I see you already got a muffin. We can share."

"*Hmm* … I know how that works." He was smiling as he made his way to the counter to order her a coffee.

Add to that another muffin. Chocolate chip.

Stephanie was a chocolate chip girl, all the way.

For the first ten minutes, Stephanie chattered non-stop, almost inhaling her muffin in between sentences. She told him all about her newest patients and how hectic their floor had been over the past few weeks. She also gave a much longer and detailed account than needed about the chart the kids made to rate the homemade cookies she brought in each week.

He couldn't get a word in.

She wouldn't let him.

Not that he tried.

No, setting his empty coffee cup on the table and leaning back in his chair, he just listened.

He watched as she spread a generous amount of butter on what remained of the muffin and popped it into her mouth. After shooting him a tentative smile, she vigorously began wiping the crumbs off the table with her napkin before she stuffed it in her empty cup.

It was more than obvious she was stalling.

He cleared his throat. "So, when are you going to tell me why you wanted to meet? What's going on? This isn't about starting up a new life in London again, is it?"

Clasping her hands together on the table, she made a face at him. "No, don't worry. I'm not planning any trips to London. Or anywhere else right now."

She frowned. "But I'm wondering if a major change in my life might be what I need."

She stared down at her hands, her words barely audible. "I'm so stupid. So, so stupid."

When he saw the natural blush in her cheeks had now become even more pronounced, he rested his forearms on the table, leaning in closer. "Hey, what happened?"

Avoiding his gaze, she told him what happened with Noah. The whole sorry mess... ending with his fiancée showing up at the hospital.

Her expression was tragic. "I can't even tell you what I said to her. When Noah joined us, I couldn't even look him in the face. I'm sure I made a complete fool out of myself, blabbering a bunch of nonsense before I finally left."

She sighed. "I tried to avoid him for the rest of my shift, but when I was leaving, he came running after me. He told me he was sorry. This was right before he asked if I could take his place at the meeting tonight."

She shrugged. "At that point, I only wanted to get away from him, so I said yes and started walking away. But he stopped me to say this in no way changed our plans. After Michelle flies back to Minnesota, we would still have dinner."

The look on her face was one of complete disbelief. "Jason, I can't do that. How could he think this would be okay? And shouldn't he have told me right from the beginning he was engaged?"

She frowned, fingering her empty cup. "Not that we ever went on a date or anything. We met in the staff lounge for a break a few times, but nothing more than that. Only when he referred to dinner after tonight's meeting as a date, I thought maybe it was possible he liked me as much as I like him."

She shoved her cup away and stared off into space. Away from what she saw as a look of pity on Jason's face.

She shrugged. "But I guess part of this is my fault. I never asked if he was in a relationship. I shouldn't have assumed that he wasn't."

Jason shot straight up in his chair. He shook his head, his expression furious. "No, don't even think of blaming yourself. This is something he should've let you know from the beginning. This would have changed everything."

She picked up a napkin from the table and began twisting it in her hands. "I know you're going to think I'm crazy, but I thought there was this connection between us, a spark of some kind. Maybe I had found my soul mate."

Her laugh was sharp. "But I guess I had that wrong." She sighed. "I'm not like you, Jazz. Men aren't falling all over me, asking me out. Instead, they seem to go out of their way to avoid me."

Jason stared at her, incredulous.

What? Was she crazy?

He reached over to cover her hands with his. "Steff, that is so far from the truth. I assure you, most men would be thrilled to be with you. You just haven't met the right one yet. But one day, and I bet this will happen sooner than you think, you will."

He scowled. "But Seriously? Next time ask the guy if he's engaged. Or, heaven forbid, married. Or send him to me. I'll be more than happy to check him out for you."

She gave him a long look. "Jason ... really?"

He smiled. "Come on, you know I'm kidding. I just wanted to see your beautiful smile."

She sent him a smile, though a very brief one, before she shook her head. "No, I'm done. I'm happy with my life the way it is. Heaven knows I have more than enough to keep me busy with work."

Worry creased her brow. "But now what am I going to do? I don't want to fill in for Noah tonight. You know that's not my thing."

She sent him a hopeful glance. "You wouldn't consider sticking around, would you? Everyone is meeting here," she glanced down at her watch, "in about fifteen minutes."

He gave her hands a quick squeeze. "You'll be fine. And, no... I have no reason to stay. Jack is our token spokesman and he should be here any minute. I'm sure he would be more than happy to help you out."

His gaze searching the room, he shook his head. "He doesn't seem to be here yet. I hope he remembers. He has a selective memory when it comes to this kind of ..."

His words trailed off, his mouth slowly curving into a smile.

Curious, Stephanie glanced over her shoulder to see a woman appeared to be looking right at him. When Jason let go of her hands, she turned to see he had come to his feet. "Do you know her?"

He smiled down at her. "Yes, I do. I'll be right back. I want the two of you to meet."

When Darcey pulled into the Café Latte parking lot, she saw Abby get out of her car and start walking to the entrance.

She caught up to her. "Abby, hi. You don't know how glad I am to see you, since I'm pretty sure you're the only one I'll know at this meeting."

Abby grinned. "Don't worry. It's usually the same people, and they're all pretty nice. Well, except for Elenore Cromley. She is the only one you need to worry about."

She rolled her eyes. "Elenore is this elderly socialite who has more money than she knows what to do with. Lucky for us, even though she had no children of her own, she has a soft spot for the Children's Hospital. But she's also very bossy and likes everything to go her way. Just so you know, she has been complaining about the 'demise' of the party center for quite a while now. She even talked about buying it at one time."

Darcey laughed. "I might just take her up on that. The job has turned out to be much harder than I expected. You don't know how many times I've thought of walking out, never to return."

A frown flitted across her face. "I hope she doesn't have a problem with what we've done so far."

Abby shook her head. "Darcey, I'm sure you have nothing to worry about. Just remember not to take what she says too personally. I know once she sees all the improvements you made, you'll be right up there at the top of her list of favorites."

Once they were inside the café, Abby turned to Darcey. "I need to go to the restroom. Why don't you find us a table?" She glanced around the room before she smiled. "Oh wait, it looks like Jason came for the meeting after all. Why don't you join him? I'll be right back."

Jason was here?

Darcey's quick glance across the room confirmed he was. There was only one problem.

He wasn't alone.

There was a woman at his table, a very attractive woman. And they were holding hands. This sent the message they were close. Maybe even more than close.

Her first impulse to run right out the door, get in her car and head for home, she began edging towards the entrance.

But before she could stop herself, she sent another glance over at Jason. This turned out to be at the same exact moment he looked over and right into her eyes.

Caught up in his gaze, for Darcey, everything and everyone else was forgotten. The slow smile he sent held her rooted to the spot.

She watched as he leaned over to say something to the woman at the table before he made his way across the room to stand in front of her.

His hands jammed in his pockets, his gaze traveled over her face. Slowly, he did this. Then, with a smile, he lightly ran his knuckles down the side of her face.

"Hi, gorgeous." At the huskiness of this endearment, just like that, she was hooked, slipping completely under his spell. Everything—his smile, his touch and the fact he called her gorgeous—sent her world spinning.

And she couldn't think of a single thing to say.

He smiled again, a very disarming smile. "What's wrong? Cat got your tongue?"

This was enough to remind her of the woman who was waiting for him. Suddenly irritated, she sent another glance in her direction, bringing him to do the same. "No, maybe I'm just a little–"

"Hey, I'm back." This came from Abby before she smiled over at Jason. "Hi, Jason, you're here."

But he wasn't listening. His gaze returning to Darcey, he gave a slow nod. "*Ah ... I think I get it.*"

He switched gears, smiling over at Abby. "Hey, Abby ... how's it going?"

Abby was grinning. It was a huge grin. He peered at her more closely.

What was she up to?

He cleared his throat. "You have that look on your face. You're not planning on getting into mischief tonight, are you?"

The grin still on her face, Abby shook her head. "Of course not. Unless I see the need. I'm only here for the meeting. I'm surprised to see you here. You only come to these meetings if it's absolutely necessary."

Jason pointed toward his table. "I have a table over there with Steff. She wanted to meet here before your meeting."

"Oh, good … I haven't seen her in a while. Our schedules always overlap. While you get coffee, I'll join her. She's probably not too happy sitting there all alone."

Something clicked in Darcey's mind, but not enough to grab on to the memory it evoked.

Steff? Why did this name sound so familiar?

She glanced over at Jason to see he seemed to be amused as he answered Abby. "I'm sure she's just fine. But go ahead. Just coffee?" At her hopeful expression, he chuckled. "A strawberry scone, right?"

He turned to Darcey. "You stay with me, gorgeous. This way, you can pick out what you want. I can also use your help to carry everything back to the table."

Abby's curious glance sent the blush rising in her cheeks. This had her shaking her head more vigorously than necessary. "I only want coffee."

"*Hmm* … you might change your mind when you see what they have. Come on, you at least need to check it out." His hand going to her back, he gave her no choice but to let him guide her over to the counter.

Darcey was confused. And becoming more irritated by the minute. Was he trying to divert her attention away from his table? If so, she had news for him.

He was too late.

Once they took their place in line, he smiled down at her, shaking his head. This made her nervous.

He's up to something. Or he knows something you don't.

Sure enough, he leaned in to whisper in her ear. "To be honest, I don't need your help. But I didn't want to yell at you in front of Abby."

Her head jerked up, her mouth falling open. "Yell at me? For what?"

He moved closer, reaching over to tuck her hair behind her ear. He knew he was taking a chance, but he liked having her close to him... as close as he could get her. The memory of how she felt under his touch was something he hadn't been able to let go. And the way things were going, it was obvious he never would.

If this wasn't proof nothing had changed between them, he didn't know what more was needed.

Taking his silence as his refusal to answer her, a frown had settled on Darcey's face. "You're not playing fair. You can't come out with a comment like that and not explain what you mean. I don't understand. What did I do?"

He leaned in even closer, his whisper carrying a hint of a smile. "If I recall, you promised you would stay home today, give yourself a little extra time to get better. Instead, where do I find you? Here ... for a meeting you didn't need to attend. And something tells me you came right from work. Remember, a great deal hinges on your recovery. We have a date coming up on Saturday."

She sighed ... darn if he wasn't making her feel guilty.

Taking pity on her, he smiled at her. "I don't know about you, but I'll be very disappointed if this date doesn't happen."

But what about the woman at his table?

She sent another glance over at her. She was pretty, she'd give her that much.

This is when she remembered Jason once telling her most of the material for his songs came from observing everything around him. There was a song to be found in any situation, he'd told her, bringing the lyrics right out of him.

Well, you certainly aren't going to give him anything to work with.

She pulled away from him, and moving over to the display case, she feigned interest in the extensive collection of baked goods.

But she really didn't care about what was in the display case. Not while she was so busy being angry. And frustrated, he was able to make her feel this way.

Jason had watched all of this. He was smiling, something he couldn't hide even if he tried. That she was jealous, and he'd be willing to bet this was exactly what was going on, had him tempted to wrap his arms around her.

He would follow this with a kiss to erase whatever crazy thoughts were going on in her mind right now.

Yep, right here in Café Latte, he would do this.

She had no reason to worry... he knew where his heart had settled.

He moved behind her, his arms wrapping around to hold her against him.

Uh, oh ...

Darcey didn't stand a chance. Her heart now beating much faster than it had only seconds ago, it was a downright struggle not to sink into his embrace.

She closed her eyes, her voice a breathy whisper. "Jason? What are you doing?"

His voice was just as low, brushing across her ear. "Why am I getting the distinct feeling you've forgotten I have a sister? Her name is Stephanie... but she goes by Steff. Or Steffi. When you were last here, you might remember I told you she was in Texas at the time, enrolled in an internship program. This is the same Steffi who is now sitting over at the table with Abby. They're good friends. I'm hoping you two will be good friends, too."

Darcey's memory had already kicked into gear.

Oh geeez ... now you remember. Stephanie is his little sister. She's a nurse and the only family he has. And they're very close.

She felt like a complete fool. And now that he knew she was jealous was obvious by the smile in his next words. "So, you have nothing to worry about, gorgeous."

She turned her face to his, the tenderness of his expression almost taking her breath away. For a long moment, they studied each other.

Then, his cheek brushing over hers, he cleared his throat. "As much as I'd like to stay right here, I think it's our turn to order. But, just to warn you, I believe we've attracted quite a bit of attention. I'm fine, but I'm not sure how you feel about this."

She pulled away from him in a flash, remaining silent while he put in the order. She didn't even protest when he ordered the special of the day, a carrot cake muffin.

For her, he insisted. Since he knew this was her favorite.

How could you refuse?

By the time their order was ready, she had managed to regain some of her dignity. Enough to nod over at the tray he was holding. "I thought you needed my help?"

A faint smile tugged at his mouth. *"Hmm ...* I did say that, didn't I? Well, I may have exaggerated a bit. But this is only because I enjoy spending time with you. So, to save face, I'm going to ask you to grab some napkins. As you can see, I've got my hands full here."

He gave her a wink before he turned and headed for their table.

She reached for a handful of napkins, almost knocking over the dispenser in the process before she hurried after him.

And yes, she knew she was smiling like a love-struck fan as she trailed behind him.

But she didn't care.

Jason set the tray on the table and, after pulling out a chair for Darcey, he nodded over at Stephanie. "Stef, I'd like you to meet Darcey Hollister. We met about three years ago. She was here in Cleveland at the same time you were in Dallas."

He glanced over at Darcey and she'd swear she saw a flash of mischief in his eyes before he directed his next comment to Steffi. "After all this time, she's still won't leave me alone. She keeps following me, showing up wherever I am."

He shook his head. "It must be my natural charm pulling her in."

As soon as this came out of his mouth, Jason wondered if he had gone a little too far. But after sending him a calculating look, Darcey turned to Stephanie. "Stephanie, I'm so glad to meet you. Jason told me how close you two are. But about what he just said? Something about his natural charm?" She rolled her eyes. "Between you and me, I think all these songs he writes have put crazy ideas in his head." She sent him a swift glance, eyebrow raised. "I hate to burst your bubble, Jason, but not all women are in love with you."

He studied her for a long moment before he responded. "I don't care about all women. I only need one."

For a brief moment, their eyes locked. Then she grabbed her cup and took a big gulp of coffee, hoping to hide she was blushing.

But, of course, he noticed. Raising his cup to his lips, he sent her a wink.

Abby and Stephanie were following this exchange with interest. To say they were surprised would be an understatement. This was a Jason they didn't know. A confident Jason. A Jason who had never before shown so much attention to a woman. And so out in the open.

Yes, this was a Jason who showed all the signs of being in love. If anything, he was knocking it out of the park.

Stephanie smiled over at Darcey. "Wow, I don't know what you did to my brother, but I love it. I wish I had met you the last time you were here." Her head tilted, she studied Jason, then Darcey. "How did the two of you meet?"

Jason set his cup on the table, lounging back in his chair before he sent a smile over at Darcey. "We met in the coffee shop across the street from The Regency. Darcey completely bowled me over when she asked if I would pay for her lunch."

In the process of cutting her muffin in half, Darcey almost dropped the knife, her mouth falling open in surprise.

The teasing glint in his eyes had her bursting into laughter before she pointed the knife at him. "Stop it. You know that's not true. I did nothing of the kind. You're giving both Steffi and Abby a very bad image of me."

She shook her head at them. "Don't believe him. That never happened. He offered. More like begged. Shamelessly, he did this. Then he asked if I would share a table with him. Which I did. Only because I felt sorry for him, thinking maybe he didn't have any friends." She sighed. "He seemed so desperate."

Stephanie and Abby both nodded.

This had Jason sitting up straighter in his chair, a surprised laugh coming from him. "Hey, wait a minute ... why do you believe her? You both know me a lot better than you know her."

Abby rolled her eyes. "Jason, get serious. Women always stick together with who's wrong and who's right, men versus women. It's a given ... the man is always in the wrong. And, before you even think of arguing about this, if you haven't noticed, we outnumber you, three to one. So, you have zero chance of coming out on top. No matter what comes out of your mouth."

With a wry smile, Jason shook his head. "I think this is a sign I need to leave before I lose my credibility."

He nodded towards the entrance. "I also see Elenore Cromley has arrived. This means your meeting will start soon." He chuckled. "She already has Jack rearranging tables and chairs. Poor guy just walked in the door and she was right there to grab him. I should probably go help him out."

A big grin coming over his face, he reached for his cup. "Nah, I'll let him handle this one on his own."

Darcey had risen from her seat. "And I should go introduce myself to Elenore. Just to be on the safe side. Save my seat."

Jason sent her a smile. "No worries, gorgeous. You've got this."

This had her blushing again as she left the table.

After Jason watched her walk away, he turned to Stephanie and Abby. They were grinning from ear to ear. This sent the heat rising in his face.

Damn ... not good at all.

He tried to make light of this, casually taking a big gulp of coffee. And what did he do? He dribbled a good amount right down his shirt.

Double damn ...

Stephanie sighed. "Jason, she's beautiful. The two of you are perfect together."

Abby was nodding. "Didn't I tell you? You can feel the vibes between them. The chemistry is there, for certain." Her sigh was long and dramatic. "Your big brother has fallen in love ..."

Scrubbing at the coffee on his shirt, Jason groaned. "Come on, you two. We're not teenagers here. Yes, she's nice. And she's beautiful. And …" here he paused, a baffled look on his face. "I don't know what it is, or how she does it, but ever since I first saw her, well … I … oh, forget it. I'm not getting into this with the two of you. Let's just say I've got to figure it all out before I make my next move."

Abby and Stephanie shared a quick glance before Abby grinned over at him. "Oh, my … did I just hear you say you're going to make your move? This sounds pretty serious. Wouldn't you agree, Stef?"

Stephanie nodded, her grin as big as Abby's.

Jason sent them a warning glance, waving his napkin at them before he tossed it on the table. "And before you get any ideas, I don't need any help from either of you. Got it?"

They both looked at each other. Stephanie shrugged while Abby sat up straight in her chair and gave him a mock salute. "Yes, sir … whatever you say, sir."

He groaned, massaging the back of his neck. "I'm screwed."

Finishing his coffee in one gulp, he hauled himself out of his chair. "Before the two of you start planning out the rest of my life, I'm taking off."

Abby held up her hand. "Wait… did you know Darcey isn't planning to attend the ball? Not as a guest, or even as part of staff. But we think she should be there. I told her it would be no trouble fitting her in at our table. Don't you agree?"

"Of course, she should be there." He was a little surprised at this. "I assumed she would be."

Abby shrugged. "Well, you assumed wrong. She said she couldn't go alone. And she had nothing to wear."

Jason laughed. "You show me a woman who doesn't say this when they need to go somewhere."

Abby made a face at him. "We already took care of that. I talked to Sophie, and she's going to call Darcey, persuade her to stop by the boutique tomorrow night. She said she would stay open just for her."

Jason shrugged. "So, what's the problem?"

"I think you should take her. I know you're playing. But she can still be your date. You've always had dinner with us in the past. And you can certainly fit in one or two dances. But you need to ask her soon. Really soon…"

His gaze went from her to Stephanie, who was nodding in agreement.

He chuckled, shaking his head. "We're going out to dinner Saturday night. So, if it comes up, I'll ask her then."

He began walking away. "And now I'm out of here for real. Before you ask any more questions or start in on something else." He sent them one final warning glance. "Remember what I said. I don't need your help."

Once he left, Abby grinned over at Stephanie. "Can you believe it? Our Jason has fallen in love. I need to call Sophie to let her know about this dinner date. A reason for another new dress, don't you agree?"

After she reached into her pocket for her phone, she glanced over at Stephanie. "What about you? Do you have a date?"

Stephanie shook her head. "No, but a group of us from the hospital have a table reserved, so I'm all set."

"Steffi?"

They both looked up to see Jack was standing next to the table. He gave Stephanie a nervous smile. "Hi. Jazz said you might need help with the meeting?"

The shy smile he gave her had her giving him a big smile in return. She, of all people, could relate to his nervousness.

"Oh, Jack … that would be great. Because, to be honest? I don't know what I'm doing."

CHAPTER 24

The gift of friendship is a wonderful thing
with the joys and happiness good friends bring.
~ Anonymous

arcey pulled into the parking lot of the Chic Boutique. Since she was about ten minutes early, she stayed in her car, trying to convince herself to go back out into the cold.

The skies had been overcast all day. And now, with the brisk wind, it seemed much colder.

At least to Darcey, it did.

She shivered. Since she'd arrived in Cleveland almost two weeks ago, she'd swear she hadn't been able to get warm.

Well, this isn't true. There was the one time. The night Jason came to her apartment bearing pizza. She could still remember how wonderful it felt to be in his arms, wrapped in the warmth of his embrace.

She plopped her forehead down on the steering wheel, a frustrated groan coming from her.

Why did you let Sophie talk you into this?

It hadn't taken her long to realize Sophie was a very persistent woman who refused to take no for an answer. Not attending the ball wasn't even an option, she had proclaimed. It was important Darcey be there, if only to represent the Hollister name.

And to do this right, she needed a dress worthy of the occasion.

After this lecture from Sophie, Darcey had gone back and forth, finally deciding if she were to go—and this was definitely still up in the air—she would only stay for a short time. Once she saw everything was under control, she would make her getaway.

There's also the fact you don't want to go alone…

But this was ridiculous. It wasn't as though she'd be spending the evening with total strangers.

Be honest, you want to go with Jason.

She wanted to walk into the Grand Ballroom, her hand in his. Letting everyone know she would always be the only woman for him.

This was when she realized she and Jason had never even danced together.

But this is probably to your advantage. Next to him, your lack of even the simplest of dancing skills is downright embarrassing.

At least, this is what David had once told her.

Jokingly, he'd said this. But you're pretty sure he meant it.

On this disheartening note, she got out of her car. Battling the wind, she ran to the entrance of the Chic Boutique.

Darcey entered the boutique, a tinkling bell announcing her presence. She had no sooner closed the door when a woman wearing glasses waved to her from the back of the small shop.

"Darcey, is that you? Welcome to the Chic Boutique, sweetheart. While I'm finishing up with a call, why don't you look around to get an idea of what we have. I'll be with you as soon as I can."

Darcey smiled. "Take your time. I'm in no hurry."

Wandering through the boutique, checking out whatever caught her eye, she came to a long rack of assorted evening gowns in all the colors of the rainbow. From elaborate to simple, jeweled to plain, there was a dress for every occasion.

She was sorting through them when the woman appeared at her side, her glasses now perched on top of her head.

She smiled, holding out her hand. "Darcey, it's so nice to meet you. I'm Louise, Sophie's aunt. I recognized you right away from the description she gave me. She should be here," she glanced down at her watch, "in about ten minutes. She's running a little late. Something about the baby sitter getting caught up in traffic."

She chuckled. "So, it looks like you're stuck with me."

Darcey smiled. "That's fine. Like I said, I'm in no hurry. And from what I've seen so far, I don't think I'll have a problem finding a dress."

Louise nodded. "You mean two dresses, don't you? One for the ball and one for this dinner date you have on Saturday."

Surprised, Darcey didn't know what to say. How did Louise know she was going out Saturday night?

She had told no one about this.

She wondered, did Louise also know who this dinner date was with?

She smiled. "*Mmm ...* I guess I hadn't even thought about what I was going to wear on Saturday. I have one dress I could wear. It's not new and very basic... a simple black sheath. But with the right jewelry, it would work."

Sending Darcey a look to let her know this would never happen, at least not on her watch, Louise shook her head. "Sweetheart, you can't be serious. When you go out to dinner with a man like Jason Bennett, you need to look your absolute best."

A stricken look came over her face. "I'm certainly not insinuating you need help in that area. Heavens, no ... not as beautiful as you are. But I firmly believe a woman should always aim higher in life, whether it be for clothes or love. After all, our reputation depends on how good you look in one of our dresses. So, we want Jason to be wowed when he sees you."

And there you have it. Evidently nothing gets by this group of friends.

Darcey nodded. "Okay, two dresses it is."

After stepping back and giving Darcey a thorough once over, Louise put on her glasses and began searching through the dress rack.

"I believe we have the perfect dress for you. It came in only a few days ago. *Ah, ha ...* here it is."

She pulled out a dress, holding it up for Darcey's inspection. A shimmery, metallic copper fabric, the front bodice had a v neckline and cap sleeves, while the back was a combination of appliqués and netting of the same metallic shade. The fit was snug to the hips, before it flared in a graceful flow of fabric to the floor and falling slightly longer in the back. The dress almost glowed in the light, changing different shades of copper with every move.

She was nodding. "Yes, I think on you, this would be spectacular, the deep copper shade of the fabric perfect with your coloring. Let's get you into the dressing room so you can try it on."

Within minutes, Darcey was in the dressing room with not only the copper evening dress, but two other dresses to try on. Louise's voice, coming from somewhere in the boutique, floated back to her. "After you get into the first dress, come out into the shop so we can see you in the big mirror. This way we'll get the full effect. In the meantime, I'll see what else I can find."

Suddenly feeling excited, Darcey began with Louise's pick. It really was a beautiful dress.

Darcey glanced down at her watch, surprised to see she'd spent almost two hours in the boutique. But as she waited for Sophie to add up the order, she decided it had been time well spent. She was now the owner of one evening gown, one cocktail dress, one pair of high-heeled sandals and a short fake fur bolero style jacket to wear as an evening cover up.

The jacket had been a last-minute splurge. She really didn't need another jacket, but as Sophie and her aunt were quick to point out, one could never have enough jackets. And she was in Ohio now, not sunny California. It was also so unique in design, it would go with just about anything, from jeans casual to evening wear.

Little did they know, from the moment Darcey had spotted the jacket on the rack, she knew it would be going home with her.

But what about the necklace and earring? Yes, they were a lot of bling. Definitely more than she usually wore. But they went perfectly with the evening gown.

Her mind made up, she pushed both the necklace and earrings across the counter to Sophie. "You might as well add these, too. You're right, they're perfect."

Sophie grinned. "Good choice. You won't regret it."

Darcey shook her head. But she was smiling. "Between you and your aunt, I didn't have a chance. I can see why the boutique is so popular. Together, you're the perfect team."

Sophie sent her a smile as she packed the jewelry in a box, "We try." She laughed. "We have our moments, though. There's always conflict between creative minds, I like to say."

She sent a glance towards the back of the store before she leaned closer to Darcey, speaking in an exaggerated whisper. "Just a heads up … I know my aunt is going to ask if you'd be interested in modeling for the fashion show we have every February, right before Valentine's Day. It's for a good cause and has become very popular. I'm surprised she hasn't already brought it up, since she is always searching for models who don't require a lot of alterations. Almost all of us get drafted, along with some of the guys. Oh, and Jason's band provides the music."

She sent Darcey a sly look. "You know his band is playing for the ball, don't you? They've provided the music for every year for this event."

When Darcey only nodded, Sophie abruptly turned away, her voice tinged with irritation. "I'll be right back. I need to get a garment bag."

She disappeared into the back room to return with the bag. Without a word, she packed up the cocktail dress and jacket. She then yanked up the zipper and plopped the bag on the counter as if she was mad about something.

Darcey was confused. Why was Sophie so angry? Was it something she said? She peered closely at her. "Sophie, is something wrong?"

Typical Sophie style, she didn't hesitate to say what she needed to share. "Yes, there is. But at the same time, there is also something so right."

She leaned her arms on the counter. "Abby and I have been friends with Jason for a long time. So, I guess you could say we know each other pretty well." She smiled, shaking her head. "When we were still in elementary school, we made a pact. No matter what happened, we would always have each other's back."

Resting her chin in her hand, she shook her head.

"Everybody thinks because Jason is this amazingly handsome and talented guy, he's all about himself, wrapped up in his success. But this is so far from the truth. Take his truck, for example. He's had this beat up old pickup truck forever and Abby and I kept telling him he needed to up his image a little. So, he finally went out and bought a Lexus SUV. Just picked it up yesterday, in fact. But I know if he had his way, he would still be driving the pickup."

She smiled. "He gave it to this kid who cuts his lawn, just gave it to him. He knew the kid wanted to buy one of his own, but needed to save his money for college."

She shrugged. "He gets all embarrassed if you bring it up. Says it's no big deal. The kid needed a truck, and he had one he wasn't using. So, it only made sense to give it to him. But he's this way with everything."

She sighed. "But he has one fault ... not a bad one, mind you. This would be his shyness, notably around women. Which is so ironic, because he could have any woman he wanted."

Darcey didn't understand.

Shy? Jason? This certainly isn't is a trait you would associate with him.
Definitely not.

She smiled. *"Hmm ...* if I had to describe Jason, shy is the last word I would choose." She shook her head. "No, if anything, I envy his confidence."

Sophie started nodding like crazy. "Yes, yes ... this is what I meant when I said there was also something so right. When Jason is with you, he's a completely different person. Even though he tries to hide how he feels about you, he can't. Abby and I noticed this right away."

She grinned. "My gosh, he's so obvious. He gets this look in his eyes when he's with you. And that same look is there even when you're not there and he talks about you." She shook her head. "Darcey, it's a look every woman dreams of getting from a man. And even more so, from a man like Jason Bennett."

She shrugged. "I guess what I'm trying to say … we want to make sure he doesn't get hurt. If you were to leave again? I don't know…" She shook her head.

Darcey put her hand on Sophie's arm. "I have no plans to hurt him. This is the last thing I would do, cross my heart." She grinned, crossing her arms over her chest. "And you know this makes it official."

Sophie was laughing as she came around the counter to give her a big hug. "Good. I hope you're not mad at me for telling you this, but I saw how Jason is with you and I had to say something."

"Sophie … Darcey …"

Her expression frantic, Louise came running from the back room. "We forgot the most important thing."

They gave her a blank look.

She pointed to her eyes. "Girls, come on … A mask. She needs a mask."

Relieved, Sophie laughed. "Thank goodness, I thought we made some huge mistake."

Already searching behind the counter, Louise pulled out a catalog and handed it to Sophie. "This is our best bet at such a late date. Have Darcey decide on one and we'll order it right away."

Flipping through the pages, Sophie pointed to a black mask with metallic gold and copper highlights. "How about this one? The black will be a great contrast to your hair and the metallic highlights will go perfectly with your dress. It also matches the jewelry you chose. We can embellish it even more if you want. If you like it, we'll order it right now."

Darcey nodded. "It's perfect."

As Sophie put in the order, Darcey checked her phone. She smiled when she saw there was a text from Jason.

> Hey, Gorgeous, Can I pick you up a little earlier tomorrow? Say, about six? I have a surprise for you. Looking forward to our date. Let me know about the time.

A surprise? What kind of surprise? She was still smiling as she answered.

> How could I possibly say no? I love surprises.
> I'll be ready at six.

When Darcey left the boutique, it was raining and the wind was blowing even harder.

But she didn't even notice. The time she shared with Sophie and Louise had sent a warmth through her that lingered on for a long time.

CHAPTER 25

*J*ason was buttoning his shirt when his doorbell rang. Singing out loud, something he always did when he was in a good mood, he almost didn't hear it.

He glanced over at the clock on the nightstand. It was 5:30.. This meant he needed to leave in ten minutes if he intended to pick up Darcey at six.

Absolutely no later than ten minutes.

So, whoever was at the door, it better be quick.

Tucking the shirt into his jeans as he went, he yanked open the door—remember; it wasn't an easy door to open—to find Caro standing on the front steps. Her face almost hidden under her big floppy brimmed hat and holding a small gift bag, she had a huge smile on her face.

Jason grinned. "Well, what do you know, our big-time traveler has returned?"

"Yes, I'm back. And I even brought you a gift." She handed him the bag. "Did you miss me?"

He could only get in a nod before she continued. "I wanted to let you know I'm home. I thought you might see my lights on and think someone broke in."

A frown flitted across her face. "I think a lot of the neighbors still aren't taking this Block Watch pledge seriously. I hope it doesn't take a break-in to get them on board."

"They will, give them time." He waved her inside. "I need to leave in ten minutes, but come on in."

She slipped past him, still chattering. "Don't worry, I'm exhausted, so I wasn't planning to stay." She laughed. "I think it's going to take me a while to recover from this trip. I'm glad to be home, but after all the attention they give you, I think it will be hard to get back to normal. And I don't want to even think about food."

She shook her head. "I swear, Jason ... I've never seen so much food in my life. I don't even want to know how much weight I gained."

Busy buttoning his shirt cuffs, he smiled at her. "You look the same to me. Speaking of food, thanks for the groceries. Since I got in late, they were a welcome sight."

"That's good to hear." She was gazing around. "I see the place still looks pretty decent." She sent him a guilty look. "I wasn't sure what to expect."

He laughed. "Hey, give me some credit. It hasn't even been two weeks since you cleaned. And I haven't been here enough to mess things up."

He glanced over at her to see she was peering up at him, a deep frown furrowing her brows.

Oh boy, this isn't a good sign.

And sure enough, her eyes abruptly going wide and clasping her hands together, she grinned. It was an ecstatic grin. "Oh my gosh, you've met someone, haven't you? The woman of your dreams. And you're going out with her tonight, aren't you?"

And darn if he didn't feel the heat rising in his face. Massaging the back of his neck, he cleared his throat. "*Ah ...* I don't think ... I ... what I mean is... well, maybe. And yes, I just so happen to have a date tonight."

She moved closer, searching his face. "*Wow ...* This is huge." Then she frowned. "Wait a minute... this woman is someone you used to know, isn't she?"

Her jaw dropped. "The photo ... she's the woman in the photo I found, isn't she?"

Their eyes met, but he broke it off, fussing with his shirt collar.

She glared at him. "You look at me, Jason Bennett. And don't even think of lying to me."

He groaned.

For your own sanity, you need to put a stop to this conversation.

Caro was in her element. Almost gleeful, in fact. There was nothing she liked better than encouraging a budding romance. She liked to think of herself as quite the matchmaker.

She crossed her arms over her chest. "I knew the photo was special. All crumpled up in a ball, it was obvious there was a story to tell. The woman meant a lot to you at one time, but your attempt to get rid of the photo was a sign she had hurt you in some way."

She was nodding. "Yep, you thought your love was doomed. So you wanted the photo out of your sight. But I bet, no matter how hard you tried, you couldn't forget her. Am I right?"

Doomed?

Jason was staring at her, a mix of dismay and bewilderment on his face. Was this that intuition thing women were always bragging about?

He groaned, dragging his hand down over his jaw. "Yeah, you've got me. Tonight, I have a date with Darcey, the woman in the photo. We met three years ago, but it didn't end well. Were we doomed? I don't think so. Instead, I went and did something stupid."

He shrugged. "Worse than stupid, I fear."

Caro's expression a sign she had something to say about this, he held up his hand. "Wait, let me finish. But it wasn't all me, we were both at fault. So, I'm hoping tonight will be our chance to straighten things out."

Suddenly embarrassed at what he'd told her, he cleared his throat. "I guess I want to see if we've still got it."

He groaned. Again, this was something she didn't need to know.

Get a grip. You're giving out way too much information. You better get out of here before you say something else.

Grabbing his sports jacket from where he had thrown it on the sofa, he slipped it on. Stuffing his wallet and keys into his pockets, he turned to her.

He held his arms out, sending her a big smile. "How do I look?"

She smiled, shaking her head. "Oh, Jason … you know darn well you look good. You couldn't look bad even if you tried." She reached over to push back the hair falling over his forehead. "But you need to stop hiding your beautiful eyes. And tone down that sexy look you've got going on. I'm willing to bet you've already got her."

He stared at her, shaking his head. "*Oh, geeez …* whatever you say. But now I need to get going. I don't want to be late."

It was after they were outside and Caro had double-checked he securely locked his door, she pointed at the shiny black Lexus SUV parked in the driveway. "Hey, I meant to ask, is that yours? Did you finally get rid of that old truck?"

He sighed. "Yes, I finally got rid of the truck."

"It's about time. This is a much better fit for you."

He chuckled, shaking his head. "I didn't know my truck bothered so many people. It seems like everyone is spending too much of their time worrying about what I do."

She grinned. "That's what friends are for."

Watching until she got to her front door, he rerturned her wave.

He was smiling as he backed out of the driveway. He wouldn't come out and admit this, but he was just as excited as everyone else about his new wheels.

He hit the audio button, music surrounding him.

The sound was amazing.

So, he'd have to agree … it really was about time.

Darcey was ready. More than ready.

In fact, she had been ready for over half an hour.

And Jason wasn't due to arrive for at least another fifteen minutes.

She had already straightened up the apartment, twice.

And now, for what was at least the third time, she began rearranging the throw pillows on the sofa.

She stepped back, giving them a critical look.

Grabbing the red pillow and switching it with the black, she stepped back to study this new arrangement.

She groaned, and gazing up at the ceiling, she shook her head.

What are you doing? It doesn't matter if the pillows aren't arranged just so. Or lined up according to color. Jason won't care. He probably won't even notice the pillows are there.

Reaching up to run her hand through her hair, this was when she realized she forgot her earrings. Muttering to herself, she hurried into her bedroom and began rummaging through her jewelry box to find a pair that would match her dress.

She was putting on the earrings when she caught sight of her reflection in the mirror. She looked nervous, extremely nervous. Like a deer caught in the headlights kind of nervous.

This certainly wasn't because of the dress. Because the dress she was wearing was perfect.

It wasn't a dress she would have chosen. Nor was it a dress she would normally wear, since the style and fit drew attention to every one of her curves. But Sophie and her Aunt Louise had made such a fuss, oohing and aahing like crazy when she tried it on, she didn't even have to think twice about buying it.

It was black.

Yes, black. But the white chiffon ruffles that formed the neckline, both front and back, softened the look. This simple addition changed the simple lines of the dress into one that was sophisticated, yet also extremely sexy.

She frowned, her reflection frowning back. Maybe it was too much?

No, she'd have to say it was perfect.

She closed the jewelry box and was about to leave when she caught sight of the necklace with the promise ring. She had left it on the dresser while she took a shower.

Picking it up, she fingered the chain.

She still wasn't sure if she was ready to let Jason know she had the ring. At least, not yet.

No, there is something you need to do first.

She set the chain back on the dresser, turned out the light, and left the room.

In about ten minutes, Jason would be here.

She was ready.

After slowly maneuvering his SUV around a group of teenagers who were using the parking lot as their skateboard arena, Jason pulled into a parking space in front of Darcey's apartment.

He glanced down at his watch to see he was about eleven minutes early.

Slowly running his hand through his hair, he peered more closely at the windshield.

What the hell? Was that a raindrop?

When this was followed by not only one, but at least another dozen drops bouncing off the glass, he groaned.

Rain was not in the forecast. He had already checked this out. At least five times.

Yeah, suddenly you've become obsessed with the weather... what's this all about?

He wanted the evening to be perfect. Including the weather. The way he saw it, he needed all the positive reinforcement he could get.

Glancing down at his watch again, he saw it was now down to ten minutes.

Would it really be such a bad thing to show up early?

Maybe?

From his experience, he found very few women managed to be ready when they said they would be.

So, you should wait a few more minutes?

But arriving early would send the message he couldn't wait to see her.

And in your case, this is true. Very true.

But when had he ever been right about what went on in a woman's mind when it came to what was expected on a first date? He'd come to the conclusion this was a no-win situation.

He sighed. If only there weren't so many mixed signals. It was enough to drive a man crazy.

Yep, you're damned if you do, damned if you don't.

But tonight? With Darcey?

Nope, with her, you're done with all of that. The time for playing games and guessing is over.

In one swift move, since it appeared the rain had miraculously ended, he opened the door and, grabbing the bouquet of white and red carnations from the front seat, he slid out of the SUV.

And why carnations, you ask?

These were Darcey's favorite flowers. If he remembered correctly, she had told him she didn't like roses. She thought they were depressing.

Depressing?

He didn't quite understand this. Wasn't a rose the flower most people associated with love?

Yes, this was true, she'd told him. But she still didn't like them.

So carnations it was.

Sprinting up to her front door, for a long moment he hesitated, his finger hovering over the doorbell.

He closed his eyes, and taking in a deep breath, he let it out easy.

You've got this ... go for it.

He hit the doorbell.

CHAPTER 26

Do magic...
Enter her heart, without touching her.
~ Anonymous

When Darcey opened the door, believe it or not, Jason didn't even notice she was there.

His back to her, he was caught up in the antics of the skateboard crazy teenagers who were now putting on quite a show, trying to up each other with their skills.

But Darcey was fine with this. This gave her time to study him up close without him knowing.

Her first thought?

Again ... how was it that one man could always be so perfect in every way?

The flawless cut of his dark grey sports jacket and crisp white shirt indicated they were hand tailored specifically for him. He was the only man she knew who could finish this look with jeans and cowboy boots and still pull off a dressy-casual look that would fit in anywhere.

She smiled when she saw the bouquet he was holding. Her favorite, red and white carnations.

He remembered ...

She cleared her throat. "So, are the flowers for me?"

He whirled around, his gaze holding hers before he smiled. It was a slow, sexy smile. A smile that, no matter how many times he aimed it in her direction, had her weak at the knees, her breath hitching in her throat.

When she swayed towards him, her lashes fluttering shut, he saw this as an invitation for more. His fingertips drifting down the side of her face to catch her chin, he brushed his mouth lightly over hers.

Her soft sigh had the corner of his mouth lifting in a smile, his voice low and husky. "Hey, gorgeous ... you look amazing."

And he meant this.

With all his heart.

But this was only to be expected. She would look good in anything. Or even better, in nothing at all.

A sudden heat barreling through him at this thought, his mind took him right back to the one night they had shared. He could almost feel the silkiness of her skin under his hands, her body fitting so perfectly with his.

He blinked.

What the heck are you doing? You're getting way ahead of yourself here. Remember, your plan was to take it slow.

His gaze traveling over her face, he shook his head. He didn't understand ... how was it, every time he saw her, something new about her captured his attention? It was something he couldn't believe he hadn't seen before.

This time, it was her eyes. Filled with a vulnerability she couldn't hide, they were pleading with him to go easy on her. If eyes really were the window to the soul, this was what she was offering him.

And this is when he finally understood what it meant to feel grounded. This woman who was standing in front of him was all he needed. As trite as this might sound, she was the song in his heart, the music of his life.

Momentarily thrown by these thoughts, he glanced down, almost surprised to see he was still holding the bouquet in his hands.

He held it out to her. "I'm sorry, but you have me so that I can't think straight. And, yes, these are for you. I remember you telling me carnations were your favorite flower. I believe this was only the red and white."

His mouth curved in a teasing smile. "I want you to know the florist suggested roses would be a much better choice. Unfortunately, when I told her you weren't the roses type of woman, she took this the wrong way and was quite frosty with me after that."

He was rambling. He knew this. But this was only because she was still gazing up at him, her lips parted, her expression uncertain. If he could, he'd pull her into his arms and erase every single one of her doubts with a kiss.

Instead, he cleared his throat. "I know I'm early. I hope this is okay?"

She came to life, her gaze dropping to the flowers. To her, they were the most beautiful flowers in the world. But he could have handed her a bouquet of wildflowers he found on the side of the road and she would've loved them just as much. Because they were from him. smiled up at him. "No, no ... it's fine. I've been ready for quite a while."

Oh geeez ... this wasn't something he needed to know ...

But now, his gaze so intense, it was her turn to start rambling. "But this is because I'm famished. In fact, I believe I forgot to eat lunch. So, now I'm hungry ... hungry for everything."

Flustered, she dropped her gaze back to the flowers

Oh, no ... that hadn't come out right either.

The fact he had nothing to say wasn't helping matters.

This had her digging herself in even deeper.

"I'm referring to only food, of course. You know, dinner..."

This is when she saw the smile tweaking the corner of his mouth.

Oh, no, no, no ... you've gone too far. Just shut up. Or at least change the subject.

She took a deep breath, and lifting her head, her smile was brilliant. "The flowers are beautiful. I love them. Even more so, because you remembered."

His gaze still lingering on her face, his nod was vague. "Like stars …"

She moved closer. But only because she didn't know if she heard right. "Stars?"

He smiled. "Yes, your eyes … they're like the stars in the sky. I told Abby I could write a song about your eyes alone."

Now she was really confused. "Abby? You and Abby were talking about my eyes?"

Damn … did you really just blurt that out?

His intention to make light of this, he gave a soft laugh. "*Ah …* you know me and music. We were talking about how I always turn everything into a song. I may have mentioned you and she started asking questions. How we met, when, where. You know, all the usual. And, well …"

His words trailing off, he shrugged.

Darcey was smiling.

This had him hesitantly smiling back at her.

After a brief silence, she glanced down at the flowers. Then she looked up at him. "I should put these in water. Do I have time, or do we need to leave?"

After a slight pause, he nodded. "We have time."

We have all the time in the world.

This is what he would have liked to say, but unsure of how this would go over, he was silent as he followed her inside.

Noting the boxes still waiting to be unpacked, he shook his head. "*Hmm …* it looks like you still haven't made much progress with your unpacking."

She laughed. "No, I'm embarrassed to say I haven't. But I'm getting much better at hunting things down." Proof of this was the vase she pulled from one box.

She waved it at him. "See? And on the first try, too." She made a face. "Though I'll admit it was a lucky guess."

He waited, watching her fill the vase with water before he spoke. "One might get the impression you don't have plans to stay."

She stilled.

Avoiding his gaze, she began adding the flowers to the vase. "I guess it all depends on how the renovations go at The Regency. As it stands now, everything is right on schedule. But you know how that goes, one setback could change everything. Fingers crossed, the plan is to have everything ready for the holiday season. With a full staff ready to take over."

She sent him a brief smile. "Already we have seen an increase in bookings for Christmas parties and other holiday events. I'm excited since I have all these ideas of how we can decorate. I was thinking maybe a winter wonderland. Or an old-fashioned Christmas theme."

Momentarily lost in thought, she stared down at the carnation she was holding.

Then she shrugged, adding it to the other flowers in the vase. "But I'm getting ahead of myself. If everything goes as planned, my job could soon end."

He had moved closer, much closer. Casually leaning against the counter, his arm brushed against her as he reached over to pick up the last carnation. When he felt her shiver at even this slight contact, searching her face, he held the flower out to her. "And then what happens?"

At a loss for words, she could only stare at him.

What happens then? Maybe you should tell him this would all depend on him?

Suddenly angry, she snatched the carnation from him. After shoving it in the vase with the rest of the flowers, avoiding eye contact, she took a deep breath. "I'm not sure what's going to happen. Or what I'll do. I haven't decided on anything yet. I …"

Her words trailing off, she began gathering up the florist paper. Horrified to see her hands were shaking, she turned away.

He wasn't sure what had brought on her anger. But when he saw her hands trembling, his next move was pure instinct. Taking the florist's paper from her and tossing it on the counter, he pulled her against him.

His words were a husky whisper in her ear. "What's going on, sweetheart? You're shaking. Why? You need to share what you're thinking. Because if you recall, this is what got us into trouble last time."

His arms holding her close, the steady beat of his heart a calming presence against her ear, was so familiar, so right.

It was as though she had never left.

Closing her eyes, she relaxed against him.

His cheek resting to the top of her head, the familiar floral scent of her shampoo had Jason swirling back into a time and place he would never forget.

This was when he knew everything was going to be all right.

Don't ask him how he knew this. Because, honestly? He couldn't say.

He just knew.

Filled with a sudden confidence, he pressed a soft kiss in her hair. His voice was just as soft. "You know what?"

She shook her head against him.

"On the drive here, I made a deal with myself."

She leaned back to gaze up at him, a smile curving her lips. "You did? What kind of pact?"

He gave her that slow, sexy smile of his again. "I decided that tonight was going to be our chance at a whole new us. We're not going to talk about the past or worry about the future. Nope, we're only going to enjoy each other's company."

Concern creasing her brow, he jumped in to re-assure her. "Don't get me wrong. We'll do all that, but not tonight." He rested his forehead against hers, his voice sinking to a whisper. "I want to spend the evening with the most beautiful woman I know. The woman who has never left my mind and will always have a home there. What do you say? Will you go along with this?"

How could you even think of saying no?

She nodded.

When he lowered his face to hers, she closed her eyes, ready for his kiss.

But this didn't happen. At least it was nowhere close to what she wanted to happen. It was closer to the kiss he gave her in the coffee shop across from The Regency. Leaving her holding her breath, thinking there had to be more.

Jason was aware of her disappointment. Hell, he felt the same. But if he kissed her now, he'd be willing to bet dinner would no longer be an option.

So, for him, this was a sign it was time to leave.

He glanced down at his watch. "*Ah* ... we need to get going if I'm going to pull off this surprise I have for you."

Her disappointment almost, but not quite forgotten, she smiled up at him. "Yes, this surprise. I'm intrigued. What do you have planned?"

"If I tell you, then it won't be a surprise." His grin was infectious. "You'll just have to wait."

He sent a quick glance around the room. "Do you have everything? Coat? Purse?"

After he helped her with her coat, and slipped the lipstick and key she gave him into his jacket pocket, he took her hand. "Okay... we're off."

Out in the parking lot, Jason hit his remote, setting the Lexus SUV lights blinking, the horn beeping

After taking in the shiny newness of the vehicle, Darcey glanced over at him. He smiled, opening the passenger door for her. "I decided it was time for a change. A new me. What do you think?"

She nodded. "It's very nice. But I remember you telling me you would never give up your truck. Too many fond memories, you said."

A worried look on her face, she glanced over at him. "I hope this 'new you' won't be too much of a change from the Jason I used to know. I wouldn't want to lose that Jason."

Framing her face in his hands, there was a tenderness in his voice. "That Jason is still here. And will be, for as long as you want him."

Unfortunately, the kiss he was about to give her was interrupted.

"Hey, Jason ..."

They both turned to see one of the skateboarders headed in their direction. After coming to an abrupt stop in front of them, he jumped off the board, flipped it up into the air, and caught it in his hand.

He shook his hair out of his face and grinned over at Jason. "Hey…"

Jason grinned right back at him. "Ben … you're a man of many talents, I see."

He turned to Darcey. "Darcey, this is Ben. We met at Café Latte, the night of the masquerade ball meeting. He was there to pick up something for his grandfather. They're both into music, both play guitar."

Darcey felt like she was looking at a wannabe Jason, hairstyle, grin and all. She smiled. "Hi, Ben."

After turning all shades of red and mumbling a greeting, Ben turned back to Jason. "I wanted to thank you for the guitar. I wish you could have seen my grandfather's face when the guy showed up at our house. He couldn't believe it was for him. Now he wants to meet you so he can thank you himself."

He laughed. "He wants to jam all the time. My mom claims it's a miracle. She wants to meet you, too."

Jason shrugged. "All the credit goes to Jack, one of my guys. He's the one with the connections. And tell your grandfather and mom I'll be more than happy to meet them. I've got your number, so I'll call you in the next couple of days. But for now, we have to cut this short. Darcey and I need to leave. We're running late as it is."

Ben grinned. "I'll tell him. And again, thanks."

After shooting a brief smile over at Darcey, he flipped the skateboard back to the ground and took off to join his friends.

Jason watched him go. "Nice kid. He came up to me at Café Latte and told me someone broke into his grandfather's house and stole his prized guitar. He had been teaching Ben how to play, but now they had to share Ben's guitar. So, I asked Jack to work his magic. I don't know how he does it, but he always comes through."

After they turned out onto the main highway, Jason glanced over at Darcey.

Her serious expression had him reaching for her hand to give it a gentle squeeze. "What's on your mind, gorgeous?"

Her heart gave a little leap.

Gorgeous ... it gets to you every time.

She leaned her head back against the headrest and gave him a lazy smile. "I was thinking about Ben. And how nice it was for you to get a guitar for his grandfather."

She shook her head. "Not only that, but Abby told me since the masquerade ball is a fundraiser for the Children's Hospital, your band plays for no charge. I can see why so many people around here love you so much."

He shrugged, uncomfortable with her praise. "It's not only me, the guys in the band are also very generous. We do what we can, give back when we can. Karma... isn't this what they call it?"

He glanced over at her. "Speaking of the ball, what's this I hear? You're not going?"

He shook his head. "This can't happen. Everyone will expect to see you there. So after thinking it over, I've decided you should be my date."

She could see he was trying to hide his smile, so she did the same. *"Hmm ...* shouldn't I have a say about this? I could already have a date, you know."

He appeared to think about this before he nodded. *"Ah ...* okay then. It looks like you're all set. That's good."

Incredulous, she stared over at him.

He wasn't serious, was he?

Why would he think, if you had the choice, you'd pass up the chance to go with him?

He glanced over at her, smiling at her bewildered expression. "But if you change your mind, or your date cancels, let me know. I'll be more than happy to let you tag along with me."

She couldn't help it ... she laughed. "You would, would you? Well, as it stands, I may have to take you up on your offer, since I don't have a date as yet."

He grinned. *"Ah ha ...* well, you do now. Me. And it appears we've settled this just in time, since we are now only seconds away from your surprise."

He had turned off the main road, and they were now on the driveway leading to the house once owned by Darcey's grandparents. Now newly renovated, it was not like the house Darcey remembered.

Peering out through the windshield, her hands went to her mouth. "Oh, Jason ... I can't believe you brought me here. Oh my gosh, look how beautiful everything is now."

Once Jason pulled up next to the house, she gazed over at him, her eyes bright. "Oh Jason, it's wonderful." And even though she tried, she couldn't hold back the tears. "I'm sorry, I don't mean to cry, but I loved this house so much. It was such a happy time in my life."

As he reached over to swipe the tears away with his thumb, he was smiling. "I hoped this would bring back wonderful memories. And now, it's going to get even better. Wait until we go inside and you can see what Sam and Livy have done. The restoration they've done so far is amazing."

With this, he was out of the SUV and opening her door. He reached for her hand, but she held back, a concerned expression on her face. "I don't want to intrude. I'm more than happy with what we've seen so far."

He tugged at her hand, pulling her from the SUV. "After the trouble I went through to set this up? I don't think so. And since I know how much Livy and Sam are looking forward to your visit, trust me when I say you have no reason to worry. It's all good."

To say it surprised him when she threw her arms around him and gave him a big kiss would be a major understatement.

But he reacted just as quickly, returning the kiss.

And if he had his way, he would have made it last a little longer.

But this was okay.

Because he saw it as a good start to the evening.

Yeah, it was a really great start.

CHAPTER 27

The setting sun had transformed the sky into a breathtaking blend of red and gold over the lake. After a quick look at his watch, Jason set his wineglass down on the table. "*Whoa* ... I'm afraid Darcey and I need to get moving. Our reservation is at eight."

He glanced over to where Darcey and Livy were discussing the plans for the kitchen remodel Sam had designed. When they both burst out laughing at something Livy said, he smiled before he turned to Sam. "Again, thank you for letting us stop by. Darcey had a pretty hard time when her father put this house on the market, so this visit means a lot to her. She told me living here with her grandparents was the highlight of her childhood."

Sam grinned. "Hey, when Livy found out Darcey was back in Cleveland, she was worried about how she really felt about us buying the house. So, this was a good idea. Next time, you'll have to come for dinner. We enjoy cooking together, so we're always looking for an excuse to try out our new recipes on unsuspecting friends." He laughed. "I can't guarantee the results, as we've had our share of failures. But I can promise you a fun evening."

"Sounds like a plan. I look forward to it."

Having said this, Jason made his way over to Darcey. "Hey

gorgeous, we should leave if we want to make our reservations on time."

Darcey gave Livy a big hug. "I can't even tell you how happy it makes me to see the renovations you and Sam have made."

Livy searched her face, worry creasing her brow. "Are you sure? You don't think of us as stealing away your family home?"

"Oh, Livy … no. I'm thrilled the house is now in such expert hands. My biggest worry was the new owners would come in and tear it down. Then they would replace it with some pretentious and modern monstrosity."

Livy sighed in relief. "Good. You'll have to come visit us again… stay longer next time. In fact, mark your calendars for the Saturday before Christmas because Sam and I are planning to have a big party. This, of course, depends on if our kitchen is done. It will be our first big event in the house."

Sam cleared his throat. He appeared to be amused. "Are you sure about that, sweetheart?"

"I think so?" Puzzled, Livy gazed up at him. Then she laughed. "I stand corrected. Our wedding was the first." She reached up to give him a kiss. "I'm sorry."

Sam pulled her against him, pressing a kiss to the top of her head. "The best day of my life." He smiled down at her. "I told Jason we'll have them over for dinner. Maybe sometime next month."

Livy was nodding. "Yes, that would be fun."

Then she waved her hands at Darcey and Jason. "But now you need to go. You don't want to be late for your reservation."

After watching Darcey and Jason leave, Sam began gathering up the empty wine glasses. He grinned over at Livy. "So, what do you think?"

Livy glanced over at him. "What do I think? Why, whatever do you mean?"

Sam grabbed a hunk of cheese from the cheeseboard and popped it into his mouth. He chuckled, shaking his head. "Come on, baby… admit it. You were analyzing every single move and look they gave each other. I could almost see the wheels turning in your head as you tried to figure out if it's serious with them."

He was smiling as he reached over to pull her into his arms. "So, what's your verdict?"

Resting her head on his shoulder, she sighed. "I swear, I'll never figure out how you always seem to know what I'm thinking."

He pressed a kiss in her hair. "It's a good thing, baby. It means I'll always have your back."

"Hmm ... that's good to know."

Her face scrunched up in thought. "But what do I think about Darcey and Jason? Well, the chemistry is there, big time. You can feel it. But something has them both very cautious. I wonder what happened? Whatever it was, I think they're afraid to open up to each other."

She frowned. "We know what can happen with that."

He shook his head. "I swear, I don't know how you come up with all of this." He gazed down at her. "What do you say, once we clean up here, we go for a walk along the beach?"

She reached up to give him a kiss. "That sounds wonderful."

Watching as he popped another piece of cheese into his mouth, she grinned. "The rate you're inhaling that cheese, we won't have anything to put away."

He grinned right back at her. "You know me. I'm not shy when it comes to food. In fact, I have an idea."

She watched as he poured what remained of the wine into their glasses. After handing her the glasses, he grabbed the cheeseboard and headed for the door to the back porch. "Come on, follow me. There's no reason we can't enjoy what's left of this beautiful evening. We'll clean up later."

CHAPTER 28

I am beginning to believe everything in my life has led to you.
Where suddenly, everything feels so right.
~ Anonymously Yours

Jason and Darcey had been seated at a table next to the floor to ceiling wall of windows in White Oaks.

A favorite of Jason's, this is the restaurant he had chosen for their dinner.

The server had cleared their dinner dishes and brought Darcey's coffee and Jason's after dinner drink, Sambuca, neat.

And now, a silence had fallen between them.

Her chin resting on her hand, Darcey was gazing out the window at the panoramic view of the heavily wooded ravine. The lighting, strategically placed throughout the trees, made the vibrant autumn colors even more spectacular.

Lounging comfortably in his chair, Jason was content to watch her, not at all bothered by the silence between them. Though the dreamy expression on her face had him a little curious.

Wouldn't it be nice if she was thinking of you?

He chuckled, shaking his head.

Look at you ... bewitched, bothered and bewildered. Just like the song.

Darcey glanced over at him and smiled.

This had him sitting up a little straighter, adjusting his jacket. His head tilted, he searched her face. "So, let me in, gorgeous ... tell me what you're thinking."

Their eyes meeting, the tenderness in his had her so flustered, she was suddenly at a loss for words. Stalling for time, she reached for her cup and took a small sip of coffee.

She cradled the cup in her hands and began chattering away. "I was thinking how the change of seasons is what I love most about this part of the country. The autumn colors are so breathtaking. And I can't even imagine how beautiful this view must be when everything is covered with a blanket of snow."

She sighed. "It must be absolutely magical."

She shivered. "But so, so cold."

"You're cold? Do you need my jacket?" A concerned look on his face, he began shrugging out of his jacket. If he hadn't been so caught up watching her mouth, thinking how he'd like to capture it in a kiss, he wouldn't have misunderstood what she said.

But he was having a hard time.

He had never been good at waiting. Especially when he knew what he wanted.

And right now, he definitely knew what he wanted.

This had him moving closer.

His offer, and the fact he was now only inches away, had Darcey almost knocking over her coffee cup when she reached over to place her hand on his arm. If only to reassure him. "*No, no* ... please, I'm fine. I was referring to the cold weather you have during the winter months."

She gazed around the room. "But right now? This is perfect."

And it was ... the aged paneled walls, soft lighting and the hypnotic glow of the flames in the fireplace gave the room a warm and cozy feeling. The ambiance was one of glamour and old money, hinting at the rich history of a mysterious and hidden past.

After she moved the coffee cup out of harm's way, she smiled at him. "I can see why this is one of your favorite restaurants. Our dinner was delicious, the service amazing. Thank you for sharing all of this with me."

Not as amazing or delicious as you ... not even close.

Jason had a moment of panic, thinking he had said this aloud. Because this definitely wasn't his style, coming on so strong.

And certainly not something he would say.

You need to cool it ...

Fingering the stirrer from his after-dinner drink, he sent her a warm smile. "There is no need to thank me. Believe me, the pleasure is all mine."

His gaze traveled around the room before coming back to settle on her. "Everything is perfect, isn't it? The view, the ambiance, the food ... everything. Along with the dessert you finally decided on, which should be here soon."

A teasing smile touched his lips. "I was beginning to think you would never make up your mind."

She had hardly heard a word he said. She was watching his fingers playing with the drink stirrer. His hands had been one of the first things she had noticed about him. She found them fascinating, their total dominance over the piano or guitar when he was performing such a contrast to the gentleness of his touch when he was with her.

You told him there was magic in his hands.

She closed her eyes, falling right back to when they first met. The day the photo was taken. The morning snow flurries had elevated into a late afternoon blizzard, shutting down the city. Sheltered in his apartment, they took full advantage of this time together, his bed becoming their own little oasis amid the storm.

It was there he showed her what it was like to be thoroughly loved. No one had ever made her feel this way before.

So, yes ... there magic in his hands. Carrying into the kisses and whispered promises he made.

"Darcey?"

She blinked. The knowing smile on his face told her he knew she was thinking about him.

And now she was flustered, her smile overly bright. "*Umm* ... the dessert? Yes, it was a hard decision. But only because there were so many choices. "She hesitated, frowning. "As I'm sure you've noticed, I'm still not good at making decisions. Or maybe I should say, I'm not good at making the right decisions."

She was unaware she was nervously fingering her bracelet, twisting it around her wrist.

But he noticed. Tossing the stirrer on the table, and leaning in closer, he reached for her hands.

For a few moments, he stared down at their hands. Then, he raised his head, a faint smile playing across his lips. "Your hands fit so well in mine, don't they?"

His voice was like velvet, lulling her with his words. But this was all Jason. Remember, his voice, if he chose to use it in this way, could wrap around you like a caress. Turning even the simplest of words into a love song.

Like now ...

Dropping her gaze to their hands, her response was a breathy muddle of words. "Yes, I guess you could say that... what I mean is, they do, don't they? Very well, as you said."

This had him moving even closer. Tracing the curve of her jaw with his fingertip, he nudged up her chin, gazing into her eyes.

The vulnerability of before? It was still there...

He sighed. "*Ah*, sweetheart ... I know I said I didn't want to talk about anything serious tonight, but now looking into your eyes, there is so much I want to say and I don't want to wait. Though I'm not sure where or how to begin, so bear with me, okay?"

She nodded, her look cautious.

He gazed down at their hands again. After letting out a slow, measured breath, he looked up and right into her eyes.

"Darcey, I acted like a fool. And for this, I am so, *so* sorry. But to be honest, when you came bursting into my life, you were like no one I had ever known before. You changed me ... you changed everything. But then, poof ... just like that, you disappeared. And I didn't know what to think."

He brought her hands to his mouth, pressing a kiss to her fingers. "This is when I realized with you, I wanted the life I never thought could be mine ... a wife, kids, the total package. And this scared me to death. How could I expect you to settle for a guy like me, coasting through life, playing in a band? You deserved a man who could give you the life you had grown to expect. So, I tried to convince myself, you leaving was for the best. But my heart refused to let you go."

A wry smile on his face, he shook his head. "I can't even tell you how many times I almost booked a flight to California, my plan to kidnap you and bring you back here."

"Jason ..." She pressed her fingers to his mouth, shaking her head. "Then why didn't you call me? Or at least leave a message? I must have checked my phone a hundred times. I didn't care if it was good or bad news. I only wanted to hear your voice again."

He hesitated, struggling as to whether he should tell her about the conversation he had with her father. The one and only time he had talked to the man, it was one he would never forget.

But, what took place between them couldn't be considered a conversation.

No, far from it. In the time span of less than ten minutes, their words had evolved into an angry shouting match, to end in an irreparable bitterness.

So, no ... you're not going to share this with her.

The man was her father. Besides her brother, the only family she had. And he of all people, knew you have to keep family close.

How many times have you reminded Steff of this?

Darcey watched as he seemed to struggle with an inner conflict before he shook his head. "I'm sorry. I ..." Then he shook his head again. Maybe someday, when they were old and gray, he would tell her. But not now.

Instead, he was going to do the one thing he had put off for way too long.

"Darcey ..."

His hoarse whisper was her only warning before his mouth came down on hers in a kiss that consumed them both.

And it was wonderful ... the kiss she remembered.

And one she knew she would never, ever forget.

Jason kissed her as if his plan was to never let her go.

And if he had a choice, he wouldn't have.

Oblivious to any of the other diners in the restaurant, he took a slow and thorough possession of her mouth, everything he had committed to his memory of what it was like to kiss her, coming back in one fell swoop.

That she responded just as passionately had him even more determined to keep the kiss going.

"Jason ..." Her voice filtering into his consciousness, he finally leaned back to look into her eyes. Clutching his arms for support, she had dazed expression on her face.

He didn't even stop to think, capturing her mouth in another kiss. But this time, he slowed it down, his kiss reaching deep into her soul.

Her eyes closed, she let out a long, trembling sigh.

How could you have ever thought you would be able to forget what it was like to be kissed by him?

Trying not to hope, wondering if maybe she was dreaming, her eyes searched his. "We ... you and I ... Jason, I ..."

He framed her face with his hands, his lips brushing over hers in a whisper. "*Shh* ... I know, gorgeous, I know. Just let me say one more thing."

Their eyes meeting, the emotion in his almost took her breath away. That she could even answer with a nod was a miracle.

He pressed a soft kiss to her mouth. "I love you, Darcey Hollister. I've loved you from the very first moment I became lost in your eyes in line at the coffee shop. Even over the past three years, I haven't stopped loving you."

He took a deep breath. "And I swear to God, I love you now even more."

He rested his forehead against hers. "I will always love you."

Closing her eyes, her response came in the softest of sighs.

"Oh Jason ... I love you, too."

The server had finally brought Darcey's dessert.

And even though Jason wanted to whisk her off to a place where they could be alone, as this was the only thing on his mind and what made sense to him right now, he was trying so hard to be patient.

Little did he know, she felt the same. In fact, gazing down at the small piece of cake remaining on her plate, she was almost embarrassed at how fast she had gobbled it up.

She set her fork on the plate and smiled over at him. "This was absolutely delicious."

He had picked up his glass , about to take another drink. A smile suddenly curving his lips, he set the glass back on the table. He reached over to cup her chin in his hand, and after brushing his mouth over hers, he sat back in his chair.

Her lashes fluttering open, she gazed over at him, confused.

His eyes danced with amusement. "You had some chocolate on the corner of your mouth. I didn't want you to be embarrassed when the waitress came back to check on us."

Color flooding her cheeks, she grabbed her napkin from her lap and brought it to her mouth. After she sent a quick glance around the room, she zeroed back in on him. "Jason, you need to stop. What will people think?"

His response was to take the napkin from her and press another kiss to her mouth. In the same exact spot. He nodded. "There... it seems I didn't get it all. But now I have. And what is everyone going to think? Only that I'm a very sweet and considerate date."

He sent her a wink. "This is what a man does for the woman he loves."

Watching as the blush became even more pronounced in her cheeks, he was smiling as he placed the napkin on the table. "Also, if you had been paying attention, you would have noticed we're about the only people still in the dining room. Everyone else has left or moved to the lounge. This means, now that I can, I'm going to kiss you whenever I want." A sudden gleam in his eyes, he leaned closer, resting his forearms on the table. "Unless you would rather I didn't?"

Their eyes locked and for a long moment, she said nothing. Then a slow smile curved her lips. "I will never tire of your kisses."

After he gave her another kiss, he nodded over at what remained of her dessert. "So, are you almost finished with that? If so, I have a proposition for you."

She was still smiling. But then, this was something she wouldn't be able to stop, even if she tried. "What kind of proposition?"

The urge to touch her again, he reached over to tuck her hair behind her ear. "So, what I'd like to know, how good are you at picking out paint samples?"

Paint samples?

She tilted her head, puzzled. "Paint samples? I'm not sure what you're asking? But if this is something you need help with, I can try."

He sat back in his chair, nodding. "Good. As soon as you finish your dessert, we'll leave."

She picked up her fork, a mischievous smile curving her lips Scooping up the last bit of cake on her plate, she held the fork out to him. "I think you should have the last bite."

A little wary, he opened his mouth. She put the fork to his mouth, smearing a generous portion of the frosting across his lips and into the corner of his mouth.

She dropped the fork on her plate. Her hand going to her mouth, she shook her head. "Oh my, we can't let the server see you like this, can we? Let me take care of that for you."

Before he could respond, the kiss she gave him should have been more than enough to take care of the frosting.

But it wasn't. So she brushed her lips over his one more time.

"Hmm ... much better. It's all gone now." She nodded, trying to hide her smile. But she couldn't.

"Darcey ..." this came from Jason in a groan, "you're killing me here, gorgeous."

Running his hand through his hair, he turned to search the room.

"Where the heck is our server with the check?"

CHAPTER 29

*Nothing is sexier than a man
who admits he wants you,
and does anything and everything he can,
to have and to keep you.*
~ *Anonymous*

Jason guided his SUV down his driveway and, coming to a stop, he shut off the engine.

He glanced over at Darcey. She was gazing over at the house.

So, he did the same, trying to see it through her eyes.

Oh boy, not good. Not good at all.

He cleared his throat. "Well, this is it … my humble abode. As you can see, it probably needs a lot more than a coat of paint. But now you can probably see why I'm looking for you to give me some suggestions."

Jumping out of the car and coming around to open her door, a glance up at the heavy clouds racing across the sky had him holding out his hand. "Come on gorgeous. I have a feeling it's going to start raining any minute. It's getting colder, too."

After they ran to the front door, just barely beating the rain, she watched as he shoved his shoulder against the door to send it flying open.

He grinned over at her concerned expression. "Don't worry, a new door is on order."

Once they were inside and he had turned on the lights, he waved his hand around at the room. "So, what do you think?"

He watched as she gazed around at the small space. This was when he saw the room for what it was … call it a mish-mash of furniture, a guy's place to crash, a bachelor pad … any of those could fit.

Hey … it's comfortable. Isn't this what's important? At least for you, it is.

But definitely not what one would call a designer's dream home. At least from a woman's point of view.

He frowned. Well, it wasn't like he didn't have other things to do. He was always on the go, hardly ever home.

Ask Caro, she would vouch for this. Wasn't she always telling him he needed to slow down? Enjoy life?

Yeah, maybe someday …

Sensing his uncertainty, Darcey smiled at him. "Jason, it's perfect." And to her, it was. This was the Jason she knew. The real Jason, not the rock star image everyone perceived of him.

He smiled as he took her into his arms, pressing a kiss to her forehead. "All this time, I've felt like something was missing. And now I know what it is … it's you."

She didn't have a chance. Swept up by his words and the huskiness in his voice, she closed her eyes, sinking into his embrace.

Now you would think Jason's next move would be to sweep her up into his arms and carry her off to his bedroom. And this is exactly what he'd like to do.

But, remember? He had vowed to take it slow. At least this was the goal.

Her hand in his, he headed for the kitchen. Picking up a bottle of wine from the counter, one he'd carefully chosen for this occasion, he held it up for her inspection. "So, I thought I'd open a bottle of wine before I give you the grand tour."

"Oh my, the grand tour?" She laughed. "You mean there's more?"

That slow, sexy smile of his came right at her again. "Yes, for you, there will always be more."

As Jason began rummaging through the kitchen drawers, Darcey noticed he had a calendar posted on his refrigerator, Walking over to check it out, she saw the photo.

Yes, the photo Jason had shown her, the photo of them.

The photo she thought had been lost.

"Jason?"

He was searching for his corkscrew. He knew he had one, had seen it somewhere. But could he find it? No. And he blamed this on Caro. She was always re-arranging things. Or searching, as she phrased it, for a more 'accessible' spot.

She even made him get rid of his junk drawer, claiming she had never heard of such a thing. Who keeps a drawer just for junk, she wanted to know?

Well, he had, until he let her clear it out. And this would be where he usually found the corkscrew.

You need to talk to her about this.

He glanced over at Darcey. "Hmm ... what's wrong, gorgeous?"

"The photo ... you found the photo."

He sent her a smile. "Yeah, I went back to the restaurant and picked it up that same night." He glanced over at the photo. "Yeah, it was suddenly important I didn't lose proof of that time. I ... well ... I wasn't sure of what was going to happen next."

He gave a nod towards the photo. "But if you remember, I did give it to you. So, you're more than welcome to take it."

Finally holding the corkscrew, he gazed over at her, his expression thoughtful.

She tilted her head. "What?"

A smile flitted across his face. "I don't know if you remember, but that photo was taken on the little disposable camera you insisted we buy to take photos of your grandparent's house. When you left it behind, I almost threw it away. But then I got it developed. Out of the entire roll, only this one photo came out."

He glanced over at the photo again. "For a while, I thought this was a sign we would find each other again. But after so much time went by, I figured fate wasn't on our side."

He sent her a wink. "But now here we are ..."

Tracing their images in the photo with her finger, she turned to smile at him. "Is it okay if we keep it here? This way, we'll always have it as a reminder of that day."

He'd swear his heart gave a leap of joy in response to what her words implied. Overcome with emotion, he stared down at the bottle before he lifted his head, his gaze holding hers. Then he nodded ... slowly, he did this. "That sounds perfect. I'd like that. A lot."

She moved closer, leaning against the counter to watch as he uncorked the bottle before taking two glasses out of the cupboard. She tilted her head, studying him. "So, where are these paint samples you want me to look at?"

He didn't answer. Instead, he lined the glasses on the counter and carefully, almost too carefully, began pouring the wine. If she wasn't mistaken, he was trying to ignore her.

She moved closer. "Jason?"

"The paint samples?" He began searching the counter for the cork, avoiding her gaze.

Ah ... so he did hear you.

Her smile grew. "Yes, the paint samples."

She waited.

He shot her a quick glance. *"Hmm ...* they're around here some-where. I'll have to see if I can find them after I finish up with this."

He then made an even bigger production out of re-corking the bottle and returning it to the refrigerator.

Still avoiding eye contact.

She tried to be serious as she slid her hand across the counter, her fingers just barely touching his. "Jason ... Maybe I'm wrong, but something tells me paint samples aren't the real reason you brought me here."

He linked her fingers with his before he dipped his head, kissing her mouth softly, briefly. They drew apart, his gaze holding hers. "And if it isn't? Will you still stay?"

Their eyes locked. Even though he already knew what he hoped for, how he wanted the rest of the evening to go, so much depended on her answer. When she nodded, he leaned in to press another kiss to her mouth before handing her a glass of wine.

He raised the other glass, tipping it against hers. "A toast ... to the beginning of a new us." Then he reached for her hand. "Come on, it's time for the tour. We'll start with the upstairs."

He smiled. "I promise we'll get to those paint samples later."

The steps leading to the second floor were flanked by double doors opening into the master suite. When Jason flicked the switch, the light from the bedside lamp sent a soft glow through the room.

He set their wine glances on the nightstand and turned to Darcey. "It's not a large space, but I like to think of this room as my hideaway from the world. I've come up with some of my best songs here."

He shrugged. "It's a place I can relax, take time to re-fuel, think about things."

It's also a place you want to make love to the only woman you have ever wanted.

To block this out of his mind, at least for the time being, he jammed his hands in his pockets, waiting patiently as Darcey walked around the room, taking it all in.

Jason liked to tell people this was the one part of the house the previous owners had done right. What had once been a dark and empty attic was now a bright and well-planned out master suite. With the high ceiling, the off-white walls and the large antique Palladian window, the space was bright and inviting. The addition of the spacious adjoining bathroom and huge walk-in closet completed the space. And up until now, all that he needed.

But this was no longer true. What had been missing, what he needed, was Darcey. She made this room complete.

Since she had reappeared in his life, most nights had him going almost crazy, his imagination having her with him. There were times she monopolized his mind to the point sleep had become a losing battle.

But now, for some absolutely ridiculous reason, even though she was here, and within reach, he was hesitant to make a move. Maybe even a little afraid.

Go figure ...

He watched as she finally noticed the fireplace, something he had been waiting for. When she whirled around to smile at him, he nodded. "Yes, gorgeous... a fireplace."

"Oh, Jason ... and it really works?"

He nodded again. "Yes ... it does." The corner of his mouth hitched in a smile. "I remember you telling me when you finally got a home of your own, one thing on your wish list would be a fireplace."

He had slowly begun to move closer. He cleared his throat. "A cold, windy night, a fire in the fireplace, soft music and a man to love you... this was your idea of a perfect love story."

Pleased he had remembered this, she nodded. "Yes, I love fire-places." They're so romantic." A long and, what came across to him as a very sensuous sigh followed this.

He studied her, a bemused smile on his face.

Hmm ... romantic? Why, yes ... you'll be more than happy to provide the romance ... as much as she wants.

Darn if he didn't have to clear his throat again. "I can agree with that. Even though I believe if two people are really in love, romance will prevail. Fireplace or no fireplace. But it's your call, gorgeous. If you want a fire, your wish is my command."

Almost holding his breath, he waited. Because, once again, her answer could determine how the rest of the evening might go.

Wrapping her arms around herself, she glanced over at the fire-place before she smiled back at him. "I think a fire would be perfect."

Just managing to hide his jubilation, he reached over to press a kiss to her mouth. "I agree, tonight is definitely a fire in the fireplace kind of night." He nodded towards the window, the heavy beat of rain against the glass even more pronounced in the silence. "After all, we already have what you consider the perfect night ... cold and windy."

After pressing another kiss to her mouth, this one lingering a little longer than before, he smiled. "You should probably make yourself comfortable, since I'm not sure how long this will take. It will be an excellent test to see if any of my training from scouts stuck with me." He winked. "I took my status as a scout very seriously. So, we'll see what happens."

Rolling up his sleeves, he got to work.

While she did exactly as he suggested ... she kicked off her shoes and nestled on the bed to watch his progress.

Jason began stacking logs as if this was something he had been doing his entire life. When, in fact, he wasn't as confident as he came across.

Yes, he had been a scout. But this had been quite a few years ago.

Remember, he was thirty-one.

But come on, how hard could it be? People had fires in fireplaces all the time. As long as he didn't accidentally set the house on fire, he should be fine.

He finally had everything stacked up and arranged for a fool-proof fire. This was according to the directions he had received from the guy at the local nursery. Yes, it's true he had sought professional advice. But he wanted this night to go without a hitch.

Now happy with the way things were moving along, he turned to Darcey, his intention to let her know it shouldn't be much longer.

The words died in his mouth ... probably a good thing since the way she was studying him, her eyes working their magic, he forgot what he'd been planning to say.

A smile slowly spread across his face.

She had kicked off her shoes and scooted further onto the bed.

Her feet tucked up under her and her chin resting in her hand, she gave him a flirty smile.

Yes, flirty ...

At least, this was how it came across to him. Enough to have him wondering why the hell he was fussing over a silly fire when he would rather join her on the bed.

He cleared his throat. "Well, you look extremely comfortable. Hopefully, in a few minutes, I'll have fulfilled your dream of a roaring fire and I'll be able to join you."

She tilted her head, her eyes wide. "My dream?"

He nodded, again taking her move as very flirtatious, sexy even.

Very sexy ...

It was driving him downright crazy.

He began searching the mantle for the matches, thinking this was where he had put them. But he could be wrong about this, as his mind had almost completely abandoned him, the little still functioning now completely focused on the woman sitting on his bed.

His fingers coming in contact with the matches, he turned back to Darcey. "*Ah* ... here we go. Let's see if this will bring on the magic."

After lighting a match to the paper, he stood back, rubbing his hands together. "Now we wait for a few minutes and if things go right, we should have our fire."

Within minutes, the paper caught fire, flames shooting up the chimney.

Jason's smile was triumphant. "Well, look at that. It appears I've still got it."

"It's wonderful ... you're wonderful." She sighed. "You're my hero."

He brushed his fingertips over her cheek in a caress. "If the position is open, I'll be more than happy to take it on."

He turned off the lamp, the only light in the room now coming from the glow of the fire. After typing on his phone, the soft sound of instrumental jazz filled the room.

His hands were suddenly on both sides of her on the bed, holding her captive.

He gazed down at her. "Darcey ... look at me, gorgeous."

She raised her face to his, the eyes that met hers alive with desire. "You've got it all, gorgeous ... the chilly night, the fire in the fireplace and even the music. Your dream of the perfect setting for romance."

And just like that, between the heat of his gaze and the deep huskiness of his voice, she fell right under his spell. But he was forgetting something, wasn't he?

She needed to remind him of this. Swaying towards him, she reached out to trace his lips with her finger. "But, you … what about you? I need you. There would be no romance without you."

He brought her hand up to his mouth for a kiss. This was the Darcey he remembered. The Darcey who needed him as much as he needed her.

Fate. Destiny. Meant to be. All of these apply. You're sure of it...

He took a deep breath for his next words. "Ah, yes … you also said you needed a man to love you. I am that man. And I always will be. As I have been from the very beginning."

Her eyelashes drifting shut, she lifted her face to his. "Then do it … love me."

In what could be less than a heartbeat, he pulled her up against him. A deep groan rumbling from low in his throat, he claimed her mouth in a kiss. It was a blinding, demanding kiss. The kiss of a man who had been waiting for a long time to make his claim on the woman he loved.

His lips slowed, pressing feathery kisses across her jaw and down the side of her neck. At the same time, he reached behind her, searching for the zipper. After one quick pull, he stepped back, watching her dress fall to the floor in a swish of fabric.

His gaze traveling over her, he leisurely looked his fill. She was beautiful, so much more than the image he had been so careful to guard in his mind. Cupping her chin in his hand, his whisper was a husky sigh against her mouth. "You are beautiful, so gorgeous. Even more than I remember."

More than he remembered?

Resting her hand against his chest, she anxiously searched his face. "But, what if …" her whisper trailing off between them, she slowly shook her head.

Yes, unfortunately, this is where the 'but' part of this love story kept coming back to haunt her. The fear what they once remembered as a love so beautiful, may have become broken over time.

Simply said, the magic would no longer be there.

And Jason?

He wasn't worried. Not anymore, he wasn't. This wasn't going to happen. They only needed to slow things down and everything would fall right back into place.

In fact, he was willing to bet on this. And he wasn't a gambling kind of guy.

So, as you can see, Jason's confidence was high. Maybe even enough for the both of them.

But first, he wanted to look into her eyes. He needed to make sure the connection was still there. He pressed a lingering kiss to her mouth. "Darcey, baby ... look at me."

One look and his words came easy. "You and me? We've got this, gorgeous. Our love will never die. Trust me on this."

They had this.

How could they not?

The connection was still there.

In the haze of desire now fogging his mind, Jason watched Darcey work her way slowly down his shirt, undoing the buttons.

It was only when she fumbled with the last button, he moved to help her. Once he shrugged out of the shirt, they took their time undressing each other, the passion building between them, intensifying with each article of clothing they discarded.

His eyes locked with hers. Easing her back with him onto the bed, he moved over her.

She could feel all of him, the hard, muscular length of him a perfect fit to her soft curves. His scent flooded her senses, sending her spiraling back to when he first loved her. To say she was overwhelmed would be an understatement.

But this didn't mean she wasn't ready for more. Because she was.

She wanted it all ... his kisses, his touch, his whispered promises. She wanted what she'd had only once before ... the feeling of being wanted by the only man she would ever love.

His forehead resting against hers, Jason had closed his eyes. That he was able to share this moment with her, a moment he thought he'd never experience again, was almost surreal to him. Because even though everything was so familiar, at the same time it was different. This was a love that had endured.

They had beat the odds.

He pulled her closer, his whisper brushing across her mouth. "I missed you … this … everything."

"I missed you, too. I love you."

This declaration of love had him lifting his head. Watching as her eyes seemed to grow brighter, bigger, he was filled with this sudden gut consuming longing.

He wanted to fulfill her every desire, her every fantasy. Simply said, he wanted it all … the passion … the heat … the forever. With her, he wanted to reach for those elusive stars.

"I love you, too."

The deep huskiness of his voice sealed his promise.

His mouth claiming hers in another kiss, Jason eased himself inside her. As he gently brushed her hair back from her face, a slow groan escaped him. "*My god,* Darcey …"

"I know, I know …" As desperate for him as he felt for her, she arched up against him. Her hands tangling in his hair, her mouth searched for his.

And now, taking it slow was no longer an option, the fire that flared between them even stronger than they remembered. His mouth never leaving hers, he guided her body in tune with his, each kiss hungrier than the last.

When he sensed she was close to the edge, his kisses slowed. He wanted to claim her all over again … heart, body and soul.

And for one breathless moment, he held her gaze. "You are mine … forever."

"Forever …" Her whisper came right before she fell apart in his arms. His mouth capturing her cries with his kiss, he fell right along with her.

Their surrender was complete, their love even more beautiful and stronger than before.

It was a love brighter than any stars.

The steady rain, along with an occasional gust of wind, sent the branches scraping loudly against the side of the house.

But within the refuge of Jason's bedroom, other than the crackling of the fire and slow jazz still playing on his phone, there was only a blissful silence.

His fingers lazily drifting through Darcey's hair, he pressed a kiss to the top of her head, smiling when this simple touch brought on her soft sigh.

He had no words.

Not even a song in the making.

This place, this moment, this love … together it was all so big, almost too momentous to take in.

He was finding it hard to believe he'd thought he could live his life without this beautiful, loving woman he was now holding in his arms. That he'd almost let her slip away so easily, now seemed unfathomable to him.

He closed his eyes, sending up a silent prayer of gratitude for this love they shared.

Passion ...

He had read about it, wrote about it, and of course, sang about it. Many times. Yet never had he understood what real passion was all about.

But now he did.

This almost sacred love he and Darcey shared?

This was real passion. More real than they ever could've hoped for.

And it would always be a part of who they were.

Darcey had no idea what was wrong with her.

She had to be crazy.

Why else would she be fighting such a desperate battle to keep from crying her eyes out? She should be ecstatic, a-singing-in-the-shower-kind-of-happy, after what she and Jason shared.

Their love had been everything she remembered. No, it had been even better. It was everything she had ever dared to believe falling in love would be.

She curled up even closer to him and closed her eyes. Maybe if she tried taking a couple of deep breaths, she would calm down.

She certainly didn't want him to know she was crying.

Yes, she had to be completely out of her mind ...

Jason was aware of Darcey's tears.

He also had an idea of what caused them.

However, he could be wrong.

Because from what little experience he had with women, he'd found tears could be caused by a number of things.

Just about anything, really.

Hell, it was anyone's guess ...

Propping himself up on his elbow next to her, he watched as another tear slowly slid down her face.

After he swiped the tear away with his thumb, he cleared his throat. "What's going on, gorgeous? Share with me. Because, I've gotta tell you, tears aren't really what a man wants to see when he just made love to the woman of his dreams." He tucked her hair behind her ears. "Unless they're happy tears?"

He watched as she let out a long trembling sigh before she slowly opened her eyes, made even more brilliant by her tears.

She reached up to trace the line of his jaw with her fingertips, her voice coming out all shaky. "I'm sorry, I don't know what's wrong with me. I think I was afraid ... that maybe after all this time, we might have lost, well ... what we had. Or you changed your mind. And now this is hitting me all at once."

She drew in a deep breath. "Or it could be I'm just crazy."

Catching her hand, he pressed a kiss to her fingers. "*Hmm* ... I had a feeling this was the reason. It's never going to happen, gorgeous. Trust me, we're here to stay." He grinned. "And, hey ... I like crazy. Makes for a more interesting life."

The faint smile flitting across her face had him pulling her closer. Then he became serious. "When you left, I tried to convince myself, even if I never saw you again, I had been so fortunate to experience such love. It was when we were given this second chance, I realized how blessed we really are."

He pressed a lingering kiss to her mouth, his voice rough with emotion. "We've got something beautiful here, gorgeous. We're what all those love songs are about. And I'm going to keep reminding you of this for the rest of our lives. That is, if you'll let me."

"Yes, I want to grow old with you, Jason Bennett." She followed this with a kiss before she settled back against him.

His lips moved in her hair. "Have I told you lately how much I love you?"

She was smiling as she gazed up at him. "Not for a while, you haven't."

Cupping her chin in his hand, he dropped a kiss to her mouth. "Well, I guess I need to remedy this, don't I?"

His eyes smiling into hers, he pulled her close. "I love you. And I promise we'll never be apart again."

But sometimes, through no fault of our own, promises are broken.

CHAPTER 30

*D*arcey was late.

She pulled into The Regency parking lot and, jumping out of her car, ran up the steps to the main entrance.

Yes, she both jumped and ran

In fact, it was almost more of a skip than a run. This was because she was in a wonderful mood. All was right in her world.

You mean in the world you share with Jason. A world you didn't want to leave.

Thinking of the kiss he gave her when she left just a short time ago, she was smiling as she pulled open the door.

Her phone vibrated, signaling an incoming text. Digging the phone out of her coat pocket, she saw it was from Jason. After she glanced around silent lobby to see no one was around, she stopped to read the text.

> Hey, gorgeous. I want to make dinner for you
> tonight. Your place or mine, your choice. I
> already miss you. I love you.

She couldn't believe how fast her heart was beating in response to this simple message.

Fingering the promise ring hanging from the chain around her neck, she closed her eyes,

When the door to the party center opened, followed by the sound of voices, she quickly typed out her reply.

> You want to make me dinner? How can I pass up an offer like this? I'll come to your place after I pick up my dress for the ball from the Chic Boutique. I miss you, too. And I love you, too.

The text sent, and her phone back in her pocket she continued in a brisk pace to her office.

She had a full schedule ahead. Both the new event planner and the chef were starting today.

She turned the corner and ran right into Rob Johnson.

He grabbed her arm to steady them. "*Whoa* ... good morning." He laughed, but it was a harsh laugh. "Even though, for me, good is not how I'd describe my morning."

His angry expression immediately had her on guard.

Please, you don't want any bad news. Least of all, from him.

Her smile was tentative. "Did something happen?"

Searching her face, and not finding what he was looking for, he nodded. "*Ah* ... so I guess you haven't heard. Good luck with that." He opened his mouth as though he was going to say more. Instead, he turned and began walking away.

She caught up to him. "Wait, you can't leave me hanging. What's going on?"

He slowed, reluctantly turning to face her. "I don't know if I should be the one to tell you this, but work on The Regency has been cancelled. It seems your father is ready to move on to the next project. This means my services are no longer needed."

Angrily shoving his hands in his pockets, he glared at her. "I want you to know I had no part in these new plans. In fact, I was let go because I refused to do something I felt was unethical."

He suddenly reached into his pocket and pulled out a key and handed it to her. "Here, this is the key to your office. I only used it once, when I left those work orders on your desk. If you want to know why I have it, you'll have to ask your father."

He gave another harsh laugh. "Yeah, you can think whatever you want about me, but I'm not a snitch."

She shook her head. "I don't understand …"

He turned to leave, his words coming over his shoulder. "Ask your boyfriend to explain it to you."

For a few moments, her head spinning with everything he just told her, she couldn't move.

Her boyfriend? What would Jason have to do with this? Maybe you should call him?

She reached for her phone, then changed her mind. She needed more information. What did Rob mean, all work was cancelled? What kind of decision did her father make? And unethical? What had Rob refused to do that would lead to him losing his job?

And the key … staring down at it in her hand, this is what confused her the most. She dropped it into her pocket, and at a much slower pace, she continued on to her office

Rob was wrong. About everything. He was lashing out, looking for someone to blame.

Unfortunately, this didn't ease the sick feeling churning in her stomach.

David Hanson was in a very sour mood.

Leaning against what he sincerely hoped was the door to Darcey's office, he was scrolling down through his phone messages as he waited for her to show up for work.

He frowned.

The Darcey he knew would have been in her office and hard at work over two hours ago.

He looked up from his phone, peering down the deserted hallway. He couldn't believe he hadn't seen a single person walk by.

What did you expect? This isn't exactly Los Angeles.

He gave a long, drawn out sigh. The last place he wanted to be was in this godforsaken city.

Cleveland?

Come on, when did anyone ever have anything good to say about Cleveland? No one he knew, that's for sure.

Massaging the back of his neck, he searched his memory. Hadn't there been a story going around a few years back about the Cuyahoga River catching on fire?

Yeah, it had become a national joke. Never mind, this was years ago and Cleveland now had so many other things going on for it… the Art Museum, The Rock and Roll Hall of Fame and Playhouse Square, to name a few.

Nope, he would still take just about anywhere in California over Cleveland.

Same goes for Texas. But he didn't want to start thinking about Texas. Not yet.

He glanced down the hallway again.

Again, where was everyone? The place was like a morgue.

He wanted to know if he was ever going to see any of the Midwest hospitality he'd heard so much about. So far, no one had even come close to giving him the time of day. Or impressed him with their so-called friendliness.

Nope … you've experienced the exact opposite.

When he had first arrived at The Regency, he waved down a woman carrying a large box to ask where he could find Darcey. Instead, after studying him for a good ten seconds, she began barking questions at him.

What was his name?

How did he know Darcey?

And why was he even in the building?

Irritated at this rude interrogation, he told her his visit was personal, Darcey was expecting him, and she was his fiancée.

So, yeah … he lied a little. Maybe it was more business than personal.

More like all business.

And maybe he had elaborated a little with his claim Darcey was his fiancée.

On the positive side, there was one thing he didn't lie about.

He gave her his real name.

But, come on ... she made him mad.

So, as he was known to do, he over-reacted.

After sending him another long stare, the woman gave a vague nod towards the back of the building. This was where he could find Darcey's office, she told him. Then, before he could get in another word, she slipped into a room off the hallway, slamming the door behind her.

Left glaring at the closed door, this was when he decided it was true what they said about red-heads, their fiery personality matched the color of their hair.

He was also still fuming about his encounter with the chef of the party center. Yes, he had walked into the kitchen unannounced. To then question why they didn't have Starbucks coffee. But was this any reason for the chef to almost physically kick him out of the kitchen? While screaming at him in Italian?

There was no reason for him to treat you like a criminal.

He only wanted a damn cup of coffee. Decent coffee...

If he could, he'd head right for the airport and get on the next available flight back to LA.

Dragging his hand down over his jaw, he groaned, knowing he couldn't do that. This was his chance to score big, with both Darcey and her father.

Somehow, and he didn't know why, her father had now decided he was the lesser of two evils. This was after he had made it quite clear there would be no rock star in his daughter's life.

David didn't know who this rock star was, or what he meant to Darcey. What mattered was her father had decided he was the winner in this contest and she would soon be his. He saw this as a guaranteed move up the ladder of Hollister Industries.

This was a reminder he should probably send her father a text to let him know, per his request, he had informed Rob Johnson his services were no longer required. He didn't quite understand the reasoning, only that it had something to do with Rob not keeping his part of the bargain.

He frowned. Johnson hadn't taken it well.

No, it wasn't good ... not good at all.

He checked the time again.

8:34 a.m..

He had now been waiting for over twenty-five minutes. Twenty-eight, to be exact. Twenty-eight minutes that had been a complete waste of his time.

Massaging the back of his neck, he leaned back against the wall. What he wouldn't give for a cup of coffee right now.

It also wasn't helping he was hungry. He wasn't big on breakfast, but now he regretted passing up the complimentary breakfast spread back at his hotel. At least grabbed a bagel or something. Maybe if he had, he would be in a better mood.

After another long sigh, he went back to checking his messages.

When Darcey came around the corner and saw a man leaning against the wall outside of her office, she slowed her pace. Something about him seemed familiar.

She came to a dead stop.

It couldn't be ... what was he doing here?

"David?"

He glanced up from his phone, their eyes meeting before he sent her a slow grin. A grin she had once thought of as sexy, one he saved for only her.

Now you know better.

She stayed where she was, eying him warily. "What are you doing here?" Then she sent a quick glance around the hallway. "Are you alone?"

Still smiling, he slipped his phone into his pocket and casually sauntered over to her. His gaze never leaving her face, he reached over to touch her cheek. "I'm here to see you, of course."

When she jerked her head back to avoid his touch, anger crept into his voice. "Hey, coming all this way, I think I deserve a better welcome than this."

She cautiously took a step back. "I'm serious. Why are you here? And why wasn't I informed you were coming?"

He shrugged. "Maybe your father wanted you to be surprised? Heck, if I know. You, of all people, know your father doesn't feel the need to explain his actions. He does what he wants, when he wants."

He glanced over at the door to her office, then back at her. "Can we at least move this into your office instead of standing here in the hallway? What we have to discuss is private."

For a moment, she hesitated. Then, brushing past him him, she unlocked the door and walked into her office. When he followed, reaching over to shut the door, she shook her head. "No, I want the door left open."

An exasperated sigh coming from him, he tossed his briefcase on her desk, trying to curb his annoyance. Things certainly weren't going the way he'd hoped.

Raking his fingers through his hair, following with a heavy sigh. "Okay, I get it. You're still mad about what happened between us. But maybe it's time you let it go. Because it looks like we'll be working together for the next several months."

He paused dramatically, his gaze fixed on her face. "The Regency has been sold."

He waited, watching as she tried to take this in. Even though she was looking right at him, he knew she didn't see him, her mind scrambling to understand.

He cleared his throat. "So, as of right now, as far as your father is concerned, your work here is done. He has already arranged for someone to take your place."

Her voice rose in disbelief. "Wait a minute ... sold? But why? I haven't even been here for a month. There is still so much we need to do. I can't leave now."

He shrugged. "He got an offer he couldn't refuse, Darcey. A very generous offer. And you know how that goes."

He checked the time on his watch, "I believe he's signing the papers to finalize the deal now as we speak. Which means this place is no longer your responsibility. You'll be moving on to the next venture. And you get to do this with me."

A stunned look on her face, she slowly leaned back against her desk.

Venture? What kind of venture? What was he talking about?

She searched his face, trying to understand. "Venture?"

David crossed his arms over his chest. A smug grin on his face, he nodded. "Yep, it looks like you and I are off to the big ol' state of Texas. Where we'll head up the renovation of Hollister's newest acquisition, an outdoor mall desperately in need of a facelift. Evidently, your father sees us as the perfect fit for this job."

He smiled. "The perfect team, I believe his words were."

The silence following this news seemed to go on forever.

This was because Darcey was speechless.

Nothing was making sense.

You don't want to go to Texas. Definitely not with David.

They weren't a team.

And they never would be.

Her silence had David a little angry. And extremely frustrated. He wasn't too keen on this recent development, either. But even though Texas fell pretty close to Ohio on his list of least favorite locations, he was willing to take on the job.

Remember?

For him, this was a double win.

Of course, this all depended on whether Darcey ever decided to forgive him.

But come on, it was about time she forgot about that stupid kiss he shared with Melanie. She has to know it didn't meant anything. He was just having a little fun.

And given the opportunity, what guy wouldn't take advantage of a moment like this?

The way he saw it, if Darcey's father thought they made a good team, this was all that mattered.

Hadn't she once told him, even though her father wasn't the most loving parent, she always respected his decisions?

Well, then ... it was time to prove she still did.

Darcey walked over to the window. Wrapping her arms around herself, she stared out at the courtyard.

How was it, after leaving Jason, her life had taken a sudden turn for the worse, spiraling completely out of control? To the point, she couldn't even think straight.

There was only one thing she was sure of ...

She was not going to Texas with David.

Absolutely not.

Taking her silence as an opportunity to check his phone, David gave a sigh of relief when he found the information he had been waiting for. The phone back in his pocket, he joined Darcey by the window. "I just received a confirmation of our flight to Texas and–"

She whirled around to face him, her angry expression putting a halt to his words. "I'm not going to Texas with you. Not now, not ever. And I am not leaving here until I finish what I started, and I've talked to my father. I need his word the new owners will keep this venue as a party center. I made a promise to the people here, and I will not let them down."

She peered more closely at him. "This Texas thing isn't your idea, is it?"

He shook his head, his look one of disgust. "*God, no.* Do you honestly believe this is something I would want? Come on, Darcey ... you know me better than that. The prospect of spending, who knows how many months in Texas, is not something I'm looking forward to."

He sent her a wry smile. "Not even with you."

Her gaze still on the courtyard, she had no comment.

He sighed. They were wasting time. He wanted to wrap this up, get everything settled and be done with it. This meant he needed to come up with a damn good reason why there was no need for her to stay in Cleveland.

He cleared his throat, nodding towards the courtyard. "Great outdoor space. I imagine it's a popular draw."

"Yes, it is." A wistful smile touched her lips. "But you should have seen it a couple of weeks ago. It was a mess." She sent him an accusing glance. "Just one of the many improvements I've helped make possible."

He sighed, moving closer. "Darcey, you're taking this too personally. You know better than to do this. The goal of Hollister Industries is to take on a property, make it look brand new, and turn it over for a profit. Then you move on."

She was shaking her head. "It's not only The Regency. There is so much more about this place, this city, that I love."

Like Jason. Especially Jason. The real reason you're even here.

And now, he was even more of the reason she didn't want to leave.

David's deep groan, maybe leaning even more towards a growl, should have been a hint of what he was planning.

Instead, Darcey was totally unprepared when he pulled her against him. His hand cupping her chin in a tight hold, his mouth came dangerously close to hers. "I think I know the way to make you forget about this place. And this musician guy, this Jason … or whatever the hell his name is. Come on, Darcey … I promise I can give you so much more than he ever could."

Musician guy? How does he know about Jason?

But before she could ask, his mouth came crashing down on hers in a kiss that was commanding, brutal. It was his attempt to ease the frustration of knowing she didn't want him. While at the same time, prove to her she did.

When Darcey struggled against him, he lifted her higher against him, his kiss becoming even more demanding.

In a panic, she closed her eyes and, giving a low moan, went completely limp in his arms. Her hope was this would fool him into thinking she was surrendering to the kiss.

It did.

He relaxed his hold, his breath brushing across her jaw in a satisfied sigh. "*Ah*, baby … nothing's changed between us. You still want this as much as I do."

In disbelief, she opened her eyes.

Nothing's changed? Was he crazy?

When he lowered his head to kiss her again, she pressed her hands against his chest, turning her face away. This was when a sudden movement caught her eye.

Jason …

He was standing in the doorway.

And for what had to be less than a millisecond, their eyes met.

Then he was gone.

Oh no, no, no, no … this couldn't be happening.

Darcey was frantically trying to untangle herself from David's arms, but he only tightened his grip. So, using every bit of strength she had, she pushed as hard as she could, shoving him up against the window.

He almost lost his balance. After letting out a loud curse, he grabbed her arm, refusing to let go. "What the hell? What are you trying to do, kill me?"

Breaking his hold on her arm, she headed for the door with him right behind her. He was furious. "Darcey, get back in here. Right now."

She didn't hear a word he said. Already out the door, she was searching the hallway.

It was empty. There was no Jason.

It was as if he had completely disappeared.

With a strangled sob, she ran back into her office. Frantically searching her desk for her phone, she finally found it and hit Jason's number.

Her call went to his voicemail.

She leaned against her desk, and staring down at her phone, she tried to stop the sobs rising in her throat.

She needed to talk to him.

Convince him what he saw wasn't what he thought.

You mean like how David tried to convince you nothing happened with Melanie?

And suddenly, she was so afraid. She didn't even want to think about how this time she may have lost Jason for good.

Warily eying Darcey, David was keeping his distance. He wasn't happy about this new turn of events. This wasn't the Darcey he knew.

You swear, this is getting worse by the minute. Texas isn't looking all that bad right now.

Massaging his arm, seriously wondering if she may have injured it, he cleared his throat. "Darcey?"

She glanced over at him, her expression blank. When he saw she was shaking, he cautiously moved towards her.

"Hey, are you okay?"

She stared at him, incredulous.

Are you okay? No, of course you're not okay. Nothing is okay. And if you lose Jason, nothing will ever be okay again.

She shook her head. "No … no, I'm not okay. I … well …" Another sob rising in her throat, she took in a deep breath. "I think it would be best if you leave. Please, I mean this. There is no reason for you to stay. I've already made it quite clear I won't be going to Texas with you."

Her voice faltered momentarily before she gained control. "So, please, just leave. I need to be alone, I need to think."

Instead, he moved closer. "Come on, Darcey. Be reasonable. You know this isn't where you belong. Your home is in California. I need you… your father needs you. You know damn well this plan of your father's is only his way of protecting you."

An uneasy feeling began building inside of her.

Plan? What kind of plan? And protect you from what?

Why was it everyone seemed to know what was going on except for her?

First Rob and now David. And the key Rob gave you? What does the key have to do with all of this?

She peered up at David.

If he knew something, he'd tell you, wouldn't he?

The searching look Darcey was giving him had David uncomfortable. But ever since Darcey's father called him into his office late last night, handing him the plane ticket to Cleveland, he felt like he was part of something he didn't understand. Whatever was going on between Darcey and her father went a lot deeper than his concern about her dating some guy in a band.

Cramming his hands in his pockets, he rocked on his heels. Now he was getting nervous.

Darcey didn't even notice this. She was more interested in finding out if he knew more than he was letting on. She held his gaze. "I'm confused. What plan, David? And what is my father protecting me from? The man I love?"

He gave a short laugh. "The man you love? Do you really think this Jason is the right guy for you?" He gave an amused snort. "You need someone stable. Someone who can give you the life you're used to."

Irritated, she moved away from him, wrapping her arms around herself. "You don't even know him. So, you have no right to make that kind of judgement."

"I'm sorry, but I have to agree with your father on this." He shrugged. "After all, you've only known this guy for what, not even a month?"

She slowly shook her head. "I met Jason three years ago when I came here with my father. I had hoped to talk him out of putting my grandparent's house up for sale. But he eventually sold it. I got to meet the couple who own it now. They've already started renovating it, so it's all good."

He leaned against the desk, crossing his arms over his chest. "So, why didn't you try to make a go of it with this Jason back then?"

She avoided his gaze. "It's complicated."

"Come on, Darcey. If he was 'the one', don't you think you would have found a way to make it work?"

He nodded. "A long-distance relationship or whatever."

She hesitated, doubt filling her face. "That was the plan. I called him when I got back to California, but he never called me back."

He raised an eyebrow.

She scowled. "Don't give me that look. There had to be a good explanation for this. Maybe I missed his call, or..."

Her voice trailing off, she tilted her head, a look of disbelief slowly filling her face.

Almost running over to her desk, her fingers began flying over the keyboard of her computer. She was mumbling to herself. *"Oh no, no, no, no ... please tell me I'm wrong."*

Puzzled, David watched all of this. "I don't understand, what are you doing?" Just when he thought she wasn't going to answer, she looked up at him. "I need to go home. My father and I need to talk."

He groaned, dragging his hand back through his hair. "You're kidding, right? You really aren't going to fly home, are you?"

The look she gave him was enough for him to realize this is exactly what she was planning to do. And nothing he could say would change her mind.

His mood now at the absolute lowest it could go, he turned on his heel and stormed out of the room.

It now appeared he would be traveling to Texas alone.

And he still hadn't had his coffee.

CHAPTER 31

Even if I have a hundred reasons to leave you,
I'll find that one reason to fight for you.
~ Anonymously Yours

Jason turned his SUV out of The Regency parking lot.

It wasn't until he was almost a mile down the road, he realized he was headed in the wrong direction.

He groaned, dragging his hand through his hair.

You need to get it together. Seriously, you probably shouldn't even be driving.

A sign for a local community park caught his eye. He pulled in and found a parking space. Resting his arms on the steering wheel, he stared out at the lake.

He let out another groan, dropping his head down on his arms.

You are a fool, Jason Bennett ... a damn fool.

What was it they said? Once bitten, twice shy?

Yeah, you got bit, all right.

Twice, this happened. By the same person.

So, now you're done.

For good.

He couldn't believe how awful he felt. Like he was drowning in a pool of anger. His heart was still pounding so hard in his chest, he'd swear it was going to explode. He wanted to strike out at something... anything ... if only to ease the pain.

A harsh laugh rising in his throat, he lifted his head. Maybe he should consider this as material for a new song? Yeah, the kind of song he had hoped he would no longer need to write.

You know the type, broken hearts and betrayal in every line.

Yeah, maybe you should switch over to country. You certainly have the material. Up close and personal.

When Abby had called him a short time ago, the last thing he'd expected her to ask was if he knew Darcey was engaged.

No, you did not know this. In fact, thinking it was possible you hadn't understood what she said, you had asked her to repeat it.

So she did.

David Hanson ...

Thanks to Abby, he even knew the guy's name. A name now ingrained in his memory.

From what she told him, she met this fiancé of Darcey's when she dropped off a cookie order at the party center. He had stopped her to ask directions to Darcey's office. Immediately becoming suspicious, she had fired a ton of questions at him. His answers were very vague, only volunteering that his visit was regarding a personal matter.

And, this is the biggie here ... he was also Darcey's fiancé.

Now he wasn't sure if this was Abby's attempt to make him feel better, but this is when she told him she got terrible vibes from the guy. She didn't like him at all. Very arrogant and condescending, she would have to say.

She had then shared every detail of their encounter.

But, still reeling from the news Darcey was engaged, his mind had almost completely shut down. So, everything she told him was pretty much a hit or miss. That he remembered anything at all was a miracle.

And there was really only one thing that mattered ...

Darcey was engaged.

And how had he responded to this news?

Like the fool he was when it concerned Darcey, the second he ended the call with Abby, he had headed straight for The Regency. His intention was to casually drop in on Darcey. If only to tell her how much he missed her.

While, at the same time, he'd straighten out what was surely only a simple misunderstanding.

But that hadn't happened, had it?

Dropping his head down on his arms again, he squeezed his eyes shut as hard as he could. But this couldn't shut out the scene he'd witnessed in Darcey's office.

It was there he'd found this David Hanson and Darcey locked in an embrace that could easily fit the requirements for a cover of one of those erotic novels women like to read. Hell, stamp the words passion and desire all over it and you'd have a best seller.

Yeah, but unfortunately, at your expense ...

And Darcey? She appeared to be thoroughly enjoying her time in David's arms, reacting to his kiss with a passion that had her clinging to him for support.

Yeah, it definitely looked like a kiss that meant a lot more than a simple hello.

For both of them.

So ... there had to be some kind of mistake, right?

Yes, it's true Darcey had told him she was in a relationship at one time. But she had given him the impression she didn't want to share any of the details. So, he had changed the subject. As far as he was concerned, this was in the past, and had nothing to do with them.

But engaged? Hell, even the word alone — *engaged* — hadn't made it into one of their conversations. Not once.

This didn't mean it hadn't been on his mind. Because it had. The more time they spent together, the more he liked the idea of a ring on her finger, a future with her.

You know, getting married, kids, the works.

He dropped his head down on the steering wheel again.

Again, you're a fool, Jason Bennett. A complete fool.

Abruptly lifting his head, he gazed out at the lake.

Wait a minute ... was she having second thoughts about her engagement? Using her time here in Cleveland as an opportunity to compare you and this David before she made her decision?

What? Are you gone completely nuts? And if this was true, would you be all right with it?

He frowned, scowling at the thought of this.

After the weekend they spent together, there shouldn't be any hesitation regarding who she belonged with.

Frustrated, he slammed his hand down on the steering wheel. He never should've gone to the party center after he got the call from Abby. Even on his drive there, he had the feeling he was making a mistake.

A big mistake.

He should have let things alone, thought out more carefully how to address this.

Have you ever heard of the phrase ignorance is bliss?

Well, Jason would be the first to tell you this was what he should have gone with. Beginning with ignoring Abby's call. Then he wouldn't be feeling so rotten right now, what David said to Darcey still so clear in his mind.

> "Ah, baby ... *nothing's changed*
> *between us ... You still want this as*
> *much as I do."*

Yeah… he certainly needed no more proof than this, did he?

His phone rang again. And as he had responded to the many other times it had rung in the past fifteen minutes, he reached over and shut it off.

But this time, he went one step further.

He turned off the phone completely.

He was in no shape to talk to anyone right now.

This included Darcey.

Especially Darcey.

He opened the SUV windows and turned on the audio. After he

gave the command for easy listening classical, he rested his head back against the seat and closed his eyes. With the sound of the waves carrying the beat, the music floated over him, through him, soothing him.

This is what music could do for him. At least in the past, this had worked.

He desperately needed to forget.

If only for a little while.

Fast forward seven hours.

His hands cradling the earphones against his ears, Jason sank every ounce of feeling into his voice. Coming to the last line of the song, he held the last note through the refrain until they both faded into silence.

His eyes closed, he remained completely still for a long moment. Then, after slowly removing the earphones, he glanced around the studio.

The tension was undeniable, everyone in the room holding their breath. He knew they were all hoping this last take made the cut and they could finally call it a day.

And you are the reason for this.

The studio manager leaned back in his chair, his voice coming out loud in the silence. "It looks like we've finally nailed it. As soon as our guys work their magic, adjusting the audio quality and making sure everything matches up, we should be good to go."

Slowly hauling himself out of the chair, he gave a long stretch before he glanced around the room, a smile finally appearing on his face. "Time to go home."

He shot a look over at Jason. "Was a tough one today, Jazz. You seemed to struggle, you weren't your usual self. Of course, it didn't help you showed up over an hour late."

Jason raised his hand to everyone. "Yeah ... I know. Thanks, guys. Don't know what my problem was. Just wasn't my day, I guess."

He grabbed his jacket, his intention to leave.

Paul came over to him. Shrugging into his coat, he was shaking his head. "Man, that was ugly, Jazz ... but I think it's still a go."

He hesitated, searching Jason's face. "How about we stop at The Home Plate for a burger and a beer? Sasha has her girl's night out, so I'm on my own."

"I don't think so." Jason picked up his jacket.

After how his day had gone, he wanted to go home, where he could get away from everyone, everything.

You just want to be alone ...

Paul persisted. "Come on... something tells me any plans you had for tonight were cancelled. And you gotta eat."

He started for the exit. "I'll meet you there."

He turned, relieved to see Jason was following right behind him.

Something was wrong. And he'd be willing to bet it had to do with Darcey. It could be his imagination, but since he was getting pretty good at sensing these things, he doubted this. Whatever it was, he was going to find out.

What better way to do this than over a burger and a beer?

Paul took a long drink of his beer before he set the bottle back on the bar. Wrapping his hands around it, he glanced over at Jason.

He wondered how long it was going to take before he finally broke down and said something ... anything.

So far, the only words out of his mouth had been to order a beer and the house burger.

And now he had completely zoned into the big screen TV over the bar. Turned on to the weather channel, from what Paul could see, there was a hurricane somewhere out in the Pacific.

The weather channel? There had to be a better choice.

He yelled over at the bartender. "Hey, Chuck ... can't you put on something more interesting than the weather? How about the game?"

After the pre-game highlights came up on the screen, Paul glanced over at Jason again.

He sighed. "Are you going to tell me what happened?"

Jason lifted the bottle to his mouth and took a drink before he set it back on the bar. Tracing the label on the bottle with his thumbs, he avoided Paul's gaze. "It turns out Darcey is engaged, to some guy from California. David Hanson is his name. Evidently, this is something she didn't think would be important enough to share with me."

Paul was relieved the server chose this time to deliver their burgers. This was because he had absolutely no idea what to say about what Jason just told him.

Engaged? What the ...?

It was only after he'd poured enough ketchup on his fries to choke a horse — Sasha's description, not his — he shot a glance over at Jason. "How'd you find this out?"

Gingerly removing the lettuce from his burger and placing it as far away from his plate as he could, something that never failed to amuse Paul, he shrugged. "Let's just say I walked in on them in Darcey's office this morning. They were so busy getting re-acquainted, at first they didn't notice I was there."

Paul nearly choked on his burger.

What exactly does he mean by getting re-acquainted? Sure doesn't sound like a good thing to you.

He cleared his throat. "I think you need to back up and start from the beginning. Because the picture you've planted in my mind is not a very good one. At least not for you."

Jason nodded ... a slow nod. "Yep, you've got that right. Not good for me at all."

Finishing his beer, he motioned to the bartender to bring another round for both of them.

He then told Paul everything, starting with Abby's phone call and ending when he walked into Darcey's office to find her with David Hanson, the man he now knew as her fiancé.

Finished, he shoved his plate away. Throwing his napkin on what was left of his burger, his voice was weary. "So, there you have it, the whole story."

Paul was silent.

Thinking he hadn't made his case, Jason was quick to add. "Abby checked him out. He's a lawyer, works for Hollister. And as we all know, lawyer trumps musician."

Paul snorted. "Hell, you are way off with that. Anyone can be a lawyer … where it takes talent to be a musician. But what you're telling me about Darcey? I don't buy it."

He shook his head. "It makes little sense, none of it. I can't see Darcey doing something like this. You talked to her, didn't you? What did she have to say?"

Jason wasn't sure he wanted to discuss this. He was now regretting he hadn't confronted Darcey when he had the chance. Asked her right out what was going on. There were also the phone calls he was refusing to take.

But this is because you're afraid of what she'll tell you.

"No, I haven't talked to her." His sigh was heavy. "I'm not very proud of how I just took off. But, it's probably for the best, because who knows what I might have said." He briefly closed his eyes. "Or how she may have responded."

Paul was thinking Jason had a lot to learn.

Again, he wasn't an expert on relationships, but the way Jason was handling this certainly wouldn't bring him and Darcey back together.

He shot a glance over at him. "Jazz, you've got to talk to her. I haven't been married all that long, but I've learned you can't hold things in. Talk, talk, talk … this is what you need to do. You run, you lose."

Suddenly curious, he decided why not ask. "You never told me … why did she leave the first time?"

Draining the last of his beer, Jason slowly set the bottle back on the bar. It was only after he centered it perfectly on the coaster, he spoke. "We had an argument. The only one we had. But it was a big one. I don't know how we got on the subject, but it came out she didn't want kids. She told me after watching her parents fight all the time and the messy divorce that followed, she didn't want to take the chance of this happening with us."

He paused, deep in thought.

He could still remember ... no matter how hard he had tried to re-assure her, with them it would be different, she'd refused to listen.

Hurt she didn't believe him, he had then accused her of not trusting him.

Something he wished he had never done.

Because the next morning when he woke up?

She was gone.

He glanced over at Paul, wearily shaking his head. "After she left, she called me once. I called her back, only to have the pleasure of talking to her father instead."

He shoved the beer bottle away, a controlled anger in his voice. "And I use the word 'pleasure' sarcastically. Let's just say he gave me every reason to believe I would never be good enough for his daughter."

He shot a sharp glance over at Paul. "Darcey doesn't know I talked to her father. And I plan to keep it that way."

Paul didn't agree with this. "Maybe you should change your way of thinking. Or have another conversation with the guy. Come on, Jazz... He shouldn't be the one to decide her future. It sounds like he might be the root of the problem."

At Jason's frown, he patted him on the shoulder. "Think about it. But right now? I'm beat... ready to call it a night. Remember, we have another session at the studio tomorrow at nine. Try to show up on time, ok?"

Avoiding Jason's murderous glance, he pulled out his wallet and, after throwing some bills on the bar, he sent Jason a nod. "Until tomorrow ..."

Jason stayed a while longer, watching a few innings of the game on TV.

And why shouldn't he?

He had no reason to go home.

The first thing Jason noticed when he turned on his kitchen light was the bottle of wine on the kitchen counter.

He had bought it from the little wine shop down the street, spending more time than usual picking it out. This was because he wanted everything to be perfect for the dinner he had promised Darcey tonight.

This is when it hit him. And it hit him hard.

She's gone.

Digging his phone out of his pocket, he sank down on the sofa. Almost reluctantly, he started scrolling down through his messages.

Darcey had called four times. It was only after her last call, she finally left a voice message.

His finger hovering over the phone, he finally hit speaker, her voice filling the room.

She was crying.

A sudden tightness in his throat, he rested his head against the sofa cushions and closed his eyes.

> *"Jason, I know you aren't picking up*
> *your phone because you don't want to*
> *talk to me. And I don't blame you. But*
> *I want you to know, no matter what*
> *you think, there is nothing...*
> *absolutely nothing, going on between*
> *David and me. This I promise you.*
> *I wish you would have stayed,*
> *given me a chance to explain.*
> *I had also hoped to talk to you before I*
> *left. But I guess this message will have*
> *to do, if you're even listening right*
> *now.*
> *Oh, Jason... I hope you are."*

In the long silence that followed, he leaned in closer to the phone.

She was leaving again? Was she coming back?

Relieved, he sank back against the cushions when she spoke again. She was still crying.

*"I think I know what happened after
I left the last time, the reason I never
got your call. And I think I know why
David came to Cleveland. But I need
to find out if I'm right.
I don't know when, but I promise I'll
be back. Hopefully, you're still
listening to this message and when I
return, you'll at least hear what I have
to say."*

There was another long pause before she spoke again.

*"If you don't, I don't know what
I'll do. I love you, Jason. I will always
love you."*

In the silence that followed, he didn't move.

It was a fire truck, siren blaring as it went racing past his house, that finally had him opening his eyes.

Wearily rising from the sofa, he turned out the light.

Yeah, he knew it was only a little past ten, but he was exhausted.

He was going to bed.

It was after a few long and restless hours later, he realized he wasn't going to get much sleep. Not as long as the same damn words kept running over and over in his head.

"So, I don't know when, but I promise I'll be back."

It appeared this promise she gave him was one he wouldn't be able to let go.

But she already left you once before. How can you believe this time it will be different?

It was simple.

He loved her.

And now?

He couldn't believe how much he already missed her.

So, he really didn't have much of a choice, did he?

CHAPTER 32

Making just one person smile can change the world.
Maybe not the whole world, but their world.
~ Anonymous

Over two thousand miles away, Darcey was fastening her seat belt for landing at the LAX airport.

From her window seat, she had a clear view of Los Angeles. Traffic was heavy, the brake lights of the bumper to bumper traffic turning the winding highways into ribbons of red.

Her forehead resting against the window, she closed her eyes.

She was running on pure adrenaline.

And now, with all the time she had to think during the five-hour flight, she was wondering if she had acted a little too impulsively.

Because as it stood right now, she was pretty sure everyone was mad at her. And if they weren't?

They soon would be … just give them time.

But there was only one person whose opinion mattered … and this would be Jason.

Her eyes tearing up, as they had every other time she thought about him, she tried not to cry, gulping back a sob.

Yeah, the poor guy next to you has been a nervous wreck the entire flight because of your emotional state.

Sending him what she hoped came across as a reassuring smile, she turned her gaze back to the window.

She hoped she was doing the right thing.

Right after she had made her flight reservations, she met with the confident and knowledgeable woman her father set up as her replacement. Then she had to do the same thing all over again with the new chef and event planner.

The rest of the day had passed in a blur. It wasn't until late afternoon she gave them the news, because of personal reasons, she was going out of town and wouldn't be returning until the end of the week.

If you return at all ...

Waving aside their shocked protests, reminding them as a team they were more than qualified to keep the venue running smoothly, she left.

Her mouth twisted into a wry smile. Her father would be proud of how she handled the situation.

It was when she walked into her apartment, greeted by the sight of all the boxes still waiting to be unpacked, the reality of what happened hit her full force.

Your life is a mess. You no longer have a job and, you no longer have Jason.

And she couldn't stop crying.

Brushing away another tear, she watched as the plane drew closer to landing. She fingered the ring hanging from the chain around her neck.

She brought it to her lips and, closing her eyes, said a prayer that Jason had listened to her voicemail.

Please, God ... let him believe what you promised him.

After traveling up the long winding driveway leading to the headquarters of Hollister Industries, the taxi pulled up to the main entrance. Even though it was after eight in the evening, Darcey saw there were lights shining from the corner windows of the top floor.

But this didn't surprise her. This was where her father's office was located, right next to the office of his long-time assistant, June Miller. It was a well-known fact her father always stayed late, and he expected June to do the same.

Yes, this was the same June who had explained the facts of life to Darcey when she was a teenager.

June had been with the company for over twenty years. She was the person who made sure everything ran smoothly in the everyday life of Steven Hollister. Both personal and business related. Darcey couldn't even imagine what her father would do without her calming presence.

After Darcey ran her I.D. card through the lockbox to activate the main doors, she took the elevator upstairs. She hurried down the long hallway to find the door to June's office was partially open.

She cleared her throat to get her attention.

June glanced up from her computer. A smile lighting up her face, she came around her desk to give Darcey a hug. "Darcey, I can't believe you're here. David called earlier to give his version of what happened, but we heard nothing from you. So, we've been so worried."

Darcey searched her face.

We've been so worried? Was your father part of this 'we'?

She seriously doubted this. She'd be willing to bet worried was low on her father list of what he was feeling right now.

Furious would be your first guess. Followed by that slow, disappointed and negative head shake of his.

She gave June another hug. "Oh, June … I'm so sorry. I know it looks like I've handled this all wrong. But I'm having a hard time trying to understand my father's reasoning. I have so many questions, I felt like I needed to speak with him, face to face."

June smiled. "Well, you know where to find him. He was in a terrible mood earlier, but now he seems tired, almost defeated." At Darcey's worried look, she shook her head. "I don't think it's all because of you. There's something deeper going on. But whatever it is, he doesn't want to talk about it."

She sighed. "I wish he would confide in me. I hate seeing him like this."

Her head tilted, Darcey studied her for a few seconds before she responded. "Can I ask you something?"

June nodded.

"Why have you stayed so long? My gosh, June … you've been with the company for over twenty years, twenty-four-seven. You need to live your own life instead of letting my father monopolize … "

Her voice drifted off at the look of longing in June's eyes. This told her all she needed to know.

She blurted it out. "*Oh my gosh*, you're in love with him, aren't you? Does he know this?"

A look of panic filling her face, June vehemently shook her head. "No, and he never will. Darcey, please promise you won't say anything."

Darcey was confused. "But what if he feels the same way?" She grinned. "I mean, come on … he must. If he didn't, you would have been gone a long, long time ago. Why, you're the only one who can tell him what to do and get away with it."

She nodded. "Everyone here sees how differently he treats you. You're in on every decision he makes. Even the big ones."

A brief spark of hope flashed in June's eyes before she shook her head. "No, I don't want him to know how I feel. Imagine how uncomfortable it would be for both of us if he didn't feel the same. I would have to leave. And if that happened, I don't know what I would do."

Darcey wasn't buying this. "But imagine how wonderful it would be if he did?" She laughed. "I bet he does, but he's clueless. I think all men are slow to catch on when it comes to falling in love. They miss all the signs."

She frowned. "At least this is what I've found out so far." A determined look on her face, she headed for the door.

She stopped to send June a big smile. "This discussion isn't over …

we'll finish it later. But right now, I need to talk to my father. I need answers."

She paused by the door, shaking her head. "You and my father. I can't believe I didn't see this coming."

"Darcey ..."

But June's desperate plea came too late. After blowing her a kiss, Darcey was gone.

Once she returned to her desk, June stared down at her hands. They were shaking. But then she was shaking all over.

She was scared to death. But at the same time?

She couldn't stop smiling.

Steven Hollister was a worried man.

An emotion he wasn't all that familiar with.

His hands clasped behind his back, he was gazing out his office window. Night or day, the panoramic view never ceased to amaze him. It calmed him.

But tonight? The photo worthy view just wasn't doing it for him. Too much was happening, leaving him feeling weary. Defeated even. Bringing him to question his life, wondering if he was going about it the wrong way.

And now there was this latest dilemma with Darcey. Yes, he was well aware she was a grown woman, having proved she could take care of herself. But ever since she took on The Regency project, he felt her priorities had changed. He feared she was heading right back into another no-win situation.

And he wasn't going to stand by and watch her get hurt again.

He frowned, jamming his hands in his pockets.

You know this is exactly what will happen if she's involved with that musician again.

That Rob Johnson had flat out refused to give him any insight on this had confirmed his suspicion she already was.

He was still smarting from Rob's sarcastic remark. That his job description didn't include babysitting for someone's grown daughter.

You didn't ask him to babysit, you only wanted him to make sure Darcey stayed focused on her job. Not the same thing at all.

He sighed, raking his hand through his hair. Ok, so maybe it was almost the same. But he would always think of Darcey as his little girl, ready to protect her when the need arose.

So, when he received the more than generous offer for the party center, at almost the same time the deal on the outdoor mall in Texas went through, he saw this as the answer to his problems.

And then there was David ...

Again, he shook his head.

Until a few hours ago, he had been banking on David's help. An excellent lawyer, personable and quick thinking, he and Darcey had made a great team.

He frowned. At least this used to be the case until they had some kind of misunderstanding a few months back. But he had hoped once they got started on this new Texas project, they would be able to work things out between them.

Instead, David was already in Texas, alone.

And Darcey's whereabouts were unknown.

That she wasn't answering her phone wasn't like her. Nor was she one to take off without sharing her plans.

Not until she met up with this musician.

So, this explained why he was so worried.

"Hello?"

At this tentative greeting, Steven turned to find Darcey standing only a few feet away. Briefly closing his eyes, he felt some of the tension roll off his body

But, as a man who was accustomed to keeping his emotions in check, his greeting was brief and to the point.

He cleared his throat. "Well, this is a surprise. We've been wondering if we would ever see you again."

Thinking she must have imagined the flicker of relief in his eyes, Darcey made her way over to him, pressing a kiss to his cheek.

She sighed, running her hand through her hair. "I'm sorry I didn't return any of your calls. But I'm sure you can understand how busy I've been, tying up loose ends and showing the new staff everything they need to know about running the party center."

Her expression turned accusing. "What made you decide to sell The Regency? Before I could finish what I started? This is such a busy time, with the Moonlight Madness Masquerade Ball coming up this weekend. A huge fund raiser, everything needs to go without a hitch." She frowned. "Everyone was counting on me to be there to help make this happen."

As Darcey expected, her father slipped right back into his business mode. "When the chance at a profitable business deal drops in your lap, it can't be ignored, Darcey. The offer we received was more generous than expected, and we would have been foolish to turn it down. The buyer is a local woman who has more money than she knows what to do with. So, before she could change her mind, we accepted the offer."

Her hand flying to her mouth, Darcey smiled. "Elenore Cromley … why am I not surprised?"

If only for a second, an actual smile touched her father's lips. "I take it you've met her. Definitely a woman with a good head for business. I am confident, after the long list of demands we gave us, The Regency couldn't be in better hands."

Hesitant to bring up what they really needed to talk about, a silence fell between them.

Turning back to the window, it was her father who spoke first. "I know about the baby."

Baby, what baby?

Confused, Darcey searched his face. "The baby? I don't understand … what do you mean?"

Jamming his hands deep in his pockets, he turned so swiftly, so much anger radiating from him, she took a step back.

She slowly shook her head. "I don't under–"

He interrupted her. "It was shortly after we returned from the trip we made to Cleveland three years ago. I came into your office and you were on your phone. You had your back to me, so you didn't know I was there."

He began to pace, obviously extremely agitated. "In your conversation you said even though you were upset about the baby, what happened was for the best. It was all taken care of and there was no reason to worry anymore."

Darcey was frantic. "But ..."

He held up his hand, a command for silence. "Let me finish. When you ended the call, my intention was to confront you about what I heard, but you ran out of the room, crying. You had left your phone on your desk, so, when it rang, I answered it. It was Jason. I lost it, tearing into him about his lack of morals, his involvement with you ... everything."

He shook his head." The one thing I didn't share with him was the news about the baby. I almost started to, but realized he could use this to his advantage. Then, before I ended the call, I warned him to never call you again."

Agitatedly running his hand through his hair, his expression was one of total disbelief. "And now you're back with him? What are you thinking?"

In shock, Darcey had sat down in one of the chairs in front of his desk. She could see he wasn't going to stop until he had his say. So she merely shook her head.

He continued to pace, the tone of his voice more desperate than angry. "Had I known Jason had ties to the party center, I never would've consented to you heading up the renovations. But, by the time I found this out, it was too late to make a change. I asked Rob Johnson to keep an eye on things. But he refused, this giving me even more reason to worry. So, when the offer for The Regency came in, I took it."

His pacing coming to a stop, he leveled his gaze at her. "He is never going to change, Darcey. This is the way these guys work. I should know, since I saw the exact same thing happen with your mother. She left me for some guy in a band. I tried to stop her, suggesting we go to a marriage counselor. Anything, I would have done anything to keep us together, but she wouldn't listen. But when things started to get nasty, I backed off, my only concern to protect you and your brother."

Briefly closing his eyes, he shook his head. "And to this day, I have no idea where she is or if she is even okay. So, I don't care how old you are, I will not stand by and let you ruin your life because of this guy."

Like a child, Darcey put her hands to her ears, vigorously shaking her head. "Please, you need to stop … please, just listen to me."

She dropped her hands in her lap, unaware she had begun to cry. "It wasn't Jason I was talking to, it was Olivia, my roommate from college. She was the one who was pregnant, not me. She was frantic, knowing her parents would be horrified. I tried to persuade her not to make any quick decisions, but she didn't listen. If that had been me and Jason was the father, I never would have resorted to that. Never."

She took in a big, gulping breath. "*Oh my god* … I couldn't understand why Jason never called me back. I realized I had made a mistake by leaving him and I wanted to tell him this. But as time went by and he still hadn't returned my call, I tried to accept he had moved on."

She pulled the necklace out from where it was hidden under her shirt. "Jason gave me this ring, but I lost it. Then, out of the blue, Livy sent it to me. When it came on the same day you sent me The Regency listing to look over, I took this as a sign. Maybe even after all this time, Jason and I still had a chance. So, this was why I pushed for The Regency sale."

Her father's head jerked up. "A ring?"

She nodded. "It's a promise ring. Livy found it in the foyer of grandparent's house."

He sat on the edge of his desk, a bewildered look on his face. "Darcey, what does my parent's house have to do with all of this? And how did the ring get there? I think it would be best if you start from the beginning and tell me exactly what happened."

So, she did.

Beginning with the promise Jason made when he gave her the ring. And ending with Jason's reaction when he walked in on her and David at The Regency.

She grabbed a tissue and swiped at another tear sliding down her face. "After David told me about your plans for Texas, I knew a phone call wouldn't do. I needed to discuss this with you in person." She shrugged. "So, here I am."

For a few minutes, there was only silence in the room. It was only when Darcey blew her nose, her father slowly began shaking his head.

Pushing away from the desk, he pulled her into a hug. A deep sadness filled his voice. "*Ah*, Darcey ... I don't even know what to say, because I'm sorry doesn't seem like enough. What I did was completely out of line, goldilocks. When I found out Jason was a musician, I guess it hit too close to home. And in the process, I almost let my own bitterness ruin your life."

He gave a long, drawn out sigh. "I think it's time for me to let go of all this anger I've been carrying around for so long. Before it turns me into a lonely and bitter old man."

Darcey lifted her head to smile at him. "Goldilocks ... that's what you called me when I was little." Pain flashed across her face. "But then everything changed..."

His hands going to her shoulders, he held her gaze. "I know I can't change the past, but I'm going to try my best to fix what I broke. But this will happen only if you can look me in the eye and convince me this Jason is the man you really want."

Darcey's brilliant smile said it all. "Yes, Jason is the only man for me. If he still wants me. After all, I've already left him twice." Her brow creased with worry. "I need to return to Cleveland. I promised him I'd be back to explain. I can only hope he will listen to me."

Then she smiled. "Does this mean I get my job back at The Regency? With the new staff finally in place, I'll be free to move on with all of my plans. At least until Elenore Cromley decides what she wants to do."

He nodded. This was the Darcey he knew. "Well, since I've always been big on finishing what you start, how can I say no?" His smile was wry. "Even though I failed to do this with this last move I made."

She reached over to give him a big hug. "I forgive you, I really do.

And I guess I understand why you did what you did. Someday you'll have to tell me the whole story."

He nodded. "I will. Both you and your brother."

Suddenly feeling better than he had in a long time, he glanced down at his watch. "Now, have you had dinner?"

She studied him, her gaze thoughtful. "Can I take a rain check until tomorrow? What I'd really like to do right now is crash. I'm exhausted. But I have a suggestion for you. It's about something you should have done a long time ago. Involving someone you've ignored for far too long."

His expression was wary. "Ignored? Who could I have possibly ignored?"

She smiled. "I think it's about time you make your move and ask June out. Starting tonight, for dinner. I have a feeling, if you do, you will make her the happiest woman in the world."

The shocked look on his face was almost comical. "June? Oh, Darcey ... I don't know about that. Yeah, we're comfortable with each other, but a relationship? I'm not sure this would be a good idea."

Darcey was grinning. "Come on, look at it this way ... she probably knows you better than anyone else on the planet. This means you already have the 'getting to know each other' out of the way. And since I'd be willing to bet she is very attracted to you, what more could you want?"

He had slowly begun to smile. "Attracted to me. You really think so?"

She nodded. "Yes, I do. But, don't think so hard. Just do it, okay?" She pressed a kiss to his cheek and was gone. Leaving him thinking about what she said.

June, huh?

He was tempted.

So tempted ...

After Darcey stopped by her office to say goodnight, June glanced down at her watch.

It was almost nine, time to go home. Where, once again, she would be alone.

But this was okay, she had no reason to complain.

She had a very full and happy life. A nice home, lots of friends and a great job.

So, what more did she need?

Or, maybe it's more like what more do you want?

Thinking back to her conversation with Darcey, her gaze drifted towards Steven's office.

Don't even go there. You know it's only a dream, nothing more.

Quickly slipping into her coat, she headed for the door. While at the same time she began searching through her purse for her keys.

And she ran head on into Steven.

She let out a loud shriek, and stumbling back from him, she lost her balance. He grabbed her arms to steady her, this leaving her face only inches away from his crisp, white shirtfront. In all the years they had worked together, she had never once been this close to him.

More embarrassed than she had ever been in her life, even more so because this was happening with him, she closed her eyes, a soft moan escaping her.

This faint sound threw Steven for a loop. A vaguely familiar heat racing through him, this brought an immediate response from an important part of his anatomy. Something that hadn't happened for longer than he cared to admit.

Even more confusing, instead of backing away, like the gentleman he thought he was, he tightened his hold on her.

He simply did not want to let go.

This had June even more flustered, thinking his reaction was because he was irritated with her. And she couldn't blame him. After all, she was the one who hadn't been paying attention, plowing right into him.

Her intention to apologize, she gazed up at him.

Their eyes locked, and for an unknown minute, or two ... or maybe even three, they didn't move.

This was because Steven was thinking about how right she felt in his arms, wondering why he hadn't thought of doing this before.

While June was desperately trying to regain her composure.

She finally took a deep breath, her intention to apologize. "I am so, *so* sorry. I wasn't expecting you, or anyone else, to sneak up on me like that."

A horrified look came over her face. "Not sneak... oh no, I'm not insinuating you would do something like that. It could have been anyone. Though it's late. And we are here alone."

She began wringing her hands. "Not completely alone. The cleaning people are also here, somewhere. And I'm sure they've seen a lot more than we could imagine."

She groaned. "Not that I'm suggesting there's something to see ..."

What are you doing? Just ... stop ... talking...

When she had finally calmed down enough to gaze up at him, she was surprised by his smile. It was a genuine smile, traveling all the way into his eyes.

He also looked confused.

And this is exactly what he was ... an amazed, surprised and totally bowled over, kind of confused. With everything hitting him at once, he wasn't sure how the hell to react.

He was definitely struggling.

It had been a long time since he had found himself in this kind of situation. He wondered, was this the reaction one might have when attracted to someone?

Nah, how could this be possible? Wouldn't this have happened before now?

He shook his head. None of this was making sense.

Damn ... this was all Darcey's fault. She's the one who put this idea into your head.

An idea he suddenly found very appealing.

In one swift move, he pulled her back into his arms and gazed right into her eyes. "Hush, it's okay. In fact, I'd say everything is more than okay. I believe Darcey has opened my eyes in more ways than one tonight. Starting with you. She made the comment you probably know me better than anyone else. I'd like to think the same holds true for me about you."

He leaned back to better search her face. "*So,* if you're free, how about we continue this conversation over a late dinner?"

She stared at him in disbelief. Then she smiled. It was a brilliant smile. "Yes, yes, I would love to have dinner with you."

Later, when thinking back to what happened next, he blamed it on the brief spark of something—he'd like to think it was desire—in her eyes that had him make such a bold move. Because why else would he have kissed her? A kiss they fell into as though it was the most natural thing in the world.

Yeah, he was taking a chance.

And maybe he was moving a little too fast.

But the man he was, when he knew what he wanted?

He wasn't one to waste time.

Especially not with something as life changing as this.

CHAPTER 33

You have the power to say ~
"This is not how I want my story will end."
~ Anonymously Yours

His hands in his pockets, Jason gazed around the newly painted room.

Dove's Song. This was the name of the paint color.

A wistful smile touched his lips. When he and Darcey had finally got around to picking out paint samples, she'd teased him about this color choice. Everything wasn't about music, she'd told him.

The memory of this, with her in his arms and laughing as she gazed up at him, sent such an intense flood of longing through him, he had to close his eyes.

She's right. Everything isn't about music ... everything is about her. In your life, everything. You'd give up music in a flash in exchange for her.

Knowing if he stayed any longer, the memories would start coming all at once, he left the bedroom and hurried down the steps.

He had just entered the kitchen, his mind on what his dinner options were, when he heard car doors slamming. This was followed by the sound of women's voices.

Familiar voices.

Steffi's voice … Abby's voice …

Raking his hand through his hair, he groaned.

Don't answer the door. Pretend you're not here. You know this isn't going to be pretty.

But he didn't have a chance of pulling this off, since his SUV was parked in the driveway in plain view. Muttering under his breath, using words not worth repeating, he reluctantly went over to open the door.

Yes, the problem had been fixed, the new door now opened like a charm.

Both women brushed past him, with Abby plopping a cranky Madeline Rose in his arms. This was verified by the tears still on her cheeks.

"Here, hold her for a few minutes. Kevin just called me and I need to call him back."

With Madeline Rose warily checking him out, he followed Steffi into the kitchen where she began pulling take out containers out of a big bag and arranging them on the counter.

He reached up to massage the back of his neck, giving a long sigh. He had only himself to blame for this.

Yeah, you shouldn't have been so dramatic when Steffi asked if you had eaten, responding with the comment you couldn't remember. Right now, it didn't matter. Food wasn't a priority.

Yeah, maybe he had exaggerated a little bit more than he should have.

Abby ended her phone call at the same time there was another knock at the door. When both she and Steffi ignored this, now searching through his kitchen drawers for who knows what, still carrying Madeline Rose, he went over and opened the door.

It was Sophie.

With Caro right behind her, a big smile on her face and proudly carrying a chocolate cake.

Damn … damn … damn … this is not good. Not good at all. What are they planning? An intervention?

If there was ever a time he wanted to take off running, this would be it.

So, when the two women walked into the house, he walked out. Standing on the steps, he gave Madeline Rose a desperate look. She returned his look, but not quite as desperate.

Then she giggled. One of those contagious baby giggles that was impossible to ignore.

He chuckled. "Tell me, little one ... are you a part of what's going on here? I have a feeling you are, if only as a diversion to keep me from running everyone out of my house."

"Jason? Come back inside. The food is all set up."

At this summons, he nodded at Madeline Rose. "Yep, they have some kind of plan in the works, bribing me with food. And even as hungry as I am right now, I have a feeling I'm not going to like it. So, I need you to be on my side, okay?"

Her reaction? She reached over, giving his hair a good tug before she giggled again.

This told him he was pretty much on his own.

Jason was beginning to wonder if he'd been a little hasty in judging the reason for this surprise visit. So far, all four women had almost ignored him, talking about people and things he knew nothing about.

If anything, he was starting to feel left out.

The only one who was paying any attention to him was Madeline Rose. Seated on his lap, she kept trying to feed him pieces of cut up cheese and grapes.

In fact, he was feeling pretty relaxed, thinking this visit hadn't turned out all that bad. It was very low key. So, maybe they really had only come to keep him company.

Hmm ...

He was also looking forward to the cake Caro was now cutting into huge slices and passing around to everyone.

Just as he put a big forkful of cake into his mouth, Abby nonchalantly turned to him "So, what are you going to do about Darcey? The four of us have spent a lot of time analyzing the situation and now wonder if this David may have exaggerated a bit with his claim he's Darcey's fiancé. Because, as Steffi pointed out, if this were true, why isn't she wearing a ring?"

Almost in unison, all four women nodded before they stared him down.

Swallowing the cake, amazed he hadn't choked on it, he set his fork down on the plate.

And here we go. You should've known it was too good to be true.

Yes, they were right, there had been no ring. But, as far as he was concerned, after what he'd witnessed in Darcey's office? This meant nothing.

Not a damn thing.

He shook his head. "From what I saw between Darcey and this guy, for them, it's not over. Ring or no ring."

Frustration filling him, he shifted in his chair, bringing a startled glance from Madeline Rose. After handing her a grape, he sighed. "Which is probably just as well, since there's no doubt he's the better catch, with a line of credentials that make me look like a loser in comparison."

In an attempt to make light of this, he made a big deal out of retrieving the grape Madeline Rose threw on the floor and tossed it over into the sink.

How was he supposed to know this would send her into hysterics, screaming for the grape?

"*Oh, baby* ... hold on, honey. We'll fix this." With these words, Jason headed for the sink. Madeline Rose still in his arms, he rinsed off the grape and handed it to her. Once he was seated with her back on his lap and her tears miraculously gone, he glanced around to see all four women were smiling at him.

He shrugged, picking up his fork and snaring another piece of cake. "Hey, when you're her age, the little things matter."

Steffi suddenly surprised everyone by throwing her napkin down on her plate, her expression livid. "You are not a loser and you know this. I don't ever want to hear you say that again, Jason Bennett."

Picking up the bottle of wine, Sophie was grinning as she refilled their glasses. "You tell him, Steff."

She glanced over at Jason. "Have you talked to her?"

He shook his head, no.

She gave a frustrated sigh. *"Jason ... what is wrong with you? Are you even planning to talk to her? I heard when she was leaving, she told the staff she was hoping to be back by the end of the week."* She frowned. "Though she never picked up her dress."

Any hope rising in Jason at what Darcey told the staff, was quickly dashed at the news she hadn't picked up her dress.

You don't know a woman alive who would forget to pick up a dress. She must have no intention of going to the ball.

He tried to push this thought out of his mind before he glanced over at Sophie. He gave a big sigh. "She sent me a voicemail the day she left. In the voicemail, she promised she'd be back. When? This is anyone's guess. So, there is nothing I can do but wait. And this is what I'm going to do. End of discussion."

He picked up his fork and began eating his cake.

Yeah, as far as you're concerned, this conversation is over.

In the silence that followed, he glanced up to see they were all watching him. What concerned him, they were all smiling ... again.

Geeez... now what? Aren't they even going to let you enjoy your cake in peace?

He raised an eyebrow.

Abby shook her head. But she was smiling. "You, Jason Bennett, are definitely husband and daddy material. You can charm even the youngest female."

He looked down to see Madeline Rose, her head resting against his chest, was sound asleep.

Steffi put her elbow on the table, plopping her chin in her hand. She sighed. "I hope the two of you straighten this out. I'm *really* ready to be an aunt."

He started shoveling in the cake as fast as he could.

He needed to get these women out of his house as soon as possible.

Husband?

Daddy?

Not that he'd admit this to these four, not even for a million dollars would he do this, but he sort of liked what they said.

Yeah, he was surprisingly okay with this.

Jason watched Caro fold the dish towel and place it on the counter. She had stayed behind when the other three left, Abby carrying a still sleeping Madeline Rose.

She turned to him, a thoughtful expression on her face.

This immediately alerted him she was about to start with another one of her lectures.

Aw, come on ... hadn't everything already been said?

Evidently not.

He watched as she crossed her arms over her chest, slowly shaking her head. "Jason Bennett, you don't know how blessed you are to have such a caring group of friends. Along with a devoted and loving sister. Why, Steffi was frantic with worry when you hid yourself away, refusing to talk to anyone."

He opened his mouth to deny he'd hidden anywhere, but she cut him off. "Don't even think of arguing with me because this is exactly what you've been doing. Hiding. Giving up. Feeling sorry for yourself."

She glared at him.

Remember when you said you hoped you'd never have to face her anger? Well, this is an example why...

Why she was so mad all of a sudden, he had no idea.

What he did know, she was on a run and there was no stopping her.

She gave an exasperated sigh. "This is not the way to face your problems. Especially when it comes to love. If you need to fight for her, then this is what you do, Jason. Your ego is the least of your concerns right now."

Pinching the bridge of his nose, he sighed. "Caro, listen to me. I know this. And believe me, I don't plan to give up without a fight. But she asked me to wait until she comes back and this is what I'm going to do. Okay?"

For a good ten seconds or so, they stared each other down. Then Caro finally smiled. "Okay. But you better not goof it up. And then I want to meet her."

Her eyes suddenly lit up. "I'll make dinner for the two of you. Something special."

She peered more closely at him. "Have you decided how you're going to go about the proposal?"

After she glanced around the room, she looked back at him. "We'll decorate the place up, candles everywhere, flowers..."

He stared at her, incredulous.

Then, a long groan coming from him, he dropped his head down on his arms.

Geeez ... you don't stand a chance.

She came over to pat him on the arm. "Now that I've given you something to think about, I'm going to take off. Dan and I are going to catch a movie."

His head shot up. "Dan? Who the heck is Dan? Do I know him?"

He'd swear she was blushing as she hurried over to open the door. She turned to him, grinning. "A friend. I think you'd like him."

He waited, knowing darn well she couldn't leave without having the last word.

Sure enough, right before she closed the door, she poked her head back in. "Think about what I said. This might be your only chance, you know. Remember, you are already in your thirties. Bye, bye..."

She was gone.

Leaving him with a lot to think about.

Caro had no sooner left when Jason's phone rang.

According to the caller I.D. it was Steven Hollister

Steven Hollister?

Staring down at the phone, his first impulse was to ignore the call.

But the fear racing through him something might have happened to Darcey, because *come on* … why else would her father be calling him, he grabbed the phone and barked out his hello.

After a slight pause, the deep authoritative voice he remembered so well filled his ear. "Jason, Steven Hollister here."

Jason immediately sat up straighter, dragging his hand nervously through his hair. "Yes, Mr. Hollister, sir … hello."

"Please, call me Steven."

In the pause that followed, Jason heard him give a big sigh before he began to speak. "I'm going to get right to the point. I'd like to apologize for all the things I said to you. At the time, I was acting on behalf of my daughter, my goal to protect her. But now, after the discussion Darcey and I had, I realize the accusations I made against you were invalid. And for this, I am deeply sorry. I'm hoping we can put this behind us and move on. Make a fresh start."

Jason was shaking his head.

But, at the same time he was smiling. Did this man ever let his guard down?

But hey, you'll take it.

He cleared his throat. "I understand. And I accept your apology."

Then he figured… what the hell? He might as well take advantage of this new truce between them.

He took a deep breath. "Darcey means the world to me. I would never do anything to hurt her, or make her unhappy. In fact, I believe this might be the perfect opportunity for me to ask you something, if only to get your approval."

Jason wasn't quite sure, but he thought he heard a chuckle come over the line before he received his answer. "I have a pretty good idea what it is, but sure, go ahead … ask."

Jason was staring down at his phone and had been for the past five minutes or so.

He was in shock, even going as far to wonder if he had imagined the whole conversation with Darcey's father.

And now? He couldn't stop smiling.

After checking his phone for the time, he grabbed his jacket and keys. He had some serious shopping to do.

Steven Hollister was feeling like a new man.

Since his conversation with Jason, he felt as though a huge weight had been lifted from his shoulders.

He was also feeling brave.

He turned off the light in his office, shut the door and sauntered his way into June's office.

And yes, saunter is exactly what he did. Hands in his pockets, his demeanor was of a man filled with a new-found confidence. If he were one to whistle, he'd be whistling up a storm.

He was also a man with a plan.

But for this plan to work out, he needed June to be on board.

He watched as she glanced up from her computer, a smile slowly traveling over her face when she saw it was him. This was followed by her sharp intake of breath when he reached behind to shut the door.

His eyes never leaving hers, he made his way around the desk. Pulling her up from the chair, he took her into his arms, his hands drifting down her back to hold her close.

"Hi ..." He followed this with a kiss to her forehead before he smiled down at her. "I want you to know I really enjoyed our dinner last night." His voice dipped lower. "It might interest you to know I had a hard time going to sleep when I finally got home. I couldn't stop thinking about you."

This was putting it mildly. The night had been almost pure agony for him. She'd refused to leave his mind, sending his imagination into high gear.

He was still finding this hard to comprehend. He was in his late forties, close to fifty, not a teenager on the prowl.

Nor did he understand how he could be in such good mood after the scant amount of sleep he'd managed to get. He'd actually caught himself singing in the shower this morning. Something he'd have to say hadn't happened in ages.

More like a decade or two.

The huskiness of his voice had June clinging to him, her response barely a whisper. "Hi … I … I did, too. Enjoyed our dinner, that is. But, Steven, the door … people are going to talk and –"

He pressed his fingers to her lips, shaking his head. "Let them talk. We're doing nothing wrong." He grinned. "After all, I am the boss. So, I should be able to bend the rules a bit."

Still keeping his hold on her, he leaned back, a twinkle in his eye. "But wait a minute, you enjoyed the dinner? What about me?" He peered more closely at her. "Did you miss me, maybe even think a little about me after we parted?"

She dipped her head, suddenly feeling shy. Again, this was all so new, to the point she was wondering if she could possibly be in the midst of a dream, soon to wake and find nothing had changed.

Smoothing the lapels of his suit with her hands, she smiled. "Of course, I did. I think about you all of the time."

Her head jerking up, she was quick to add. "When I'm here, that is. When we're in the office, since we do work together." She hesitated. "I try not to think about you when I go to bed. If I did, I wouldn't get any sleep."

The second these words came out of her mouth, she wanted to just die.

How was it the twenty-plus-years of professionalism they'd shared, with never a slip-up of any kind, had now flown right out the window? Leaving her unsure of how to act, rambling on like an infatuated school girl.

She took a deep breath. "What I meant to say, it's hard not to think about you after I leave the office. But it's not like I'm only thinking about you. This would be work-related. Since this is what we do all day, five days a week. Not that I'm complaining…"

Her words fading, she closed her eyes.

Oh my god … you need to stop talking. He's going to think you're crazy.

But caught up in the blush filling her cheeks as she stumbled over her words, Steven wasn't really thinking at all.

It tickled him he had her so flustered. Not because it made him feel powerful. Oh no … he simply saw this as a sign he wasn't imagining this chemistry between them. This had his confidence soaring even higher.

His fingers slowly sifting through her hair, he smiled down at her. "Good… this is good. Hopefully this means you'll be open to an idea I have. Let's make this coming weekend a long one. We'll drive up along the coast, visit a few wineries, share some great food and stay at whatever cozy bed and breakfast we find along the way. How does this sound to you?"

Her answer came in a long sigh. "It sounds wonderful … absolutely wonderful."

She hadn't even realized her arms had gone up to wrap around his neck, her body relaxing into his.

If this wasn't a dream, she had been so wrong thinking her life had been complete.

This moment … this man … was proof of this.

CHAPTER 34

*C*hris Gardner threw his bag in the trunk of his car and, after slamming it shut, he glanced up at the sky. There wasn't a cloud to be seen. This meant it was going to be the perfect night for the Masquerade Ball.

He knew how much Carrie was looking forward to the event.

He had been in New York all week with a demanding client who still couldn't accept he had left the city and moved to Cleveland. So, his time there had been hectic.

In fact, the past few weeks had been crazy for both him and Carrie, with very little time together. And now, he only wanted to be with her.

He smiled, just thinking about this.

Yeah, he knew he would be home in less than fifteen minutes. But he couldn't wait. For all he knew, she might need something and he could pick it up on his way home.

He hit call.

She answered on the first ring. "Hi …"

This coming out in a long sigh, he frowned. This wasn't the Carrie he knew. She sounded exhausted, out of sorts.

"Hi, princess. Hey, what's wrong? You don't sound too good."

She gave another long sigh. "I don't know what wrong with me. I've had an upset stomach all day."

"Hmm ... do you think it was something you ate?"

"I don't know. And I'm so tired. I almost fell asleep at my desk earlier this afternoon. So, I came home. I thought if I had a nap, I might feel better by tonight. I hope I don't have some kind of flu or something."

"Hmm ... maybe?"

She didn't know he had started to smile. Or what he was thinking. If she had, she would have been very surprised.

After he pulled into the parking lot of a drugstore close to where they lived, he turned off the ignition. He was still smiling. This was something he had been thinking about, waiting for the last few days to happen. "Well, I should be home in about ten minutes. I called to see if you need anything."

She sighed again. "No, just you. I miss you. Maybe you're the reason I'm in such a funk."

This turning his smile into a chuckle, he quickly cleared his throat. "I guess I very well could be. See you in a bit, princess."

Carrie was frowning as she laid her phone on the coffee table. She was a little upset Chris didn't seem very concerned about her. He almost sounded like he was laughing. Maybe this was only because he was in a good mood, happy to be home? After all, he had been gone for a week.

Chris found Carrie still on the sofa. Burrowed under a quilt, her eyes were closed. Thinking she was asleep, after he took off his coat and threw it on the chair, he pressed a kiss to her cheek.

Her lashes fluttering open, she gave him a faint smile. She watched as he made room to sit next to her.

He had a bag in his hands.

He smiled, nodding at the bag. "I brought you something. I'm hoping it will make you feel better." He cleared his throat. "In fact, I brought you three things. They all sort of go together."

Intrigued, she struggled to sit up.

He pulled a container of ice cream out of the bag.

She made a face, shaking her head. "Oh, no… I don't want any ice cream. Please, I don't even want to look at it."

So, he pulled out a jar of pickles.

She stared at the jar before she looked over at him, puzzled. "Chris, what in the world? Pickles? But isn't this …" Comprehension dawning on her face, she stared open-mouthed at what he had pulled out of the bag and was now holding in his hand.

It was a pregnancy test kit.

He handed it to her. "Princess, I might be wrong, but …" His words trailing off, he waited.

For the longest time, she stared down at the box. Just as he was about to say something, her hand going to her mouth, she looked up at him. He could see she was on the verge of tears.

"I … oh my gosh, Chris… I… do you think? I never … but why didn't I pick up on this? When did you … how did …"

He smiled, tucking her hair behind her ear. "Well, I started going over the past few weeks and, well, it seemed it could be more than possible. Very possible."

She was shaking her head, sending the tears flying. "I've been so busy and everything has been so hectic. I just thought … I never …" She glanced down at the box before she gazed up at him. "But what if I am? I thought you wanted to wait until things–"

He pressed his fingers to her mouth. "*Shh …* Sweetheart, if you're pregnant, I will be the happiest man in the world. There is nothing I'd love more."

He rose to his feet, pulling her up with him. "So, come on, let's do this. I can't wait to see if we're going to be parents."

Fifteen minutes later, Chris was exactly what he told her he would be.

He was the happiest man in the world.

CHAPTER 35

When the light has faded and you've lost your way,
Let another's love guide you.
It could turn even the blackest night into day.
~ Anonymous

It was a beautiful September evening. A perfect night for the Moonlight Madness Masquerade Ball.

Stephanie Bennett pulled into a parking space at The Regency, where for a few minutes she remained in her car. Her eyes closed, she needed a moment to relax.

She had been on the run all day. And now she was still running.

Well, not actually running. Because no one could run in these strappy, and what felt like six-inch heels Sophie had talked her into. Yes, she would agree they looked absolutely stunning on, but already her feet were protesting.

She was thinking Cinderella hadn't merely lost her shoe, as told in the story. No, the actual story was, after dancing the night away with her prince, her feet had been killing her. So, her goal had been to kick off those uncomfortable glass slippers in order to beat the clock.

Unfortunately, she could only kick off one shoe.

But this all worked out for her in the end. She got her prince. Something you certainly haven't been able to do yet.

Enough of this ... she was letting her imagination run rampant again.

Carefully sliding out of the car, careful to keep the hem of her dress from dragging on the pavement, she grabbed a large box and her masquerade mask from the back seat.

The box was heavy, filled with the programs donated by the staff of the Children's Hospital. Specifically designed for the event, they were to be placed at each place setting. But, somehow, they were left behind at the hospital.

So, guess who volunteered to pick them up and make sure they were on the tables?

Yep, you guessed it ... Steffi.

But she was all right with this. It would give her a chance to check out the decorations in the Grand Ballroom before the guests began arriving.

She set the box on the hood of her car and slipped on her mask. After all, the rules were clear ... the decorative masks were to be worn until the dinner was served.

Now, feeling not only excited but also very mysterious, she picked up the box and headed for the party center.

After she set the box down on one of the tables, Steffi wandered around the Grand Ballroom, taking it all in.

Once again, the decorating committee had gone far and beyond what was expected of them, turning the space into the perfect setting for a night of mystery and glamour.

The chosen color scheme was black, gold, silver, and red. The floor length table coverings were black, with alternating metallic gold and silver fabric toppers. Candles were everywhere, tucked here and there around the place settings of fine white china and sparkling crystal glassware.

The centerpiece on each table featured a clear glass vase with an arrangement of white and black ostrich plumes, red roses, gold stars, and an elaborately decorated mask. The vase, nestled in a swirl of glittery tulle, sparkled with miniature lights. These lights, along with the candles at each place setting, cast a mysterious glow over each table.

Additional garlands of glittery tulle, miniature lights, and gold stars decorated the twig trees arranged throughout the room.

And best of all? At each place setting was one of Abby's cookies. Tucked in a cellophane bag and tied with a gold ribbon, each cookie was in the shape of a masquerade mask, each a unique design and a work of art.

At the sound of voices out in the hallway, she glanced down at her watch. The guests would start arriving in less than thirty minutes.

This meant she needed to get busy. The programs certainly weren't going to hop onto the table by themselves.

Grabbing a handful of programs out of the box, she got to work.

Evan Marshall slowly trudged up the steps of The Regency. This was when he realized he was practically shuffling.

You're walking like an old man. Come on, you should at least try to look like you're having a good time.

After he entered the lobby, stopping to pull the camera strap further up on his shoulder, he gazed longingly out at the parking lot. If he could, he'd turn around and walk right back out the door.

He blamed most of his attitude on the tuxedo he was wearing. Not accustomed to wearing one, he felt like a fool. He had to rent the stupid thing. Then, to top it off, he must have spent at least fifteen minutes trying to figure out how to tie the annoying bow tie.

Even after checking online for directions, the result was still far from perfect. No, it was more like a mess.

But it was this ridiculous masquerade mask he was told he had to wear, this is where he had almost put his foot down, refusing to work the event.

Whoever came up with this idea had to be out of their mind. You're surprised they didn't force you to wear hats to match.

Like party hats.

Birthday party hats ...

He closed his eyes, another one of those crippling waves of grief barreling through him without warning, memories flooding his mind until he felt almost ill.

Today would have been his fiancée, Kelsie's twenty-fourth birthday. She loved surprises. If he closed his eyes, he could still see the excitement on her face when he brought out the gifts he'd wrapped for her.

This birthday would've been the first one they celebrated as husband and wife, had her life not been cut short only two weeks before their wedding. Texting while driving, a teenager had plowed right into the motorcycle Kelsie and her brother were on, killing them both on impact.

Since then, nothing had really mattered. His only goal was to make it through each day at his job as a photographer for the local news.

He covered mostly social events, new city projects and some sports. This was because he refused to do the heavier stuff, his mind still raw from the horror of what happened to Kelsie.

When he wasn't working, he kept to himself. He missed Kelsie too much, nothing felt right without her. And he was almost ready to accept nothing ever would.

As he made his way down the hall, he decided he would take as many photos as he could, and as quickly as possible. Then he'd sneak out, go home and grieve in solitude for this lost day.

He finally found what he was looking for. The Grand Ballroom. His plan was to take photos of the room before the guests began arriving. Walking around the room, he began scoping it out, looking for the best angles, assessing the lighting.

And this is when he saw her.

He blinked.

An angel ... this is the only way he could think of to describe the woman who was flitting around the tables, adding something to each place setting. In the candlelight, she was dazzling, a vision of pure beauty, her long blonde hair and ivory colored evening gown giving off an almost luminous glow.

The décor of the room completely forgotten, he began moving closer, his goal to get the perfect shot.

He couldn't believe how much he needed this.

If only as proof she was real.

More people had gathered in the reception area outside of the Grand Ballroom.

Now down to her last table, Steffi took a moment to scan the crowd. Unfortunately, Jason wasn't among them. Since she hadn't heard from him since they had all been at his house the other day, she was worried. After she finished the programs, she intended to find either Jack or Paul to see if they knew where he was.

Now in a hurry to finish, she scooped up the programs left in the box and turned to put them on the table.

There was a man standing only a few feet away, his camera aimed right at her.

She cried out and, without thinking, she flung the programs right at him. Completely taken by surprise, he ducked. After they watched the programs fly in all directions, he turned back to her.

For the briefest of moments, their eyes held. The first to look away, he began gathering up the programs.

He was struggling. This intense attraction to a woman, one he had just met, was something he never thought he would experience again.

It was also one he wasn't ready for.

All the programs safely in his hands, he glanced over to see she hadn't moved, almost as if she'd become frozen in place. Moving closer to hand her the programs, he was relieved to see a slow smile curve her lips.

He just as slowly smiled back at her.

"Are you okay?"

Her smile still there, Steffi nodded. For some odd reason, she didn't want to talk. She wanted to savor the moment, make it last.

Drawn to this man in a way she couldn't explain, almost as if this moment had been set in motion by a power so much bigger than the two of them.

He moved even closer, reaching out to brush his fingertips along the curve of her cheek. "Who are you? I feel as though you're not real. A princess, or a mythical fairy of the best kind."

She laughed, a sound like the music of a million tiny ringing bells. The blush deepening in her cheeks, she shook her head. "No, not a princess. Or a fairy. Just plain old me."

He wanted so badly to remove her mask so he could frame her face in his hands. If only to get closer so he could gaze into her beautiful eyes, maybe even get lost in them. But thinking this could very well scare her, he dropped his hand to his side.

And now he was the one shaking his head. "No, there is nothing plain about you. You're absolutely beautiful." He hesitated, searching her face before he spoke. "I want to tell you, I didn't want to be here tonight. I ... well, let's just say, it's been sort of rough lately and I haven't wanted to do much of anything. But, since work called—I'm a photographer—here I am."

His voice dipped to a whisper. "And now I find you." He suddenly frowned. "But I imagine you're with someone, have someone."

"*No, no* ... I'm with no one." This was delivered swiftly, emphatically, as if she wanted to assure him he had no reason to worry.

And this was when she did something so totally uncharacteristic for her. Later she would wonder if this was something she'd only imagined, wishing she had been brave enough to do.

She reached over to adjust his bow tie.

His eyes closed, he stood completely still. It was only when he felt her step back, he opened them. He smiled. "Thanks, I had a little trouble with that."

"I could see that." Again, her laugh was the sound of all those tiny bells. They seemed to fall over him, surrounding him. Making him not only happy, but filling him with such a feeling of peace.

She sent a quick glance over at the entrance to the room before she reluctantly backed away from him. "But I really need to get these programs on the tables. And I imagine you need to get your photos taken before everyone comes in."

He watched as she turned away, his brain scrambling to come up with something to say that would make her stay. At least for a little longer.

This is when she turned to look back at him. Again, she was about to do something so unlike her. After a slight hesitation, she gave him a tentative smile. "Are you going to be here all evening?"

Even though this was not what he had planned, he nodded.

She smiled. "Maybe we can share a dance? I'm a nurse, so I'll be sitting with my friends from the hospital at table number twelve."

He hesitated. Kelsie was the last woman he had danced with. Her goal to have him dancing like a pro for their wedding, she had signed them up for a dance class. But by the end of the first class, she laughingly pronounced him hopeless.

He gazed into space, lost in the memory.

"It's okay, I understand if you would rather not. I shouldn't have asked."

This coming from this angel standing in front of him, her embarrassment so obvious, his answer came out in a rush. "No, no, no ... I would love nothing more than to share a dance with you. But, I'm not a very good dancer. Plus, I don't even know your name."

She rewarded him with her smile. "Good, neither am I. We can stumble through it together. And my name is Stephanie, but my friends call me Steffi."

"Stephanie ... such a beautiful name. It suits you. I'm Evan."

He slowly shook his head. "I can't even tell you how glad I am to have met you, Stephanie. But now I'm going to leave. So you can finish your work and I can take my photos. Until our dance, then?"

At her nod, he turned and walked right out of the room.

He knew his departure was sudden, but he needed to think. There was so much going on in his mind, so much he was having a hard time with.

But there was also something else ... and if he wasn't mistaken, this was a feeling of hope.

It was only the smallest glimmer, but it was a start.

He slowed his pace, closing his eyes.

Please, God ... let this happen ...

It wasn't until he glanced down to see his camera in his hand, he came to an abrupt halt. He had completely forgotten why he had gone into the Grand Ballroom to begin with.

He turned around and walked back in.

The room was empty. There was no sign of Stephanie. Almost as if she had never been there.

He wondered ... had he imagined the whole encounter?

Then, clear as a bell, he could see Kelsie's face.

She was smiling.

And for the first time since he had lost her, her presence didn't fill him with such an overwhelming sense of grief.

Yes, the pain was still there.

But he was also able to smile.

CHAPTER 36

arcey was running late.

Really, *really* late.

From the moment she first woke up at the ridiculous hour of three-thirty this morning, she had been trying to make up for lost time.

Why?

Because everything that could... had gone all wrong.

Starting with the massive traffic jam on the way to the LAX airport that had her missing her flight. She booked another flight to Cleveland with three—yes, three—layovers, thinking she was all set. But her final layover turned into a two-hour delay because of a massive storm front in a slow crawl across most of the country.

Yes, massive... biggest storm of its kind.

Why were you even surprised?

So, it was already late afternoon when she arrived at her apartment, where in the time span of less than forty-five minutes, she took a shower, did her hair and applied her make-up.

She had planned to pick up her dress at the Chic Boutique herself, but with her late arrival, she called Louise to see if, by any chance, someone could deliver the dress to her office.

And this was the important part ... no one, *absolutely no one,* was to see or know about this.

Nervously fingering the ring on her necklace, Darcey was relieved to see The Regency parking lot was still empty when her taxi pulled up to the main entrance.

There was no sign of Jason's SUV.

She grabbed her bag and, after waving her thanks to the driver, she went running up the steps.

Once she was in her office, she scanned the room before sagging against the door in relief.

As promised, the dress was hanging on the coat rack.

Then she did something that could be the first in a chain of events to determine how the evening would go.

She reached into her purse and pulled out a small box tied with a ribbon. There was a note attached. Tucking it in her hand, she headed for the equipment room.

After she unlocked the door and slipped inside, she placed the box on the desk.

A prayer on her lips, she left as silently as she had arrived.

At almost the same time, Jason was studying his reflection in his bathroom mirror.

If he said so himself, he was looking pretty decent. Not one to dwell on his looks, this was the one time he made an exception.

He needed a boost to his confidence.

A huge boost.

You need this ... badly ...

He couldn't believe how nervous he was. He was pretty sure he broke his own daily record of checking his messages, this happening in the morning alone.

But this had been the norm since Darcey had left.

Yeah, he was trying to hold on to what she said in her voicemail, but come on... of course, he was a little skeptical. She was over two thousand miles away. Anything could happen.

He was slipping his mask for the masquerade ball in his pocket when his phone rang.

Jumping on it like a madman, he groaned when he saw it was only Paul.

He hit answer. "Yeah? What do you want?"

After a brief silence, Paul responded. "Geeez ... you're really testing my patience. And now I'm wondering if I should even tell you why I called."

Jason all but growled out his response. "Don't play games with me. Trust me, I'm not in the mood."

This was when Paul knew he had the advantage. It was also when Sasha, who was listening in on the call, smacked him on the arm. She was giving him one of those looks of hers. The look telling him to take this seriously, or she would have a lot to say after he ended the call.

He groaned. "You're lucky Sasha likes you, otherwise I'd hang up right now."

He paused, if only to make Jason sweat it out a little. "I got a text from Jack. He said he saw Darcey. In fact, he saw her coming out of the equipment room. So, he ducked into the men's room so she wouldn't see him. Why the hell she was in the equipment room is anyone's guess. Thought you'd like to know this. And yes, you're welcome."

He chuckled. "That's all I got ... see you in a bit."

Gripping the edge of the vanity, Jason stared down at his phone. Then, lifting his head, he watched in the mirror as a goofy smile slowly spread across his face.

At the same he felt the tension leave his body in one big swoosh.

She was back.

Like she promised.

CHAPTER 37

True love doesn't mean
you won't ever grow apart or break up.
True love means you'll always find
a way back to each other.
~ Anonymously Yours

Once she was back in her office, Darcey changed into her dress and made some last-minute repairs to her hair and make-up.

Twenty minutes later, she was pacing back and forth. She didn't know what to do. There was still no sign of Jason.

This meant she didn't know if he had found the box she left on his desk. Or if he had gone straight to the Grand Ballroom when he arrived.

Then again, maybe he hadn't even arrived yet.

It was also very possible he didn't want to see her. So, for this reason, she had hoped to meet up with him in private. So she could explain … apologize … or even beg … if this is what she had to do. She would do whatever it took to make him see how much she loved him.

She glanced out at the deserted courtyard. Crowded only a short time ago, now all the guests had moved on to the Grand Ballroom to find their table assignments for dinner.

But you're still here. In the dark, and alone. What are you waiting for?

When she began searching through her bag for her high-heeled sandals, she came across the jewelry she bought at Chic Boutique to go with her dress. She had completely forgotten about it.

She hesitated, reaching up to finger the promise ring.

It was gone.

The whole necklace was gone, chain and all.

Oh no, no, no, not the necklace. Not now ...

In a panic, she began searching the floor, even almost crawling under her desk. Not the easiest thing to do while wearing a long evening gown.

She emptied her purse, shook the garment bag upside down, and searched through her bag.

Twice she did this.

There was no sign of the necklace.

Pressing her fingers to her forehead, she tried to think back to when she last felt it around her neck. The last she could remember was when she arrived at The Regency. Thinking about Jason, she had been fingering the ring while she was in the taxi.

This meant the ring had to be somewhere in the party center.

She froze

What if it fell off when you were in the equipment room?

Trying not to panic, she checked her phone for the time. It was now 8:14. Dinner was to be served at 8:30.

Surely no one would be in the equipment room now. She would make it quick. She would also be able to find out if Jason had found the box she left for him.

You don't have a choice. You need to find the necklace. So much depends on this.

For a moment, she thought of not wearing the beautifully embellished mask she had found in the garment bag with the dress. But thinking this might keep her identity a secret if she came across someone, she slipped it on and left her office.

Little did she know, there was one person who would know her anywhere.

No matter what.

Mask, or no mask.

Jason ...

Jason was singing as he drove his SUV up to the front entrance of The Regency.

Not loud. No, only enough for him to hear. This was something he always did before a performance.

This was his way of loosening up, getting in the mood.

And yes, he was late. He probably should have arrived over an hour ago. Paul's numerous texts were a reminder of this.

But he wasn't worried. As long as he was there before the band took the stage after dinner, he'd be fine.

Jumping out of his SUV and handing the parking attendant his keys, he started up the steps.

Something shiny caught his eye. Coming to a halt, he reached down to pick up a fine silver chain.

Hanging on the chain was a ring.

For a moment, he was confused.

After he glanced around to see he was alone, he looked down at the necklace in his hand.

Are you imagining this?

He went sprinting up the rest of the steps, coming to a halt right inside the entrance. Holding his breath, he checked the inside of the ring.

It was engraved.

DH and JB

His heart thundering in his chest, he raised his head, slowly taking in his surroundings.

How was it that everything looked the same, so familiar? While, for him, everything felt different? As though his life was about to change, something momentous waiting to take place?

His fingers curling around the necklace, he slowly shook his head. What were the odds, with all the people who used these steps tonight, he was the one to find this?

Maybe a million to one?

More like a billion.

Slowly dropping the necklace into his pocket, almost afraid to let it leave his fingers, he made his way down the hall. In a daze, he walked right by the entrance to the Grand Ballroom and headed for the equipment room.

He needed to be alone.

He needed to think.

Darcey had searched every inch of the floor, beginning with her office and all the way into the equipment room.

After locking the door behind her, she began rummaging through everything on the desk.

She was slowly losing hope, mumbling to herself. "Please, please be here … because I don't even want to think what I'm going to do if you aren't. Please …"

At the sudden click of the lock, she froze.

Her heart racing, she listened to the sound of footsteps coming in her direction.

When Jason saw Darcey crouched down by the desk, he came to an abrupt stop. And for the second time in the past few minutes, his heart began pounding in his chest.

Déjà vu …

Yep, this all felt so familiar.

He watched as she slowly stood. Gripping the edge of the desk for support, she avoided his gaze.

She took his breath away.

She looked stunning. Exquisite. Everything—her dress, her hair, the mask—together, they were the perfect combination of sophistication and mystery.

And to him, so desirable, so, *so* sexy.

Resisting the urge to erase the distance between them in record time, if only so he could kiss her until they both couldn't think anymore, or at least block out everything that happened, he paced himself, coming to stand only a few feet away.

After patting his pocket to make sure the necklace was still there, he crossed his arms over his chest.

He slowly shook his head, the huskiness of his voice revealing his emotional state. "My goodness, what do we have here? I must say, the last thing I expected to find was an absolutely gorgeous and mysterious masked woman rummaging around my desk. This reminds me of a similar encounter about a month ago. Might you also remember this?"

When she didn't give him an answer, or even move, he nodded. "Yep, same woman, same place."

Darcey slowly turned to face him.

Even as worked up as she was, she found it so hard not to stare. Just as she had thought, Jason in a tuxedo was perfection. Words like seductive, magnificent, hot, mind-boggling, sexy and so many, many more came to mind.

If she wasn't in such a quandary, not sure what he was thinking, she wouldn't have hesitated to run right into his arms and tell him this.

His head tilted, his expression was unyielding, giving nothing away. It was obvious he was in no hurry, more than willing to wait for her explanation. She opened her mouth, but nothing came out.

This had him moving a little closer. "May I ask what you're looking for? Because you probably won't find anything of value here. At least, not that I know of."

This time, she found her voice. "I … I lost something. And I thought … well, I thought it might be here."

The necklace …

The flicker of a smile passing his lips, he nodded. *"Hmm ... I see."* And now the urge to take her into his arms, if only just to hold her against him, was even stronger.

Instead, he reached over to remove her mask. First, he needed to see her face ... all of it. Especially her eyes, her beautiful eyes. He wanted to see if the connection was still there.

And it was.

The relief that ran through him had him clearing his throat. "So, let me get this straight. You lost something. And you think I might have it?"

Wringing her hands, like him, she was having a terrible time. He was so close. The heat radiating from him, the scent of his cologne and again, the superb fit of his tuxedo ... all of this was messing with her senses, making it hard for her to breathe, let alone think.

She wanted to walk right into the safe haven of his arms. So, she could explain why she left. And why she had come back.

But most of all, she wanted to tell him how much she loved him.

Gazing up at him, and after a deep breath, everything came out in a rush. "The first time Livy and Sam saw my grandparent's house, they found the promise ring you gave me. Thinking it might belong to me because of the initials, Livy sent it to me. So, I've been wearing it on a chain around my neck ever since. I had it on tonight, but just now, I realized it was gone. And since I had come here earlier," at his raised eyebrow, her gaze darted over to the small box on the desk, "I thought you might come here before you went to the Grand Ballroom and I wanted to leave something for you."

Her voice caught, bordering on a sob. "Something I was hoping you might wear tonight."

She reached for the box and handed it to him. At his curious glance, she nodded. "Please, open it."

He untied the ribbon to remove the notecard and, after a slight hesitation, he read the note out loud.

Jason,
I hope you will wear this as a

promise of my love for you.
I love you. I've always loved
you. And I always will.
Darcey

He glanced over at her again before he reached inside the box to take out a ring. It was a promise ring, an exact match to the ring he had given her.

The ring she didn't know was now in his pocket.

DH and JB

After reading the engraving on the inside of the band, this taking him so long she was beginning to worry, he raised his face to hers.

Totally unprepared for the emotional state he was in, he didn't trust himself to speak, instead slowly shaking his head.

But she didn't see it this way, thinking this gesture she had made was too late. Her bottom lip quivering, she could barely get out her next words. "I guess … well, I thought I'd be giving you the same promise you gave me and we'd be okay. But now maybe it's too late, because… because now, the ring you gave me is gone …"

When her last words rose in a sob, he reached over, gently tucking her hair behind her ear. There was a huskiness in his voice. "Close your eyes, gorgeous."

Her eyes closed, she felt his fingers brush over the back of her neck. He fastened the necklace, the familiar weight of the ring resting against her skin.

She drew in a sharp breath. *"Jason …"*

Framing her face in his hands, he pressed the softest of kisses to her mouth. "You can open them now."

Darn if this didn't put her face to face with that sexy smile of his. After reaching up to finger the ring, she searched his face, stumbling with her words. "How … where … I don't understand…"

His hands sliding in her hair to bring her closer, he pressed a kiss to her forehead. "After I dropped my SUV off for valet parking, I saw the necklace on the steps. Almost as if it was waiting there for me." He brushed another kiss over her mouth. "Proof of what we've both known all along ... we're meant to be."

His gaze held hers, his searching. Met with the love shining in hers, his sigh brushed over her cheek. "*My god,* gorgeous ... I missed you. So damn much."

And she was gone, completely falling apart. The tension and uncertainty weighing her down for the past few days erupting in a flood of tears.

She tried to stop, but when he pulled her against him, she cried even harder. While she tried to tell him about her father, David, why she left and why she came back.

He tried to make sense of the mish-mash of words muffled against his chest, but truthfully? He didn't care. That she was back in his arms and where she belonged, this was all that mattered.

There was only one time he reacted. This was when she started babbling about her father's confusion about the baby.

He groaned, pulling her closer. "I had such a hard time with that. He was so angry, where I was confused. For the longest time, I told myself I must have misunderstood what he was trying to tell me." He hesitated, leaning back to search her face. "But it didn't help you told me you never wanted to have kids..."

She closed her eyes, but not before he saw the flash of pain there. "Oh, Jason ... I was such a fool. I was angry, confused... thinking if you couldn't even come out and tell me you loved me, how could I trust you to always be there for me? Convinced we'd end up like my parents, I used them as an excuse to keep from getting hurt."

Linking her fingers behind his neck, she gazed up into his eyes. "But now, I would trust you with anything. And I'd do anything for you. I'd have a dozen kids with you if this is what you want."

His lips slowly curved into a smile. "A dozen, you say? Wow, that's a pretty high number."

His head tilted, he studied her. "You're sure about this? Because if you are, I'm more than willing to give it a try."

"Jason ..."

He chuckled, shaking his head. "Too late, you already committed. But because I love you, I'll try to go easy on that number."

A sudden seriousness in his gaze, he rested his forehead against hers. "We both said things, or should I say, didn't say things we should have. And when you left this time, even though you promised you'd be back, I was so afraid I had lost you for good."

She pulled away from him and, taking the ring out of the box, she slipped it on his finger. Relieved it was a perfect fit, she gazed up at him.

"So, it's a promise?"

"It's a promise. For always, gorgeous."

His look one of such unconditional love, she wrapped her arms around his neck. "Then kiss me ..."

And he did. Slowly, deeply, thoroughly.

As with every other time he kissed her, his plan was to take his good old time, keep the kiss going for as long as he could.

After all, it had been a long three years...

This meant they had a lot of lost time to make up.

Unfortunately, the sound of someone clearing their throat put a quick stop to Jason's plan. Reluctantly raising his head, he glanced over to see Paul was casually leaning against the doorjamb.

His hands in his pockets, he had a huge grin on his face.

"Umm ... I hate to break up this romantic interlude you have going on, but there's a lot of speculation going on whether you're ever going to make an appearance."

He shrugged. "So, guess who they sent to check it out?"

He nodded. "Yep, none other than yours truly."

He shook his head. "I gotta tell ya, I'm glad you two finally figured it out. Because I seriously don't know how much more I could take."

When Jason's only response was to raise an eyebrow, Paul pointed to his watch. "They're just about to serve dinner. So, you better get a move on."

He was grinning as he walked out of the room.

Jason nuzzled his face in Darcey's hair, his words coming out in a long groan. "Sweetheart, right now I'd give anything to whisk you away from here."

He chuckled.

She leaned back, her heart leaping into high gear at his mischievous grin. "Maybe even get started on one of those dozen kids you promised."

The seductive tone of his voice had her swept up right along with him, wanting the same. She buried her face in his chest. "Jason... what have I done? You do realize I was only caught up in the moment. Never did I think you'd run with it."

He was smiling. "*Ah* ... but you were so convincing. And now I'm having a hard time thinking about anything else."

After he glanced down at his watch, he picked up her mask, gently adjusting it over her eyes. "Come on, gorgeous. Since we're late, we'll try to sneak in. Hopefully, no one will even notice us. Are you ready?"

She nodded, her smile as brilliant as the gems on her mask.

This had him shaking his head. "It just doesn't seem right to hide your beautiful eyes. Thank goodness, I can still see your smile."

He reached for her hand, giving her that slow smile of his. The one he had every woman dreaming about.

But this didn't bother her.

She had his love.

CHAPTER 38

Dancing with the feet is one thing, But dancing with the heart is another.
~ Anonymous

*A*pparently, Jason had miscalculated his popularity when he told Darcey they should be able to sneak into the Grand Ballroom unnoticed. Because as soon as they walked into the room, everyone at their assigned table erupted into a cheer.

This set the rest of the room buzzing, everyone trying to get a good look at the woman Jason was with, speculation about this possible relationship traveling through the room like fire.

Darcey didn't notice any of this. Clinging to Jason's hand, she was still in somewhat of a daze, wondering if she may have dreamt the whole encounter in the equipment room.

And Jason? For him, this was all part of the job. But even though this kind of attention was what to be expected, it certainly didn't mean he liked it.

And right now?

His concern was for Darcey.

He placed his arm across the back of her chair, his hand a comforting presence on her shoulder.

He leaned in close. "Hey, gorgeous ... are you okay?"

His look was so tender, so sincere, she impulsively leaned in to press a kiss to his mouth.

His fingers catching her chin, he didn't give her the option to pull away. His lips brushing across her mouth, she was carried away by the huskiness of his voice. "I don't think I even told you how beautiful you look tonight. You take my breath away."

The kiss he gave her was just as soft. And it would've been longer had they not been interrupted ... again.

"Hey Jason ..."

They both looked over to see this was coming from Abby. Her chin resting in her hand, she was grinning right at them. "It's so good to see the two of you finally straightened things out."

She nodded over at Jason. "Are you teaching a new dance tonight? You do know everyone will be expecting this."

He gave her a blank look.

Teach? A dance?

He smiled, shaking his head. "Sorry, my mind is a little occupied right now."

Abby laughed. "*Hmm* ... trust me, we're all aware of this."

He slowly shook his head, a sheepish grin on his face. "Yeah, don't worry, I've got this. Thought I'd try something different this year. My plan is to go back in time, do a little waltzing."

Sam and Livy were following this conversation with interest. Sam loved dancing with Livy. But Jason's news was a little disappointing. He had been hoping for something more exciting. Like a rhumba or tango.

He frowned. "Isn't the waltz a formal type of dance?"

Jason grinned. "Yep, but we're going to jazz it up a little with the Viennese version. A more modern type of waltz. Quicker moves, sweeping turns and fast footwork."

Sam was shaking his head. "Sounds complicated to me." Then typical of Sam, he pulled Livy into a hug before he grinned over at Jason. "But, hey ... I've got my favorite dancing partner with me, so I'm game."

Jason laughed. "Remember, it's about having fun." After glancing down at his watch, he rose from his chair. He dropped a kiss to Darcey's cheek. "Duty calls. I'll be coming for you in a little bit, gorgeous."

With one backward wink, he was off, running up on stage.

This left Darcey alone to face all of the smiling, waiting faces. Hoping to avoid any questions, she glanced over to where Jason was talking to Paul up on stage before she shook her head. "I'm a terrible dancer. He doesn't know what he's in for."

Carrie, who along with Chris had been very quiet during dinner, smiled at her. "Darcey, you don't need to worry. You can't be a bad dancer when you're with Jason. It just doesn't happen."

Sophie was nodding. "Seriously, he can turn anyone into a great dancer. Just about any woman in this room would jump at the chance to dance with him."

A pained expression crossing her face, Carrie suddenly pushed her plate away. This had Chris jumping up from his chair. "Here, princess, I'll move this out of your way." Once the offending plate was out of sight, he sat next to her, a concerned look on his face. "Is there anything you want? Ginger ale? Tea?"

Livy, Abby and Sophie all sent a swift glance at each other before they all looked over at Carrie.

Sophie was the first one to get it out. "Oh my gosh ... Carrie, you're pregnant? You are, aren't you?"

Carrie didn't even have to answer. The big smile on Chris's face was enough answer for both of them.

After this? Darcey's lack of dance skills were all but forgotten.

After the final last notes of a rousing rendition of Shout, Jason reached for his water bottle and taking a long drink, he scanned the room.

He was looking for Darcey. When he finally spotted her, a grin on his face, he unhooked the microphone from the stand and jumped off the stage. When he was in the middle of the dance floor, he raised the microphone to his mouth. "So, is everyone having a good time?"

A big cheer was his answer, anticipation filling the room.

He was smiling as he slowly began walking the floor, his voice loud and clear to the now silent crowd. "Before we get into the serious dancing part of the evening, I have an announcement to make. Sean Young, are you here? If you are, stand and make yourself known."

A big grin on his face, Sean waved from where he was standing by the bar with Hannah.

After he made his way over to them, Jason turned to face the room. "I want all of you to know, today Sean pitched the perfect game. No hits, no runs for nine innings. An accomplishment like this deserves a huge round of applause, maybe even a standing ovation, don't you think?"

The noise was deafening, only to die down when Jason handed Sean his microphone.

His arm wrapping around Hannah in a hug, Sean grinned. "Thanks everyone. I have to confess, the outcome of the game probably surprised me more than anyone. I couldn't have picked a better team, a better place or a better group of fans to have this happen."

He smiled down at Hannah. "And of course, I do it all for this little beauty."

Tipping his ever-present cowboy hat, a signature trait of his, he sent another grin around the room. "Thanks again."

Jason returned to the dance floor and smiled around at the crowd. "What a great guy. Are we lucky here in Cleveland, or what?"

Again, he waited for the applause and cheers to die down before he began sauntering around the floor as he spoke. "But now it's time to get down to business. Those of you who've been coming to this event over the years know I always try to teach you a new dance. Tonight is no exception. We're going to work on the waltz, but we're going to perk it up a little. Maybe you'll like it, maybe you won't. It's definitely not like some of the freeform dancing I've seen from a lot of you tonight." He slowly shook his head. "I don't think moves like that can be taught."

Laughter greeting his remark, he grinned. "But, this is okay. Remember, our goal here is to always have fun."

His gaze searching the crowd, he began walking towards the one woman in the room that, as far as he was concerned, made every other woman appear pale in comparison. "And now, if I'm going to teach you a new dance, I need to find a willing partner to help me demonstrate."

"Me, me, Jason."

"Pick me. Please, pick me."

"Over here, Jason."

Ignoring these and all the other cries coming at him, he made his way right over to Darcey. After a slight bow, he held out his hand. "Will you do me the honor of sharing this dance?"

Her apprehensive nod, along with her tight grip on his hand, had him leaning in to kiss her cheek before he whispered in her ear. "Baby, you're going to do just fine. Just follow my lead. I won't let you down."

Bringing them back out to the middle of the dance floor, he kept hold of her hand as he spoke. "I'm sure you've all heard of the classic waltz. But did you know the word "waltz" comes from the Italian word "volver" which means revolve or turn? Your feet never leaving the floor, you glide around the dance floor in a counterclockwise direction using right and left box turns. It is one of the first dances where dancers closely faced each other, almost touching. As you can imagine, when first introduced, this was considered quite scandalous."

He grinned. "I know ... sounds complicated, right?" He shook his head. "It's not. But it is very formal. So tonight, we're going to go with the Viennese Waltz, a much faster paced dance than the classic waltz. The elegance and charm of this style of waltz is what you'd expect to see at the glamorous balls in the palaces of Europe. It is a quicker, rotating dance, much faster-paced. The steps are small and compact, with a gentle swing action to each bar of music. With each sweeping turn, this results in a delightful, lifting feeling as you rotate gracefully around the dance floor. This is, of course, is if you do it right."

He sent a smile around the room. "This is definitely the dance for all you ladies to show off your beautiful dresses. Think of Dancing with the Stars, where you've probably already seen different variations of this dance, if only a lot more elaborate."

He shot a quick grin over at Darcey. "We won't be attempting any of the lifts just yet." He raised an eyebrow. "Unless you're feeling brave?"

After Darcey vigorously shook her head, bringing a laugh from the crowd, he continued. "Okay ... Darcey and I are going to show you how a Viennese Waltz is meant to be done. I'm sure you'll recognize the song we've chosen. Our band's own version, jazzed up a bit."

This is when he hesitated, sending a thoughtful glance over at Darcey. It had suddenly dawned on him, this would be their first dance. And it didn't seem right this would happen while they were wearing masquerade masks.

He wanted to be able to see her face, gaze into her eyes ... her beautiful eyes.

He couldn't imagine anything less.

So, what are you going to do about this? You're in charge, right? So, change the rules.

He was smiling when he turned to address the room. "But first, we're going to spice things up a little. Since the waltz is considered as one of the most romantic dances of all times, wouldn't this be the perfect opportunity to let your partner know how you feel about them?"

He slowly gazed around the room. "So ... this is what we're going to do. If you're with the love of your life, before you take your first step on the dance floor, take off your mask, show your face. Use this moment to let them feel your love."

He cleared his throat. "Let me demonstrate ..."

He turned to face Darcey and slowly removing his mask, he slipped it into his pocket. Crossing his arms over his chest, he gazed right into her eyes — at least into what little he could see, not hidden behind her mask.

Without breaking his gaze, he addressed the now silent room.

"And now, it will be up to your partner to let you know if they feel the same."

For a long moment, Darcey didn't move. It was when he saw the smile slowly beginning to curve her lips, he chuckled, taking a step closer. Because of the silence, his voice was barely a whisper. "You do realize my reputation is on the line here, don't you?"

Laughter bubbling up in her throat, she nodded. She leaned closer, also whispering. "So, what will you do for me if I do this?"

A kiss ... yes, you'd definitely give her a kiss, You'd give her a dozen, or even more, if this is what she wants.

But the sudden reminder they were not alone, had him rethinking this move.

Slowly shaking his head, he smiled at her. "*Anything* ... For you, gorgeous, I'll do anything. *Always* ..."

Right now, she would happily settle for a kiss. Or two. Or three. Whatever he wanted to give her.

Instead, she nodded. "It's a deal."

And, very, *very* slowly, she removed the mask. A move that had everyone in the room joining in a huge sigh of relief.

After she handed him the mask, she leaned in to whisper in his ear. "I wanted this moment to have a lasting impression. This way, everyone will always remember you're mine."

He slowly shook his head. "Gorgeous, you're killing me here." Giving her that slow smile of his, he tossed the mask over to Paul, who earned a huge cheer from the crowd for his leaping catch.

Reclaiming her hand, Jason addressed the room. "Ah... and there you have it... you've both declared your love and you're ready to celebrate this with a dance. So, let's get started."

He slipped his microphone in his pocket and facing Darcey, he took her one hand and guided it to his back. Holding her other hand at shoulder height, he smiled. It was a teasing smile. "Are you ready?"

She smiled right back at him. "With you, I'm ready for everything. I really do love you, Jason Bennett."

He stilled, momentarily lost in her eyes. Then he smiled. "I love you, too, gorgeous."

He nodded over at Paul.

The band started right into a polka, a very loud and instrumental screeching, out-of-beat polka. Enough to make everyone put their hands to their ears even as they laughed.

His hands going to his head, Jason whirled around, sending the band a threatening look.

They all merely shrugged.

Shaking his head, he waited until the chatter died down before he turned back to Darcey, again positioning their hands correctly.

He sent another glance over at the band. "Okay ... now that you've had your fun, let's try this one more time. Remember, it's a waltz, not the horrible mess you just gave us."

And again, he nodded over at Paul.

And this time they got it right, their rendition of Can't Help Falling in Love filling the room.

When Jason first began leading Darcey around the dance floor, under what to her suddenly felt like the watchful eyes of every single person in the room, she was so nervous she was completely out of sync. She began stumbling over her own feet as she desperately tried to follow his lead.

She gazed up at him in a panic. "Jason, I can't do this. Look at me. It's like I have two left feet."

He smiled, tightening his hold on her. "Relax, sweetheart. You're trying too hard. You need to close your eyes and let the music move you. I won't let you go, so you'll be fine. Trust me."

And amazingly, after a few more turns, she was dancing as she'd never danced before. Floating across the floor, her steps in perfect time to the music, she mastered each sweeping turn like a pro.

The awe in her expression when she gazed up at him, had Jason smiling.

He'd be the first to tell you, this was the magic of music.

The dance was coming to an end and now more couples had joined Jason and Darcey on the dance floor.

After guiding Darcey to the middle of the floor and out of the path of the swirling dancers, Jason slowed his steps, almost bringing them to a complete stop.

And, as the final strains of the song filled the room, he cradled the back of her head in his palm and captured her mouth with his. The kiss he gave her was a long, sweet kiss, lasting until the last note died away.

It nearly stole her breath.

It definitely stole her heart.

In the early years of the waltz, this would've been considered more than scandalous.

But now? Once again, Jason had taken it upon himself to shake things up a little.

He wanted to give Darcey the perfect first dance. With even more of a perfect ending.

Looks like he nailed it.

Stephanie gathered up her purse and mask from the table.

She had stayed behind, offering to help sort out the items still waiting to be picked up from the silent auction. But now she no longer had a reason to linger. Giving the Grand Ballroom one last sweeping glance, she headed for the parking lot.

She was happy the night had been a success, thrilled with the record amount raised for The Children's Hospital. She was also glad everyone seemed to have had such a good time.

And yes, she was so happy for Jason and Darcey. They were obviously so much in love.

It was just that ... well, she had been so sure Evan would honor the promise he had made to dance with her.

But halfway through the evening, he disappeared. When the band began warming up, she had looked over to where he had been seated with the rest of the members of the press.

His seat was empty.

It wasn't that she hadn't danced. Because she had ... at least a half-dozen times. But for her, this had been so stressful, her shyness making it so hard to relax.

Except for the one dance you shared with Jack. You never realized how nice he was. Or so funny, making you laugh.

She came to a dead stop in the middle of the parking lot, suddenly filled with a horrible thought.

Oh, no, no ... did Evan leave just so he wouldn't have to dance with you?

Blinking back tears and muttering about how, once again, she'd let herself be fooled, she plopped her purse on the hood of the car. She began rummaging through it, searching for her keys.

Even though Evan had taken more photos than he needed, he had fully intended to stay at the ball so he could dance with Stephanie, as he'd promised.

But it was after the dinner was over and the band had begun to warm up, a woman's laugh carried over to where he was seated.

A laugh just like Kelsie's.

And as had happened so many times before, his thoughts were no longer his to control, his mind fast forwarding through one memory after another.

Memories centered around Kelsie.

This was when he knew he had to leave.

But, when he was finally back in his condo, still in his tuxedo and sprawled out on the sofa, staring blindly at nothing, he knew he'd made a big mistake.

There was something about this woman, this Stephanie, that had him thinking, even praying, she could help him. Maybe even give him a reason to smile again.

And if he didn't take advantage of what she was offering, be it friendship or something more? He would regret it for the rest of his life.

His mind made up, he drove back to the party center.

When he pulled into the parking lot to find it was almost empty, he thought he was too late. He turned the car around, his intention to leave.

He abruptly hit the brakes.

Completely still and almost in awe, he watched as the woman he had already begun to think of as an angel, come down the steps. She began walking towards a car parked on the other side of the lot.

He jumped out of his car and headed in her direction.

At the sudden crunch of gravel underfoot, Stephanie glanced up from her purse. A man was running towards her.

It was Evan.

Her breath catching in her throat, she waited.

He stopped right in front of her. Breathing hard, he searched her face. Unable to get a read on what she was thinking, he finally spoke.

"Hi."

She didn't respond. Her eyes wide, she studied him.

He cleared his throat. "I'm sorry. I wanted to stay, I really did. But it suddenly seemed all wrong. So, I went home."

Shoving his hands in his pockets, he shook his head. "I knew I had to come back. If only to tell you how sorry I am."

She tilted her head, still studying him. "It's okay. Don't worry about it."

He shook his head, suddenly angry. "No, it's not okay. I made a promise to you and I broke it. But, I ... well, I ..." His words trailing off, he glanced away, a frustrated sigh coming from him.

He turned back to her, his eyes bright with the tears that always seemed to come at him so unexpectedly. He searched her face. "Have you ever been to The Glass and Grape?"

Her heart starting to beat faster at the intensity of his gaze, she shook her head.

"It's a little wine and jazz bar right down the street. I know they're open late. Would you consider going there with me now? I want to explain, tell you why I didn't stay." At her hesitation, he smiled. "You can follow me in your car if this would make you more comfortable."

Then he pulled out his wallet and began handing her one card after another. "Here, this is my driver's license. Here is my work pass. And here's my insurance card. All proof I'm who I said I was, and not some crazy person."

A smile flitted across his face. "Though it would be understandable if you thought this with how I'm acting."

So much hinging on her response, he waited.

She finally lifted her head to smile at him. "Okay, I trust you. I'll follow you." She held out the cards.

But Evan had pulled out his phone.

He had an idea.

After typing something on the phone, he set it down on the pavement.

An instrumental version of The Way You Look Tonight filled the air. Carried by the breeze blowing off the lake, the beginning notes of the song rose over the deserted parking lot. It was the perfect invitation for a dance.

He held out his hand. "Will you share this dance with me? I know this may not be an ideal place or time, but after all, I did promise you a dance. And now, since you're not wearing your mask, I'll finally be able to look into your beautiful eyes."

So, they danced.

And contrary to their claim of not being able to dance, the dance they shared on this night, on the uneven pavement and under the light of the moon and a billion stars, was far more beautiful than they could've ever imagined.

When I'm awfully low,
When the world is cold,
I will feel a glow when I think of you,
And the way you look tonight.

CHAPTER 39

*W*hile Jason finished up with the band, Darcey waited for him in the courtyard.

She shivered, wrapping her arms more tightly around herself. At this late hour, with the slight breeze blowing off the lake, it had grown much cooler. Unfortunately, in her hurry to get to The Regency, she had forgotten her evening jacket.

"Hey, sweetheart … I'm finally here." This greeting came at the same time she was enveloped in the warmth of a jacket falling over her shoulders.

Jason's jacket.

She looked up and right into his smile. His hair mussed from performing, his tie undone, and the top buttons of his shirt unbuttoned, he looked so unbelievably hot, this sent a rush of desire surging through her. She didn't even stand a chance of hiding the longing in her eyes.

His smile disappeared, his mouth swooping down to cover hers in a kiss that had her clinging to him for dear life. After ending the kiss, he pulled her up against him, his lips moving in her hair. *"My god, gorgeous* … when you look at me like you just did, you have me wanting to take you right here and now."

His mouth finding hers once again, the kiss he gave her this time was slower, gentler. Just enough to bring them both back down to earth.

For the time being.

He took her hand to lead her out of the courtyard. "Come on, I thought this night would never end. And now I want to take you home with me."

On their drive to his house, their talk was casual, covering the events of the evening. But this was overshadowed by their awareness of each other, the desire building between them, something they couldn't have fought even if they tried.

So, by the time they got home, that they made it to Jason's bedroom was a miracle.

It was a passionate, almost overwhelming love they shared. It filled their hearts and fused their souls. Exactly the proof they needed their love was finally back with them for good. Yes, the past few years had been lost, but now they had the rest of their lives to make up for this.

Remember Jason's belief true love would prevail, fireplace or no fireplace?

Well, not to give him too much credit, but he was right.

Her hand drifting across Jason's chest, Darcey linked her fingers with his. She sighed.

"What's on your mind, gorgeous?" He pulled her closer. "You have me a little worried with the serious look you have going on."

Her gaze was searching, her words hesitant. "I guess I'm still finding it so hard to take in everything that happened. Losing the ring, you finding it, my father's part in all this. But…"

He sifted his fingers through her hair. "But what?"

"I don't understand. Why didn't you tell me about the phone call you had with my father? Or if only you had called again, taking the chance I would answer. So much could have changed."

She sighed against him. "I waited for so long…"

He pulled her closer. "Oh baby, I know this now. But he's your father … you're family. I didn't want to come between you, take the chance of ruining the fragile relationship you shared."

He sighed, running his hand through his hair. "That conversation with your father was a wake-up call for me. When I woke up that morning to find you gone, I honestly thought I was going to lose my mind. Suddenly, I was the guy in the songs I sang... love gone bad kind of songs. I couldn't concentrate on my music or much of anything. I blamed everyone I could think of... myself, you, everyone. The guys in the band were at a loss, they didn't know what to do with me."

He shrugged. "Then you called, giving me hope. But, as strange as this may sound, when I called back and your father answered, he helped me more than he could have known. By the end of that call, he had me convinced he was right. I wasn't good enough for you. You deserved better, someone with a brighter future. So, I got serious about my music. I began looking into new opportunities, found different outlets to use the band's talents more productively. And now I can honestly say I have a solid plan. I know what I'm supposed to be doing in my life. I also have so much more to offer you."

She curled in closer. "Oh, Jason … I'm sorry this happened with my father. And I don't need more. I only need you."

He pressed a kiss to the top of her head. "You have no reason to be sorry. I believe this is the road we were meant to travel to get to where we are now. Together, we've got this, gorgeous."

When she remained silent, he looked down at her.

She was smiling.

This had him smiling, too. "*Uh, oh...* now what's going on in that beautiful mind of yours?"

She pulled herself up against him until she was looking into his eyes. Her smile was still there, but now it was one of those flirty, sexy smiles that had him ready to agree to anything.

She traced his lips with her finger. "Don't you think it would be nice to have a fire in the fireplace? It's the only thing we're missing right now. And you did make me that promise on the dance floor. Remember? Anything I wanted, you said."

He chuckled. *"Ah ...* but that was in the heat of the moment."

A thoughtful look came over his face. *"Hmm ...* very similar to the deal you made with me earlier." He slowly shook his head. "All those kids ... wherever shall we put all of them?"

"Jason..." She was trying not to laugh.

"You started it." He was grinning.

She sighed. "I love you. So much."

"I love you, too. So much."

She snuggled closer. "The fire?"

He lifted his head so he could see her face. "You really want this. Now, you want this."

She gave him one of those flirty smiles again. "I promise I'll make it worth your while ..."

Their eyes held.

After he pushed himself off the bed, he smiled down at her. *"Ah ...* how can I refuse?"

He was humming as he began stacking the logs.

Buying this house with the fireplace?

This was by far the smartest thing he had ever done.

CHAPTER 40

We can't always change the past,
But we can start a new chapter to get that happy ending.
~ Anonymously Yours

ere it was, only Monday, and already Darcey was exhausted. This came from spending the entire morning and most of the afternoon with Elenore Cromley.

Not only was the woman a ball of unending energy, she was relentless.

Not a thing got past her, not a single detail. You would never know she had just celebrated her eighty-seventh birthday. Obviously very proud of her age, several times she had reminded Darcey of this.

But Darcey was to learn very quickly, Elenore was also an extremely honest and generous person.

Under her direction? The Regency would be just fine.

After she watched Emily's driver pull out of the parking lot, she pulled her phone out of her pocket. There was a text from Jason.

> Hey, gorgeous. When you get a
> chance, call me.

Believe it or not, this little message alone had her heart beating in a frenzy. Smiling, she hit his number as she began walking back to her office.

Jason was drying his hair when his phone rang. Hoping it was Darcey, he grabbed it off the vanity.

It was.

So, he was smiling when he answered. "Hey, beautiful … I've been waiting for your call, wondering if I might have to come to your rescue. I know first-hand how crazy Elenore can get when she's got a new project going on. Did she just leave?"

A dreamy smile on her face, Darcey had become lost in the sound of his voice. Even over the phone it had this way of wrapping around her, making her feel like she was in his arms.

"She did. The woman is unstoppable. You wouldn't believe all the plans she has for the party center. But they're all good. And I'm happy, because she loved my decorating suggestions for the holidays."

Now in her office, she sank into her chair, closing her eyes. "I miss you. I can't believe how much. How did your day go? What are you doing now? Do you miss me, too?"

He chuckled. "Yes, I miss you, too. Very much."

After giving his hair one more rub with the towel, he opened his closet doors. "I was at the recording studio most of the day and after going for a run, I just got out of the shower. I am now staring into my closet, trying to find something to wear. I've got big plans for tonight."

He pulled out a white and grey pinstriped button-down oxford shirt. Giving it a quick once over, he nodded.

It would work.

Satisfied with his choice, he was smiling as he sank down on the edge of the bed. He wanted to look his best. He had a plan in place and he wanted it to work out personally.

"Jason?"

"*Ooops…* sorry. I was thinking of you, have been all day, in fact. I believe I'm addicted to you. All of you. Just like the song." He chuckled again. "You know … addicted to you, addicted to love, I can't get enough …" And he was off, singing into the phone.

Between this and picturing him just out of the shower, Darcey's mind had gone sailing off on a whole new train of thought. She'd give anything to be with him right now.

Seriously, anything…

She sighed. "I can't wait to see you. And what do you mean about having big plans tonight? What kind of plans?"

He smiled, this coming through in his voice. "Plans involving you."

She was grinning. "Me?"

"Yes, you. I want you to put on your sexiest dress and be ready at seven. Someone will pick you up."

Sitting up straighter in her chair, she laughed. What was he up to? "Picking me up? Who? Jason, what is going on?"

He chuckled. "Remember how I'd planned to make dinner for you, but then you ran off and left me? Well … we're going to try again. But this time, we're going to go all out. *Hmm …* maybe I'll even teach you some new moves …" He left this last word hanging between them and now had her complete attention.

"Moves? What kind of moves?"

He chuckled again. "*Ah …* baby. Where is that mind of yours taking you? Of course, I'm talking about dance moves. If you're going to be hanging around with me, you've gotta know all the moves. And after dancing with you Saturday night, I'm pretty sure you have the poten-tial to be a fantastic partner and I want to be the one to teach you everything."

She was silent. Even though he would deny this, she knew he wasn't talking about dance moves. Which was fine with her … more than fine.

"Hey sweetheart … are you still with me?"

She sighed. "You're driving me crazy. But something tells me you know this, don't you?"

He was smiling. "Have I told you lately how much I love you?"

A rush of every kind of emotion coming right at her, she closed her eyes.

She didn't think she would ever get used to hearing him say these words to her. It still felt like a dream ... him, her, the two of them, everything.

She swallowed, her voice coming out all shaky. "I love you, too. So much. I ... I guess I'm still trying to believe this is all real."

There was a slight pause before he spoke, his voice almost as emotional. "It's real, gorgeous. More real than anything. But, like I've already told you, we've got this, okay?"

Even though she knew he couldn't see this, she was nodding as she responded. "Okay."

And just like that, his smile was back in his voice. "So, tonight ... You'll be ready at seven?"

"I'll be ready. I wouldn't miss this for the world."

It was now 6:58 p.m.

Leaning against her kitchen counter, Darcey was scrolling down through her messages.

Since she had been ready for over fifteen minutes, this was her attempt at staying busy while she waited.

Right after she had ended her call with Jason, she had locked up her office and headed for the Chic Boutique.

If Jason wanted sexy, then this is what she was going to give him. At least this was her plan.

A faint smile on her face, she looked up from her phone, thinking about what happened when she had walked into the boutique.

After running over to give her a hug, as though they were the best of friends, Sophie's Aunt Louise had nodded, a big smile on her face . "Darcey, I had a feeling you were going to stop in. You're here to find a special dress, right? Something flirty, maybe even a little sexy?"

A guilty look coming over her face, she had promptly shut her mouth. She led Darcey over to a rack of cocktail dresses, and chattering non-stop, she began sorting through them .

Then, without giving Darcey a chance to say much of anything, she ushered her into the dressing room with three dresses to try on.

Forty-five minutes later, Darcey was out the door, a garment bag holding a new dress slung over her arm.

She shook her head. She couldn't believe how swiftly news traveled through this close group of friends. She'd be willing to bet they all knew about this dinner before she did.

But she liked it.

You like it a lot. Yeah, you do.

And now, smoothing down the skirt of the dress, she knew she had made the right choice.

She loved everything about the dress.

The color was a deep shade of garnet, the fabric a soft brocade. The bodice featured capped sleeves, a round neckline and was fitted to her natural waistline. The gathered skirt fell just to her knees.

The only jewelry she wore was the necklace with the promise ring. And her diamond earrings that had once belonging to her grandmother.

Louise had told her the dress was Sophie's favorite style, vintage forties. A little flirty and a whole lot of sexy was how she described the dress. A woman couldn't help but feel beautiful when wearing a dress like this, she claimed. Darcey had to agree.

So, yes ... she was ready.

More than ready.

Exactly at seven, her front door bell rang.

Flying across the room, she opened the door, surprised to find Ben standing on the front steps. Dressed in what looked like a chauffeur's uniform, he gave her a slight bow.

She gave him a big smile. "Why, Ben ... how nice to see you again."

Avoiding eye contact and his face already turning all shades of red, he nodded. Then he cleared his throat. Twice he did this. Even then, his voice started out with a bit of a squeak. "Good evening, Ms. Hollister. Mr. Bennett has assigned me as your driver for this evening.

He also wanted me to assure you that I'm a very cautious and experienced driver."

He suddenly smiled, looking right at her. "Don't worry, I've had my license for almost a year now. I told Jason ... I mean Mr. Bennett ... he could trust me. He said he did, otherwise he wouldn't let me drive his new Lexus."

His smile grew bigger. "It's so cool. I can't wait until I can someday have one of my one. The sound system is ..."

Realizing he had strayed from the formality of his position, he once again cleared his throat, becoming serious. "So, are you ready to depart?"

His seriousness had her responding in the same. "Why, yes I am. And if Jason trusts you, then I trust you, too."

He held out his arm, giving her a genuine smile this time. "Okay. Here, take my arm then. So we can be on our way."

They were both fairly quiet during the drive.

Ben was concentrating on his driving.

While Darcey was reluctant to distract him.

When he finally pulled up next to Jason's house, before she could even say a word, he dove out of the SUV and sprinted around to open her door.

He grinned, again holding out his arm. "I promised Jason ... *umm* ... Mr. Bennett, I would walk you to the front door. This is the proper protocol a man should follow when on a date, he told me. It's important a woman knows how much she is treasured and admired."

He cleared his throat. "You look very nice tonight."

Panic immediately marked his features. "Not that you didn't look nice the last time I saw you. You always look nice. Honest, you do."

Slowly shaking her head and managing to hide her laugh with a smile, Darcey patted his arm. "Oh, Ben ... thank you. If you keep listening to Jason, which I assure you is a good thing, you're going to drive the girls crazy someday. If you haven't already."

This had him turning all red. Nervously clearing his throat again, he opened the front door, gesturing for her to go in front of him. "After you, Ms. Hollister."

He took her arm, leading her through the silent house until they came to the door that opened to the back deck. A big smile now on his face, in part because his job was almost over, he gestured to the door. "When you open this door, you'll find Mr. Bennett waiting for you, Ms. Hollister."

He gave a slight bow. "I hope you enjoy your dinner."

"Thank you, Ben."

But her words were delivered to empty air.

Ben had already disappeared into the kitchen.

Darcey hadn't known what to expect when she opened the door.

But never in her wildest dreams had she thought such a beautiful setting would be waiting for her. Caught up in what could only be described as a moment of pure magic, she slowly took it all in.

Candles were everywhere.

Not only were they on the table set up in the middle of the deck, they were arranged in clusters on the deck floor and lining the railings.

Miniature lights twinkled in the tree branches, clustered in large pots in the corners of the deck. They were also tucked in the garlands of ivy wrapped around the railings

The table was covered with a floor length white linen table cloth and set for two. The cut crystal stemware, fine white china, and sterling silverware sparkled in the candlelight.

If this wasn't enough, white carnations were everywhere. They were in the centerpiece on the table and tucked in the ivy wrapped around the railings.

There was only one red carnation.

This was in Jason's hand as he slowly made his way over to her, a smile on his face at the stunned expression on hers.

His gaze leisurely traveling over her, she could see the approval in his eyes.

He held out the carnation.

"Hey, gorgeous." He tilted his head. "So, what do you think?"

What did she think?

She was thinking this was by far the most romantic thing anyone had ever done for her. A moment she would remember and cherish forever.

She wanted to tell him this, but even though she tried... and she really, *really* tried, she couldn't. The words wouldn't come. Her eyes bright with the tears she was trying so hard to hold back, she kept shaking her head.

It was when he reached out to brush the back of his hand down her cheek, the words she wanted to say came out in a flood of tears.

"Jason ... I ... you ... *Oh my gosh, Jason.* You did all of this for me? I ... this is so amazing. I love you *so, so, so* much."

And, somehow, she was in his arms, the carnation crushed between them.

His answer came in a murmur against her cheek. "I confess I can't take much of the credit for this. I lit the candles. And I helped string some of the lights, but for the most part, you can thank Steffi and Caro. Abby and Sophie, too."

He pulled her closer, pressing a kiss to the top of her head. "They told me I needed to do this right." He chuckled, shaking his head. "Believe me, I had advice coming at me from all directions."

"It's perfect. Absolutely perfect. You're perfect. I couldn't ask for anything more." Her cheek resting against his chest, the steady beat of his heart against her ear, she meant every word she said.

You would stay here in his arms forever if you could.

And what about Jason?

Suddenly, his plan for a romantic dinner, followed by what he had planned as a formal declaration of his love?

This no longer felt right.

And the words he had practiced over and over, spending more time than on any song he ever wrote?

Yes, those still needed to be said.

But they needed to be said now. There was no reason to wait.

What mattered was the woman he now held in his arms gave him the only answer he would ever need.

Gently pulling away from her, he went down on one knee.

Darcey stilled, her hand automatically going up to finger the promise ring.

A bewildered expression on her face, it was obvious this was the last thing she expected.

This brought a smile to Jason's face as he reached into his pocket and pulled out a small jeweler's box. But before he could even open his mouth, she came to life.

Giving a small cry, she was in his arms, pressing kisses over his face. He could feel her tears, along with a few of his own, wetting his cheeks.

And now they were both on their knees.

He was grinning as he reached for her hands. "*Ah*, gorgeous ... I take it from your reaction, your answer is a yes. But how about if we start over? Do this right? I don't want our future children and grand-children—if you remember, there might be quite a few of them—thinking I didn't know what I was doing."

Her smile was brilliant. Her eyes never leaving his, she nodded.

Still holding her hands, he cleared his throat. "Okay, here we go ... Darcey Ann Hollister, from the moment I looked into your eyes, I knew you were the woman for me. You will always be the song in my heart and the music of my life. I want to spend the rest of my life with you, grow old with you. Maybe even take you up on your more than generous promise of a dozen children, give or take a few."

Here, he stopped to wink at her before he continued. "So, before there is even the slightest chance I might lose you again, will you please marry me?"

She had been nodding the whole time. And she continued to nod even as she gave him her answer.

"Yes, yes ... I will marry you. And you'll never lose me again, *never*. I promise you this."

After he put the ring on her finger, she gazed up at him. "It's perfect."

Resting her cheek to his, she sighed. "It's so perfect."

He smiled. "Ah … gorgeous, you're right. It's all perfect. Together, we're perfect."

He kissed her.

Then he kissed her again.

And with them still on their knees?

Yes, he kissed her again…

Jason pulled them up from the floor of the deck.

He was smiling. At the same time, he was shaking his head. "I know I do this a lot, but this is a moment I can't let pass by. I have been working on this song for so long and never have the words meant as much to me as they do now."

He stepped back, holding out his hand. "Dance with me?"

So, with the deck as their own private dance floor, the moon high in the sky and the stars sparkling like diamonds, he led her in a slow dance.

The smooth tone of his voice was like velvet as he sang to her in the night's silence.

This is not just another love song,
Words scribbled on a page.
No, this is the real thing, baby,
My way of asking you to always be
mine.

This is just not another little moment,
Fading from our memory in time.
No, this is the real thing baby,
It's fate, destiny and all of those signs.

You weren't what I expected,
You weren't what I planned.
But one look in your eyes and

everything changed.
You showed me what love is.
You showed me what love is.

These words just didn't come to me,
From any other love song
No, this is the real thing, baby,
What I've been saving for you all
along.

You weren't what I expected,
You weren't what I planned.
But one look in your eyes and
everything changed.
You showed me what love is.
Yes, you showed me what love is.
What real love is.

A love that is forever ours, this time...
This time...

The last words of the song fading in a whisper against her cheek, he pulled her even closer. "*Ah, gorgeous...* and there you have it, *Darcey's Song.*"

It was the perfect September's moonlight serenade for the woman he loved.

Linking her fingers behind his neck, Darcey smiled up at Jason. "Thank you, I love it ... it's beautiful."

His response was to press a big kiss to her mouth. He was on the top of the world, happy about everything. For him, life couldn't get any better.

But at the same time, he was also very hungry.

Starving, would be more like it.

He grinned. "I don't know about you, but I'm famished."

She burst out laughing. *"Oh my gosh...* so am I. When I walked into your house, whatever was going on in your kitchen smelled absolutely heavenly."

He nodded. "Caro, Steffi and Abby have been cooking up a storm all day. I'm sure they would be insulted if we didn't take advantage of everything they've done to make this evening so special. Come on, let's go tell them the good news."

He headed for the door to the house, taking her with him. "Hey, everyone ... it's official ... she said yes."

As soon as he yelled this out, as if they were waiting right by the door, which was exactly what they were doing, they came running out onto the deck.

Ben was right behind, champagne bottle and glasses in hand.

There was so much to celebrate.

CHAPTER 41

True love doesn't have a happy ending.
Because true love never ends.
~ Anonymously Yours

Jason crumpled up more paper, stuffing it between the logs in the fireplace.

After he lit the paper with a match, he stepped back. Hands in his pockets, he watched the flames come to life.

Thinking back to the first time he made a fire in this fireplace, he smiled as he turned to Darcey.

She was sitting on the bed. Her hand held out, she was admiring her ring. Sensing his gaze, she glanced up and smiled back at him.

And again, you guessed it. For him it was a sexy smile. And just as flirty, if not more.

Déjà vu?

Probably.

But this time there was something a little different between them.

The promise of the ring.

A sign she finally belonged to him. Just as he would always be hers.

He joined her and pulling her up with him on the bed, he settled her next to him, his arm around her. His next words came out a little hesitant. "About the wedding…"

"Jason …" Laughter bubbling up in her throat, she gazed up at him. But at the seriousness of his expression, she became silent.

He pressed a kiss to her forehead. "I need to say this. If I had my way, I'd run off with you right now to get married. The last thing I want is the wedding and everything else, turning into some huge extravaganza with months in the planning. We've already lost three years as it is and I don't want to wait any longer. I just want to marry you, be able to call you my wife."

Tucking her hair behind her ear, he suddenly grinned. "After all, we do have your father's blessing."

Her eyes wide, a smile slowly curved her lips. "My father? You told my father you wanted to marry me?"

He nodded. "I wanted to wait until after I proposed to tell you this. After all, I wasn't sure what your answer would be." The teasing glint in his eyes told her he'd thought no such thing.

"Jason … I swear, if you hadn't asked me, I would've asked you by now."

"Oh, is that so?" He was grinning. "Well, just for the record, if you had… my answer would've been, and always will be, a definite yes."

After he confirmed this with a kiss, she gazed up at him. "About my father?"

He nodded. "*Ah, yes …* your father. It must have been after the two of you talked, he called to apologize. It wasn't an emotional apology, but that he made the effort was more than enough for me."

He smiled at the memory. "While I had him on the phone and knowing this would probably be the one and only time I'd ever have the upper hand, I told him I intended to ask you to marry me. But, before I did this, I wanted his approval. And he gave it, under the condition I would always honor our marriage vows."

Still a little amazed at how that conversation had gone, he shook his head. "I told him with you, this would be easiest thing I'd ever have to do."

Slowly searching his face, she didn't know whether to laugh or cry. Never had she loved him more than she did at this moment.

She reached up to give him a kiss. "Jason, I would be more than happy to run off with you and get married."

His eyes lit up. "You would? Well, then—"

She pressed her fingers to his mouth, cutting off his words. "But you know we can't. Everyone who has worked so hard to get us back together would be so disappointed. And look back at all the weddings your band has been a part of. You know it's not just about the bride and groom ... it's about family and friends. It's about celebrating one of the most sacred of events in two people's lives."

Here she stopped to grin at him. "We don't have to plan a huge extravaganza, as you just called it ... or spend months to make it happen. But we can still have a celebration that will make both us and everyone else happy."

She gave a huge sigh. "And something tells me we'll have plenty of help. Probably more than we could possibly need. If I've learned anything since I've been here, it's that everyone is very involved... with everything." She smiled up at him. "But I love it."

He was frowning. But at the same time, he wasn't surprised.

She was right.

All hell would break loose if they didn't have the wedding everyone believed they should have.

There was no doubt in his mind Steffi would be horrified if they told her they wanted to keep everything low key. Paul, too.

And, hey, wouldn't it be kind of fun to be on the receiving end for once?

He gave a long, resigned sigh. "I guess you're right. But if things start to get out of hand–"

Her kiss put a stop to his words before she smiled up at him. "Have I told you lately how much I love you? Because I do, so much."

His gaze holding hers, his response came in a husky whisper. "Stars, like the brightest of stars. I will never grow tired of looking into your eyes. I love you, too."

She reached up to give him another kiss, this one slower, lingering long enough to bring a soft groan from him as he pulled her closer.

She smiled. "Then show me ..."
And so, unable to refuse her anything?
He did ...

*Love is a very complicated thing. Did
you know it is actually made up of five
different emotions?*

*When we love, we can feel joy, sadness, anger,
the same time.*

*So, this means you can't plan ahead,
surprises are inevitable. Instead, you need
to just dive in, hang on and embrace every
single glorious moment.*

*Your hope is there will finally come that
one time, that one day, you'll have found
the love of your life.*

*Jason and Darcey experienced pretty much
all of these emotions. So, it's not surprising,
even though their journey had so many
ups and downs, in the end? Everything still
turned out so overwhelmingly right.*

*Think of it as a not so ordinary, fairy
tale kind of love.*

When Jason told Caro carrot cake was Darcey's favorite cake, she searched through her cookbooks to find the perfect recipe.

So, she was beaming with pride when the cake received rave reviews the night of Darcey and Jason's engagement. Even from Abby.

Before she left, she cut a large slice to take home. She had promised Dan she would save him a piece. He later told her he ate it on one of his breaks between surgery duty at the hospital. He claimed it was the best carrot cake he'd ever had. The recipe is as follows:

Cake:
  2 cups white sugar
  3/4 cup vegetable oil
  3 large eggs
  1 teaspoon vanilla extract
  3/4 cup buttermilk
  2 cups finely grated carrots
  1 cup flaked coconut
  1 (15 ounce) can crushed pineapple, drained
  1/2 cup raisins*
  2 cups all-purpose flour
  2 teaspoons baking soda
  2 teaspoons ground cinnamon
  1-1/2 teaspoons salt
  1 cup chopped pecans, lightly toasted

Cream Cheese Frosting:
  3/4 cup butter
  12 ounces cream cheese, slightly softened
  1-1/2 teaspoons vanilla extract
  5-1/2 - 6 cups confectioners' sugar
  Additional coarsely chopped
  and toasted pecans for garnish.

Directions:

1. Preheat oven to 350 degrees F (175 degrees C). Line the bottoms of 2 (8 inch) round cake pans with parchment paper, grease and flour the paper and sides of pans for easy release.
2. In a large bowl, mix together sugar, oil, eggs, vanilla, and buttermilk. Stir in carrots, coconut, vanilla, pineapple and raisins. In a separate bowl, combine flour, baking soda, cinnamon, and salt; gently stir into carrot mixture. Stir in chopped nuts. Spread batter into prepared pans.
3. Bake for 40 - 50 minutes or until toothpick inserted into cake comes out clean. Remove from oven, and set aside until cooled.
4. In a medium mixing bowl, combine butter or margarine, cream cheese, vanilla, and confectioners' sugar. Beat until fluffy. Don't over beat or it will become too soft.
5. Place one cake layer on serving plate. Spread top with frosting and add second layer. Frost top and sides of cake. Garnish with toasted pecans.

*To plump up the raisins, soak them in hot water for about 15 minutes, drain well and dust lightly with flour before adding to the batter. The flour will keep the raisins from sinking to the bottom of the cake layer.

ABOUT THE AUTHOR

L. B. Joyce lives in Chagrin Falls, Ohio. A freelance artist by day, with designing Christmas ornaments her specialty, she is also a writer by night. She loves getting lost in a good book, has redecorated almost every room in her house more times than she'd like to admit, loves baking up a storm in her kitchen, hates housework with a passion and will drive just about anywhere because of her fear of flying.

To keep up with news of the first eight books of the Twelve Months, Twelve Love Stories series - *A Million Decembers, For the Love of July, February's Angel, Promise Me November, An Unexpected June, A January to Remember, September's Moonlight Serenade, and Goodbye Heartbreak, Hello May* - along with the first book of the new *Holidays in White Oaks Valley* series, *A Grand Slam Kind of Christmas,* make sure you check out the website/blog at:

lbjoyceauthor.com

Or visit on Facebook:

https://www.facebook.com/AuthorLBJoyce

Email: lbjoyce12@gmail.com -

She'd love to hear from you!

Credit due:

I Only Have Eyes for You - Composer, Harry Warren. Lyrics by Al Dubin.

The Way You Look Tonight - Composer, Jerome Kern. Lyrics by Dorothy Fields.

Darcey's Song (Chapter 40) - Copyright © 2020 by L. B. Joyce

In My Arms (Chapter 9) - Copyright © 2020 by L. B. Joyce

www.ingramcontent.com/pod-product-compliance
Lightning Source LLC
Chambersburg PA
CBHW061938130726
47909CB00013B/2041